MW01056395

TIME AND CHANCE

TIME AND CHANCE

❦ BY ❧

GWEN DAVENPORT

DONALD I. FINE, INC.

NEW YORK

Copyright © 1993 by Gwen Davenport

All rights reserved, including the right of reproduction in whole or in part in any
form. Published in the United States of America by Donald I. Fine, Inc. and in
Canada by General Publishing Company Limited.

Library of Congress Catalogue Card Number: 93-70901

ISBN: 1-55611-373-0

Manufactured in the United States of America

10 9 8 7 6 5 4 3 2 1

Designed by Irving Perkins Associates

This novel is a work of fiction. Names, characters, places and incidents are either the
product of the author's imagination or are used fictitiously. Any resemblance to actual
events, locales, organizations or persons, living or dead, is entirely coincidental and
beyond the intent of either the author or publisher.

I returned, and saw under the sun, that the race is not to the swift, nor the battle to the strong, neither yet bread to the wise, nor yet riches to men of understanding, nor yet favour to men of skill; but time and chance happeneth to them all.

—ECCLESIASTES, 9:11

❧ 1 ❧

A BIRTH UNDER GEMINI

The twins' birthday was an easy date for the family to remember because it was the same as the day of Queen Victoria's accession to the throne. Maria Wrox-Hampden had started in labor nearly a fortnight before the estimated date of her confinement, and the trap had been sent for the doctor in the middle of the night. Instead of taking the old Roman road, which was longer but would have shortened the driving time, Tole, the coachman, chose to go by his own back ways, instinctively following unmapped lanes worn deep into the land by centuries of passage. They were now so rutted after the winter's frosts and the rains of spring that the doctor was jolted thoroughly awake. He clutched his leather bag with one hand and with the other the side of the rickety carriage. Like everything else pertaining to the Wrox estates, it was in need of repair or replacement. The doctor's corpulent body was jammed against that of the coachman in his shabby livery, for the trap, hardly bigger than a chaise, was a tight fit. Dr. Pipkin was made aware, even in the open air of the mild June night and despite the strong, acrid-sweet odor of the hawthorn hedgerows, that the coachman must have been regaling himself while he waited for his passenger to dress. It was Tole's wife who brewed the beer for the Wrox laborers, so he always had access to it and carried its odor about on his person. It had made him garrulous.

He complained monotonously about having had to get up in the middle of the night because the Wroxes had no consideration for poor folk who worked all day "and as if that warn't enough, they have to rouse me up to go to work while everybody else gets to sleep. *I* need my sleep as much as any—aye, more than most—"

"I, likewise, was roused in the night," the doctor interrupted at last, thoroughly provoked. "It's me job, just as it's yours." The tiresome complaining of the coachman was typical of all the Wrox servants and laborers; they were a shiftless lot.

Half an hour after the trap had left the market town, Bunbury, it was turned into the unkempt park of Wrox, through rusting gates that had been left open beside an untended keeper's lodge. Inside the park there loomed up on the right the ivy-covered, empty tower and half-built wall of an artificial ruin erected by the old squire, Henry Wrox. In the doctor's youth the bogus ruin had been the refuge of an ornamental hermit, an emaciated whitebeard dependent on the Hall for his few necessities. An object of terror to the boy, the poor creature was now, in retrospect to the man, an object of pity. One day he had simply disappeared from the countryside and, on returning some months later, was thought to be his own ghost; as such, he had been avoided and had starved to death. It was now believed his real ghost haunted the Wrox park by night, begging from anyone who happened to be abroad. The doctor would not have been surprised to catch sight of a wraithlike figure, but nothing moved across the path of the trap except a low-flying owl that emerged suddenly from the shadows of a roadside spinney and disappeared into a dark grove of abeles. "Did ye ever see the hermit?" he asked the coachman.

"Aye—many a night. He don't mean no harm. I leave him a bit o' meat now and then, and 'tis allus gone by daybreak."

Presently the bulky facade of Wrox Hall loomed ahead. It was a massive and ugly house, of no particular architectural style or period, appearing, as it had no adequate base or balustrade, to have been thrust up like a volcanic rock out of the ground, rather than erected upon it. Projecting circular bows were attached to the front corners. Offices, outbuildings and additions had been haphazardly appended over the past century. Lights were now showing in the first-floor windows of Mrs. Wrox-Hampden's bedroom.

In the drafty hall the expectant father was pacing the carpet in front of a cold hearth, observed only by dim portraits hung on the walls between dusty assegais. Although Arthur Wrox-Hampden was an exceptionally tall man, the chimneypiece was well above his head; the fireplace could have stabled the children's pony. Beside it a giant long-case clock was measuring the night.

The squire heard the sound of hooves and wheels on gravel, at last, as the trap bringing the doctor approached the door. His big mastiff, asleep on the spot where it had worn the carpet threadbare, pricked up its ears and rose with a growl. Wrox-Hampden went to the door, the dog at his heels. "Doctor—come in, come in," he said in a deep bass, roughly pulling open the door. The entry, or vestibule, was small and narrow. As the door was flung open, its handle went through a priceless Sir Joshua of Caroline, Countess of Moulds; it always did go through it.

The mastiff continued to growl and slobber, the doctor recoiling involuntarily from its size and strong odor to which its master seemed indifferent. "Get back, Caesar," the squire ordered, reinforcing the command with his boot. The dog bounded away, then pushed past both men and took off into the night before the door was closed. The men shook hands, the doctor's stubby fingers disappearing into Wrox-Hampden's enormous grasp. Everything about the squire was outsized; his head was even large for his big body, and his nose and ears were big for his head. His clothing looked as if he had outgrown it, or as if his tailor had skimped on material and tried to cover the huge frame with a bolt of cloth sufficient only for a normal-sized man.

"How is your wife?" the doctor asked as he removed his cloak.

"She's taking the devil of a time about it. I'm glad you're here. You know your way upstairs."

Partway up, Dr. Pipkin turned to remark, "By the way, Silly Billy is dead. You may not know. I just heard this evening when the mail coach came in. He died early yesterday."

"God save the Queen," the squire replied automatically, and as the other man disappeared into the dark upper part of the Gothic staircase, he told himself he should drink to the health of his new sovereign, Victoria, barely eighteen years old and now Queen of England. He poured a beaker of West Indian rum and settled down in an armchair, feet on the sooty fender, to anesthetize himself while his wife, without such benefit, got the business in hand over with. From time to time he could hear her cry out, the intervals between the outcries becoming of ever-briefer duration. It could not be much longer now. Would it be a boy or a girl? No matter. There were already plenty of both, and in any case it might not live. He reflected sentimentally on his legitimate children—the illegitimate ones, actual and putative, seldom entered his mind—and remembered the first to live beyond infancy, Henrietta, who had died at eighteen as a result of eating ices when she became overheated at a ball. Her sudden death had caused him real distress, the more so since there had been reason to hope for her marriage to a certain widower of substance. The three boys who had died in infancy had been too young to be remembered as persons, so on this account he wept an appropriate tear at the notion that he was unable to mourn them.

A prolonged, piercing scream came from upstairs. There was another interval of silence, but no baby's cry. Maria moaned loudly again. Wrox-Hampden poured himself more rum, and after a while he ceased to hear the distressing sounds and ensuing ominous silences.

Sometime after daybreak Dr. Pipkin came down the stairs to find the squire snoring by the empty hearth. The candles had long since burned down and gone guttering out, but the sun slanting through the dust motes from the oriel window showed the huge man lying grotesquely half in, half out of the chair into which he fitted no more comfortably than he did into his clothes. Wrox-Hampden was a man of immense physical and mental activity; his days were spent outdoors, riding to hounds, fly fishing, trapping, shooting, breaking in hunters or otherwise imposing his will on Nature. His enormous animal energy was enthusiastically expended on any and all physical enterprises that could not conceivably be called useful. He ate and drank with huge appetite and was always ready, when inactive, to fall soundly asleep.

The doctor shook him by the shoulder.

The squire roused, regained consciousness and remembered the events of the night just past. "Is it over? Is Maria all right?"

"Your wife is safe and resting. It was an exceptionally difficult labor, and she is worn out. You may see her for just a minute."

"Very well. Oh—by the way, have I a boy or a gel?"

"You have one of each. They are delicate but appear to be well formed."

"Oh, merciful God!" The father buried his enormous head in both hands as if it were too heavy for his neck to support. *Two* more to provide for! Provision for a boy to enter the Army or the Church . . . a dowry for a girl—and she might not even live to marry, like poor Henrietta.

"You may see your wife and the babies for a minute," Dr. Pipkin repeated. "I must make arrangements immediately for a wet nurse. Will you call the trap?"

"You cannot start back to town without some breakfast. You must be hungry." Wrox-Hampden dragged himself to his feet, yawning, shaking his heavy head on which the graying thatch still carried undertones of its original ginger color. He pulled a handle attached to a wire on the wall, setting a bell to jangling in the distant kitchen, where the cook was already up and busy rousing the fire in her range. Outside, a pheasant began to crow in a coppice, joining the whistles of blackbirds from the lawn and the song of a thrush in the shrubbery.

"Thank you, I shall be glad of a bite," said the doctor, envisioning with hope a pigeon pie or perhaps some kidneys.

When a manservant appeared from the back regions, yawning and pulling on his jacket, the master ordered him to see that breakfast was laid for him and the doctor, and the trap brought around after they had eaten. Then he went slowly up the staircase, straightening his crumpled clothing. In the upper hall Nurse passed him, arms full of soiled linens, and said, "Two bonny wee ones, sir, and Madam well, the Lord be praised. I'll send her up some milk pudding."

Maria lay still, exhausted, in the big velvet-hung bed in the recess. Her thick brown hair, only recently become streaked with silver filaments, had been brushed and freshly plaited by Nurse, who had just withdrawn. On her bony, waxen face the strongly marked eyebrows stood out like broad streaks of black paint over the deep sockets of her closed eyes. The two tiny babies, swaddled in blankets, were asleep head to feet in a bedside cradle. They looked at once brand-new and ancient.

The husband leaned over the bed. "Maria? Are you sleeping?"

She opened her eyes and looked up at him, a look expressing nothing but weariness and contempt. She turned her head away on the pillow. "This is the last time," she stated, her voice surprisingly strong. "I shall have no more children."

"You cannot be certain of that, my dear. Remember Aunt Sophia Cheycester had Algernon when she was forty-nine."

"But I *am* certain. I shall never have another child," Maria said positively.

"If God chooses—"

"It is not His choice, Arthur. It is mine." She moved her head to look him full in the face once more.

"Well, well, we shall see. One cannot tell." Arthur ran a hand over his rough chin. The fingernails were not clean. He needed a shave. His stock was soiled, and the smell of spilled rum was mingled with the customary horsy odor of his clothing. He saw her glance and said apologetically, "I have been up all the night."

"Drinking."

"Only to the health of our baby—of our babies. And to the new Queen. King William died early yesterday."

"Oh?"

"Long live the Queen."

"Poor young thing."

"Why should you say that? She is Queen of England."

"She is a woman."

This was undeniable.

"We shall have to name the infants," their father said, looking down at them and thinking they were so small they could easily not survive and had best be christened quickly. He remembered that they had agreed a boy was to be named Edward, with the additional names of his godfathers. "Who are to be godparents?"

"I don't care in the least," Maria said indifferently. "Whatever you decide."

With all the other children, she had already had names and sponsors picked out before their births. It did not occur to him that what had been done ten times would not be done the eleventh.

"You know I can't do that!" he cried. "They're your babies."

"They are yours, Arthur. I had no choice in the matter."

"Well, I'll be damned!" he exclaimed.

Again she gave him that shriveling look. Then she closed her eyes and turned over on her side, away from him and the cradle, as if she were turning her back on life. Once she had embraced it eagerly, when as a young widow she had found irresistible Arthur Hampden's compelling vitality and animal charm. The intervening years having revealed these to be all he had, her feelings for him had now swung as far as they could go in disillusioned reaction.

Her husband regarded her uncomprehendingly, with the disdain of the healthy for the sick. He could not understand a person who did not, on its most elementary levels, enjoy life. He hovered at the bedside, feeling helpless, then after a moment shrugged and walked off. Women were inclined to get depressed after childbirth, and the best thing to do was to leave her alone until she recovered. He would absent himself all day from the house. But first, he was hungry. He joined the doctor in the dining room.

Cook had sent to the sideboard silver-covered dishes well filled with bacon and eggs, toast and cold boiled beef. Arthur poured two mugs of stout and proposed the health of the newly born Wrox-Hampdens. "Though God knows what will become of them," he said as he tucked a napkin under his chin. He launched into a tirade against the evils of the taxation that was ruining the country. "And where is the money coming from to pay them? Nothing has been the same since the war. My father-in-law used to get fifteen pounds for a cow twenty-five years ago, and my overseer told me yesterday he's lucky to get three."

"But wages are down along with prices," the doctor pointed out. "As I very well know. A laborer who gets eightpence a week can't pay much for the setting of a child's broken leg."

"Things will never be right again until we have another good war," Arthur declared, thus dismissing the subject of business affairs, which he regarded as no concern of a gentleman. There was always money from the Wrox estates, which had become his upon his marriage. As the impecunious son of a Hampshire clergyman he had been fortunate to win Maria's hand and, by assuming the additional surname of Wrox, ensure his own prosperity and an inheritance for his children.

"If I weren't so old, I think I'd emigrate," said the doctor, after his plate had been emptied and refilled. "All the sensible fellows are emigrating. Two carpenters, a bricklayer and a smith left Bunbury within the past twelvemonth. They say they'll be worth their weight in gold in America."

"Oh, to be sure, it's the sensible fellows who leave," the squire agreed. "It's not the aged, the halt and the ailing. Those remain for us to take care of. There must be a dozen such at Wrox, not really worth their wages." He sighed, partly from satisfaction at being replete. "Yet now I'm supposed to produce from the estates provision for two more hungry mouths."

"Be thankful they are living."

"Yes, yes, of course. I hope it may never be said they'd be better off dead. Only, by Jove, I wish there were some way to see to it there won't be any more of them."

❧ 2 ❧

THE FAMILY IS INFORMED

Lucy Wrox-Hampden, who was seventeen, had been awakened in the night by noises coming from the direction of the stableyard. Her sister Marietta, just one year younger, lay asleep beside her in the big bed. Lucy got up and padded silently to the window, which looked down on the courtyard leading to the kitchen door and the surrounding outbuildings. Luke, the stableboy, carrying a lanthorn, was in conversation with Tole, the coachman, who had evidently been awakened by the same call Lucy had heard. Tole's quarters above the stables were lighted, and he was leaning out the window in his nightshirt.

"Hurry up!" the boy was saying. "You're to go to Bunbury and fetch Dr. Pipkin right off. It's the mistress."

"Get the trap ready and harness Cavalier, then," said Tole, "while I put me clothes on."

There followed all the sounds connected with the carrying out of these instructions, but they seemed to disturb no one except Lucy. After she had watched Tole's departure, she went back to bed to await his return and found Marietta still sleeping. Lucy deliberately drew up her knees, lifted her sister's nightgown and laid her cold feet against Marietta's warm bare thigh.

Marietta woke, pulling in her breath with a little hissing sound.

Lucy laid a hand across her sister's mouth. "Sh-sh!" She changed position until she could put her lips to the younger girl's ear and whisper, "Tole has just gone to Bunbury to fetch Dr. Pipkin."

Marietta blinked. "What's the matter? Who is ill?"

"Mama is going to have a baby."

"Will the doctor fetch it?"

"Oh, Marietta, you are an *idiot.*"

"Why does he bring it in the middle of the night?"

"He does not, you simpleton. The baby is inside Mama."

"How does it come out?"

"The same place it got in. The doctor pulls it out. I'll tell you in the morning. No—listen, I'm going out and you're not to say anything."

"Going *out?*"

"Out of the room." Lucy slipped off the bed and dragged the bolster into a position alongside Marietta under the bedclothes, where it might be taken for her sleeping self. Three minutes later she was prowling the drafty corridors of Wrox, an unscrupulous eavesdropper and invisible spectator of the night's drama, leaving Marietta wide-awake to mull over the puzzling scraps of information.

Concealed at the turn of the stair, Lucy heard her mother's groans and caught glimpses of preparations for the delivery of an infant brother or sister. She watched the arrival of the doctor and shivered as the groans became cries and the cries increased to shrieks behind the closed bedroom door. Lucy had watched animals rutting, mares foaling and humans coupling behind a haystack; she could perfectly well imagine what had been and was going on. She was built in the image of her father—tall, gaunt, big-headed and red of hand—and it was generally conceded she "should have been a boy." She had no interest in clothes, needlework or music but lived outdoors whenever she could escape the schoolroom. She knew the location of every fox's earth and every poacher's traps. She was privy to the secrets of the hedgerows that enclosed the fields and sheltered the wildlife. Today she was almost the first person at Wrox to know of the King's death and the twins' birth. Nurse, carrying away for disposal the messy aftermath of the latter event, encountered her at daylight at the head of the back stairs and assumed she had just got up. "You'd best get dressed before you catch your death," she said. Lucy was as unlikely to be affected by wearing scant clothing on a drafty staircase as the household cat, but she was generally expected to behave like a young lady even in the face of evidence that she did not.

Nurse scurried down the stairs with the covered basin and its bloody contents, meeting at the foot the ascending water boy, Adam, who had no surname. He could neither read nor write, he was big and ungainly, but he was strong, easily bearing his double burden of filled pails. Adam carried clean water up and dirty water down again, making climb after climb until all the bedrooms had been supplied.

Lucy had taken his existence for granted all her life. He was about the age of her brother Arthur. He lived with his mother, a laundress, in one of the old thatched wattle and daub cottages on the home farm. Now, suddenly, seeing him from a new angle, sandy head coming up into the light from the dark well of the stairs, long body foreshortened and shoulders bowed under the heavy weight of the buckets, she was struck by something unfamiliar in his appearance; he did not look like the Adam she had never really looked at. He reminded her of someone else, someone she had seen before, often. She watched him uneasily, then was suddenly visited by a moment of revelation. It was herself she was looking at. It was her own big body, ginger hair, pale eyes, disproportionately large feet and hands.

Adam reached the landing, stepping over the broken tread on the next to last step. As he came slowly about, keeping his swaying burdens in balance, he ducked his head respectfully in her direction; had he had a free hand, he would have touched his forelock. Frozen, she stared at him. He looked exactly like her father—who, of course, must also be his own.

Lucy's heart thumped so hard she felt it knocking against her ribs. Why had she never noticed before? It was so obvious that everyone must know: Mama, and Arthur, all the servants and tenants, the whole village of Wrox and the town of Bunbury. Perhaps Adam himself. Color flooded her face, which she covered with her big hands as if she would never dare show it again, stamped as it was with those so clearly recognizable features. She hated her father because she, like this beast of burden, was made in his image, instead of being smaller and pretty, as Marietta was and Henrietta had been.

With the morning the household came gradually to life. The doctor had left; the squire gone to Bunbury to see the saddler and hear the London news. Breakfast was laid for Miss Wetherby, the governess, Mr. Reddle, the tutor, and their charges. One by one they were informed as they came downstairs that two new Wrox-Hampdens had been added to the family, a boy and a girl.

The births immediately affected the tutor and governess as much as anyone, meaning as they did that the need for their services might now be extended by many years. Augustus, at ten, would soon be sent away to school, the elder girls' educations soon be complete, but now there was another boy and another girl.

Osbert Reddle hardly knew whether to be glad or sorry. His position was not a proud one; he felt he should be elevating and educating in the classics the minds of young gentlemen instead of trying to hold the attention of Augustus, who would never be a scholar. Yet the tutor was an unassertive person, and the prospect of a measure of security—meager though it was—tempted him. He held no degree, but he was a keen naturalist and knew a great deal about the land and its creatures that the squire hunted so mindlessly. He loved the environment of Wrox, a hinterland still preserving a sense of remoteness, netted by secret lanes, with thick copses between the open farmlands. He decided that if asked, he would stay. "Walking out this morning, I saw a redwing!" he remarked with enthusiasm. When no one showed any interest, he added, "They are rare in June, very rare. It was remarkable. Most of them who winter here have left by mid-April."

Miss Wetherby was a kind and likable young woman of thirty who put up with much for a small compensation, but to the children she was often a figure of fun, shortsighted, her fusty black dress ornamented with a gold brooch containing a lock of her deceased mother's hair. Alone in the world, with no money and no connections, she was kept from giving in to despair only by pride in her education and in her ability to teach. She had been educated at a boarding school for the daughters of clergymen and at home by her father, who had thought that if she did not marry, she could find a vocation as a teaching nun, thereby leading "a useful life"—his goal for her.

She was possessed of soft hair, a beautiful skin and a well-formed figure; she could have been pretty, if only someone had told her so. She longed to love and to be loved, and she lavished the unspoken love of which she had so much on the young ladies in her charge.

She regarded them now. Poor Lucy, so big and plain, so unlikely to marry soon, if at all. Marietta at sixteen was pretty and amiable enough to find a husband readily; certainly she would be gone from home before the newly born girl was ready for a governess. Lottie, the twelve-year-old, looked like her mother and had her mother's matter-of-fact nature. But she had a good mind. It was a pleasure to teach the child, who was clever at sums and had quickly picked up the French language as taught by Miss Wetherby, including her atrocious accent.

Elsie Wetherby prayed to be asked to stay on at Wrox. She fingered the brooch containing her late mother's hair, hoping the deceased approved. She often hoped her mother was thinking of her, because there was no one else to do so, in this world or the next.

Lottie accepted the new births as children do accept the natural conditions of their lives. It seemed to be more interesting news that far away in his London palace there was a dead King.

"I'm glad he is dead," said Augustus. "Papa said he was a dangerous revolutionary."

"Now, now," Miss Wetherby reprimanded him. *"De mortuis nihil nisi bonum."*

Mr. Reddle explained, "That means speak only good of the dead."

"Why?" said Lucy. "They can't hear. It makes more sense to speak only good of the living; it might get back to them."

"It is for History to judge the late King, not his subjects," said Mr. Reddle rather sententiously.

"Yes," Miss Wetherby agreed, "in time *la vérité se fera jour.*" She spoke with a dreadful accent, despite which she continued to lard her remarks with French phrases; it was the fashion, and she wished her pupils to fit into the mold of fashion, perhaps obscurely seeing her own chance for advancement in the event of a good marriage for one of them. No Frenchman could have understood a word she said, but her pupils had no trouble understanding since they had never heard a Frenchman speak and would not have understood *him.*

"We shall say henceforth 'God save the Queen,'" Miss Wetherby went on. "How I should love to go to London for the coronation. Had my dearest mother but lived a few years longer, she might have seen the procession." The children all knew that Miss Wetherby's mother, a clergyman's widow, had lived in London lodgings during her last years; the location and poverty of these had never been described to them.

"The Duke will go, won't he?" asked Marietta. She referred to the premier nobleman and landowner of the county, a peer with great estates in other counties and a seat in Scotland. This personage she had seen only once, at the dedication of the new workhouse.

"Oh, he'll be in Westminster Abbey, of course. So will Lord Edge, I shouldn't wonder."

This brought the coronation closer to home, for the Edge lands adjoined those of Wrox, and Edge Park was distant by only half an hour's drive. The Dowager Lady Edge was Maria Wrox-Hampden's nearest neighbor (of those called upon) and girlhood friend. Although her son, the seventh viscount, was not yet of age, he was decidedly the most eligible young man in the county. Miss Wetherby began mentally matchmaking. Marietta would be just right. The governess wondered if Mrs. Wrox-Hampden and Lady Edge had considered the possibility. If so, Marietta should have been provided with some pretty and becoming clothes instead of Lucy's outgrown and cut-down wardrobe.

"Before we can think about a coronation, there will have to be a funeral," Mr. Reddle remarked. "It will be a very grand one."

"Shall we have a holiday?" Augustus asked, with his mouth full.

"Perhaps. We shall see. Eat your bread and milk," the tutor added unnecessarily.

"And you, Lottie—you are not eating your breakfast."

"I don't like it; it's not good."

"Now, now," the governess reproved her, "one does not talk about the food."

"No," said Lucy. "The less said about it, the better."

"That is not what I meant," said Miss Wetherby, although it struck her now that this might have been the original reason why to speak of the food was not *comme il faut*. "Even if the food is particularly delicious, it is rude to remark on it, as if one were surprised or as if to imply that delicious food is an exception in the house."

"But good food is one of the good things of life," said Lucy, "like good weather. Why not talk about it?"

"Ladies and gentlemen do not."

"Well, you can't ignore it. It's very necessary."

"One cannot qualify the adjective 'necessary,' " said Miss Wetherby patiently. "A thing is either necessary or it is not."

"I think food is an interesting subject," Lottie put in.

"It has been said that interesting people have interesting food," Miss Wetherby quoted, "and dull people have dull food; the same platitudes go into the mouth as come out of it."

"Now who's talking about food?" said Augustus rudely.

Miss Wetherby flushed. In a voice that trembled from mortification she brought forth the automatic reproof: "Don't talk with your mouth full."

"Full of what?" Lucy asked.

"Full of porridge, of course."

"There you go again!" Lucy shouted, and gave a laugh like a whinny.

Seeing that his colleague was trying not to cry, Mr. Reddle felt a rising of compassion for her, much as he would have felt for a helpless animal being baited in a trap. The humiliation of her position, and by extension of his own, struck him. He turned on Lucy in anger. "How dare you to be so unkind!" he said sharply, his long-pent-up dislike of her breaking out in the tone of his voice and in the scornful look accompanying his words. Lucy stared back in surprise. As it happened, he had surprised her no more than himself, speaking as he had after years of placating her for fear of what she might be capable of in retaliation. Now he felt good. He felt like a knight in armor. In standing up to this horrible child, he had come to the rescue, as it were, of a damsel in distress. Elsie Wetherby needed him. Without him she could have been reduced to tears in front of her tormentors. He rang the bell on the linen cloth (none too clean) in front of his place at the table—the master's place, Osbert Reddle's only in the master's absence—and when the footman appeared, he ordered (not requested) fresh tea. A subtle but significant change had just taken place in the dining room.

The tutor's neck was disproportionately long for his height, and it contained an Adam's apple that traveled up and down its length when he spoke, sometimes disappearing altogether as if it had been swallowed. When young Arthur (now at Oxford) had been Mr. Reddle's pupil, he had found the phenomenon to be so distracting that in order to understand what the tutor was saying, he had had to avert his eyes or close them, giving the impression he was not paying attention when, in fact, the opposite was true. Lucy for years had tried to mimic Mr. Reddle, but lack of the cartilage made her attempts less than successful. Now nobody noticed it anymore, and Miss Wetherby, being shortsighted, had never remarked it in the first place. Its owner himself was unaware of its existence. "Augustus," he said happily, "I think you also owe Miss Wetherby an apology." Lucy had given none. "You spoke to her with rudeness."

Augustus had to wait until he had chewed and swallowed before saying, "I'm frightfully sorry, Miss Wetherby."

"There is no occasion for fright," said the governess. "It is enough to be sorry."

Nurse appeared in the doorway, an important personage again with the nursery to reactivate and nursery maids to train. "Miss Lucy," she said, "your mother would like to see you after breakfast."

What have I done now? was Lucy's first thought. Neither parent ever summoned her except to chastise or punish. But curiosity to see the newborn infants took her to her mother's room promptly from the breakfast table; customarily she might have ignored the summons and said later that she never got it.

The twins were asleep. To have more than one in a litter was like an animal rather than a human being, Lucy thought as she leaned over the cradle. It was uncharacteristic of her mother.

"Don't touch them!" Maria said sharply from the bed.

Lucy withdrew the big hand she had laid on the blanket to pull it back.

"If you were to pick them up, you would be sure to hurt them," said Maria, reminding her daughter of countless chipped teacups, broken windows, smashed robins' eggs, unhinged gates and dropped puppies—results of her uncontrollable clumsiness.

Lucy clenched her hand into a fist. "Well, I did not know they were considered so precious!" she said in a loud, defiant voice. "Are all Papa's children so precious?"

"What are you talking about?" her mother replied with impatience.

Adam, Lucy mouthed silently.

"They are certainly weak and helpless," Maria went on. "And here before they were expected. That is why I sent for you. I want you to help Miss Wetherby write letters to everyone who must be told.

"First," she said, "there is your half brother, Robert, in London at this season, I suppose. The addresses you will find in the book on my writing table. Then to your father's relations Uncle and Aunt Hampden at Stoke-sub-Ham, and Uncle Charles and Aunt Georgiana. They must all be told they have a new nephew and niece."

Lucy wondered, in the light of her discovery in the stair hall that morning, how many such relations the aunts and uncles might have of whose births they had never been informed. But she felt pleased at the opportunity to write the letters her father should obviously have done. Miss Wetherby's assistance would not be solicited. She, Lucy, would impart the news very dramatically. "Which was born first?" she asked.

Maria was startled. "I do not know. You must ask someone else. Dr. Pipkin."

One of the babies awoke and began to cry, a thin bleat. It made little noise, but even that seemed like a lot to come from so tiny an instrument as a pair of lungs no bigger than a wren's wings, and the cry wakened the other infant, who promptly doubled the volume.

Lucy turned to leave.

"Wait a minute," her mother said. "Be sure to get Miss Wetherby to help you."

"Mama, I am not going to misspell any words or blot the paper!"

Later in the morning, excused from the music lesson, Lucy sat at her mother's small boule escritoire, with shoulders hunched and arms akimbo, her large feet hooked on the stretcher of the frail chair, looking like an ungainly bird crouched over a toadstool. First she wrote to her half brother. She covered Maria's letter paper with the carefully formed words and phrases of her dramatic narrative. She began with her own awakening in the dead of night (a nice phrase), the arrival of the doctor, the long labor with its screams of anguish and at last, on the third page, the arrival of not one but two new Wrox-Hampdens—"two more unwelcome additions to the population of this troublesome world, as both our mother and my father are greatly annoyed at the birth of two more children. All hope this will be the last." Lucy signed this "Yr. aff. sister," and addressed it to Maria's eldest child, Robert Fox, Esq., Villa Brozzi, Rome, the address immediately following his name in the book.

Before sealing the letter, Lucy reread it as if she were to be the recipient, and she was satisfied that it could not be improved upon. Accordingly, she copied it word for word for the benefit of her father's brother Cuthbert and his wife, Aunt Esther, then again in a letter to the Chipping aunts and finally to Uncle Charles and Aunt Georgiana.

It happened that the letter announcing the births to the Charles Hampdens crossed with one from Aunt Georgiana (Mrs. Hampden), sealed in black, that told of the sudden death of "my beloved husband, Arthur's beloved brother Charles." (The brothers had not seen one another for ten years and had never got along.) "Charles had suffered a chill but had no premonition that the end was at hand," wrote Aunt Georgiana in her thin, precise and legible script, "but being ever prepared during the days of his journey here on Earth for the Great Journey into the Beyond upon which we must all one day embark, he expired full of faith, hope and resignation. We were permitted ten years, eleven months and three days of Perfect Happiness together, and now he has left me for a Greater Happiness in the company of our precious little Departed Boy. I shall be lonely indeed without both of them, but knowing that they are Together in Paradise must be my Consolation from here to the Grave."

Arthur Wrox-Hampden read the melancholy tidings aloud to Maria, who was still bedridden. She had turned the babies over to the wet nurse, Sally Hill, wife of a village carter, who had an abundant supply of milk for her own month-old infant as well as for the tiny, delicate newborns. Relieved of responsibility for them, their mother had been resting and doing a great deal of thinking.

"Poor Charles," she said, but in spite of Georgiana's moving eloquence, she shed no tears for her late brother-in-law. If he was indeed in Paradise—as his uneventful earthly life left no reason to doubt—there was no occasion to mourn on his account. Georgiana, she supposed, was the one to be pitied, for in her loss she had no immediate family left.

"It must have been his heart," said Arthur, handing Maria the letter. "Georgie had obviously not yet heard about the twins when she wrote."

"She *must* be godmother," Maria said. "And she must come for the christening. We'll call the boy Charles—Edward Charles—and he could very well fill the void in her life. If she sees him, so small and helpless, she's bound to want to do something for him. Heaven knows someone will have to."

"Good God, Maria, he's only two days old! Nothing has to be done for him beyond keeping him alive!"

"They have to be christened, Arthur. For that they need godparents. Georgiana can hardly refuse." Aunt Georgie was well connected, being the daughter of an Honorable who was the third son of a fourth earl. She had recently lost her only child of water on the brain, and as she was thirty-nine, had never had a second child and now never could, it seemed likely she might feel a particular sense of responsibility toward a godchild.

⇛ 3 ⇝

"ONE SHOULD NEVER SEPARATE TWINS"

The christening was arranged to take place on a Sunday morning preceding the regular service in the village church of Wrox. There was a chapel connected to the Hall, but it had not been used for so many years there was some question of its being still in a state of consecration. In any case it contained no chairs or prayer books, as Arthur Wrox-Hampden was not in the habit of holding family prayers, leaving such things to the tutor and the children. As the day of the christening was pleasant and sunny, the little congregation walked to the village green, following the carriage containing Maria and Nurse with the two infants, well wrapped against the first outdoor air to which their frail bodies had been exposed. Arthur escorted his sister-in-law Georgiana, who was dressed in widow's weeds that concealed the features of both face and form. It was impossible to tell anything about her person beyond the fact that she was short. They were followed by Uncle Cuthbert (Archdeacon Hampden) and his wife, Esther, Miss Wetherby and her three charges, then Mr. Reddle with Augustus, young Arthur—who was down from Oxford—and two friends of Maria who were to be proxies for the absent godparents. Lady Edge was standing proxy for Grandaunt Augusta

Pounceby, for the Chipping aunts never went anywhere; it was too risky for their health to quit the vicinity of the waters.

Aunt Georgie had arrived two days before with young Arthur, who had accompanied her on the journey that had involved an overnight stop at Hatche Castle. She had been very tired, so had spent the day following her arrival in retirement. No one had really had a chance to talk to her, and her recent bereavement put a further constraint on everyone.

The small congregation filed into the church, which held the damp of centuries in its ancient stones, and gathered around the font. Georgiana Hampden handed little Edward Charles to the vicar, promising in the child's name to keep God's holy commandments and walk in the same all the days of his life. When the tiny creature felt the touch of icy water, he started a shrill cry and refused to stop, even after having been handed back to Aunt Georgie, dried and rocked against her shoulder. It was next the turn of his twin, Violet Augusta Maria Louisa, and she did not wait to feel the freezing water before adding her voice to her brother's.

"The devil has left them," Lucy whispered to Marietta. Aunt Esther Hampden, standing in front of the two girls, lifted her head and turned around to frown. As soon as she had resumed her position and again bowed her head reverently, Lucy stuck out her tongue at the narrow, erect back. All the children feared and disliked Aunt Esther. "To know her is to hate her," young Arthur had said after spending a holiday visiting in her house, Stoke Rectory. She was what is generally described as "a fine woman," meaning she was rigid, self-righteous and humorless. She had informed on Arthur, when she caught him sampling his uncle's port, "for his own good," and for the same noble reason made him stay all day in his room repenting, while the other young people in the neighborhood had a picnic on the downs.

After the christening, Aunt Georgie insisted on keeping possession of her godchild. She was a quiet, soft-spoken woman with pink cheeks and round, prominent eyes that looked made of glass, being clear and expressionless. That afternoon at tea she made known to what lengths, as godmother, she was prepared to go for her late husband's infant nephew. Immediately after she had been so suddenly widowed, Aunt Esther had proposed she should move into the rectory at Stoke-sub-Ham with her and Cuthbert, for reasons of economy as well as companionship. Every chair in the drawing room was occupied, and Maria was seated behind the tea table for the first time since her confinement. Among those present were the vicar, Mr. Smallwood, his wife and his maiden daughter, Miss Theodora, who gave the Wrox young ladies their lessons on the pianoforte. All the grown-ups who had attended the christening, including the father of the twins, were there when Georgiana Hampden made her petition. "I have given this much thought, Maria," she began timidly, "and have discussed it at length with Esther and Cuthbert, with whom I am to fix my future home. I feel deeply the loss of my dear husband, but I feel almost as strongly the fact that I have also lost the child who might have been the solace of my widowhood."

"I incline to believe there is no accounting for the ways of Providence," remarked the archdeacon.

"Quite," agreed Arthur Wrox-Hampden. "Some of us have none of what others have too much of."

Georgiana's doll-like eyes were turned to him pleadingly, a-glitter like glossy twin lakes. Only her rosy face and the pale fingers holding her teacup were visible of her person; all the rest was covered in unrelieved black. She was like a deputy of Death himself, and it would have been unthinkable to have made of the afternoon anything resembling a tea party. Arthur felt uncomfortable and averted his face from those pleading eyes and quivering lips.

"Maria"—Georgiana turned to her sister-in-law—"could you be persuaded to give up to me little Edward Charles? I mean, give him up altogether, to be my adoptive son?"

Aunt Esther nodded emphatically, indicating her approval. Uncle Cuthbert leaned forward, ready to add his considered opinion of the desirability of such an arrangement. Arthur, who was standing on the hearth, abruptly fell into the nearest empty chair, taken aback by the suggestion. One did not give the pick of a litter to a godparent, as one gave a bitch's to the owner of the sire.

Everyone looked to Maria, to see her reaction. With scarcely a second's hesitation and without looking toward her husband, she said warmly, with a smile, "My dear Georgie, how very kind of you! Yes, certainly, the baby shall be sent as soon as it is weaned, and if anyone else would like one, would you kindly recollect that we have others."

"I say!" exclaimed the children's father. "What's this?"

He was not the only surprised witness to this scene. Georgiana herself was astonished by the enthusiastic acceptance of her tentatively phrased suggestion. Only Maria remained unmoved, as if she had been asked to give fruit to a bazaar or lend an embroidery pattern.

Aunt Esther spoke first. "Georgie does not mean simply to have the child on loan," she said.

"No," Georgiana concurred, certain she had been misunderstood. "Cuthbert and Esther and I have discussed it at length, as I told you—"

"And what we intend," Esther interrupted her, "is that Edward is to be altogether Georgie's. That henceforward you are to have no claim on him whatsoever. That Georgie's parents are to be regarded as his grandparents, and you, his natural parents, as his uncle and aunt."

"We shall, of course," said the archdeacon, "see that he is brought up in the fear of God and educated as befits a Hampden. He will not be a white elephant around Georgiana's neck, as Esther and I shall relieve her of much of the burden."

Arthur Wrox-Hampden sprang up to his immense height. He was much agitated and began to pace the floor, rattling teacups in his passage. "This is a dreadful decision to make!" he cried out. "The baby is, after all, my own flesh and blood—"

"One should never separate twins," murmured Lady Edge from a corner. "It is bad luck for both of them. Mark my words."

"I am in a terrible taking!" exclaimed the father.

"I advise you to agree, Arthur," Aunt Esther said calmly. "It will be in the child's best interests."

"Certainly," Maria announced, as if it were all settled. Since neither the Cuthbert Hampdens nor the adoptive mother had any heirs, it was as if little Edward Charles had just come into an unexpected fortune. It would be very wrong to snatch it from him. "Edward is assured of his future. I wish we could see as bright prospects for Violet."

"How can you give up our child!" exclaimed the squire. "It is against Nature."

"Nonsense," said Maria, pouring tea with a steady hand. "Nature herself is wasteful. She produces an overabundance of all kinds of animal life, not to mention seeds. Why should humans be an exception?"

Everyone who heard this remark was profoundly shocked. The whole company had been feeling embarrassed by the open hostility between husband and wife and was already inclined to side with the husband, whose sentiments were more suitable, while agreeing with the more sensible ones expressed by the wife. However, the lumping of Man in with the rest of Nature was not to be tolerated.

Cuthbert Hampden, vicar of Stoke and an archdeacon, in the act of passing around the curate's assistant with its offerings of thin bread and butter and tea cakes, set down the stand abruptly in the center of the room. There was a sudden, uneasy silence. After a moment, "As God's humble representative among us," he intoned, "I believe I am correct in saying that He would not wish one of His innocents to remain with a parent capable of comparing it with the beasts of the field. It seems to me beyond dispute that the infant Edward should be raised in a Christian household of which I am the head."

Georgiana's chinalike eyes filled with ever-ready tears. Aunt Esther nodded vigorously, as if to say, "Hear, hear!" The infant's father, defeated, left the room to seek comfort in something stronger than tea. Lady Edge said, "Still, it is a mistake to separate twins. Mark my words." She was not an unsympathetic woman, but she could not be expected to put herself in the place of her girlhood friend and to know what it would be like to have lost four children involuntarily and to believe sincerely that the voluntary losing of a fifth was for its own good.

In fact, Lady Edge was an intelligent woman with a literal mind. On her husband's deathbed she had assured him that she would never remarry, that she would uphold the Edge high standards of behavior, that the infant heir would be reared properly according to his station and would at the right time take a suitable wife. These promises she intended to keep faithfully. When the taking of tea had been resumed following the interruption, and the squire had returned to the room, the conversation was turned to the subject of the proposed new railway from London to Bunbury. The company had become divided, as was customary, by a process as imperceptible as osmosis, into two groups divided by sex, ladies at one side of the room, gentlemen at the other. Because Edge lands might be involved, Lady Edge joined in the gentlemen's conversation with cogent questions, while the other ladies languished in boredom or whispered among themselves on female subjects.

It was young Arthur, down from Oxford for the christenings, who introduced the matter of the railway, he, as the heir to Wrox, being naturally interested. He resembled his father only in appearance, having decided to take orders and eventually occupy the family living. He had heard in the town that the Great Western Railway wanted to pass through Wrox village and near Edge Park on the route from London to Bunbury.

"Who gives them permission to do this?" Lady Edge inquired.

"The Bunbury Town Council will not have it near the street," said the squire. "They will have nothing to do with its noise and vulgarity."

"But certainly the railway would follow the main coaching road?" asked Lady Edge. "And if the coach should ever be replaced by the railway, how would travelers get from London to Bunbury?"

"They will not do so, of course," said the squire. "They'll come by way of Wrox and Edge. Ruin the hunting."

"Scare the sheep and cattle to death, I shouldn't wonder," said young Arthur.

"I venture to say it is contrary to the will of God," said the archdeacon. "Wrox village was never meant to be a railway stop. Has no posting inn, no livery stable, no town hall—"

"Would they not pay handsomely for permission to use our land?" inquired Lady Edge.

"Madam, if they go through your land, you will have no land left. And you can have no idea of the frightful noise and the dirt. We must stop this ruination of our countryside."

"Lady Edge." The archdeacon, still on his feet, walked across the carpet to stand over and address her. "You must have some influence in London. It is a shame your son is so young. Perhaps you yourself could appeal to the Duke? He of all people would have at heart the best interests of the whole countryside—"

As everyone turned to look at her, Lady Edge felt the weight of the responsibilities that were hers until her son was of age. She decided to trust the advice of her bailiff, a most competent and reliable man who had successfully managed the estates since her husband's death.

The course of the conversation was changed with the arrival in the drawing room of the daughters of the house. They had been sent downstairs to join the grown-ups: big, ungainly Lucy, taciturn and awkward; pretty Marietta, so clever and amiable; timid Lottie, serious and courteous. Marietta was induced, after only a little becoming reluctance, to play for the company. She removed the felt cover from the pianoforte, opened it and sat down at it demurely, while her mother directed to Lady Edge a look that said, See, Emma, is she not clever and amiable?

Yes, my dear Maria, Lady Edge said to herself in silent reply, and she does indeed play with accomplishment, and I am quite well aware that her virtues are being displayed for my benefit, that I may see her cast by Fate to be the future Viscountess Edge.

Before leaving, Lady Edge took Maria aside and spoke her mind. "I do not think it right to give the infant to those persons," she said. "They are too old; they know nothing of raising children. He will be an only child among them, with none of his own kind to play with or even talk to. It cannot be for his good."

"Perhaps he will grow up the sooner," said Maria. "What is the harm in that?"

"The harm is that he will have no childhood. Children are not little grown-ups. And he will have no father."

"He will have Cuthbert."

"Archdeacon Hampden? My dear Maria, he is not cut out to be a father."

"And is Arthur, do you think?" Maria asked bitterly.

Lady Edge gave up. She could not indeed hold the squire to be a better exemplar of paternal suitability than his elder brother. She embraced her old friend warmly and took her departure.

Aunt Georgie, the widow Hampden and now baby Edward's mother, was to leave in the early morning, Tole having been instructed to bring the carriage around at ten o'clock to drive her to the Bird and Bottle in Bunbury, where the coach stopped. But before six o'clock Aunt Georgie, fully dressed, appeared downstairs in the hall and was waiting there when Arthur and Maria came down. They found her in a state of great agitation.

"I simply couldn't sleep," she complained. "There were the most dreadful noises all night, as if someone were throwing things around the room. I got up once or twice and made a light, when the sounds ceased. Nothing had apparently been disturbed. But directly I blew out the candle there began a horrible knocking underneath my bed. I could not remain in it."

"It is nothing harmful," Maria assured her. "Put it out of your mind."

"Indeed, I cannot," protested the timid woman, who was still trembling.

"Which room were you in?" inquired the squire.

"You know very well, Arthur," said his lady sharply.

Georgiana had been assigned the chamber off the landing at the turn of the stairs, a room known to be haunted by the Wrox house ghost, that of an egregiously obstreperous child who had been incarcerated there as punishment in the early eighteenth century, had died of a fit and been buried beneath the floorboards. In Maria's lifetime he had been heard from no more than half a dozen times, and why he should choose to terrify the blameless Georgiana was unaccountable.

Georgiana thought: The sooner I get my child away from this dreadful house, the better for everyone. In ordinary circumstances she would have stayed on at Wrox for weeks or even months, but the recent death of her husband required her return to Wiltshire.

The Cuthbert Hampdens, having no pressing need to depart, had said nothing about when their departure might be expected. "Let us have them moved into the haunted room," Arthur said to Maria, "and we may hope they follow Georgie."

"That would be useless," Maria replied. "Esther would not be disturbed by the ghost—quite the contrary. She would soon have it silenced."

"I do not think so," said her husband. "The ghost has more right to be there than has Esther; it belongs in the house."

❧ 4 ❧

UNCLE CUTHBERT DOES HIS DUTY

Cuthbert Hampden had left in the care of a temporary curate his parish at Stoke-sub-Ham. He felt no sense of dereliction of duty; his only remorse was concern about the terrible loss suffered by his flock in being deprived of his weekly sermons. These lasted several hours, the happiest hours of his week because he regarded them as the most useful to his parishioners. He had left with the curate a supply of them to be read every Sunday for the duration of his absence. This cleared his conscience, as far as his being absent in person from Stoke went. Still, it bothered him that he was not making a useful contribution to life in the little world of Wrox, and he had offered to read aloud in the schoolroom every morning following prayers, which he, of course, led. Neither Mr. Reddle nor Miss Wetherby being in a position to refuse, his self-indulgence took the place of regular lessons for the children, to whom he referred as his "little flock of Christ's lambs." Slates and copybooks were laid aside in favor of the archdeacon's readings, which included selections from the Scriptures and from the writings of various Anglican divines.

After the first two such sessions the tutor, resenting the high-handed taking over of his domain, had suggested that the archdeacon might read aloud from one of the three-volume novels sent around by the circulating library to which the household subscribed. "I would like the children to associate reading with enjoyment," Mr. Reddle said. "A love of reading is a lifelong pleasure."

The clergyman dismissed the suggestion out of hand; in his view, it was dangerous. "In my humble but informed opinion, reading is for edification, for instruction, not for pleasure," he declared. "It is not a frivolous pursuit. Our duty is to remove from these impressionable young minds any tendency to frivolity."

"They receive what instruction they need in the course of the regular lessons," said Mr. Reddle.

"I venture to opine, sir, that there is no such thing as a sufficiency of instruction. One cannot be too well informed. Let us not forget that what we feed into these so-to-speak empty heads is as important for their health as what is fed into their bodies."

If there is such a thing as mental food, Mr. Reddle thought, then surely an appetite for it is necessary for nourishment. What good could these readings aloud do the listeners if they did not listen? "We have a new story by Captain Marryat, just published; it is called *Mr. Midshipman Easy*. I should like to hear it myself."

"You have not read it then?"

"It is only just arrived."

"How then can you know it to be edifying? It is better we read those authors whose works have stood the test of time."

Mr. Reddle sighed, then patiently conceding that contemporary works of fiction might be considered trivial or unimportant, "We should all enjoy listening to your reading of, let us say, *Emma*," he said.

The older man stared down from his physical and moral height. "You cannot be serious, sir. Miss Austen's portrayal of the clergy amounts to being irreligious. Mr. Elton, the vicar of Highbury, is portrayed as irresponsible and self-seeking—a disgrace to the cloth."

Mr. Reddle forbore to say that the archdeacon appeared to be thoroughly familiar with the frivolous Miss Austen. He then suggested readings, suitably edited, from the works of Fielding. "He was a most moral man, not in the least frivolous. In fact, in *Tom Jones* he pours contempt on hypocrisy, on meanness, on all types of vanities—"

"He married his deceased wife's maid," said the archdeacon with finality. Picking up his copy of Keble's sermon on apostasy, he cleared his throat and waited to resume the reading of it and of his pleasure in the sound of his own voice.

Mr. Reddle made one further attempt to stem the flow that was about to inundate them all in a sea of boredom. "Young people will not form a taste for reading if none of the reading matter offered them is to their taste," he said.

Miss Wetherby, boldly allying herself with him, added, "We do not wish reading to be associated with ennui."

"*En*-wee Who?" asked Uncle Cuthbert.

The children burst into laughter, hiding their faces to smother it.

"Just *en*-wee," Mr. Hampden. We do not wish them to associate reading with boredom."

"Oh—on-*wee*," said the clergyman, while the children dared continue laughing. Indeed, they could not have stopped. The contagion spread as the grown-ups caught it and tried to hide their smiles. (From then on Uncle Cuthbert would be known behind his back as *En*-wee Who.) Perfectly unconscious, as ever, of any effect he had on his audience, the archdeacon went calmly about his business of creating the intangible damage he had come to inflict.

In a glass case under the window was Mr. Reddle's collection of butterflies he had made on walks with the children, all the while giving lessons in lepidoptery. Each bit of flying, living color had been netted, identified and pinned down with spread wings as if still in flight: there were the Fritillaries, the Swallowtails, the Wood Nymphs and the tutor's special pride, a brilliant, lemon yellow Great Sulphur, never before identified in this part of England. How happy those walks had been! Would he and the children ever walk freely again along the hedgerows with their nets? Or were they doomed to remain thus, like the butterflies, pinned into place in the schoolroom throughout eternity?

Lucy had escaped these readings by simply absenting herself. There was no person among those who heard them, child or adult, who would not have absented himself had he dared. The voice went on and on, rising and falling in a cadence that set Mr. Reddle's head to nodding in accompaniment and Miss Wetherby's eyes to glazing over as she strove to keep them open. The children squirmed and wriggled, coughed as loud as they dared or stared at the long hand on the wall clock as it crept imperceptibly around the face. After nearly an hour Mr. Reddle's head was jerking up and down on his neck as he tried spasmodically, from his semiconscious state, to hold it upright. Miss Wetherby emitted an unladylike nasal sound that could only have been a snore.

The sudden cessation of the sonorous voice that had been filling the room brought the small congregation to consciousness, awakened by the silence. *En*-wee Who was fixing the governess with a stare like that of a bird of prey waiting for its opportunity. "You, Miss Wetherby," he said in a terrible voice, "are supposed to set an example."

She sat frozen in fright, unaware of the reason for having been singled out. "Yes, Mr. Hampden," she said.

"Well—?" he asked.

"She did, Uncle Cuthbert," said Augustus. "She did set an example."

"A good one!" cried Lottie, and in the general laughter that followed this remark *En*-wee Who gathered up his papers and left the room, going in search of his brother, Arthur, to report on the shocking lack in his children's lives of a Christian education.

"I find myself," Cuthbert complained, "in the position of one casting pearls before swine. Mind you, it is not my own words of divinely inspired wisdom that I give them—Heaven forbid I should presume to do so—but on this day it happened to be a sermon of John Keble's—very *founder* of the Oxford Movement—and, mind you, they all *laughed* at him, led, I might add, by the tutor and governess who are supposed to guide them not only in their education but in their behavior. I hope my esteemed Oxford colleague will never hear of this."

"Rest assured he will never hear it from me," said the squire. "So they laughed at Keble—eh? Dashed if I can see why. Fellow never wrote anything amusing that I know about. Still, if you don't like 'em to laugh, why don't you just read 'em somethin' that's not funny? What about *Lives of the Saints*? Smallwood—our rector, you know—thinks a lot of that, says it's capital. Unless, of course, you think it might be too entertaining. Haven't read it myself. But why do you have to read to 'em at all, Cuthbert? That's what Reddle and Miss Wetherby are here to do. I pay them, and then you come along and do their job. It's as if I were to hire a dog and then do my own barking. Waste of money."

"They do not read what the children should hear," said Cuthbert. "It is my duty—however unsuccessfully I may perform it—to see that they listen to what is edifying and uplifting. And I make it a point to leaven the readings with stories from the Old Testament, such as Daniel and the lion's share."

"And very good of you, I'm sure," said his brother.

"My dear Arthur, it is not notably 'good' to do one's duty. It would certainly be very bad to fail to do so."

Cuthbert gave up trying to talk sense to his brother, whose grasp of it was so slippery one always felt that it eluded him. The archdeacon sought the company of his wife, a woman of immense sense who commiserated with him and said he must not on this account allow the unappreciative swine to go without a regular casting of pearls, for if he failed to persevere in casting them, their lack of appreciation would be his own fault and not theirs, since how could they be expected to appreciate pearls of wisdom that were not cast before them?

So on the following day the reading was taken up at the exact place where it had been stopped by Elsie Wetherby's snoring. None of the captive listeners had the courage to interrupt with a snore or any other manifestation of on-*wee* until, after nearly two hours of *The Christian Year*, Lucy came clattering into the room, breathless.

"There are Gypsies on the common!" she announced.

Miss Wetherby regained full consciousness. "You don't say!" she cried. Then, seeing the Reverend Mr. Hampden's appalled look turned from the intruder to herself, she added lamely, "You are late, Lucy."

No one else spoke. Uncle Cuthbert merely glared; he had never before been interrupted. Poor Miss Wetherby, flushed with embarrassment, said to Lucy, "Go to your room immediately, and remain there for the rest of the day."

"Are you *punishing* me?" asked Lucy.

"That is my intent."

"Then make her *stay*," said Augustus.

"No, no," said Uncle Cuthbert, "she must not be permitted to stay; she must go. She must learn that she cannot do as she pleases, regardless of the convenience of others. She must not be allowed to stay."

Lucy departed immediately, slamming the door behind her, and her high, raucous laugh could be heard outside, diminishing in volume as she went farther away along the passage.

The reading aloud was resumed, after some searching for the lost place, which was found a full page back from the stopping point. The insistent voice, rising and falling, went on and on, until the reader himself at last was sated.

It was teatime before Lucy reappeared, having ignored the instruction to remain in her room; she was hungry. She was not reprimanded, for she was a welcome link between the isolated world of the schoolroom and the events of the surrounding countryside, of which she was always knowledgeable.

"So the Gypsies have come back!" Miss Wetherby remarked, putting down her cup. "How extraordinary! They come on the same date every year, just as if they knew."

"But they couldn't know, could they?" Lottie asked. "They don't have calendars."

"And yet," Mr. Reddle volunteered, "it is said they gather in southern France from all over Europe on a certain day at a certain time, when they elect the Gypsy king. They seem to know, just like migratory birds. Frost is the great enemy, and they move south just ahead of it in autumn, north just behind it in spring. I remember once on Dartmoor—"

"But how did you know, Lucy?" the governess asked, interrupting him.

"Me?"

"Yes, how did you know the Gypsies were come?"

Lucy hesitated, biting her lip. The common was off limits, which never stopped her from going there, only from telling about it. "I had to go with Tole to take Skittles to be shod. You know he wouldn't have gone without me." Skittles was the newly acquired Welsh pony.

Miss Wetherby seemed satisfied with this. Lucy ate her bread and butter greedily, not elaborating on the visit to the common. She and Tole had taken Skittles to the blacksmith's only to find a queue of farmers waiting with their working horses at the smithy. Skittles seemed to know something was up. Only half broken, he possessed an almost untamable spirit. It had taken Tole, Lucy and the stableboy to hold him in line. When at last they got to the smith in their turn, the pony had shown the whites of his eyes, snapped his jaws, lashed out in all directions, twisted his body, rolled, kicked and even tried to crawl away to avoid being shod. Everyone around had been watching the struggle when a small Gypsy boy appeared, suddenly and silently. He was tiny—impossible to guess his age—but well made, ragged and barefoot, with dark eyes burning under a mat of black, clotted hair. Fearlessly he walked up to the wild Skittles and reached for his bridle, saying, "I hold him, miss." And strangely enough Skittles immediately became a different creature. He allowed the smith to shoe him and afterward stood still in surprise, lifting each foot in turn, as if trying on shoes and finally deciding to take them.

"Now you ride him, miss," the Gypsy child had said, holding out a filthy, small hand.

Tole had pushed him aside, snarling, "Get off with you," but he continued to stand there, holding out his hand to Lucy. She was without money. When she thanked the boy, ignoring the outstretched hand, she thought a sly, furtive look appeared in his eyes. He gestured to the far side of the common, where the Gypsy pitch had been set up in a thorn thicket with the barrows on the verge and ponies wandering. Lucy nodded, wordlessly promising to take him money later.

Now she said nothing of this episode, merely remarking, "Augustus and Lottie can now ride Skittles perfectly safely."

"Homeless creatures wandering around the world," Miss Wetherby was saying.

"They have their own world," Lottie observed; "they take it with them."

She was a thoughtful child, who already looked as she would in womanhood, when the fine, strong features would have more than made up for a lack of childish prettiness. All the children bore the family stamp, but what in Lucy was exaggerated to grotesqueness was in Lottie conventional and in Marietta understated, her eyes large but not prominent, the ginger hair a fetching auburn, the height merely pleasingly an inch or two above the average.

"You are none of you to go near the *bohémiens*," Miss Wetherby ordered. "They are dangerous. They have been known to abduct babies."

Augustus was intrigued. "How ripping! I wish they'd take me. I'd like to live in a caravan and travel all over and not have to take lessons."

"Really, Miss Wetherby, you shouldn't have said that," Mr. Reddle rebuked the governess. Augustus was his particular responsibility. He essayed to describe the discomforts and filth of the bohemian life, the thieving and trickery of the tribe, and succeeded only in making Augustus regard the Gypsies as something like Robin Hood's Merry Men on wheels.

"There is nothing romantic about such a life," the tutor continued. "They steal children, bleed them to death and sell the bodies to anatomists."

"Above all, beware the Gypsy's curse," Miss Wetherby added.

"Grrrr—" cried Augustus, attempting to sound like a Gypsy cursing. "I curse you, with my eye of newt, toe of frog, hair of bat—"

"Mr. Reddle, I see you have succeeded in implanting some knowledge of *le grand Shakspeer*," said Miss Wetherby.

Lucy, gulping tea with her mouth full of Marie biscuit, felt what Miss Wetherby would have called a *frisson* of fear. She saw the dark boy's eyes, narrowed, inscrutable, threatening something dire if she did not get money into that hand stretched out to snatch it. Where could she get it? How could she take it secretly to the common before some curse was laid upon her, or some covert act of vengeance carried out? She possessed only one penny, which she had held out of the tuppence given her for the offertory on Easter Sunday, twice the amount allotted on ordinary Sundays.

When they were getting ready for bed that night, Lucy confided in her younger sister, who thought it foolish to be afraid. "But you weren't there, Marietta! You didn't see how Skittles just stood still the minute the Gypsy boy put a hand on him. There was something strange about it. And then the way he looked at me and held out his hand. If I don't give him money, I'm afraid they'll do something to Skittles, perhaps put the devil back in him—or even steal him."

"If they try, Tole will catch them, or someone will. You can't pick up a pony and carry it off as if it were . . . a tortoise."

Lucy clutched her sister, digging her fingers into Marietta's soft upper arm. "They could carry off a baby," she whispered. "You heard Reddle say they steal children."

"Let go, you're hurting me!"

"Be quiet! Wetherby will be here at any minute. You've got to help me."

"How can I? You know I have no money."

"You'll have to give them your locket."

Marietta wrenched her arm out of her sister's grip. The locket had been given to her at her christening by Grandaunt Augusta Pounceby, for whom she had been named Marietta Augusta, and contained a picture of that lady; it was the young girl's sole piece of jewelry and was worn on Sundays and special occasions. "Of course, I won't give them my locket. It's mine! Let them take Skittles if they want to. Papa can get us another pony."

"What if they don't want to? What if what they do is steal one of the babies?"

"You're demented, Lucy; indeed, you are." Marietta began to cry. She got into the bed, where she turned her back and continued to sob, half fearfully and half in anger. She did not see Lucy put on her nightdress over her clothing before she climbed into the other side of the bed.

When the house was quiet and Marietta had cried herself to sleep, Lucy got up silently and removed the nightdress. She felt her way about the familiar room without needing to see where she had placed her slippers, where lay the beadwork box on the chest of drawers that contained the locket. In a few minutes she was on her way down the back staircase, avoiding from long familiarity the missing board and those that creaked. Her way out led through the back passages of the kitchen wing, where no one slept, through the servants' hall, with twelve deal chairs placed around a rectangular board, the stillroom, where a mouse scurried into the wainscoting, to the water room. Here a door was always left open for Adam to come in before daylight and draw the water for all the needs of the upper floors; water had been laid on only in the kitchen and sculleries.

The moon was on the wane but still gave sufficient light to make visible any figure walking abroad. Lucy's foreshortened shadow preceded her along the narrow road that led through the park to the village. She had never before in nocturnal wanderings left the immediate vicinity of the house. Every sound from a distant barnyard or nearby coppice was alarming. She walked swiftly, keeping to the cover of trees or hedges, clutching the locket, fearful of encountering the ghost of the hermit.

In the village no light shone from the cottages, the church, the vicarage, the public house or the two small shops, all of which surrounded the common. Far across the green could be seen vague outlines of the wagons of the Gypsy pitch, and there the remains of a fire glowed, showing Lucy the way to her destination.

The dog scented her first, before she was halfway across the common. He came streaking out of the shadows, a fiendish-looking yellow cur, barking a warning. She stopped. The dog stopped, facing her, growling. She trembled. After a long moment it advanced, sniffing around her. She took a step forward. The dog took one backward. In this manner they arrived at the caravan, with the dog on guard and facing the girl.

A canvas flap was lifted from a tent, revealing in the pale light a bed of rushes or bracken on which several figures sat or lay. A man emerged, half dressed; he was small, well knit, with the look of a highwayman. An acrid smell mingled with that of smoke from the flickering embers of the campfire.

"*Gajo,*" the man said to someone behind him, coming forward. Another larger dog was with him.

Lucy tried to speak. "Boy," she said two or three times before she was understood.

"Boy," the man repeated.

"The pony. He kept the pony from hurting itself." Lucy advanced and held out the hand clutching the locket. As she opened her fist, a dying log burst into sparks and gold flashed in her palm like a firefly. "For the boy," she said.

Dark fingers had taken the locket before she knew it and without her feeling their touch.

The man went back into the tent. The cur growled low. Lucy turned and walked slowly off, feeling as if something were crawling up her neck at the back of her head. She tried to hear if the cur followed, and when it seemed the growling had ceased, she broke into a run, lifting her skirts as she stumbled over them. Without stopping, she ran as if in terror for her life all the way home. Once inside the water room, she stood leaning against the wellhead, panting like an animal, feeling the trembling of her limbs, tasting blood in her throat.

A quarter of an hour later, when she crept back into the bedroom, the sky was lightening and Marietta was awake. She was not crying now. She was angry.

"My locket is gone," she said as Lucy came in.

"Shhh!"

"I shan't. I'm going to tell Mama."

Lucy grasped her sister by both arms, forcing the younger girl on her back. "You lost your locket," she said between clenched teeth. "You lost it! Do you hear?"

"I did not."

"Yes, you did. Say you did!" The pressure of fingers was increased. Marietta whimpered in pain. "If you tell Mama, I'll put a Gypsy curse on you. Say you lost it!" Marietta, terrified, looked up at her sister's face. "I lost it," she whispered.

Soon after, the Gypsies left Wrox common, taking with them a variety of trinkets, some cash, a supply of vegetables, a number of chickens and a pig belonging to the squire's overseer, Mr. Spence, who had suggested to them in strong language that they should move on. Early in the morning, before the village folk were abroad, they were gone along the old cambered Roman road toward Bunbury, quarreling, thieving, laughing, singing Romany songs, taking with them all their world.

❧ 5 ❧

BREAKING UP OF A HOUSEHOLD

Maria Wrox-Hampden had been married young to Matthew Robert Charles Fox, Esq., of Foxbridge Abbey while her elder brother, heir to Wrox, was still living. She had borne a son, Robert, posthumously, his father having been killed in a hunting accident. Had Maria remained at Foxbridge Abbey as the widowed mother of the heir, she would have drawn a jointure for her lifetime from the Abbey estates, but the death of her brother of Roman fever (contracted on a visit to the papal capital while on the grand tour) had changed the course of her life. Had she not remarried, removed to Wrox and produced an heir, Wrox would have passed by entail to a cousin who had emigrated to New Zealand in 1820, since which time he had not been heard from. For all anyone knew, he had married a savage and fathered half-breed children. Robert Fox was left in the custody of his grandparents at the Abbey; Maria returned to her father's house and the destiny that awaited her.

Maria had been entirely serious in declaring, after the birth of the twins, that she would have no more children. Since their birth she had refused her husband her bed. Twice he had forced himself upon her, shouting and cursing so loudly in the doing of it that she had submitted from fear the Cuthbert Hampdens would be aroused. Following the welcome departure of this formidable couple at the end of July, she took to locking the door to Arthur's dressing room, ignoring the late-night poundings upon it.

Even in a household the size of Wrox, the atmosphere was permeated by the tension between master and mistress, although their bitter exchanges took place behind closed doors. Things came to a head one day when Arthur asked Maria in honest indignation, *"Why, Maria—why? Why do you turn your back on your duty as a wife? It is unnatural. Indeed, it is downright wrong, it is sinful."*

"Let us just say I do not wish to suffer childbirth and its consequences," she said coldly.

"That is to shirk your duty."

"You also have a duty to me."

"I have certainly performed that duty. What on earth is it you wish?"

Maria was seated in a chair by a window that overlooked the deer park and the home farm, with the church steeple over the village beyond. This was the Wrox estate as it had been for generations. It had been hers as the old squire's heiress until her marriage, when its ownership had passed to her husband, the entail to their eldest son. The production of that son had not been Arthur's sole duty, as he seemed to think; in return for all that he had received with the heiress, he could be expected to love and cherish wife and children and to look after the Wrox lands, now badly in need of good management. In Maria's view, he had not done his plain duty. But of what use would it be to point this out to him? He simply did not understand. She murmured, "I wish no longer to be treated as a kind of vessel into which you relieve yourself when you feel so inclined."

The man was utterly taken aback. "You are monstrous!" he exclaimed. "You are impudent! It is unwomanly to be so cold, to regard yourself as an inanimate vessel—I never heard of such a thing! It is unnatural," he repeated.

On the edge of tears, she lashed out at him. "Unnatural? Every other female creature in Nature has the right to refuse the male if she is not ready for him, if the time is not appropriate; she has a right to be treated with consideration. As for me—for us—you never considered whether or not I wished your attentions. If I were in my period, even when I was so ill with the fever from the mumps—" All the pent-up resentments of years were loosed; she could not stop their flow. The recital went on, of times when she was bleeding, was simply tired to death or even really ill and had not been allowed control of her own body. He listened, appalled, until she fell silent at last.

Utterly bewildered, Arthur sought to find somewhere in his experience an explanation for this outburst. The only possible way to account for the tantrum was her time of life; he had heard a lot about that, of course, and supposed he must put up with it when the time came. But he could not see any present connection with the subject of marital duty. "My dear Maria," he asked, "what do you think marriage *means?*"

In a low, even voice she said, "Marriage is making legitimate the mating between men and women for its sole purpose, which is the procreation of children. And since I decline to bear further offspring, I decline further mating."

These were words shocking in their bluntness, putting Christian marriage, the first miracle wrought in Cana of Galilee, on a level with the copulation of dumb beasts. "You took a solemn oath to obey me!" he cried.

"As you vowed to forsake all others and keep only unto me. Since you have not done that, I intend henceforth to keep only unto myself."

"I do not know what to do," he said, "upon my word, I do not—"

Now she said, her voice strained, "You can do as you have done before, go to the churchyard."

And so it was. The back of the churchyard, which lay behind a low wall along the common, served as a public toilet and on warm nights as a place where a man could find waiting some of the Wrox field girls, laborers who were seeking to augment their ninepence a week. Arthur could now repair there without feeling a pang of remorse since it was Maria herself who had driven him to seek his relief among the tombstones.

With this crisis past, life went on, if not in quite the same manner, and the Wrox-Hampdens faced having to make decisions regarding the immediate future. They had disposed of Augustus, who would soon go to school in Hampshire, and of baby Edward, who was to be taken by Nurse to the Stoke rectory in Wiltshire. Now came up the matter of Mr. Osbert Reddle, the tutor. "We can no longer afford to keep him," Arthur said to his wife, "what with the fees for Augustus."

"He should not remain," Maria agreed. "He has mentioned to me on several occasions how much he likes this country and the life here at Wrox. It would not surprise me to find that he even has designs on one of our girls."

Arthur dismissed this notion. "Impossible. He would never aim so high."

"It would not surprise me," Maria repeated. "He lacks humility, and they are perforce thrown much together. You will advise him that his usefulness is at an end. I daresay you'll find him reluctant to leave, which will prove my suspicions to be correct. The sooner he leaves, the better. As you said, we shall need the money, it has been wasted on him, he never taught Augustus anything."

Augustus was destined for the Army; he would not need to know Latin or botany or Blake's *Songs of Innocence*, for all of which he showed not the slightest aptitude. What he did like was music. From the age of four he used to go to the pianoforte and play simple tunes. He hung about when his older sisters were having their music lessons, and by the time he was ten he could play as well as their teacher. Mr. Reddle, after trying his best to interest Augustus in anything other than music, had advised the parents that in his opinion, the boy should have lessons along with his sisters.

Arthur Wrox-Hampden rejected this idea out of hand. "It's all very well for the gels, but whoever heard of a man playing the pianoforte?"

"I can't think where he got it," said Maria. "None of the Wroxes had an ear for music—nor the Hampdens, that I know of."

"Aunt Sophia Cheycester was very fond of singing," said Arthur. "She used to go all the way to London to listen to that Swedish woman, Madame Birsten. But still, that was a long time before Augustus was ever born. Music will never do him any good, it's all indoors, he ought to be out-of-doors, like a man."

"He does not much care for out-of-door sports and games," said his tutor. "I can't see what harm it would do to let him play music, perhaps on rainy days when he cannot be out-of-doors."

"It will never get him into Winchester," said Arthur. "All the Hampdens go to Winchester. Let alone get him into the Army," he added. "Music is of no use to anyone in the Army. Bands are made up of common soldiers, enlisted men. Can't have Augustus hanging around the barracks."

Mr. Reddle made one more effort. "There is a public school at Blitchley, north of London, that offers music lessons as part of the curriculum. It is very well thought of. Many boys go there who are, shall we say, uninterested in attending Winchester or Harrow."

"Hampdens are not Harrovians," said Arthur. "Naturally they are uninterested in attendance there."

"If, as you say," Maria put in, "Augustus does not apply himself to his studies, I suggest that you instruct him to better effect. That is what you are employed to do."

The tutor managed to hold his tongue and hold on to his temper. After swallowing hard, he said, "Madam, one can lead a horse to water, but one cannot make it drink."

Both Wrox-Hampdens looked at him in surprise, Maria because he had come very close to being impudent, Arthur because he saw no reason for changing the subject from Augustus's education to the behavior of horses.

"Do not tell us that Augustus would be incapable of learning his lessons if they were properly taught."

Mr. Reddle, flushing, held on again as hard as he could to his pride and his good manners. "The lessons are well taught, madam, and Augustus is perfectly capable of mastering them. He is simply not interested in anything but music. He is highly intelligent. He has taught himself to read the notes—at his age! For all we know," Mr. Reddle went on, in an attempt at jocularity, "he might have been another Mozart had he had Mozart's early opportunities—"

"Heaven forbid!" cried Maria. "Mozart was a total failure, nobody ever paid any attention to him, he died a pauper—worse than a pauper, he was in debt! Would you wish upon Augustus a life like that? And a death so dreadful, at so young an age? Why, Mozart was an absolute nobody, a failure, until after he was dead and buried. Buried in a pauper's grave at that!"

Recognizing a stone wall when he was up against it, Osbert Reddle left the drawing room, without slamming the door. (What would have been the use?) He returned to his schoolroom. He did not tell Augustus about his efforts on the boy's behalf, but he did advise him not to play too loudly, preferably to play only when he knew his parents were out or away. Meanwhile, he persisted in his dogged efforts to make interesting to the children those subjects on which he himself was so keen.

Mr. Reddle had been informed in due course that his services would not be needed after September, when Augustus would be sent away to school and baby twin Edward would be taken off forever to live with his adoptive family in Wiltshire. It was in this way that the news of Edward's adoption first reached the schoolroom.

"How dreadful!" said Lucy, and Marietta echoed her.

"Yes, dreadful," she said.

"Thank you," said Mr. Reddle, touched. "I shall miss all of you."

"I meant how dreadful for baby Edward," said Lucy. "He will have to live with Aunt Esther."

"Aunt Georgie will be his mother. She is not so bad."

"But they are to live with Uncle Cuthbert and Aunt Esther."

"How dreadful!" said Augustus.

"The family is breaking up," Lottie said, with a troubled look for Mr. Reddle, who had been a familiar part of the household for so long.

"Perhaps it is merely expanding," Miss Wetherby suggested. "Your brother will have his own family in addition to this one."

"He is not to be our brother," Lottie said. "Aunt Georgie is his mother. How can he have two mothers? There is something wrong." Lottie had overheard Betsy, the parlormaid, telling Nurse that Lady Edge had said it was terrible bad luck to separate twins, something shocking awful would happen to both of them. She repeated this now. "Everyone knows it is very bad luck to separate twins," she declared.

Osbert Reddle understood all the logical reasons why his services should no longer be needed, but the unspoken reason—that he might have a wish to better his station by marriage—had never occurred to him. The very idea that he would aspire to enter the Wrox-Hampden family circle would have made him laugh aloud. No future could have appeared bleaker to him than one spent among these people who rode across the country without seeing its life, who killed and ate animals about which they were ignorant, who hired others to do any work that required mental or physical labor and believed themselves superior for the very reason that they possessed these negative qualities. However, following the decision that he was to go, there happened something that changed his whole outlook.

He fell in love.

He must have been in love for a long time, unconsciously. Now he asked himself how he could have been so imperceptive. He did not want to leave Wrox if it meant being parted from Elsie Wetherby. He did not want to leave her here unprotected, she who was so vulnerable, so timid, so sweet. He thought her beautiful. He wanted to dress her in pretty clothes that would show off her slender figure. He wanted to make her his own true wife, to have and to hold, to live with him and bear him children. He longed for a home of his own, with her beside him. In his dreams and reveries he went so far as to consider asking her to elope. How foolish he was! Elope where? Live where? On what?

He resolved he would not leave Wrox without speaking to her of his passion. If she could not return it, she would at least know of it, and know that she was beloved. Then he realized in despair that it would be unfair to her to make a declaration without being able to follow it with a proposal of marriage.

On the morning of his departure he asked her to join him in a walk in the shrubbery, between the house and the kitchen garden, out of sight from any of the buildings.

"My dear Elsie," he began, "if I may so address you?"

"Of course," she said, her fingers going automatically to the brooch containing her mother's hair.

"I hope you will think of me as Osbert," the tutor continued. "I have never been so bold as to tell you this, but I admire you more than I can say." He summoned up all his courage. "In fact, I think you are the most wonderful person in the world."

Tears sprang immediately to Elsie's eyes. Her knees grew suddenly weak. She stumbled and would have fallen if Osbert had not caught her and held her up. He kept his arm around her waist, thinking how slim she was, how frail, how lovable, how altogether precious. "I cannot bear to part from you," he said. "May I write to you? It will be less unbearable if we may keep in touch through correspondence."

"Oh, yes!" she said. "Please do so. I shall so look forward to hearing from you." She raised her shortsighted eyes to him with a look that made her face indeed beautiful.

He bent and kissed her on the lips.

❧ 6 ❧

LUCY AND THE YOUNG LORD

Lucy was now too old for the schoolroom and temperamentally disinclined to the usual female occupations of needlework, playing the piano, painting, reading or writing fiction. Like her father, she preferred physical to mental activity and spent long days covering the countryside for leagues around on horseback, astride one of the hunters, with skirts tucked under the saddle and petticoats showing, frightening sheep and cattle on the farmlands. She took to dropping in on the farmers and their families, becoming acquainted with their livestock, sometimes helping with a calving or a foaling. She heard their complaints about Mr. Spence, the overseer, who lived in a comfortable stone house a mile or so distant from the Hall. His house was the only one in good repair, his barn the only weatherproof structure on the home farm. Weeds were growing rampant in a cornfield. Fences needed mending. A stile was missing here, a pump handle there. Poachers had the run of the land; one of the traps had injured a sheepdog. Back in the early spring, which had been unusually cold, Nettle's little boy had been hired for sixpence a week to scare the birds from daybreak to sunset on a lately sown field. He had received only fivepence, as Spence said he had run home to get warm and eat his dinner, instead of bringing it with him, so for three hours of the week he had left his post.

Lucy reported all this one morning to her parents. "Spence is incompetent," she declared, "if not downright dishonest. Farmer Nettle told me two of his pigs had been sold at Bunbury market, but he never saw a farthing from the sale. I think, Papa, you should look into Spence's account books."

"That is what Spence is paid to do," her father said in an aggrieved tone of voice.

"He does not do it. He is ruining the value of the land."

"I have little use for people who fail to do what they are paid and expected to do," said Arthur self-righteously.

"You must speak to Spence," Maria said. "Someone has to see that he is kept in line."

"Papa, Mama, let me do it!" Lucy exclaimed. "I can do it. I know I can! The farmers all trust me; they will work hard for us. They don't work for Spence because they get no reward for doing so."

"They are a lazy lot," Arthur said.

"Only because they have no reason to be otherwise," Lucy insisted. "Please, Papa, Mama, let me try to bring Wrox back to what it used to be, in Grandpapa's day."

"My father," Maria said, "was a very extravagant man. He it was who, instead of spending money on the farms, wasted it buying Italian pictures and the Reynolds portrait and all that French furniture—"

"Mama, please! We are not talking about Grandpapa. I beg of you, let us talk about now, not about then. Something must be done *now*. Won't you do it, Papa?"

"I don't know how we could replace Spence, after all these years. He is well known in the county; his people have been at Wrox as long as the Wroxes, when you come down to it."

"And so have Nettle's," said Lucy.

"For that very reason they expect special consideration," Arthur grumbled. "But I shall look into it."

"In the meanwhile, Lucy," her mother put in, "do you not think it shows a lack of propriety for you to be consorting with the farm people? It only gives them ideas; they think they can complain to you when they would not dare do so to your father."

Lucy left the room without another word, slamming the door after her.

Maria drew a deep sigh. "I do not know what to do with her; indeed, I do not. She must be got away from Wrox; she is a bad influence. It cannot be good for the younger children. I wonder if the Chipping aunts might take her; she might be of use to Aunt Augusta—"

"In what way could she be of use to anyone?" asked Arthur. "She has no accomplishments, and Heaven knows her appearance is not prepossessing."

"She takes after you," said his wife.

This remark would once have led to a possibly violent quarrel, but husband and wife had been across stormy seas and had now reached a shore which, although rocky, had provided a resting place. Recriminations belonged in the past. Decisions had to be made in the present.

Maria had long thought about taking the older girls to Rome. It was possible to live there comfortably on 250 pounds a year. There was a large English colony with many balls and entertainments. Young English gentlemen making the grand tour always stopped there for stays of indefinite duration. Robert Fox, of Foxbridge Abbey, half brother to the Wrox girls, was in residence there for a good part of the year, and it was known that he moved in the highest society; certainly he would "do something" for his near relations.

The question was money. Two hundred and fifty pounds was not a great sum considered as annual living expenses for a family, but there would have to be found money to transport that family to Italy, with their servants, and to provide the ladies with wardrobes suitable for high society life in a great city. Yet it did seem as though the best chance for Lucy and Marietta lay in removing them from the backwater of Wrox into a larger society. In Marietta's case, a year abroad would bring her to marriageable age and add to her accomplishments the polish of the Italian language, art and literature.

"How can we afford it?" asked Arthur. He said nothing about the possibility of his missing a wife and daughters who would be absent from him for a twelvemonth because he would not in the least miss them.

"I suppose we shall have to sell one of the farms," said Maria. "However, it is a big step. Say nothing about it to anyone for the time being."

James Almeric Mountjoy FitzJames, seventh Viscount Edge, was all that a nobleman should be, as well as being handsome. He was tall and slender, with classic features on a narrow head. He was intelligent without being an intellectual. He was clever enough to be about to go up to Oxford to read history at Christ Church until he should be of age, when he would assume all the responsibilities of his inheritance. He was immensely rich; the first viscount, a vice admiral and hero of a famous naval battle, had been granted land with a very respectable pension and, as brother-in-law to a subgovernor of the South Sea Company, was in a position to make a fortune before the Bubble burst. But better than all the young viscount's obvious assets was his character: he was thoroughly nice, as considerate of his inferiors as of his peers. An only child, he had been lonely, wanting the playmates he had never had, until at the age of twelve he went to Eton from the hands of a private tutor.

On this afternoon in late September the young lord was out riding with his bailiff to look over the fields where it was proposed that the railway pass in avoiding the main coach road to Bunbury. James had once seen a railway engine and cab in a London station and had thought it a marvelous thing. People said it was noisy and dirty, so it was understandable that it would not be welcome in the famously beautiful market town of Bunbury, or in the vicinity of a gentleman's residence. But the proposed route through the village of Wrox was sufficiently far from both Edge Park and Wrox Hall to inconvenience their inhabitants in no way. The field in which the railway would cut across a corner of the Edge estate could be diverted from cattle to crop, and having the railway station as close as Wrox village would be excessively convenient, providing a direct connection to London and to the West Country. The bailiff was pointing out to his young lordship the exact path of the proposed rails when a figure on horseback appeared in the distance, headed at a gallop across the fields in their direction. While they watched, horse and rider jumped hedges and ditches without slackening speed, and presently they saw it was Lucy Wrox-Hampden, riding astride like a man, with unpinned hair flying out behind her like a mane. She went past them, then slowed, turned her horse around and rode back to where the two men were watching. Her face was flushed, and she was breathing hard, not at all like a young lady out for an afternoon's exercise.

The bailiff touched his cap. "Good afternoon, miss," he said, the barely polite tone of his greeting expressing disapproval of this young woman who, everybody agreed, "should have been a boy." "I've no use for a crowing hen," he said later to his wife, after he had watched the two young people race each other back across the countryside in the direction of Wrox. They should have asked him to accompany them; they knew very well they should not be going about unchaperoned.

James had lifted his hat to the girl and said courteously, "Good afternoon, Miss Lucy."

Without returning the greeting, she had called out, "Come along, I'll race you to Sheerwater," and after a moment to recover from his surprise, the young man said, "Done!" and off they went, neck and neck, over hill and dale toward Sheerwater Pond, some miles distant. Sheerwater was now in view from the upper floors of the west front at Wrox, because the squire had caused a hill to be leveled so that he might see without leaving the house when the migrating geese had arrived in their southbound journeys and were ready for his sport and his dinner table.

Lucy won the race, of course, but told James, "Never mind, I know the lay of the land better than you, and I have the better horse. See." They stood with their mounts on the bank, letting the animals drink, and she pointed out to James the difference between his horse and hers. "Ironsides has the better formation. He not only stands half a hand taller, his forelegs are better placed to support the rider's weight. Feel his shanks, how strong they are. He is a bonny creature, and I keep him fit. I see that he gets exercised every day, I groom him myself, one cannot trust the stableboys. Here, hold him, please, I am thirsty myself." And handing James the reins, she pulled up her skirt and flung herself facedown on the bank, leaning far over to plunge her face into the water. When she had drunk, she rose to her knees, leaned back and shook the water from her head like a dog. Then she ran a hand over her mouth, looked up at him and said, "Well—what shall we do now?"

That day they rode back to where they had met, where James showed her the proposed route of the railway. Lucy pointed out the difference between the condition of the Wrox lands and those of Edge. She confided in him, describing the recent scene with her parents and, without criticizing them, declared herself better able to oversee the running of the estate than was Spence, but of course it was out of the question.

That day James found the childhood playmate he had never had.

In the next fortnight they rode out daily, exercising the horses, going in various directions until they had almost covered the country. They took a picnic to the White Horse on the chalk downs. They fished the river Sheer where it formed part of the boundary between Edge Park and the Duke's estates. They rode the wild country beyond the pastures, over Knip barrow and the Giant's Grave, where men had lived and moved on before the dawn of history. One day they climbed a big linden, something James had never done, and Lucy dared go higher than he even though, she pointed out, she probably weighed more. There was a lot of laughter, sometimes accompanied by physical contact that would have horrified the respective parents. James discovered things he did not know he had been missing—the laughter, for one. There had been none at Edge.

On a warm afternoon they went hunting mushrooms in Edge Park. James was to leave for Oxford next day to take examinations. He knew this was the end of summer, of this happy interlude spent with a playmate in his remote, beautiful home country. They tethered their horses in a beech grove and went wandering among the trees, looking for edible fungi to take home to the kitchens. When they stopped to rest on a mossy slope, Lucy threw herself prone on her back and, as James sat beside her, pulled up the layers of petticoats and skirt covering long, well-shaped legs that now appeared before the astonished and fascinated eyes of the young man. What happened next was foreordained. Lucy, though more hot-blooded than James and more mature, was really no more the seducer than he; he could have—he should have—risen immediately and walked off. But he did not. It was a natural, inevitable coming together of two healthy young creatures on a sunny afternoon under sheltering branches with the open sky above and the good earth of the home land all around. Their music was the gentle sound of cowbells drifting over from Wimborne Chase.

↬ 7 ↫

Mr. Share Comes to Stay

Benjamin F. S. Share, Esq., was a professional man—a professional guest. It was thus that he made his way in the world, and it was a way at which he was expertly good. The cycle of his year took him on a round of extended visits to country houses, one or two of which might even be called great. He had no fixed domicile and was possessed of an income sufficient for his personal needs. By the time he was forty years old he was, in a manner of speaking, part of the ecology in the shires.

He was a snob. He claimed royal blood—never proven—by means of descent from a younger son of Edward I. Little was known about more immediate forebears; it was believed he stopped from time to time with a widowed mother somewhere in the West Country. He was low in stature, slender and neat, with small, exquisite hands and feet. His facial expression in repose was rather melancholy, because of a mustache that drooped at the ends on either side of a narrow chin. His visits were everywhere eagerly anticipated, for in his professional skills he was without peer. He played a good game of whist, danced with all the ladies at assemblies and balls, was a gifted raconteur of scandals, gossip and ghost stories and was a talented artist, giving his hosts at the end of each visit a well-executed watercolor of some part of their houses or gardens. His sketch pad and diary, both much used, traveled everywhere with him. A great virtue was his ability to engage the young people. He played with them indoors at rook or cribbage, at bowls and quoits outside. Charades, sack races, all sorts of games were in his repertoire; at stalking he was tireless. Also, it was greatly in his favor that he never made a derogatory observation about any person.

Mr. Share arrived at Wrox in early October of 1837, bringing all the news from Hatche, his previous stop. He could not wait to hear the family news (he was distantly related to Georgiana Hampden) so that he might write it back to Hatche. In the past he had several times stayed a full month at Wrox, but a few years before this Lady Edge, sitting next to him at dinner, had been so charmed she had insisted he come from Wrox to Edge for the second fortnight, a move he was only too happy to make; there just might be an opportunity one day, at Edge, to be introduced to the great Duke himself.

On this visit Mr. Share was housed, at his own request, in the haunted room. He was much interested in spiritual phenomena and hoped, having heard of the manifestation to Georgiana Hampden, that the ghost of the refractory child might disturb him. After dinner one evening he held the attention of a party consisting of twelve of the neighboring gentry with the account of what had happened to him the previous May while staying in Sussex, near Bognor.

"I had retired for the night and was preparing to sleep. The weather had been frightful, and the night was stormy, with intermittent bolts of lightning and lashings of rain at the windows. For this reason I had not opened a window. My bedroom door was of course closed but left unlocked so that the servant could enter before daybreak to light the fire of logs already laid in the chimney place. The time must have been about midnight, as I had been reading quite late, Mrs. Trollope's account of the manners of Americans, a book that makes one thankful to have no reason for visiting their shores. I had extinguished the candle and was lying quietly when suddenly . . . I had the very strong sensation that I was not alone—"

Mr. Share's delivery was quite as arresting as the stories he told. His pauses for effect were dramatic. His voice could be lowered to compel attention or raised to a pitch of excitement that raised his listeners' hackles.

"I was not alone in the room. I heard under the noise of the storm a heavy, labored breathing coming from the direction of the window, which had not been opened. No more had the door. I lay still as if petrified. Presently I felt some kind of Presence approaching the bedside. Then I heard a scraping sound by my head, and the candle on the table there was lighted.

"In my terror I jumped up and hurled the candlestick to the floor. I heard it strike the boards, and the flame went out before I could see by what means it had been lighted. There was a sound of footsteps retreating across the room, then silence."

The raconteur allowed the silence to last exactly the right amount of time before resuming his narrative. "In the morning I begged my hostess to allow me to be moved to another room in a different part of the house. When she insisted upon learning my reason for not wishing to remain in that bed, she told me the following:

"Her husband's great-grandmother, the dowager lady, had dismissed a maid she insisted had stolen a valuable ring. The maid denied having committed the theft and insisted the ring was lost or misplaced somewhere in the lady's room—the room in which I had been sleeping. A thorough search revealing no trace of the ring, the maid was dismissed in disgrace, charged with theft (never proven) and found herself unable to find employment. Sometime after this, when the episode had been forgotten, the dowager was found burned to death in her bed. It was assumed she had seen someone or something that so frightened her she had lost consciousness and been set afire when the bedside candle fell or was knocked over onto the bedclothes. All her clothing had been burned off her, and the flesh charred to the bone. On the skeletal remains of her blackened right forefinger was the ring."

Mr. Share's audience reacted as expected with delightful shiverings and credulous sympathy. "It had happened on a very stormy May night," he said, "exactly one hundred years before."

The lengthy letters that flowed out from the pen of Benjamin Share, following his passage across the country like a wake behind a ship, were as entertaining as his stories and were read as eagerly as the tales were heard.

Benjamin F.S. Share, Esq.
from Wrox to Mrs. Bellwood at Hatche

My dear friend,

What a delightful fortnight it was at dear Hatche! Quite the most original of all English castles, with the placid waters of its moat reflecting the grace of swans, the beauty of water lilies and the old stones of its walls. I do hope the small watercolor I left for you is to your taste and captures something of its charm.

You will wish to know of the recent happenings at Wrox. There have been troubles involving a tutor who had to be dismissed because of his attentions to the daughters of the house, and on the estates the farmers have fallen into lax habits despite the efforts of the overseer. Maria Wrox has with the utmost unselfishness divested herself of all responsibility for the twin boy in favor of your cousin Georgiana Hampden, who had recently lost her own infant son. The child Augustus has been sent to a school in Hampshire run by a Mr. Plumptre, who, I believe, was formerly a fellow of Oriel—long before my time there. At any rate he is an educated man who may be presumed to pass on something of Greek and mathematics to young Augustus, who has shown no inclination toward scholarship.

We have not been a dull party. Last night I presented a magic lantern show with some new slides I had brought from London, showing the Zoo, the Houses of Parliament etc., which was much appreciated. We have also been entertaining ourselves after a most unusual fashion, thanks to the presence of a Mr. and Mrs. Warnfield (she is an Honorable) whose acquaintance Maria Wrox first made while staying at the seaside at Torquay. It is said that Mr. Warnfield has never been known to laugh. This makes him an object of much interest to the children, who have been attempting (with the cooperation of some grown-ups) to make him do so.

First it was determined that verbal wit would not unlock those compressed lips. We recounted some of the droll remarks of Sydney Smith, which never fail to cause merriment. It was in vain. Mr. Warnfield remained grave. The children next thought to see if he could be induced to laugh at the sight of some physical grotesquerie. Making faces (at which Lucy is very good) merely caused him to avert his gaze. An elaborate scheme was devised to insert a thin piece of flannel in a slice of butter cake, conceal its presence with icing and make certain that this piece was handed to Mr. Warnfield. His attempts to bite through the cake, with the puzzlement of his expression, were most amusing, as the more he chewed, the more the piece of flannel became lodged inextricably between his tongue and teeth. All who were in on the joke could scarcely keep their faces straight, but the Man Who Never Laughed got up and, without even excusing himself, left the room. A well-placed pun did not cause even a glint of understanding, let alone amusement, in the stony eyes that look out from the mask that is Mr. Warnfield's face. Last Saturday at dinner champagne was served with the dessert in honor of Arthur's birthday (his fifty-third). It appeared that Arthur drank rather too freely in all the toasts honoring himself, for the next day (Sunday) he failed to come down to breakfast and excused himself from attendance at church on account of having a most dreadfully painful headache. "It may have been champagne last night," said I, "but it is real pain this morning." All the company laughed heartily in appreciation, with, of course, the exception of the Man Who Never Laughed. I daresay his is a unique distinction.

You will be interested to hear how the venerable man whose ghost haunts Wrox park came to be there. Maria told me her father, in the year 1775, replied to a notice in the *Gazette* that read as follows: "Young man wishes to retire from world and live as a hermit, is willing to engage with any nobleman or gentleman who may be desirous of having one." Squire Wrox thought an aged person with a long gray beard doddering about among ruins would be a spectacle to delight the eye, so he responded to the notice, caused the ruins to be built, and had the young man fitted with a wig of gray hair to wear until such time as Nature would have given him his own.

The weather having been pleasant, the gamekeepers have been employed and there has been a great deal of outdoor sport of a kind in which I do not join. I do not understand why the hunting of animals and the shooting of birds are called sports. They are so unfair. In true sport both sides should be equally armed and stand an equal chance.

I have been much occupied in sketching various scenes. I have made a sketch of an old grove of abeles that look like living things (which, of course, in a sense they are) in their twisted configurations; and a view over lush meadowland to the distant downs, almost purple in a certain light, lends itself admirably to the medium of watercolor. Mrs. Warnfield was kind enough to tell me, when accompanying me on a sketching walk, that my work was on a professional level.

I shall await with much anticipation a letter from you directed to Edge Park, where I betake myself the day after tomorrow, after an agreeable sojourn here at Wrox.

Faithfully yours,
B.F.S. Share

❧ 8 ❧

A Day in Bunbury

In the attics of Wrox, the cook, the housemaids and the scullery girl slept under the eaves in one set of rooms. In similar cramped accommodations on the other side of the house were the butler (who had his own sitting room) and the menservants. Between these two sets of sleeping quarters was a large chamber lighted from above by a window in the roof where Mrs. Cluster, the dressmaker, had her workshop with her assistant, a seamstress. Mrs. Cluster lived in the village and walked to the Hall every day. She made all the clothes of the Wrox ladies from patterns sent from London; her taste was much admired, and her work was exquisite. She taught the young ladies to be fine needlewomen as well as to do embroidery and woolwork. The seamstress, in addition to helping the dressmaker, had the care of all household linens, which were mended, patched, darned and turned until they had become rags and were assigned to the scullery.

While the seamstress mended linens, Mrs. Cluster created dresses and the young ladies practiced on fine seams and embroidery stitches. Miss Wetherby, seated in a straight chair under the skylight, read aloud, holding the book up within two inches of her eyes. She chose *Childe Harold* because his pilgrimage provided a history lesson on the countries through which it passed. She read *The School for Scandal*, taking all the parts quite creditably, for its lesson in morality. *Evelina* was a favorite, read because it was such a romantic, altogether delightful and satisfying love story. "When you read," she told her pupils, "you keep always the best company."

Twice yearly, in spring and autumn, after consultation with Mrs. Cluster and measurements taken, Miss Wetherby and the three oldest girls were driven by Tole to Bunbury. The carriage and pair waited for them in the innyard while they spent an entire day among the draper's, shoemaker's and milliner's shops, ending with the treat of a lavish tea at Theobald's in the High Street. Bunbury was a charming town, with an ancient cross in the market square surrounded by shops and offices. Besides the coaching inn, with its big courtyard and stables, there were a public house, the Duke's Arms, a bank, the Duke's estate office, the attorney's house that was also his place of business, the apothecary's, the town hall with assembly rooms behind and all those shops that purveyed the necessities of civilized life. The High Street contained some handsome houses, including that of Dr. Pipkin; it was steep and cobbled, dangerous to horses, especially when the stones were wet. At its top the tower of the fine church, completed and pewed three hundred years ago, surveyed the buildings of Bunbury and the undulating downland beyond.

The day of the autumn visit to Bunbury was a happy one. Marietta, who was now old enough to attend the winter's balls, was allowed to pick out the stuff for her own gown, the first she had ever had that had not previously been Lucy's. Marietta's pleasure was clouded by the realization that Miss Wetherby never chose for herself any pretty patterns, because she either could not afford them or had no place to go where she could wear them, so the girl shared her own pleasure with the governess, asking her opinion and advice about the stuffs laid out on the counter and choosing one that Miss Wetherby particularly liked. "I do so much want to be pretty in it," said Marietta. "Do you think it wrong? Vanity would be wrong, would it not?"

"Oh, no," said Miss Wetherby, "to wish to look nice is not vanity; it is a courtesy owed to others who are obliged to look at you. That is why your appearance should be pleasing to the eye."

Lucy, hearing this advice, regarded the governess from top to toe with amused contempt, noting her fustian clothing and her hair worn (as she had once described it to Marietta) in a manner resembling the ears of a spaniel. However, she did not snicker, as she might have done; instead she turned her attention to herself and, without being urged, chose a very pretty stamped velvet for a jacket and skirt. She had never before shown the slightest interest in her clothing. Miss Wetherby was pleased, and was even more so when later Lucy tried on several bonnets and chose one she thought the most becoming, giving the governess some hope that Lucy might be changing for the better as she grew from girlhood into womanhood. Perhaps the day would come when it would be possible to like Lucy—never as she loved the sweet-natured Marietta, of course, but at present, try as she might, she could not bring herself even to *like* Lucy. If it were not for Lucy, Elsie Wetherby could have been happy at Wrox, in spite of missing Osbert Reddle quite dreadfully.

At the draper's, E. Hole & Son, Son himself waited upon the Wrox ladies. He was a pleasant young man, well spoken, very keen on his trade and knowledgeable about it. For a provincial town E. Hole & Son was an unusual establishment. The merchandise was the equal of any in London, with a wide choice of patterns and materials. Son showed a line of woolens as fine and soft as the choicest imported merino and told the ladies it was made locally, from downland sheep's wool that was carded, spun and woven under his own supervision as a home industry. Many cottage wives roundabout thus found gainful employment. The woolen stuff was much in demand; E. Hole had customers from all the large towns in the neighboring shires. It made into beautiful shawls. "This that you see here will be gone before the real winter weather," said Son, "and there will be no more until next year. Only yesterday Lady Edge purchased enough of this agreeable shade of green to make a dress and cloak. Her ladyship said she saw no need to pay London prices for inferior goods."

After the girls had made their selections and instructed Son to deliver them to the carriage, Miss Wetherby begged their indulgence while she did an errand for herself. Twice yearly she took to the bank her savings of the previous six months and left them for safekeeping against her old age. Mr. Maule, the banker, always waited upon her himself and assured her that her economies would double or even triple in value long before she would have need to call upon them.

Theobald's tea was sumptuous and included trays full of the delicious Bunbury cross tarts that were the specialty. They cost two for a penny, and once Lucy, on a dare, had consumed fifteen. This year Lucy finished one and had started on a second when she suddenly stopped eating it and pushed it across the table to Lottie.

"That's very kind of you, Lucy," said Miss Wetherby. "I am happy to see you sharing with your little sister."

"I don't want it," said Lucy. "Lottie might as well have it as the cat."

When the party of four had finished tea, they walked back down the High Street to the inn, where they found E. Hole's Son waiting by the carriage with their parcels. Tole had left one of the horses between the shafts and Cavalier tied to a post with his feed bag on; the horse had eaten all he could reach and was standing patiently, surrounded by pigeons and sparrows pecking and darting about at his feet, squabbling over the spillings. Tole was nowhere in sight. "Oh, dear," said Miss Wetherby, "I fear we shall have trouble on the way home."

"Let me fetch him for you," offered Son. "I daresay he is no farther off than the Duke's Arms." And so it proved. The young man returned after a quarter of an hour with the coachman in tow. Tole's hat was on at a strange angle, and his livery looked as if it had only just been donned in haste. He opened the carriage door and stood waiting for the ladies to enter, leaning upon the door rather than holding it open. Lucy removed Cavalier's feed bag.

"Allow me to accompany you young ladies back to Wrox," said Son, taking in the situation. "I can ride up with the coachman."

"There is no need," said Lucy. "I shall drive. Help Tole to get up on the box."

"I am afraid he will fall," the young man said.

Lucy shrugged. "Never fear. If he should fall now, it would not hurt him at all." She took charge of the reins and horses while her sisters and Miss Wetherby got into the carriage and the draper's son handed in the wrapped bundles of cloths.

Young Mr. Hole lingered at the carriage door with a hand at the window. "Miss Marietta," he said, "may I look forward to the pleasure of seeing you at the December Assembly?"

Surprised, but too kind to show it, Marietta hesitated before replying, "Why, I daresay I shall be there with my parents—"

"I shall certainly recognize you in your beautiful new brocade gown," said the draper's son. "Good day, ladies. I wish you a safe journey home."

There was much to talk about among Lucy's passengers on the way back to Wrox, for they left it so seldom any detail of the day away held interest. Theobald's renowned tarts were not as good as (or were they better than?) last year's. To whom belonged the newly built house they had just passed? Was or was not the brocade for Marietta's gown the most beautiful offered by the nice young man who was the Son of E. Hole? Marietta could now be sure of one partner at the Assembly, and he was certainly a pleasing young man with good manners. Mr. Maule, the banker, must be a secret admirer of Miss Wetherby, as he always came out to the front of his establishment to attend her himself as soon as he saw her enter.

The conversation was interrupted only once, when Lucy pulled Cavalier and his mate to the side of the road and stopped the carriage to allow passage to a vehicle approaching from the other direction. There were two outriders accompanying a somewhat shabby, dusty carriage, undistinguished but for a crest coronet on the door. Inside was a lone passenger, a small gentleman sitting with his head dropped forward and eyes closed.

"That was the Duke," said Miss Wetherby. "He must be in residence; there will be his standard flying over the castle."

"*That* was the Duke?" asked Lottie incredulously. "That little man?" She had expected him to ride in a gilded carriage with liveried and bewigged postilions, himself dressed even more splendidly and wearing a golden coronet. "Is *that* what a duke looks like?"

"Judge not by appearance," quoted Miss Wetherby.

"How else should I?" Lottie asked reasonably. "You told Marietta she should look pretty because she owes it to others who must look at her. Should not a duke look like one?"

"But he *does* look like one because he *is* one," Miss Wetherby said. "You entertained false ideas of what a duke should look like because you had never seen one."

"Do you think most persons look like what they are?" asked Lottie. "Do you think you look like a governess?"

Miss Wetherby thought a moment and then said, "I suppose I do, yes."

"Then, if I did not know you and I were to look at you and judge you from your appearance to be a governess, would I not be judging by appearances? And is not that what you told us not to do?"

Miss Wetherby threw up her hands. "Lottie, I declare you are growing to be too much for me! There is a name for your kind of logic that is illogical, but I do not know what it is. If only Mr. Reddle were with us, he could tell us. He is so wise, he knows so many things on all sorts of matters." She remembered the day he had kissed her. A blush appeared on her cheek that did not escape the notice of Marietta, whose romantic heart was touched. She reached over and squeezed the hand of the governess, whereupon the blush deepened. Embarrassed, Miss Wetherby sought to divert attention from herself and the talk from the subject of Osbert Reddle. "Speaking of the Duke," she said, "he has six daughters."

"No wonder he looked so despondent," said Lottie.

Lucy drove the little party home as competently as ever a sober Tole had done. The next time Elsie Wetherby was taking tea at the vicarage with the Smallwoods she remarked upon it, whereupon Mrs. Smallwood made the usual observation that Lucy should have been a boy.

"I used to think so," Elsie said, "but of late I have remarked a difference in her attitude and behavior. I believe she will change."

"No person—or thing, for that matter—can change in kind," said Mr. Smallwood, "only in degree."

"Papa," said his daughter, "as a vicar of God, do you not believe a person may change? A sinner be reformed?"

"He will still be a sinner," said Mr. Smallwood, "though he may be a reformed one."

"That does not seem to me to be a very Christian attitude, Jonathan," said Mrs. Smallwood, who was sewing aprons for the poor when she was not pouring tea. Her hands were never idle.

"My dear, if the sinner be a Christian, his sin will be forgiven," said her husband. "That is very different from expunging the sin as though it had never been committed. If we behave well in this life we may be assured of our reward in the hereafter."

"I should prefer to get my reward in this life," said Mrs. Smallwood. "Then I should be sure of it."

"You would not then have it to look forward to," said her daughter.

"It is dangled before me like a carrot before a donkey, always just out of reach, and I am not to have it until I can no longer enjoy it."

"You are both under a misapprehension. The reward is in the very looking forward to it," said the rector.

"You are saying the means and the end are one and the same," his wife said, "which is not possible."

"Oh, please," Miss Theodora begged her parents. "Do not start your quarreling, you are always quarreling, I cannot bear it—and in front of Miss Elsie—"

The two looked surprised. It had not occurred to either of them that they were engaging in a quarrel; each was thoroughly enjoying the airing of differences. Mrs. Smallwood was a kind, well-intentioned woman who automatically disagreed with whatever statement was made to her; that was her role in life and its chief purpose. If told the weather was fine, she called attention to a distant cloud. She routinely expressed dislike for whatever another had praised, were it a thing to eat, wear, read or listen to. Her husband, equally opinionated, held views opposite to hers. Thus they were ideally suited to each other and enjoyed their differences in perfect happiness.

"I am sure it is for Miss Elsie to say, Theodora, and not you," said her father. "Come, Miss Elsie, tell us what are your feelings about this noisy railway that is to bring the world to our door?"

"Indeed, sir, I have no opinion on the matter."

"It may prove to be a means of spreading the Word of God more widely," said the rector.

" 'Wherever God erects a house of prayer/The Devil always builds a chapel there,' " quoted Mrs. Smallwood.

❧ 9 ❧

AN EXCHANGE OF LETTERS

On leaving Wrox, Osbert Reddle had gone to stay at his parents' home in Devon, where his father was a dealer in wine and spirits, while he made up his mind about a future course of action. He could have readily found another tutorial position, but he wished now to find employment suitable for a married man. His parents welcomed him and would have been happy to see him settled nearby. However, no congenial occupation presented itself, nor did he wish to live in the family home in the town. The neighbors and family friends, sensible and kindly folk, for the most part tradesmen, were not even aware of the interests that were Osbert's obsession. He had started a collection of the wild flowers found in the country around Wrox, pressing, sketching and cataloging specimens he hunted in the woods and on the downland. Second only to Elsie Wetherby, he missed the opportunity to finish this work after leaving there.

He was ideally suited to be a schoolmaster. He had no what is called small talk and was a poor conversationalist, since his idea of a conversation was telling others what he knew that they did not; sometimes he persisted in telling them what they did already know. Children, who could not interrupt or contradict him, made perfect companions. He determined to find a way of life where he could exercise his special talents and have Elsie Wetherby as his helpmeet.

Excerpt: Letter from Osbert Reddle
at Truro to Elsie Wetherby at Wrox   *December 18*

. . . I was interested and not surprised to read that Mr. Plumptre's reports of Augustus's first term at school are not promising for the boy's future.

. . . I always take an interest in any local news you have to tell. Pray let me know the current state of negotiations for the extension of the railway into the neighborhood. This is of importance to me—likewise, I hope, to you, my dear Elsie—so kindly keep me up-to-date on the developments. . . .

Excerpt: Letter from Elsie Wetherby at Wrox
to Osbert Reddle at Truro   *December 31*

. . . I write on the eve of the New Year in reply to your letter posted on 18 December, arrived by this morning's courier. It appears to be settled that the railway will indeed cross the home farm and there will be a station at Wrox, to the great relief of the citizens of Bunbury, who will be spared all the attendant noise, disruption and dirt. The posting inn will still remain in the town for the convenience of travelers by coach, for whom the railway has no provision. Mr. W-H is greatly worried about the adverse effect the railway will have on the value of his property, and especially on the village, for no one will wish to live in the vicinity of the railway. The household has all been suffering greatly from chilblains in this severe weather. They are bearable during the daytime if one avoids getting too close to the fire, but very painful at night once one has retired and begun to get warm. I should prefer to live in a house less grand with small rooms that are warm. Christmas passed with no visitors except for young Mr. Arthur and a friend of his from Oxford whose people are in the West Indies, so he had nowhere else to go. They have been quite gay with parties in the neighborhood, to which Marietta is now old enough to be invited. Her mother accompanied her to the December Assembly, where, according to Mrs. W-H, she received many attentions from young gentlemen, especially young Hole, who is the son of the Bunbury draper; he is a personable young man, and although he is in trade, it is a respectable one that is prosperous. Mrs. W-H also said that young Lord Edge had singled out Marietta for attention at several parties and seemed to enjoy dancing with her. Mrs. Cluster's gowns had everywhere been much admired. Baby Violet is very pretty and does not cry much. She did howl all night as if her little heart would break when the baby Edward was taken away to Mrs.

Charles Hampden at Stoke-sub-Ham. Nurse reminded me that it was said at their christening that to separate twins would bring ill luck. Lottie and I think that all the ill luck is brought to baby Edward, who has to live in the house of Archdeacon and Mrs. Cuthbert Hampden. Little Edward will have *no* brother or sister or other companion to share his fate at the hands of those people. It is said their intentions are good, but there is a screw loose somewhere if good intentions can produce such unwelcome results. Lucy has not been at all well. She did not attend any of the parties; she remained at home with me and much to my surprise wished me to read to her every evening until she fell asleep. Some time ago she complained of being sick, and even though she eats nothing, she seems to gain weight. Dr. Pipkin has attended her several times, but the physic he prescribed did her no good. He told Mrs. W-H that it was possible she suffered from a new ailment called, I think, hypokondra, that is imaginary! I well knew there was nothing *imaginary* about Lucy's *malaise* as it was I who helped her when she was sick in the morning; there was nothing imaginary about it. Dr. Pipkin says this *mal-de-terre*, to *ainsi dire*, is quite commonplace but usually occurs in persons much older than Lucy, who has just turned eighteen. Her birthday was not a happy occasion, since it was on her eighteenth birthday that Henrietta W-H died so suddenly. As you well know, I have never found it possible to like Lucy, an *enfant terrible*, if ever there was one, but I am now inclined to feel sorry for her; it does not seem right that her eighteenth birthday should go unobserved because an older sister did not survive her own. . . .

❧ 10 ☙

TWO ROADS TO ROME

"I do not believe it," said Lady Edge.

She and the Wrox-Hampdens were sitting in the small drawing room at Edge Park. It was a fine room, designed by Robert Adam, with a specially woven carpet that reflected the pattern of the elaborate plaster ceiling. The butler and two parlormaids, who had brought in the tea service, had withdrawn and closed the door. The two ladies and one gentleman were seated before the hearth, where a coal fire provided a little warmth against the chill of a sunless winter afternoon.

Maria had waited for the servants to leave and the tea to be poured before coming straight to the point of her and Arthur's visit to her old friend: Their daughter Lucy was pregnant. Lucy had told her parents that James Edge was responsible. "Lucy has never told an untruth," said her mother, unconscious that she had herself just uttered one. "Dr. Pipkin confirms it."

"My dear Maria, I do not doubt her condition," said Lady Edge, "but I do not believe James to be responsible for it."

"You remember they were seen together a good deal last autumn before James left," said Lucy's father.

"Because you did not exercise proper control over Lucy. You let her run wild, with total lack of propriety, and now everyone's disapproval of the manner of her upbringing is fully justified. Small wonder she is now a fallen woman. You are reaping what you sowed."

Maria came to her own defense. "I was perhaps lacking in judgment when I trusted the supervision of Lucy's behavior to the governess. Miss Wetherby is wanting in character; she lacks the firmness necessary to control a girl as high-spirited as Lucy."

"If so, you should not have entrusted to her the duties you were certainly capable of performing yourself."

"Lucy is not controllable," Arthur murmured.

"Every animal goes to the end of its tether," said Lady Edge.

"Lucy has so much . . . energy, let us say," said her father. "Once she is married, a husband will no doubt know how to tame her, as it were—"

"I wish you luck in finding her such a husband," said Lady Edge, "and if you are to succeed in his pursuit, it had better be soon, had it not?"

"Her husband should be the man who is responsible for her plight," Maria said boldly.

"That might be any man among the farm folk around," said Lady Edge. "It is well known that she consorts with them, while her parents are not even apprized of her whereabouts."

"She says the father is Edge," Arthur said.

"There is no way to prove that," the widowed mother declared. Far from being on the defensive, as Lucy's parents had expected, she moved to the attack. "Edge is not yet twenty years old," she said. "He cannot marry until he is of age. When he does marry, it will not be with one who is already pregnant with a bastard child. He does not even know of its putative existence. He has not even seen the disgraced young woman for many months. And I forbid any mention to him of this altogether lamentable affair. And now, Maria—may I pour you some more tea?"

Maria got to her feet. "Thank you, no, Emma. Since you have accused me of not supervising my daughter's actions, I feel free to remind you that you yourself were unaware that behind your back your precious James was seducing a girl of good family. Come, Arthur, we shall take our leave—"

Lady Edge sat erect, facing the fire, in a tall chair whose back her own had never touched. She was a rather short woman, but her posture made her appear taller and lent its uprightness to her moral stance. She rose, crossed the floor and rang for the butler to show her guests out. It required a full two minutes for him to walk from his pantry to the drawing room, during which time she remained standing to emphasize

Maria's decision that further conversation on this painful subject was futile.

After the Wrox-Hampdens had taken their departure, Lady Edge did not resume her seat but walked back and forth in front of the fire, turning over in her mind what course of action she should take. Even if the inadmissible were true (although unthinkable) that James could have violated Lucy Wrox-Hampden, it could only be because Lucy had entrapped the innocent youth. His marriage to her was out of the question. Not only was her son of high rank, placed in an exalted position in life, but he *was*, in a sense, that position; it had existed before he had and would exist after him. The position was of more importance than its temporary occupant. Lord Edge was patron of four livings. He was curator, rather than owner, of the valuable paintings, sculpture and furniture that filled the great rooms at Edge Park. The estates were for his lifetime only in his custody rather than in his possession.

The great privilege of being a peer of the realm carried grave responsibilities attached thereto. For example, only recently, one of the livings had fallen vacant and Lady Edge had had to decide upon whom to bestow it. The letters of application were many and from clergymen of all sorts, some pitiful in their descriptions of need: many children, no private means; appeals to her ladyship's charity; letters from obviously suitable applicants who were too elderly or who had private incomes and were not in need. She had lost sleep over having to make this agonizing decision.

Edge could not raise to the peerage a wanton woman and her ditch-conceived child whose paternity was problematical. None but a suitable consort could wear the Edge coronet and bear its heir. These facts were self-evident; it should not have been necessary to point them out to the Wrox-Hampdens. Lady Edge sat down again, alone, to consider how she should behave in this dreadful situation. She found her eyes filling with tears that she did not try to control, and after she had indulged in a long fit of crying, she got down on her knees and asked her deceased husband to ask God for His guidance.

Later on, in the night, an answer from Heaven came in the form of Benjamin Share. James should leave the country until the birth of Lucy Wrox-Hampden's bastard was well over and done with. It would be more than logical, it would be a providential solution, for James to tour Europe—Switzerland, France, Italy—with a suitable guide and companion. Who better than Mr. Share? He was well educated, well read, with excellent taste in art, and he was perfectly trustworthy. He would never introduce his charge to any form of vice or allow him to succumb to any temptations of a vicious nature to which an innocent youth with a great deal of money might be exposed in Rome or Paris.

Negotiations were undertaken that resulted in James Edge's being sent to join Mr. Share in lodgings in the papal city. Correspondence back and forth had settled on a handsome recompense to Mr. Share for his time. He was given no specific instructions about James's education except, wrote Lady Edge, "James must not become exposed to the dogma of any Papists. I have heard that many Englishmen, including even adherents of the Oxford Movement, have succumbed to the constant pressure and proselytizing of the Papists. I hope you have yourself no inclination in that direction." Mr. Share assured her ladyship that he abhorred Papism in all its forms and although the highest Roman social circles included some of its adherents, he himself took no part in their staurolatry. In fact, he wrote:

. . . Such Papists as I have now and then encountered have behaved in most peculiar fashion. There was an Irish landowner staying at Naples, a Mr. Flannagan of Kerry, who had the habit, from time to time, of not speaking to his wife when she had in some way displeased him. The period of silence was determined by the gravity of the offense. Mr. Flannagan once did not speak to her for an entire week, the unfortunate woman having no idea of the reason for her disgrace. At the end of the week he told her she had been punished for having eaten meat on a Friday. These people infest the Italian hill towns and particularly Rome in hopes of meeting the Pope in his person and receiving his dubious blessing, for which they pay handsomely toward the maintenance of his princely style of life.

. . . Your ladyship will remember a Mr. and Mrs. Warnfield whom we met while I was staying at Wrox last autumn; you were so kind as to entertain the whole company at dinner. Mr. Warnfield was famous for never having been known to laugh. I happened to encounter Mrs. Warnfield not long ago at Capri, where I had an opportunity to be alone briefly with her in the sitting room of the hotel. She gave me the melancholy news that Mr. Warnfield had recently been laid to rest as the result of an apoplectic stroke. I ventured to bring up the subject of her husband's unique distinction and asked her the reason for his eccentricity, thinking she might say he had suffered from an unhappy childhood or some form of melancholia. Not at all, said she, he was a most agreeable man, but he had very bad teeth. . . .

Mr. Share traveled to Dover to meet the young lord and accompanied him back to the papal city on the first stage of his grand tour.

On the day before this departure James was with his mother at a hotel in Dover. She had wanted to talk to him before he left for the Continent but would on no account let him come to Edge Park on his way there. "Once you have attained the age of one-and-twenty, James," she said, "among the responsibilities of your position will come the great one of your marriage."

"Ah!" said James airily. "I am in no hurry to get married; you need not worry about that."

"You will find there will be many young women ready to throw themselves at you."

"That would be an interesting sight, Mother. I could probably manage to catch one if all did not throw themselves at once."

"Do be serious, son. Most young men have to seek out their future wives and court them. You will have to turn them away. Your choice will be immense, beginning with either Lady Anne or Lady Eleanor Stuart."

"Why only those two?" said James. "Why not the Duke's other four daughters? All are surely old enough for one to make as good a cradle snatcher as another. Oh, I think I shall take the one that loves me best, not the one most desperate for a husband."

"All will love you, my James," said the doting mother, "for indeed, you are very perfection; you would be irresistible even without your high rank and fortune. Just as was your dearest father. I wish for you to be as happy in your marriage as we were. And as to children, your father used to say the dam is as important as the sire."

"My dear Mother," asked James, "are you trying to give me the lecture about the realities of life that my father would be expected to do?" There was nothing about life or women, he thought, that his mother could tell him. He was already a man. "I acknowledge that I am very lucky, Mother. I can marry the girl I love, no matter what her station. Thanks to good fortune, I have no need to marry an heiress."

"That, of course, is well known to every girl in the kingdom who is of marriageable age. However, if you do not marry a young woman already well placed, how can you know you are not being married for your money and title? One of the Duke's daughters, for example. You could be sure she is not marrying for the sake of improving her station."

"She would be improving her station if she married a groom," said James. "Any station is an improvement over that of an unwed maiden immured in those medieval towers."

"Ah, well, you have years yet before it becomes imperative that you marry at all." Lady Edge embraced her son and gave him her blessing. The parting was very hard for her, yet she felt a profound sense of relief in the knowledge that James was beyond reach of her scheming former friends at Wrox, who had attempted to take advantage of his youthful innocence and her own old attachment to Maria.

Mr. and Mrs. Wrox-Hampden had left Edge Park on that chilly afternoon in an indescribable emotional state. They were forced to travel home in silence lest Tole should get wind of the state of affairs, but it was a silence waiting to be broken with a sound of thunder as soon as they found themselves alone. As the carriage left the great house and rolled through its park to the gates surmounted by the Edge arms, Maria thought: All this should one day have belonged to my grandchild. Both she and Arthur had been certain that James's mother and Maria's old friend, being upright and moral, would force her son to make an honest woman of the girl he had wronged. Instead she had turned everything around to make him the one wronged, even forbidding them to apprize him of his impending fatherhood. To do so would now be futile, resulting only in Lucy's open disgrace. This disgrace must now be avoided by all means. So far only Dr. Pipkin was aware of her condition. It must be kept from the world, including the younger children and all the relations.

There was no time to be lost. Some of it had already been wasted in recriminations, accusations and arguments. At last it was decided, after much discussion, that Maria and the two eldest girls should go for a sojourn to Rome, as had before been considered, taking two maids. Maria would appeal to her son Robert Fox to find them proper lodgings and launch Marietta in Roman society. Lucy's presence there would be kept a secret while she awaited her confinement, after which a suitable disposal of the infant would be decided upon.

Funds for this expensive undertaking were to be found from the sale of land, preferably that nearest to the railway and in the village where the proposed station would be situated, "if we can find a purchaser for land now useless for either grazing or agriculture," said Arthur, "not to mention human habitation." However, he undertook to see the land agent in Bunbury and arranged to find a purchaser. Mrs. Cluster was put to work day and night letting out clothes for Lucy to wear until she could find in Rome a dressmaker who would, so to speak, take over where Mrs. Cluster's work had been forced to come to a stop. It was put forward that Robert Fox had requested the presence of his half sisters at his Roman villa, they being now of an age to appreciate all the advantages of a visit to that city. Miss Wetherby was to be left in charge of the household at Wrox and the education of Lottie.

Mrs. Wrox-Hampden sent for the governess to inform her of these arrangements. Although she could not blame Miss Wetherby for Lucy's condition without revealing it, Maria did inform the governess that Lucy had never had proper supervision; her attendance in the schoolroom or required hours of practice at the pianoforte had never been insisted upon; her removal to Rome was ostensibly to provide her with the cultivation she had lacked under the aegis of Miss Wetherby. It was to be hoped that Lottie would not be as much neglected, if not downright mistreated, as Lucy had been. In addition, Maria informed the governess that as she would henceforth have only one pupil, her stipend would accordingly be less.

The departure for Italy came on a day when the squire was in Bunbury seeing to his affairs, so he did not witness the leave-taking when the two young ladies bade Miss Wetherby good-bye. The latter was in tears as she embraced Marietta. "I am truly sorry if I failed you and Lucy," she said humbly. "I did my best for you. I tried to form your minds and your tastes as they should be—"

"Oh, dear Miss Wetherby," said Marietta, herself beginning to cry. "Did I never tell you how much I owe to you? I feel guilty indeed for not having told you that you are much appreciated and loved."

The words Elsie Wetherby had longed to hear had been spoken at last. Gratitude caused her nearly to choke on her tears as she said, "My dear Marietta, you did not need to tell me. You showed me."

❧ 11 ❧

JAMES MOVES INTO THE *Haut Monde*

The *haut monde* of the Continent was a country without boundaries. Its inhabitants circulated among the great cities of Europe, at home in all, and stayed in the grand villas and castles of Italy, France, Germany, Austria and Switzerland. In the *haut monde* several languages were spoken, and its denizens understood the unspoken international language of classical music. They ate delicacies and drank vintages that did not grow on or in English soil. They read Gibbon, Mme. de Sévigné, Ariosto. They frequented rooms where hung the works of Canaletto, Rembrandt, the newly adopted Corot. It was in this world that Benjamin Share was to act as the guide to the young Lord Edge.

They arrived in Rome in early February, traveling by hackney carriage through the Apennines, their two menservants following in a second *vetturino*. To James the whole countryside was of immense interest: the plains covered with withered grasses and thistles on which wandered herds of strange creatures called buffalo; crumbling hill towns crowned with towers; occasional clumps of flowers Mr. Share identified by the poetic name of asphodels. It was all of interest to James mainly because it was so different from his home landscape, to which he now felt the first stirrings of a longing to return. Mr. Share kept up a stream of talk; he was familiar, it seemed, with the highways and byways that made up "All

Roads Lead to Rome." Then on a distant hill there appeared the great dome of St. Peter's, containing its storied history that Mr. Share recounted on the way through the wretched suburbs until the arrival at the Piazza del Popolo, where rooms had been engaged in the Palazzo Arvati.

Word of this arrival soon spread. Mr. Share had laid out for his charge a course of study which soon proved difficult to pursue, as invitations to parties, balls, audiences, weddings and even funerals came to the lodgings. Some were from ladies of English or Irish birth married into noble Roman families, some from French royal duchesses, others from Spanish exiles.

It was to the home of an exiled Spanish *duquesa* that James went to a ball on the evening following his first day in Rome. The *duquesa* lived in a villa, rather than a palace, on the outskirts of the city, whither Mr. Share had arranged for a hired carriage to take them. For James it was to be his introduction to the *haut monde*; he cut a handsome figure in the London-tailored clothes that he wore, despite his youth, with the aristocratic air that was his birthright. Benjamin Share was beside himself with happiness to be so closely associated with the distinguished young lord. He climbed into the carriage after James and directed the coachman to take them to the Villa Lambrosi on the Rivoli road. "The *duquesa*'s ancestors are most distinguished," he remarked. "She is a great-niece of Marie Antoinette! She is nearly related to Queen Isabella of Spain. Her suppers are famous, as you will see, for the delicious viands. It is said the Pope wanted to marry her, which, of course, would not be *comme il faut*, unless the Risorgimento—mostly clericals, don't you know?—should get its way. They would like to see a federation of Italian states with the Pope as president, and of course, if he were to be president of a state, he would have to have a consort—not for reasons of succession, a president does not need to produce an heir any more than does a Pope, but a head of state needs an official hostess, as a Pope who is not also a president does not. You will find politics much discussed wherever we go here. You had best keep quiet and not appear to take sides. There are too many sides to be taken—unlike what we are accustomed to at home, where one is either a Whig or a Tory, and now with Melbourne in the saddle one would be advised to be a Whig. In Italy you will find it is all vastly more complicated—ever since the Bonapartes—so it will be well for you merely to listen and appear to agree with whoever is talking. Well, here we are. Driver," he said in Italian, "be at the door for us at four o'clock, not one minute after."

The Villa Lambrosi was magnificent, every window glittering with light, approached through laid-out gardens by an avenue of silver candelabra. Inside there was music, the hum of conversation, the movement to and fro of guests in *grande tenue*, many of the women wearing tiaras. On the threshold James was struck by a paralyzing shyness as he looked over the great rooms filled with strange persons bearing strange names and speaking in strange tongues. He would have given much to be back at home, where everyone knew him and he knew everyone. "Come along," said Benjamin Share, taking his elbow, "they are *dying* to meet you, and you need not be in awe of the *duquesa*. She is not the wife of the Pope— not yet, at any rate—and in fact, her husband was a common soldier, no more entitled to be called a duke than you or I."

So James entered the *haut monde*.

Among the invitations that overflowed a silver bowl in the salon of the two gentlemen's lodging was one for a ball at the house of an Englishman who wintered in Rome, Robert Fox. "You must meet Mr. Fox," Mr. Share said to James, "as he is quite the leader among the English colony. He is, by the way, the son of Mrs. Wrox-Hampden, your neighbor at Edge Park, but you will find him exceedingly unlike those relations."

Robert Fox was indeed different in every particular from the Wrox-Hampdens. He owned the renowned English country house Foxbridge Abbey, where he stayed twice a year on the way to and from his Scottish shooting box. He had a house in Mount Street where he spent the London season. He was now twenty-eight years of age. He had been called a dandy, but although it was true he paid great attention to dress, he was by no means a fop; he found the company of women just as enjoyable in his arms as in the drawing room. In the little Roman Piazza San Claudio he kept an Italian mistress who was not accepted in the *haut monde*, and in London it was openly known he had been the lover of the Countess Hopeford. Invitations to his parties were as eagerly sought as they were carefully issued.

When his mother wrote to him in Rome from Wrox, demanding that he receive her and his two half sisters, he was appalled. He had never expected Wrox-Hampdens to set foot in the *haut monde* (it was not their style); besides, he had heard that his mother—at her age!—had produced twin infants who could not yet be more than a few months old. How could she leave them? Surely—Heaven forbid—she did not intend to bring them! At one time Robert had even sought to lay claim to the Wrox estate, but his lawyer, after looking up old wills, deeds, inheri-

· 73 ·

tances, agreements and entailments, had advised him against proceeding; not only would such a claim be difficult, if not impossible, to prove, but the estate was hardly worth the trouble and expense it would take to restore house and lands. So Robert, who was good-natured and not in the least vindictive or greedy, had decided to behave like a gentleman toward his half relations and leave them in possession of their dubious claim to what might possibly be his own inheritance.

But receiving these rural folk in his beautiful Villa Brozzi, and in the height of the season! And being expected to introduce them to the Borghesi and the Santa Croci as his mother and sisters! He might just as well send out for three millstones to wear around his collar in full view of all Roman society.

Maria Wrox-Hampden and her two daughters arrived in Rome on the eve of Robert's annual ball. His house was undergoing all the preparations for that event, including cleaning, polishing, decorating, unpacking and washing of china and crystal, ironing of linens. It was impossible to put up his relations in the *villa*, he explained, so he had arranged for lodgings near the Piazza Navona, whither he accompanied them to see them settled in. Their appearance was both better and worse than he had feared. First, there were no infants or young children in the party, he thanked God, and the three women were well dressed and well shod. (One can always tell a lady by her shoes.) He found himself genuinely glad to see his mother. He had forgotten what a handsome woman she was; his own wide forehead and dark eyes, his proudest features, were her inheritance. He customarily saw her only once yearly, when she spent a week at the Abbey, and he himself never stopped at Wrox, there being no time in his full schedule when a visit there could be fitted in. Or so he had always maintained. Thus he had never seen any of his half brothers or half sisters, and it was with natural curiosity that he now met Lucy and Marietta.

Marietta was exceedingly comely, with a sweet expression and becoming manners; Robert would not mind presenting her to his friends, he could even do so with pride. But Lucy! She was even taller than himself, excessively plain and . . . enormous, there was no other word for it; she must weigh at least fourteen stone. And then her manner! She acknowledged the introduction without a smile, jerking her large head about in an awkward way. He had meant to invite these relations (they were, after all, near ones) to his ball. Now he felt he really could not do so. Yet they knew the ball was impending. What was he to do?

Maria herself extricated him from this very real quandary. She said without ado that she must speak alone with him, as soon as possible. She suggested that the two girls busy themselves with helping the maids unpack and settle in, after which they would need to lie down and rest after the journey. She would accompany Robert back to his house.

So it was that Robert found himself alone with his mother in his garden, in a sheltered spot in the sun where they could be warm. The house was swarming with the people preparing for the ball, and Maria had insisted upon privacy. They sat on a stone bench set against a wall between espaliered plum trees.

"I shall speak to you frankly," Maria began. "Lucy, as can now be readily seen, is with child."

Robert Fox was in every sense a man of the world, but he had never faced a situation such as this one. He was shocked. "And is she not married?" he inquired.

"She is not."

"How could this have happened to her?"

"In the usual way, I suppose."

"I mean, Mother, how could you have allowed it to happen? Was she not at all times under supervision?"

"You do not know Lucy—" Maria began.

"It appears that I am about to do so," said Robert, "much to my regret." Having risen to his feet, he began to pace the gravel, feeling almost faint in contemplation of what this might mean to him. These women had thrown themselves at him in their misfortune, expecting him to do something about it. Why could they not have stayed quietly at Wrox, shut Lucy up in the attics and smuggled her brat when it was born to one of the cottagers' wives? Such things happened all the time. Why did they impose themselves on *him?* They had no claim on him, none whatsoever. If anything, it should be the other way around: He could lay claim to Wrox and throw them all out, Wroxes and bastards alike. He stopped in front of his mother and asked, "What do you expect me to do? Can't you get the father to marry her?" Even as he suggested this, he remembered the ugly, sullen mother-to-be and knew no one would willingly marry her. In fact, why had any man been tempted to cause the disgraceful condition in which she had got herself? She had no fortune. It was only thanks to himself, when you came to think of it, that she had so much as a roof over her head. Still, in a way it was a mercy: Lucy's misshapen appearance was at least only temporary; she could not always look this way.

Maria's head was bowed. She put a hand to her forehead, smoothing the thick brows. The fine dark eyes beneath were closed. In a voice almost humble, she said, "No one at home knows. Except her father, of course."

"Are you telling me that the man responsible does not even know?" Maria shook her head.

An appalling thought struck Robert. "Does Lucy herself know who is the father?"

"She says she does."

"Well?"

"His identity must remain confidential."

"My dear Mother, this makes no sense. Whoever he is, he must know if responsibility for this—this impending catastrophe—could or could not be laid at his door. Cannot Lucy's father confront him?"

"It is not possible," said Maria, now beginning to lose her composure.

"Then the scoundrel is already married?"

"No, not that."

"Then I can only conclude he is one among several—or even many— men who might or might not be responsible."

"Lucy says not. But believe me, Robert, there is no way of forcing him to make the child legitimate. No way on earth."

"So what is it you propose to do?" asked Robert.

Maria laid forth her proposal. Lucy was to be kept sequestered in the Roman lodgings until the time of her confinement. Everyone at home knew she and Marietta were spending a season in Rome. No one in Rome need know Lucy had even left England. Meanwhile, Robert would see that Marietta had the happy time here that she deserved. Did he not see how winning was his younger sister, how deserving of a chance at life that Lucy must not be allowed to spoil? When it was time for Lucy to be brought to bed, Robert's knowledge of Roman ways could certainly provide a doctor or a midwife to attend her without anyone's knowing of it. She, Robert's mother, was not asking him for any other assistance; she expected to defray all the expenses; she needed his help because she had no one else to whom to turn. The barriers of Maria's natural reserve, always so strong, began to crumble here under the southern sky so far from all the scenes of her previous life. Robert was her firstborn, the nearest person by blood to her in all the world. She poured out her heart, calling him "my little kit," as she had done when he was a babe, a kit being the name for a young fox. Had her brother not died, she would have remained at the Abbey and been mother to Robert, her only child. Then she had been told it was her duty, as the heiress, to return to Wrox, marry again and produce a son, to the end that Cousin Wilfrid Wrox, now in New Zealand, should not inherit. Why should he not have done? If he were a future landed squire, he would not ever have gone to New Zealand to seek a fortune he would not have needed. Maria had left Foxbridge Abbey and the Fox family, had married Arthur Hampden and borne all those children, living and dead, for no reason except to keep the estate intact for her father's direct descendants.

As she recounted all this, she could hear her own voice rising to a shrill level in self-justification but was unable to stop it. Ever higher it rose as she aired her grievances. "I have felt like a broodmare, with no reason to exist but to bear these children, and they die, Robert, one after another they die, or they turn out to be no better than Cousin Wilfrid Wrox's children, who would not have been savages had I not married Arthur, and Cousin Wilfrid then not gone to New Zealand—" She heard herself and stopped suddenly to get out a handkerchief and blow her nose. "I am sorry, Robert," she said. "It is just that I feel I had no choice—and now this, Lucy putting us all in this dreadful position, it is unfair."

"Please don't cry, Mother," Robert begged her. He thought it equally unfair to include him in this dreadful position, as Maria put it, especially on the eve of his great day, the day of his annual ball; one would think they could be more considerate. "I really can't talk about it any more just now, Mother. There is so much I have yet to do against tomorrow. Keep Lucy at home by all means, at least until dark, but do not let her go out after dark on any account, as the streets are not safe, unless, if she must venture out for necessary exercise, she has a trustworthy companion. I shall see what I can do. And now I shall expect you and Marietta here tomorrow night, at eleven o'clock."

With this Maria contented herself for the time being. At the moment they were at least safely settled; if Robert had not offered help and protection, he had not actually turned them away, and Marietta was to have a chance to meet people who lived in a world less circumscribed than that of Wrox.

Lucy was forced to recognize she was wholly dependent upon her parents. Their help, if not their goodwill, was a necessity. She had been brought to Italy that her disgrace might not be known at Wrox, but she could not have borne permanent exile from the beloved place where she had spent all her life. "I knew no one would ever want to marry me," she said. "And I don't care! I shall have my child, and Papa will give us one of the cottages to live in, and we can say it was adopted in Italy."

"Adoption will do well enough, something of that sort," said Maria.

"What shall we tell Miss Goody Two-Shoes?" Lucy asked.

"I suppose Marietta will have to know at some time," said her mother. "But her discretion may be counted upon." To Marietta, in a separate conversation, she explained that it was for reasons of health Lucy must quit the climate of England for a sojourn in the south. Dr. Pipkin had recommended it. The trouble was nothing that could prove fatal, just a bloated condition.

"What is the cause?" asked Marietta.

"The doctor did not say. But she must remain indoors in Rome. That is most important."

"Then what is the advantage of the Roman climate over ours?"

"It is reputed to be more salubrious. But no one in Rome must ever know she is there. Promise me you will tell no one. The Italian people are ignorant in matters of hygiene; they might turn her out if they knew."

"Is it catching, then?" asked Marietta, terrified. "I am the one who shares her bed, who sleeps with her!"

"No, no, Dr. Pipkin assures me it is not contagious. You need have no fear of catching it. In any case, you will no longer be sharing a bed; you are both too old for that. Just think of what a happy time you are going to have. Think of the places you will see and the people you will meet."

Robert Fox's annual ball was anticipated eagerly by the English residents, temporary and permanent, and was always well attended. Guests came from as far as Orvieto, Terni, even Cassino, staying overnight with Roman friends. They not only mingled with their compatriots but could count on some sort of entertainment out of the ordinary. This year was no exception. Robert had imported a band from Leipzig to introduce into Italy a dance step called the waltz. It had a rousing tempo that caught the fancy of his guests, to Robert's satisfaction; failure would have ruined his reputation as host. Soon adherents of the new rhythm were revolving enthusiastically to the tune of *"Ach, du lieber Augustine,"* working up an appetite for the delicacies to appear later on the dining tables.

Maria Wrox-Hampden was reigning as mother of the host, receiving his guests as he brought them up to her, and introducing her daughter. Robert was glad, after all, that his female relations had descended on him (as he put it) for it added a surprise to the evening's entertainment, and they were a nice-looking pair to present: Maria majestic in a purple ball gown (not in the least provincial in style), wearing the pearls that had been her great-grandmother's; Marietta, in an agony of shyness, dressed in a becoming shade of peach that looked well with her complexion and hair.

Maria was enjoying herself. Then she glimpsed in the doorway a familiar figure. Could it be? Here of all places? It was. Benjamin Share was approaching across the floor. She should not have been surprised to see him, for this was exactly the sort of place and kind of occasion where he could be expected to appear, ever the welcome guest. He would translate for those who spoke little or no English, waltz easily with the young ladies, wait upon the elderly at supper. She was glad to see him. Somehow it was as if his appearance had put the final stamp of success upon the ball; had he been left out, a necessary part would have been missing. He filled a gap that would not have existed, so to speak, had he not created it by appearing in order to fill it. Maria was prepared to greet him with cordiality when she perceived that he was not alone. At the sight of his companion her blood ran cold.

James and Marietta saw each other at the same instant. Had they been at a party at home, they would have greeted each other politely, danced once or twice and perhaps later remembered the evening with pleasure. But here—far from home, where there was not one familiar face—they positively fell upon each other in mutual joy. No person, boy or girl, had ever been so welcome a sight. James greeted Marietta's mother with his usual good manners, remarking on the unexpected pleasure of finding her here; then he gave his arm to Marietta and carried her off into another room where they could find seats. Maria was dumbfounded. She had no idea James Edge was any closer than Oxford. She had not seen or spoken to his mother—and vice versa—since the awful visit to Edge Park when she and Arthur had been dismissed from her presence like beggars. Offering a hand to Mr. Share, who bent over it, she patted with her closed fan Marietta's empty place beside her, indicating that he was to take it.

"My dear lady," he began, "how delightful it is to find you and Miss Marietta here. I remember her fondly from many happy days at Wrox. She has grown into a most comely young lady, has she not? I see that she and James have met. Of course, they are friends from childhood, just as are you and James's dear mother, Lady Edge." There was not need for him to identify the mother of James to Maria, but he could not resist the feel of the title on his tongue and its sound in his ear. "I did not expect to find you at the Fox ball, although, of course, I realize that none has a better claim to be here than has Mr. Fox's mother. Still, I had not been made aware of your pending arrival."

"No more had I of yours," said Maria. "Let alone in the company of James Edge. May I ask why he is here in the middle of term?"

Mr. Share explained that Lady Edge had decided quite suddenly, soon after the New Year, that it would be a good part of the heir's education to take at least some of the grand tour, the highlights certainly, and that he, Benjamin Share, had the honor of being thought the best possible cicerone to accompany James on such a journey. "In fact," he said, "James and I are settled in quite decent lodgings—in the Palazzo Arvati." These chambers were as luxurious as any in the city, hence the *snobisme* of referring to them as being "quite decent." "We intend to visit every place of interest," he continued, "which will be a treat for my sketch-book, and it is hoped James may embark on his way to becoming a man of the world—the *haut monde*, that is."

Now Maria thought she understood the reason for James's sudden removal from England; it must have been to get him far away from Lucy and Wrox and the scandalous birth lest word of it reach him. And now here he was settling down in the same city as Lucy! Marietta must be reminded to say nothing of Lucy's presence here, and Lucy must be kept out of sight, even after nightfall. Maria smiled wanly at Mr. Share, who must on no account get wind of the state of affairs.

Mr. Share departed from her side after sitting a courteously sufficient length of time and took himself off to ply his trade. James and Marietta, in a corner beneath the great staircase and partly hidden by tubs of oleanders, were chattering happily. Marietta at home would have been shy even of James, but here it was he who had relieved her of her shyness. She glowed. "Oh, I am so glad to see you, you can have no idea! I was so very afraid that some person whom I do not know at all—indeed, I know no one—I was afraid he would invite me to stand up with him in this dance they are doing, and I am certain I should not be able to do it."

"We can try it together," said James, "then if neither of us can do it, that will matter not at all, and if it happens that one of us can master it, he or she can teach it to the other."

"It is not only that I cannot dance," Marietta said, "but that I cannot converse with them. They are speaking Italian, but I was told I would get along because everybody speaks French, and I am quite good at French, yet they do not seem to speak that either."

"They have lamentable accents," said James. "Thank goodness you and I both speak English."

They remained together until the carriages were arriving to take away the last of the guests. Robert's efforts, at Maria's urging, to bring partners to Marietta had resulted only in her saying she was engaged for the next dances, while periodic attempts by Mr. Share to see that *le tout beau monde* was presented to the young peer met with no better success. "Of what use is it," Mr. Share complained to the wife of the British consul, "to bring the young man all the way to Rome for the express purpose of introducing him to the *haut monde* only to have him turn his back on it and spend the entire evening with a little country girl he has known all his life?"

❧ 12 ❧

JAMES AND MARIETTA

On the morning after the ball Mr. Share rose at his usual hour of nine o'clock. James still slept; he was too young to manage on only four hours' sleep. He was allowed to remain abed until midday, when his cicerone waked him to say that half the day had been wasted, there would not be time left to do more than walk about looking at buildings and fountains; for serious visits such as to the Vatican galleries or the Baths of Caracalla a whole day must be consecrated. After luncheon they set off for their walk, Mr. Share with his sketchbook, James carrying a book of Italian lessons and an English-Italian pocket dictionary.

"It is odd your mother did not tell us that the Wrox-Hampdens were to come," Mr. Share remarked as they crossed the Piazza di Spagna. "She must have known, being so close to Mrs. Wrox-Hampden. I daresay she did not wish you to associate with persons not of the *haut monde*, for you will never learn the ways of it unless you inhabit it, so to speak. Tonight we shall go to the Princess Santa Montagna, and you must circulate among her guests. For the most part, they are a dull lot, but *crème de la crème*."

"Did you not tell me that to be dull is the greatest social sin?" James asked.

"Certainly," said his companion, "but with you and me there it will not be in the least dull. The princess's palace is the only haunted house in Rome. Two statues of former cardinals who were defrocked and imprisoned for apostasy are in the long gallery. Sometimes they come off their pedestals and rattle their chains along the marble floor, but they do no harm except to frighten the servants, which is not all for the bad, as it keeps them on their toes—the servants, I mean to say, although come to think of it, the same could be said for the cardinals."

"Shall Miss Marietta be there?" James asked.

"I should not think so, unless she accompanies her brother Mr. Fox. But your mother would surely not expect you to travel all the way to Italy to be in the company of Miss Marietta Wrox-Hampden."

"Then I shall not tell my mother we have met her."

Mr. Share pointed out the famous Palazzo Simonetti, which they were then passing, and gave an account of its story, which occupied him until they came into view of the Ponte Salario, of which he wished to make a sketch. They found a bench and sat while he considered how best to arrange his view of the bridge.

James had been enjoying the company of Benjamin Share ever since they left Dover, as his mother and Benjamin Share himself had felt sure would be the case. James also found, as he came to know Benjamin on more familiar terms, that his companion was not so simple a character as at first acquaintance he had appeared to be. He was snobbish, of course; he thoroughly enjoyed the company of even the dullest person if that person was highly placed, for the place meant as much to him as the person. It might even be said the duller, the better, for the more he himself shone by comparison. He did not seek company in order to be amused, he did not need to, for it was he who supplied the amusement. *Au fond*, as he himself would have put it, he was *sérieux*, a true scholar; he knew a lot about history, languages, literature and art, and his taste in every field was selective, rejecting any work not of the highest quality. James was coming to appreciate the worth of his companion and perhaps to discover the weakness—if it were that—wherein lay Mr. Share's Achilles' heel. This was his self-esteem. He was the person in all the world most appreciative of his own superiority to all the rest. Therefore, he might be subject to flattery.

"If we are not to meet Miss Wrox-Hampden in the evenings," James now said, "why could we not take her with us in the day when we visit the museums and churches?" Watching Mr. Share's face, he saw no sign that this proposal would be answered in the affirmative. "She could profit from your knowledge of the world as well as I," James continued, trying flattery. The other's expression changed from positive rejection to possible consideration of the idea. "It seems a pity, Mr. Share, that all the knowledge and experience you have to offer should be offered for the benefit of one listener only. It would be such a waste."

The look of consideration then became one of acceptance on the face of Mr. Share. "I see no real objection," he said. "She seems like a young person who has a great deal to learn. Very well, we shall ask her mother if she may accompany us tomorrow, when I plan to visit the Forum and the Palace of the Caesars."

March retreated into the past as the month of April came in, bringing its own Italian sort of spring, with a hot sun, the bright colors of marigolds and pansies and other flowers familiar to the English, as well as strange ones like the cyclamens. The hills around Rome were fragrant with the scent of rosemary, thyme and bay. Mr. Share's excursions, which had covered the monuments and sights of Rome, now moved out of the city and sometimes comprised all-day trips, such as one spent at Corneto and the sepulchers at Tarquinii. James and Marietta were much in each other's company—never, it goes with saying, out of Mr. Share's sight and seldom out of his hearing.

They found they had more in common than the frequent company of Benjamin Share. Both had been homesick. "I was unprepared for that," Marietta confessed, "and I found it to be a real illness. I had difficulty in sleeping and eating. I wished that I had never come to Italy, and now, of course, I am thankful we did. Mr. Share has made it all so interesting. I hardly think of home anymore, and that may be wrong of me. It seems as if I did not care for it, which is not so."

One day the three members of their little party had finished a picnic luncheon at Castel Fusano. James and Marietta were sitting in the shade of a cypress tree while Mr. Share, at a little distance, was setting up his easel preparatory to executing a large drawing of the site. He walked back and forth, cocking his head now to this side, now to that, seeking the most picturesque *point de vue*. Marietta watched him, leaning against the tree, feeling intensely happy, wishing this day could go on forever. "Why does he use all those French phrases when he is in Italy?" she said to James.

"I think the Italians do the same. I think it is the fashion throughout the *haut monde*, which itself is never spoken of in any other language."

"I thought when in Rome one was expected to do as the Romans. Let us call Mr. Share by his Italian name. Now, what would that be?"

"I have no idea."

"Look it up, you have the dictionary."

James consulted the small red leather volume and said, "It is not here. There is no 'share.' "

"Hmm. Well—what about trying 'portion'?"

"Very well." Pages were thumbed. "I cannot find any 'portion' either."

"They *must* have shares and portions," Marietta persisted. "What is another word for 'share'? Or 'portion'?"

" 'Part'?" James suggested. He moved back a page. "Here is 'part,' " he said. "It is the same word—part—only it has an *e* on the end." He tried it out. "Mr. Part," he said.

"The *e* would be sounded, would it not?" asked Marietta. "*Par*-tay."

"Signor *Par*tay," said James.

They had been suppressing laughter during this exchange, and now it burst out as they exclaimed together, "Signor Partay!"

Mr. Share, hearing the laughter, turned to look for its reason and saw that it stopped immediately. He sensed he might in some way be its source. He believed wholeheartedly in young persons having an enjoyable time, but not at his expense. "You must continue with the lesson," he admonished them, raising his voice that they might hear, "else you will never learn to understand Italian, let alone converse in it."

"Yes, Mr. Share," said James. He bowed his head over the book of lessons and whispered, "*Si*, Signor Partay." Marietta found this vastly amusing.

Mr. Share turned back to his self-imposed task, while the young people obediently memorized *buono giorno, buono pomeriggio* and the correct phraseology to use in ordering meals in a *ristorante* or (less formal) a *taverna*. When the artist had finished his rendering, he called them over to admire it. It was really very good; Benjamin Share understood perspective and what to include, what to omit, for best effect. He stood proudly awaiting laudatory comments. "Oh, I say, how very good," said James. "I can't think how you manage to show light and shadow like that. Jolly difficult, I should think."

Marietta thought she should sound a bit more enthusiastic and tried to remember the right words of praise for a work of art. "Oh, it *is* good, Mr. Share!" she exclaimed. "It is such a good likeness!" She looked from the viaduct in the middle distance to the finished drawing beside her. "A splendid likeness. I should know it anywhere."

Mr. Share was satisfied. He broke camp, so to speak, packing up all his paraphernalia preparatory to returning to the city. "I try to vary the monuments we visit," said he, "among those left by the ancient Romans, such as this and the Colosseum, and the buildings of our own civilization, like San Gregorio, which we shall see at our next opportunity. It will certainly be our last, as James and I are to leave for Paris in three days. We shall go to Paris by way of Firenze and stop there for a week." He did not refer to Florence by its English name, the young people noted, yet he did not pronounce Paris as do the French and call it Paree. Such nuances in usage were obviously of the *haut monde* and must be mastered if one hoped to enter it.

The two gentlemen accompanied Marietta to her door, where her mother was expecting her, but found on arrival there that Mrs. Wrox-Hampden could not receive them. James lingered in the doorway before taking his leave while Marietta was thanking both gentlemen for the delightful day. "I shall remember it always," she said.

"And so shall I," said James. Leaning closer to her, he whispered, *"Felicissima notte,"* before turning away to follow Signor Partay. They were expecting guests later for a grand reception they were giving *pour prendre congé* and to repay the hospitality that had been lavished upon them. Mrs. Wrox-Hampden and her daughter were not included in the company. They did not qualify for inclusion, never having received the *haut monde* in their own lodgings.

Maria was lying fully clothed on her bed in a darkened room, her door closed against interruption of her turbulent thoughts. She had just returned from an unsatisfactory interview with her son Robert Fox at the Villa Brozzi. Every word of it was still echoing in her aching head.

"I should think, Robert, that you would remain here until after Lucy's confinement. I shall need your help and support."

"My dear Mother, I never remain here any later than this. The London season is about to begin; I must go to Foxbridge before London. I cannot be expected to turn my life upside down because you failed to keep your daughter on her leash."

Maria had swallowed her pride. "We need your help," she pleaded. "Can you not help us? It seems you live only for your own pleasure."

"For whose else should I live?" asked Robert. "You cannot expect I should live for yours. Or even for your convenience."

"But I was counting on you," persisted his mother. "We must decide upon what disposition shall be made of Lucy's child."

"I assumed you would take it back to England with you."

"What future would it have there? The father will not acknowledge it." Maria, who had been sitting throughout the conversation, now rose to her feet as if the increase in stature would place her in a more commanding position. To plead or beg was entirely foreign to her nature. Standing upright might make her sound less importunate as she said, "It had occurred to me that you might adopt the child."

Robert Fox was stricken dumb. He stared at his mother with an expression of complete incredulity as his mouth fell open.

"It is—will be—your niece or nephew," she went on, "your sister's child. Your half niece or half nephew, I should say," she added, taking note of his expression. "Since you show no sign of intention to marry and produce a child yourself, surely you might consider adopting one who is, after all, of your own flesh and blood."

He continued to stare without speaking. There were no words available to him in his vocabulary with which to reply to this monstrous, wholly unexpected suggestion. After a long silence he got up, tottered to a bellpull on the wall by the mantel and summoned a manservant. When the man appeared, he managed to say, "Show Mrs. Wrox-Hampden to her carriage." He made no move to see her out. He did speak once, as she was walking toward the door. "I am shaken to the very depths of my being."

His mother stopped and turned. "My dear son," she said, "I am afraid you have no depths. There are only shallows."

So Maria, despite having had the last word, went down to defeat and returned to the lodgings where there awaited her the terrible problem of Lucy and her ill-begotten child. She remained secluded in her room and lay awake until dawn, by which time she had decided to make one final effort to enlist the help of Robert, this time on behalf of Marietta. The younger girl should not be obliged to remain in Rome and be exposed to the ordeal that lay ahead in this small, exiled household. Maria wrote a letter to Robert asking that in the name of Christian charity he take Marietta with him back to England and Foxbridge Abbey; Foxbridge was not far from Hatche Castle, and Mrs. Bellwood of Hatche would obligingly send for the girl and see that she was safely conveyed home to Wrox. The letter was taken around to the Villa Brozzi, and as Maria had hoped, Robert could not decently refuse this request. In fact, it was so much more reasonable than her earlier demand that in his relief Robert was almost glad to grant it.

The grand reception at the Palazzo Arvati was a brilliant success. The two hosts slept late next morning, their last in Rome, as they intended to depart for Florence very early on the following day. The afternoon being delightfully warm and sunny, Mr. Share sent word to Marietta that there was time for one last visit, to San Gregorio.

The three arrived there in midafternoon. Mr. Share delivered his usual talk on the history and artistic merits of the church and of its spectacular site overlooking the city. James and Marietta sat upon a low wall to listen, while Mr. Share faced them on a folding stool he carried about for use while sketching. After a few minutes they found themselves joined by several passersby, obviously English-speaking, who stopped to listen. Then more arrived, until there was a small gathering, including an American family that was making the grand tour. It was all immensely gratifying to Mr. Share until, after he had brought his interesting little talk to a conclusion, the American gentleman thanked him and held out a bank note of large denomination.

Mr. Share stared down in silence at the outstretched fingers containing the money. He remained so for such a length of time that James thought his companion was for once at a loss for words. That was not the case. The pause was for effect, and it did have the intended effect of leaving the American gentleman standing foolishly in front of the onlookers holding out in midair a large bank note. Mr. Share well knew the exact length of time a pause should be held. "Take it back, Father," the American lady said, pulling at her husband's arm; "some people have no sense of gratitude." Mr. Share had turned his back on them and was opening the large case in which he carried his artist's equipment. The crowd dispersed.

Then the artist discovered he had by mistake brought the wrong materials. He had made a very effective sketch of San Gregorio on a previous visit, when he had been the guest (always welcome) of an Irish lady married to a Roman of high position. On today's visit it had been his intention to make a watercolor to present to Lady Edge, but he had omitted to bring the right paper and paints. "What a nuisance!" he exclaimed. "I have only my sketching materials. Wait—I have a thought. Let us have a little lesson on the art of sketching. You have seen me draw monuments, castles and views. They are relatively easy to do. It is more difficult to capture the likeness of a person. Suppose I draw a portrait of James; it will make a memento for him to take home to his mother. Come, James, sit here on the wall with the view behind you, and I shall set to work."

Marietta watched, while James remained very still, as instructed to do, holding his young head proudly erect, as he habitually did. He was *so* handsome, the girl thought, and if handsome is as handsome does, he was the handsomest person in the world because he was the best. James had had his twentieth birthday in March; in less than a year he would be a man. She now had a perfect excuse to stare at his face for as long as she wished, and so she did until Mr. Share declared himself satisfied with his handiwork. "It is, of course, not a finished piece," he said, "just a rather hasty sketch, but it will suffice to show the technique employed in making a likeness. Come, James, you need sit still no longer." The sketch was presented to its subject for his appraisal.

James stared at the picture that showed how he appeared in the eyes of Mr. Share. It bore no resemblance to his own idea of his appearance. Did he *really* look like that to others? Or only to Benjamin Share? Was Mr. Share's impression of James Edge's appearance a truer one than that of James himself? Mr. Share was awaiting an opinion, smiling in anticipation of a favorable one.

"I am not the person to ask," said James after a minute. "No one can know what he himself looks like; that is well known. Let Miss Marietta say if it be a good likeness."

Marietta had been afraid she would be asked for an opinion and was dreading the moment. In her turn she examined the drawing. She saw no likeness except in the clothing. "The buttons on the coat are very like," she said. "I would know them anywhere. And that corner of the church that appears over his shoulder, that is excellently well rendered, I would recognize it anywhere." Mr. Share was satisfied, if not flattered, so the last delightful excursion in the papal city ended on a happy note.

"I shall miss her," James said to Mr. Share after they had dropped off Marietta at her mother's lodgings. "I shall miss the sound of her voice." Marietta's voice was charming—soft and well modulated but full of vitality. Listening to it, one felt certain she would say something interesting or amusing, but James sometimes did not hear what it was she said because he was listening to the sound of her voice, as if to a song without words.

James and Benjamin Share, dining out for the last time in Rome, did not stay out late because of the necessity to arise and depart early the next morning for Firenze. They were being driven home along the Piazza Navona when James, aware that Marietta dwelled nearby, suddenly told his companion that he wished to walk the rest of the way. Before Mr. Share could stay him, he had ordered the coachman to stop, in quite passable Italian.

"I cannot allow that," protested Benjamin. "It is dark; there may be footpads about; it is not wise. Your mother would not approve."

"I shall not tell my mother. I shall be home directly. If I am not, then you may tell her."

The last thing Mr. Share desired was to upset Lady Edge in any way that might cause her to cut off the source of the delightful life he was currently enjoying in the *haut monde*. Better than being a perpetual (albeit welcome) guest, he was now also a surrogate host, in splendid chambers, with limitless funds for entertaining, and with no necessity to abandon his profession of guest *sans pareil*. To be thus the welcome guest in his own house was to have arrived at the acme of happiness. "Be certain then, James, that you do come directly home," he said.

"I shall," James replied, setting off on foot. He intended only a slight deviation from the direct way home, just to look briefly at the house in the street that contained Marietta. Ahead of him, walking rapidly, was a tall figure in a long black cloak with hood. He remembered having seen the man before several times when driving at night near the Piazza Navona; he must be, James thought, some sort of priest or monk on his way to or from a midnight mass or late service of some sort. He was surprised when the figure turned into the street for which he was himself headed. When he rounded the corner, he saw the man walk right into the Wrox-Hampden lodgings, as if expected.

James stopped still in astonishment. Could it be, he wondered, that the Wrox-Hampdens were being secretly inducted, under cover of darkness, into the rites of Papism? They would, of course, not wish it to be known; that would explain the arrival at their house of a priest or monk in so secretive a manner. But if any such thing were afoot, he thought, would not Marietta have told him? He waited for the mysterious figure, whoever it was, to emerge from the house, but as he watched, the lights were extinguished room by room, and poor Lucy did not reappear.

❧ 13 ❧

The Crime Against Elsie Wetherby

The schoolroom at Wrox now held only Elsie Wetherby and Lottie. Miss Theodora Smallwood walked from the village twice weekly in all but the most inclement weather to give Lottie her music lessons, staying on for tea and bringing the neighborhood news. Miss Theodora had contracted smallpox as a child of twelve in the widespread outbreak of 1809, which had taken a younger brother and an older sister. Her own life had been spared, but at the terrible price of a face so disfigured by pit marks that she sometimes wished that she, too, had been taken. She suffered painfully on meeting new people, but in the common room at Wrox, taking tea with her friend Elsie Wetherby, she lost her shyness and was able to forget her affliction. Elsie, shortsighted and too well bred to stare, had long ceased to notice it at all; in looking at Miss Theodora, she saw only the agreeable face of a dear friend and envied Theodora her happy home with both parents. Theodora it was who never failed to stare at her friend's face, envious of Elsie's smooth, fair complexion.

Mrs. Cluster, with now virtually nothing to do there, had left her position in the attics and in March, according to Miss Theodora, had gone into trade with E. Hole & Son. She was established in an atelier behind the draper's shop, where she made dresses for the Hole customers on the spot from the fine stuffs the draper carried. His shop was now expanded to include a room where at first patterns were on display; then gradually appeared ribbons, buttons, laces, trimmings, even needles, threads, scissors and thimbles, so ladies who did, or did not, wish to avail themselves of Mrs. Cluster's services could find in the one place all things needed for making fashionable clothes. In April, with the advent of spring, business at the draper's became so brisk that Mrs. Cluster needed two assistants; the seamstress therefore disappeared from Wrox; Miss Wetherby mended Lottie's petticoats and let down the skirts of her last summer's dresses.

All winter there had been no visitors in the house that had heretofore been so full. Mr. Benjamin Share did not come in the spring, nor did anyone from Edge Park, nor any of the Hampdens from Wiltshire, nor the Bellwoods from Hatche. Elsie Wetherby found less and less to write about in the letters that linked her to Osbert Reddle; she reported baby Violet's first word ("ga-ga") and the sale of part of the home farm and village cottages, to whom Miss Theodora did not know, but she did know that the route of the railway was included and in the summer the tracks were to be laid.

Excerpt: Letter from Elsie Wetherby at Wrox
to Osbert Reddle at Exeter   *May 14*

It has been long since I received your letter of May 1, and you will I trust forgive my delay in replying when I tell you the reason therefor. We have had a terrible scare of the typhus that has wrought havoc in the whole house. Tole reported that a vagrant had been found sheltering in a pile of straw in the stables. When he was roused and ordered to move on, it became apparent that he was most desperately ill and was quite unable to do so. It was two days before Dr. Pipkin could come, and when he did, he declared that the man was suffering from the typhus in its final stages and he could not be saved. It transpired that a fearful epidemic has been spreading; the doctor said that in the town of Bath this past winter three hundred persons had died of it. The hearse was sent to remove the vagrant from the stables to the workhouse, but he expired on the journey. The doctor ordered us to observe a quarantine, and I was instructed to write no letters to be carried out into the country. Then two of the housemaids became ill, and it devolved upon me to care for them. It quite wore me out going continually between attics and kitchen, with Adam, the water boy, fetching water up and down so I could keep the women tolerably clean. Fortunately it turned out they were suffering only from severe colds with a fever, and we are back to normal in the house—or what is now normal with our sadly reduced numbers.

They are laying the track for the railway. There will be a station built in the village, as it is not welcome in Bunbury. Some cottages, trumpery little dwellings, have already been put up to accommodate some of the workers who swell the numbers of our community. It will soon be not at all as you remember it. A grocer's shop has been opened, which I must say is a convenience for us here at the Hall. The water boy Adam has found other employment in the construction of the railway. The butler has threatened to leave unless the squire has water laid on to serve the bedrooms. It appears this is now possible with the wonderful new piping that can make water from a rain catchment run uphill, so to speak. The spring has never been more beautiful; how I wish you could have been here to hear the cuckoo and see the wild flowers in the woods and on the downs. In the first week of June the Duke's gardens will be opened to the public, and it is planned that Lottie and I will be driven over to visit them, as you remember we did two years ago with all the children and took a picnic which we ate in the home park and Lucy fell into Sheerwater Pond and would have drowned in her heavy skirts had you not shown great presence of mind and saved her. I shall write to tell you who bought the land as soon as I have heard his name. . . .

On the day after the above letter had been posted, Elsie learned the identity of the purchaser from the squire himself. He had taken occasionally to eating his dinners with her and Lottie and his great dog, Caesar, who now had the run of the dining room. Elsie had proven herself to be very helpful to him in running the household and paying the wages and performing other duties that Maria had always done. This day he sent word requesting her to come to the first-floor sitting room after Lottie was in bed; the child should not be concerned with the affairs of house and estate about which he wished to talk.

When Elsie knocked on the door, she heard the great dog begin barking on the other side of it. She had always been rather afraid of Caesar, as well as disliking the hairs he left on carpets and furniture and his unpleasant odor. Indeed, her regard for the dog was not greatly different from that which she held for its master. While she waited for the squire to open the door, she prepared herself for an attack from the animal; however, as usual, it meant her no harm and pushed itself against her skirts in a manner in no way threatening as she entered the room after the door had been opened.

Maria's writing table was covered with pages pertaining to the business of Wrox that the squire had obviously been going through, turning over and putting into disorder. "Sit down, Miss Wetherby, do," he said. "I need to ask your help; there are matters on which I cannot consult Spence."

"Indeed, sir," Elsie began, "I do not know how I can be of assistance in such matters. If only Mr. Reddle were here—" She looked around for a chair that showed no trace of Caesar's occupation and sat carefully on the edge of the armchair beside Maria's workbox, which was half full of unfinished netting, as she had left it. Arthur Wrox-Hampden remained standing, awkwardly trying to decide how he should begin what he had to say. Elsie had not seen him for some time and thought he looked disheveled and distraught. She knew he had been frequently seen at a gambling room in Bunbury, where games of faro and loo went on, and she wondered if he had suffered losses. Could it be that her services would now be dispensed with? Her hand went to the brooch at her throat, to seek counsel from her dead mother.

To her great surprise, the big man now said, "Miss Wetherby, I wish to tell you that it was not right for your wages to have been reduced. Far from having less responsibility after the departure of my wife and daughters, you now have a great deal more. I intend to increase your remuneration to compensate for the amount by which it was reduced."

Elsie flushed scarlet, as quick tears came to her shortsighted eyes. The color was becoming to her usually pale face. "Oh, sir, I do not know what to say, you are so kind—"

"No, no, it is only right," he said. "And I must ask your further help, as I said. I have told you that there are matters I cannot discuss with Spence."

"Yes, sir, so you did say."

"I think you have heard," the squire continued, "that the land agent has secured a purchaser for a considerable part of the home farm and the village."

"Miss Theodora Smallwood did tell me that that is so, sir."

The squire began pacing about the room. There was a silence broken only by the thumping of the dog's tail upon the carpet where it had stretched itself out. At last the man stopped at the fireplace, laid an arm along the mantel, whence he faced the young woman again, and said, "Perhaps Miss Smallwood also told you that the purchaser was Spence."

"Oh, no!" cried Elsie. "Oh, dear, how—how—"

"How abominable!" Arthur interrupted with a shout. "Yes, behind my back Spence has been robbing me and using my own money to ruin me!"

"But this is terrible, sir," said Elsie. "Did you not know what was going on?"

"I trusted him. He took advantage of my good nature. Everyone knows I am a good-natured fellow, wouldn't hurt a fly—"

Elsie wondered why a good-natured fellow would not hurt a fly but would slaughter larger, equally defenseless creatures right and left. Fly hurting probably was beneath him, not a gentleman's sport.

"Everyone knows I would never willingly hurt anyone," the squire continued. "Why should Spence turn on me? I trusted him. He was not open and aboveboard. I am not good at business myself—no time for things like that—I trusted Spence to do what he was engaged to do. Do you not think a man should do what he is engaged to do?"

"Certainly," Elsie agreed. She felt compassion for the squire. He had been kind to her, and it was not his fault, really, that he was incompetent and—well, let it be thought but not said—stupid. She rose and went to him, laying a hand on his arm. "I wish I could be of help, sir; indeed, I do. I can only suggest that you consult Mr. Weston, the attorney. Surely Mr. Spence can be forced to open his books and be discovered." She looked up sympathetically at the face on the leonine head more than a foot higher than her own.

When the squire suddenly grabbed her, lifted and half carried her through the open door into Maria's bedroom, she thought he had gone mad and was attacking her, as if it were somehow her fault that he had been cheated. Before she understood what was about to happen to her, what was happening, what had happened, it was over. She felt acute pain, then a battering of her helpless body, then the man lying still on top of her, breathing heavily. She strove to struggle free of the leaden weight. At the foot of the bed the great dog was barking, slobbering and jumping up, as it had been since the assault began. She was being smothered in her own dress, which had been thrown over her head. It required more strength than she thought she possessed to tear it away from her face. The man rolled over and slept. As she escaped, the dog snarled and jumped, following her as she fled through the dark passages of the old house. She found her way to her room, entered it and shut the door. The dog retreated along the passage.

Curled up on her bed, Elsie Wetherby could not believe, much less accept, what had happened to her. She put up a hand to her throat, automatically invoking the help of her dearest mother. The brooch was gone! This was a loss as bad as that which had gone before. Her mother had deserted her, left her to her shame.

She sobbed uncontrollably, hour after dark hour, until exhausted. Gradually the realization came that she had been violated and was now in that shameful condition about which she had read in novels without comprehending its meaning. Toward dawn she got up and washed herself, over and over again. Shame and humiliation overcame her; she returned to her bed and lay there without movement. She was found in the morning by Lottie, who, wondering why her governess had not appeared for breakfast, went in search of her and found her lying motionless, her life in ruins.

It was not only her body that had been violated, but her very soul. She had been brutally robbed of her unique, private self-respect and pride. The gentility she had held on to so bravely, for so long, at such cost, had been taken away in an act that she came to perceive as the exercise of a *droit du seigneur*. She had been handled like a farm girl when she knew herself to be a lady, respectably born and, but for circumstances, the equal of any Wrox-Hampden.

For three days she remained in a kind of limbo, refusing food or drink, with consciousness coming and going. Lottie was terrified. She and Nurse did all they could, without success, to bring the governess back to the real world. Once Lottie encountered her father in the hall and he asked her, "Where is Miss Wetherby? I need her to assist me in composing a letter."

"She is not well, Papa."

"Oh! What a nuisance," said he. "This is very sudden. She was perfectly well two days ago. I shall go to see Mr. Weston by myself then. Let me know when she recovers."

"If you are going to town, Papa, please stop by the doctor's and ask him to come."

"Has it arrived at that?" The squire was surprised.

"Nurse and I think it advisable. Please, Papa."

"Very well," he agreed. "If you see Miss Wetherby, tell her to keep her chin up—what?" He rode his best hunter into Bunbury, where he had so much on his mind to discuss with the lawyer that he forgot to stop by Pipkin's house; it was out of his way, in any case, up that steep hill paved with great cobblestones that were hard on the horses.

After the third night had passed without alteration in Miss Wetherby's frightening condition, Nurse took it upon herself to have Dr. Pipkin summoned. He arrived as soon as he heard he was needed, to be met by Lottie in tears. "She will neither eat nor drink," the girl said; "she just lies there as if she did not even hear us when we speak to her."

Dr. Pipkin was a long time in Miss Wetherby's room while Lottie and Nurse waited in the passage. When the doctor joined them, closing the door behind him, he said, "I cannot account for the original cause of this condition, but the immediate cause is the need for nourishment and for water. She must be made to swallow something—warm milk, broth. I have left medicine she is to be given immediately. As for the primary cause, I incline to believe her to have suffered some sort of shock. I know Wrox Hall is haunted, inside and out. Could she have had an encounter with a ghost or a spirit?"

Nurse said the house ghost had never been known to leave its room at the stair landing, and in any case Miss Wetherby had passed by there daily for many years without any manifestation on the part of the difficult child. Lottie said the ghost of the hermit that frequented the park went abroad only by night—as Miss Wetherby did not—and had not been seen since just before Henrietta died. "Its appearance heralds a death in the family," she said, and then was stricken with a dreadful thought. "It could not be that Miss Wetherby will die, could it? She is not exactly family—"

"She will not die if she receives nourishment," said the doctor. "She is sound in body, in excellent physical health. Now, be sure to give her the medicine I left, it will relax her, so she should not refuse nourishment. I shall return tomorrow morning without fail." Starting down the stairs, he turned back to say, "You might send for Mr. Smallwood. It can do no harm, and words of spiritual comfort may well reach her consciousness."

Luke, the stableboy, was sent to fetch Mr. Smallwood, who hurried to the bedside, carrying his psalter. Nurse and Lottie, having administered the medicine, were forcing between Miss Wetherby's lips spoonfuls of a thick, milky gruel. They thought her cheek showed a faint color, which was encouraging. The vicar made the sign of the cross over the stricken woman and, opening his book, began to read. His voice was a very pleasing one; it could always be heard and understood in the back of his church, and now in this quiet room it was lowered to a murmur audible only to the two women standing by the bed and the one lying upon it. "The Lord is my shepherd: therefore can I lack nothing. He shall feed me in a green pasture: and lead me forth beside the waters of comfort . . ."

He read through the Twenty-third Psalm, and as the sound of his voice died away, Miss Wetherby opened her eyes, saw the concerned face of the clergyman leaning over her and whispered, "Amen."

Nurse crossed herself.

Lottie was quietly crying. "Don't die, Miss Wetherby," she begged. "We need you." She felt a faint, heartening pressure from the hand she had been holding in hers throughout the reading.

❧ 14 ❧

OSBERT REDDLE RESCUES HIS LOVE

Osbert Reddle's inquiries about the coming of the railroad to Wrox (referred to by the squire as an encroachment upon it) had not been idly made. He had formed an ambitious plan for his future life and Elsie's. He had visited the school run by Mr. Plumptre, where Augustus was now a pupil, and several other institutions of the same kind. Mr. Plumptre had made the most favorable impression. He had explained his method of what he termed "constructive punishment": "If a boy hurts another boy, or any living creature, he will get a severe caning where it hurts *him*—on the seat of punishment, as it were, and I do not spare the rod. If he misbehaves otherwise, he is not put to writing out one hundred times that he will not again commit the same transgression; he is put to memorizing some worthwhile speech or a sonnet of Shakespeare. He will have it by heart for the rest of his life. That is constructive punishment. I may put a boy in a corner with a duncecap on his head, but he will not sit and stare at the wall, he will work a difficult sum, and only when that is completed to my satisfaction may the duncecap be removed."

"It is most sensible," said Osbert. "I never myself had to cane a boy because his father was there for that purpose. The squire would never let anyone but himself give the boy a whipping."

Osbert foresaw the growth of Wrox, with the railroad station situated there, and the consequent diversion of commerce from Bunbury. He intended to establish in the neighborhood the Reddle School, with himself as Headmaster and Elsie as his Wife, Helpmeet and Partner in the Enterprise. Indeed, he would not, and could not, undertake the founding of such an establishment without Elsie. Day pupils would be drawn from Bunbury with its neighboring towns and villages, and when the School's reputation had become established, boarding students would arrive by rail from more distant places. In his daydreams he sometimes saw himself and his School as Mr. Arnold and Rugby, Master and School inseparable.

He had carefully saved his money and given it into his father's keeping for investment, and his father had offered to help further by lending money toward the start of his venture. He knew that Elsie had placed her own savings against the future with Mr. Maule, the Bunbury banker. Her future was now to be identified with his own, and her savings, like his own, would help establish their School. If they were lucky, Osbert thought, they might find a building suitable for a school already in existence.

Osbert dreamed of this ideal School. It was to be in or near the village, close to meadows, streams and woodlands. Eventually there would be a small farmyard, with chickens and ducks for the table, a vegetable garden, ponies for the youngest children to ride, cricket games on Wrox Common. On Sundays a crocodile of pupils would walk over to hear Mr. Smallwood's sermons, with Mr. and Mrs. Osbert Reddle bringing up the rear.

Elsie's letter telling him that work on the railway had begun, and that there was certainly to be a station at Wrox, emboldened him to approach her on the two subjects—marriage and the school—that were closest to his heart. He went so far as to write that he hoped to see her before long, as he had a matter of some urgency he wished to discuss with her.

He never received an answer.

Weeks went by, during which Osbert wrote almost daily, begging Elsie for a reply. When he had heard nothing by mid-June, he became alarmed, and one day, when he could bear it no longer, he took the coach to Bunbury, where he arrived after dark to find the Bird and Bottle fully booked. "It is the railway coming through over at Wrox," he was told. "They are building a station there. There are no rooms to be had for miles around. The contractors and engineers are stopping here."

Osbert decided to go straight to the Hall without announcing himself first, as he had intended to do. He asked if he could hire someone to drive him over to Wrox. "Hold on a minute," said the landlord. "I think the Wrox coachman is at this moment in the pub; his horse and buggy are still in the stableyard."

So Osbert, very much later, found himself beside a drunken Tole being driven in the trap toward Wrox. The night was foul, a driving rain had begun and the cloth covering that should have been available to raise from the back of the seat had long been gone from the empty rack that lay there. A chill wind blew the rain down his collar and around his ankles. Tole was uncommunicative, having long passed beyond the loquacious stage of inebriation. The horse Cavalier was heading home to Wrox at a slow walk, in no hurry now that he knew he was going there. Tole's silence was not as boring as his conversation, but Osbert broke it, wanting information. "Can you tell me anything about Miss Wetherby?" he inquired anxiously. "Is she at the Hall?"

"Aye, she be. I reckon."

"Has she been away?"

"The missus is away. And Miss Lucy."

Osbert gave up. It was nearly midnight when Cavalier pulled into the stable at Wrox; he had refused to be led out of his direct way there in order to leave Osbert at the door of the Hall. Not a light showed anywhere in the massive bulk of the forbidding structure as the man walked toward it, carrying his valise. Had it not been raining so hard, he would have sought shelter somewhere on the grounds until morning, but the deluge was so vile that it was not possible even to look for a refuge. There was over the door a roof of sorts supported by two posts, but the rain was not coming straight down, and lashed by the wind, it was being driven against the door itself.

Osbert drew a deep breath, summoned his courage and raised the heavy brass knocker shaped like the head of a lion. The sound it made as it fell could barely be heard for the howling of the wind. There was no wind *inside*, he reasoned, so someone in there should be roused if he continued to pound on the outside. He did so. Presently a light appeared in a window. Osbert continued to raise the lion's head and bang it back against the door. Someone opened it.

It was Arthur Wrox-Hampden. He loomed in the doorway, dressed in shirt sleeves, obviously roused from sleep. He carried a lanthorn. Beside him was the great dog, Caesar, in a menacing stance. "What the devil are you doing here?" demanded the squire. "What in Heaven's name do you want at this time of the night?"

"It is I, Osbert Reddle, Mr. Wrox-Hampden. You must remember me. Please allow me to enter."

"Why do you come here now, for the love of God?"

"Please, sir, allow me to enter. I shall explain everything. Do not, for the sake of Christian charity, turn me away!"

"Oh, well, I am getting soaked—come in then, quickly." Arthur pulled the door wide, throwing it back against the wall where the handle went through the hole it had made long ago in the painted skirt of Caroline, Countess of Moulds. Osbert stumbled inside, nearly falling over the dog. Water was running off his hat and his outer garments, even dripping from the valise. The entry was crowded with boots, walking sticks, riding crops and outdoor garments hanging on the walls. The fireplace in the great room was cold, the atmosphere dank and chill.

"I thought you were gone," the squire said. "But I suppose I cannot very well turn you out on a night like this, can I? You had better stay until morning; then we shall have it out."

"Tell me, sir," Osbert entreated him, "what of Miss Wetherby? It is to see her I have come. Is there anything amiss?"

"Amiss? Oh, she was indisposed for a time, I believe, Pipkin could not say why, but she recovered and is in good shape. You did not need to present yourself here at this hour in order to inquire after the health of a perfectly healthy young woman. Extr'ord'n'ry thing to do."

"Thank Heaven she is well," said Osbert. "I hope I may see her in the morning."

"Yes . . . well . . . I see no reason why you should not. Haven't seen her myself for some time now, not since she took to her bed that day, wouldn't help me write a letter. Well, sir, do not stand there dripping all over the carpet. You may as well go to your old room; there is no one in it now. We can talk in the morning. If there is anything about which to talk."

Osbert now remembered his plans for a School near Wrox and the need for a suitable building. Hoping to establish a logical reason for his arrival, he said, "There is indeed something, sir. I am looking for a property hereabouts with a view to its purchase, and you may be the very person to know of one."

If Arthur Wrox-Hampden had been surprised by a midnight call made for the purpose of inquiring after the health of Miss Wetherby, he was much more surprised—he was utterly astounded—by this new reason given for the tutor's unexpected appearance. "Upon my word," he said, "you are a peculiar chap. Maria always said so, she thought you were after something. I never heard of such a thing . . . in the middle of the night . . . raining as if the heavens had opened . . . don't care if people get any sleep . . . knock up the dead if you could—most extr'ord'n'ry!"

Osbert started up the great staircase that disappeared over his head into the darkness under the high ceiling. He had not gone far when Wrox-Hampden called after him, "It is no use your asking to return here as tutor; there is no place for you!"

"I would not return here were it to be as lord of the manor himself," Osbert muttered under his breath. He groped his way along the passages to his former room, which, when he found a candle and looked about, bore no sign of having been even entered since his departure nine months before. He found a change of clothing in his valise and hung up those that were sopping wet. Then he lay awake on his old bed until daylight, thinking of Elsie and asking himself over and over what reason she could possibly have had for the sudden cessation of the correspondence that had been so precious to both of them. Why had she not replied to his letters? Elsie would never, under any circumstances, have been so unmannerly; her ladylike manners were among her attributes that he most admired and considered desirable in the Wife of a Headmaster. In the darkness and his unhappiness his body ached with the love for her, right through to the marrow of his bones. The wind went on tearing at the slates of the roof and rattling the windows, as if trying to get in.

By morning the rain had abated, and the pale sun appeared, although a strong wind was blowing still, chasing flocks of white clouds across the sky like sheep across a meadow. Trees bent before it. The fields appeared empty of all living things, great or small. The squire should have been abroad early, looking to see what damage the storm had left behind on his properties, but he had a double excuse for not attending to this duty: first, he had been roused up in the middle of the night, so needed to sleep in; second, that tutor chap was in the house, and his reason for the extraordinary intrusion must be explained.

No one was in the dining room when Osbert went downstairs in the morning. The table was not laid. Without hesitation, he rang bells until a man appeared from the pantry. Osbert was determined to assert himself. Mr. Wrox-Hampden could do no worse than have him thrown out of the house, and the storm being past, he could walk back to Bunbury if necessary. Preparations for breakfast were put under way, and the ravenous Osbert was devouring the last kipper from what had been a full plate when Elsie Wetherby and Marietta Wrox-Hampden entered the room.

The first thing that struck Elsie's lover was how thin she had become. Her clothes—he recognized them as those she had always worn, as much part of her as her skin—now hung on her frame as from a peg on the wall. She had been slender (he liked to think of her as slim), but skin and bones are not the same as slender and slim. Her dear remembered face was now a sickly ashen color until she saw him, when it became suddenly flushed, as if all the blood in her veins had run to her head. She stopped short in the doorway, putting a hand to her throat with her familiar, automatic gesture. Then he noticed the brooch with the lock of her mother's hair was gone.

He sprang up and ran to her and encircled her in his arms. "Oh, my dearest," he cried, *"what have they done to you?"*

Lottie Wrox-Hampden was behind her older sister and the governess when they entered the dining room. She saw Mr. Reddle leap up from the table and rush toward Miss Wetherby, then Miss Wetherby's virtual collapse into his outstretched arms. The servant gaped. Mr. Reddle and Marietta led Miss Wetherby between them to the nearest chair and helped her to sit. "Fetch something!" Mr. Reddle ordered the servant. "Fetch water, a damp cloth, anything!"

"Mr. Reddle!" exclaimed Marietta, becoming aware of his identity. "What are you doing here? Why have you so frightened Miss Wetherby? She has not been well; you have caused a relapse—"

Osbert assured her that whatever had caused Elsie to collapse, it was not of his doing. He kept his arms around the trembling frame of his love. "Something terrible has happened to her," he said.

"However that may be, it can be no concern of yours," said Marietta. "It was you who upset her. Why are you here now?"

"Why, indeed?" came an echo in a deep, loud voice as Arthur Wrox-Hampden entered the room. "He appeared in the middle of the night, no rhyme or reason, woke everyone out of a sound sleep, said something about doing me out of some land, as if Spence and the railway had not done enough. Well, my dear young lady," he said, advancing toward Elsie, "do not let him upset you."

Elsie's head was sunk upon Osbert's chest. She did not raise it, but at the sound of this new voice she began to shiver from head to foot as if taken by a sudden, violent chill.

"Dear Miss Wetherby, what is it?" Marietta cried. She saw that Mr.

Reddle's arm was laid across the governess's shoulders. "Mr. Reddle, leave her alone. You are distressing her!"

Osbert Reddle was armed with all the strength of his righteous indignation. "*I* would never cause her distress!" he declared, "as she very well knows. I insist that I be allowed to see her to her room and to talk to her privately."

"I shall come with you," said Marietta.

"And I," said Lottie.

"I shall be glad of your assistance to help her upstairs," said Osbert. "But once we have conveyed her to her room, I shall talk to her in private. We shall be left alone together."

Miss Wetherby was assisted up the stairs and into the schoolroom by Mr. Reddle and the two young ladies. She sat in her old place by the window with closed eyes and her thin arms crossed on her chest that was lifelessly flat—not at all as Osbert had remembered and dreamed of it. Beside her was the glass case containing Mr. Reddle's collection of butterflies, reminder of happy days long past.

"She has been so much improved," Lottie said. "I do not understand it."

"I knew she had been unwell while I was away," said Marietta, "but she seemed to be recovered. We shall send her up some breakfast," she added, as she and Lottie withdrew. "Please call us if we can be of any assistance."

Alone with his beloved, Osbert drew up a chair and sat facing her. "Please look at me, Elsie," he begged.

She opened her eyes and looked into the face so full of loving concern.

"Why have you not replied to my letters?" he asked.

"I could not."

"Why could you not?"

"I cannot tell you."

He reached for both her hands and held them between his own. "You must tell me. There must be some reason. Elsie, look at me! I have come to ask you to do me the honor of becoming my wife. We shall go away from this house and make a home of our own, for ourselves. Perhaps, if God wills it, we shall have a family of our own to instruct and to care for. I cannot go on with my life without you at my side. You will marry me, won't you? Elsie—Elsie—" The very way he spoke her name made it an endearment.

Tears began to run down her thin cheeks.

"What is it?" he begged her.

"I cannot marry you, Osbert."

"Do you not love me?"

"I cannot marry you or anyone. I can never marry."

Now the man began to see why there might be a real obstacle to the realization of his dreams for the future. Elsie had been taken ill; Dr. Pipkin could assign no cause; she had refused to reply to his own letters in which his intentions toward her had surely been made manifest. It must be that she suffered from some fatal illness, perhaps the worst, the most dreaded, the most agonizingly painful of all—

There came a knock at the door. Osbert went to open it and admitted a housemaid carrying a tray. He recognized Maggie, a woman who had been a Wrox servant since she had come to the scullery at the age of thirteen. She was one of the two women who had accompanied Mrs. Wrox-Hampden and her daughters to Rome. Maggie was the lucky one who had come home with Miss Marietta by way of Foxbridge Abbey and Hatche Castle. She knew Miss Wetherby of old, had always respected her and had been sorry, on returning from abroad, to find her looking so poorly. Now, however, as she set the tray down on Augustus's desk, she looked at the unhappy governess without sympathy. Miss Wetherby, Maggie knew (and she was the only one who did), had brought all her troubles on herself; those that lie with a dog get up with fleas.

"Try to eat something," Osbert said to Elsie.

The maid had moved back to the door, but she did not leave the room. "Please, sir," she said. "Mr. Reddle—"

"What is it, Maggie?"

"Please, sir, can I have a word with you?"

"Certainly. What is it?"

"In private, like, sir. I wouldna want no one to hear." Maggie held open the door but did not leave the room.

Osbert tried to hold on to his temper; it was not easy to do. The interruption of his most deeply personal conversation was hard to accept, but excusable, for Elsie really did need to take nourishment. But when the woman Maggie hung about talking of some foolish irrelevancy, he snapped at her. "What is the matter with you, woman? Leave us alone, I beg of you."

"I must speak with you, sir," she persisted stubbornly, still holding the door ajar. "In private."

He gave up. "Very well, if you must," he said. "Elsie, my dearest, I beg you to have some breakfast; it is most important that you should. I shall not leave you for long."

Out in the passage, with the door to the schoolroom closed behind them, Maggie looked around to make sure she and Mr. Reddle were alone. No one was about upstairs. She approached him and spoke in what was almost a whisper. "It has been on me mind ever since I come home, but there was nobody I could tell it to, sir. You will see why—" She lifted her apron and felt under it in the pocket of her skirt. When she withdrew her hand, it was closed over some object that she held out toward Mr. Reddle. She opened her fingers. In her palm lay Miss Wetherby's brooch.

"Take it, sir," said Maggie. "I don't want nothin' to do with it no more."

Osbert was certain the woman had stolen the brooch and was afraid of getting caught with it. "How do you come to have it in your possession?" he asked.

"I was dusting in the mistress's bedroom," Maggie said. "I went to straighten up the bed, it was all mussed up, like. This was on the floor just under the bed, sir; I near stepped on it. I didna want to tell anyone; I wouldna want Miss Marietta nor Miss Lottie to know. Nor the master, I wouldna want him to know I found it, nor no one on or about the place. When I seen you, I thought you could be the one to give it back to her; you see, sir, you not bein' here no more it wouldna matter if you knew. I wouldna wish it to be found on me, they'd think I took it, they would, but if I had of left it there in the mistress's room, she woulda knowed or the master woulda knowed—"

Osbert was standing with the brooch in his hand and his feet on a floor that he felt was moving away beneath him. He put a hand against the wall to keep from falling. The woman Maggie went on, half whispering, "I wouldna give it back to Miss Wetherby, sir, she woulda knowed that I knowed, and I never told no one, I didna—"

Osbert managed to interrupt. "Very good, Maggie, that will do. Please go now, and do not return for the tray. I shall see to that. Thank you."

She went off down the passage and through the baize door leading to the back stairs and that back world so close to the front and so remote. Osbert returned to the schoolroom.

Elsie Wetherby was sitting as he had left her, the breakfast untouched. He stared at her and thought, No wonder she looks as she does; it is a wonder she can look anyone in the face, knowing to what depths she has sunk. And the squire saying to her not to let *me* distress her, I who loved her—how could she have done this terrible thing to me?

Elsie looked up, as he walked toward her, with a pitiful expression that he interpreted as an effort to win his sympathy. Without speaking, he laid the brooch down upon her lap.

"Oh," she cried. "Oh, I am so thankful! I lost it, I know not where, I was *so* unhappy!" She smiled as she put up her hand in the well-remembered gesture, holding the brooch to her throat. "Thank you, Osbert, thank you! Where was it found?"

He sat again to face her. "I may as well tell you," he said. "It was found by the bedside in Mrs. W-H's room. I assume that is where you lost it. It was unwise of you to have worn it there and very ill luck to have left it behind."

Elsie was so happy to have her treasure returned that for a full minute she did not grasp the import of Osbert's words. Then she realized that he must believe she had gone purposely to the squire's chambers and lain willingly in his bed. She was horror-stricken.

"Oh, no, oh, no, no, Osbert, no—oh, it was horrible, the dog, the dog was slobbering, it was barking the whole time, I could do nothing, he is so strong, he smelled so bad, the dog was trying to jump on the bed, I did not know what to do, I could do nothing, I cried out but no one answered, no one heard, the dog was barking, he was so heavy, I did not know what he was doing, I could not stop him, he hurt me, he breathed all over me like an animal, the dog kept barking, he must not do it again, what he did, he hurt me, the dog was slavering, he could have gone for help, it would have been too late, I could not get clean, my mother must not know, she will be so ashamed, no one must ever know, the children would not love me, no one but the dog knows, he cannot talk, he just slobbers, I could not get cl-clean—"

The words came pouring out through Elsie's sobbing. Her voice rose as she became more and more hysterical. She could not stop, and Osbert knew now what was the terrible thing that had happened to her and left her the wreck of the woman he had loved. Did love. Still loved. Would always love.

"Hush," he said, pressing between his own her hands, which had been clawing now at the air, now at her head. "There is no need for tears. It is all over. It will not come back." He took the brooch from her lap and pinned it at her collar, where it belonged.

"We are leaving this place now," he said. "Together. I shall take you to the rectory, to the Smallwoods; you shall not spend another hour under this roof. Marietta and Lottie will help you to pack. They need not know our reason for departing. They know you have been ill, and I am here to take you away. Come, now, it is all in the past; we shall go together into the future. Come with me, Elsie, dearest."

He took her to her room, which he had never before entered. It was immaculately clean and neat. His heart ached when he saw how comfortless it was, and how she had tried to adorn it with her few treasures: amateur likenesses of her parents, her Bible at the bedside, a beadwork cushion in bright colors, a vase containing pink velvet roses made by Marietta at the age of twelve. On the wall was an allegorical picture of Christ as a shepherd leading his flock across the green pastures of some ancient land.

He helped Elsie to sit in the big chair that held the beadwork cushion, then went downstairs in search of the two young ladies. He requested their assistance for Miss Wetherby's immediate departure from the house. He instructed the manservant to take a message to the rectory informing the Smallwoods that they were to expect the imminent arrival there of Miss Wetherby and himself. He sent orders to Tole to have the carriage brought around to convey them there.

As Mr. Reddle and Miss Wetherby were leaving with Tole, Lottie clung to the governess, weeping. "Whatever shall I do without you?" she cried.

"Good-bye, dear Miss Wetherby," said Marietta, taking her sister's hand to draw her away. "It will be all right, Lottie. I shall take care of you until Miss Wetherby comes back."

"Miss Wetherby is never coming back," said Mr. Reddle as he climbed into the carriage after her.

It was very romantic, Marietta thought: Miss Wetherby's mysterious indisposition was now explained; she had been lovesick, pining away with love she had thought to be unrequited, and now her lover had come to carry her off—not, to be sure, on a white steed to some distant castle, only as far as the rectory in Tole's carriage, but it was romantic all the same. Who could ever have imagined that mousy, drab Miss Wetherby would be the heroine of a romance? Or that Mr. Reddle would play Romeo?

The sisters watched as the carriage receded from view along the road through the park, toward the ruin and the gates. Both of them saw the same thing at the same moment, and in broad daylight: the figure of a white-bearded ancient atop the ruin. It, too, was turned away from the house but facing across the fields toward Sheerwater. When the carriage passed behind a beech grove and disappeared from sight, so did the apparition.

Lottie squeezed her sister's arm. "Did you see him?" she whispered.
"Yes," Marietta whispered back.

"What can it mean?" asked Lottie fearfully.

"I do not know," said Marietta. She did know that the ghost was a
harbinger of death. She hoped its appearance did not mean that Miss
Wetherby, leaving here, was destined to continue the journey forever, far
beyond the gates of Wrox, to the ends of the earth and the end of the
world and beyond.

The ghost had never before been known to appear in daylight. It was
always by night that it made off with food or clothing that had been
placed in the ruin by some charitable hand. On the eve of old Squire
Wrox's death it had been seen by moonlight when the moon appeared
between black clouds driven by a bitter wind across a February sky. The
beautiful young Henrietta had been called above in summertime, soon
after the phantom had been seen hovering at night over Sheerwater.

❧ 15 ☙

THE SQUIRE IS EXCOMMUNICATED

Mr. Smallwood and Osbert Reddle sat in the room overlooking the garden where the rector wrote his weekly sermon, sometimes following an argument with Mrs. Smallwood about fine distinctions among various words like "composition," "reference," "attribution," "quotation" and "outright plagiarism." The first pages of the next Sunday's sermon lay on his desk beside a pile of books, just as he had left them when interrupted that morning by the arrival from Wrox Hall of the two unexpected guests. It was now early afternoon. Mrs. Smallwood, Miss Theodora and Elsie Wetherby were upstairs, well out of earshot. Mr. Reddle had requested a private meeting with the clergyman. It was evident to Mr. Smallwood that Osbert was extremely distraught. He refused to seat himself.

"I should like to kill Wrox-Hampden!" he burst out.

The vicar regarded him in astonishment. He was in the habit of receiving confidences (had he been a Papist, he would have had a confessional), but never had he heard anything like this. "My dear sir, are you mad?" he asked.

"I would kill him," said Osbert, "if it did not mean that I should hang instead of him, who should be hanged!"

"Try to calm yourself, Mr. Reddle, else I shall never understand what it is you are talking about. Why should you wish to kill the squire?"

Osbert got hold of himself and told the rector the whole dreadful story of what had been done to helpless, innocent Elsie Wetherby, "as if she were his chattel, his slave girl, and he owned her."

Mr. Smallwood had never before experienced such a shock. At the conclusion of Osbert's recital he was rendered speechless. When he found his voice, he said, "This is a terrible sin. It is a sin worse than murder, for men may murder and call it war or vengeance, or may commit it without knowing they are so doing. But this is the worst possible sin. Let us hope the awful damage done will not prove to be irreparable."

Osbert said, "He does not even know he has done damage."

"He must repent of his sin," said the rector.

"He does not even know he has sinned," Osbert said. "He is a monster. He should not be allowed to live. Yet I cannot accuse him or bring him to book without doing further irreparable harm to Elsie were the whole thing to be made public knowledge. Why should she be made to suffer for his crime? I should enjoy killing him!"

"It must never be made public knowledge," the rector agreed. "Mrs. Wrox-Hampden and her children must never know, for they, too, are innocent. He must repent this great sin."

"He does not know he has sinned," Osbert repeated. "And were he to know, how could that help Elsie? It is worse than a sin; it is a crime, for it was committed against an innocent victim. You must make him realize what he has done. You are the only person who can tell him that he is going to spend the hereafter burning in hell."

"He will not burn in hell if he does not first repent," said the clergyman. "Torture is pointless if one does not understand the reason for it."

"Mr. Smallwood, I do not understand you; indeed, I do not. Do you say he must acknowledge his crime before Almighty God will punish him?"

"In a way, yes. That is, only his own conscience can punish him. If he does not recognize himself for a sinner, punishment would be meaningless; it would be punishment for a crime he did not, to his own way of thinking, commit. He must be made to acknowledge his sin and repent it."

"Whereupon, I suppose," said Osbert, "it will be forgiven and he free to go his way and sin some more. I must say I do not follow your line of reasoning. But in any case, only you, sir, can tell him he has sinned because that is what you are here to do."

Mr. Smallwood examined his soul, then did a very brave thing. "I shall go to him and tell him he has committed a terrible crime, and you shall come with me to confront him as accuser and witness. He shall be made to see the evil of his ways."

It was brave of the rector to do this because he was dependent upon Arthur Wrox-Hampden for his living. If the squire was to take it away, Mr. Smallwood was too old, he knew, to find another. He had little means of his own and, without the living, no way to provide a comfortable home for his wife and daughter.

The two men walked the mile from the village to the Hall. Wrox village was a different place from the backwater Osbert remembered; it swarmed with activity connected to the laying of the railway tracks and the building of a station. Next to the common were two great shiplike long-distance carriers' wagons. Laborers, bricklayers, masons were everywhere; the public house was busy. In front of jerry-built shelters children, chickens and pigs spilled over onto the common. The encampment of the navvies who were the laborers for the railway was on the other side of the village by the Bunbury road.

"I wonder if the Gypsies will come back this year," Osbert remarked.

"Quite possibly they will find better pickings than ever," said the rector, "and there will be even more of them. There will be more of tramps and mendicants likewise. They come from all parts of England, along with the railroad. We used to be able to take care of our own poor, but these are not our own, and who will take care of them?"

As the two men turned their backs to the village and headed toward the Hall, leaving behind the noise and activity, the countryside had never appeared more peaceful, washed clean by the rain, the rolling uplands cropped close by sheep moving slowly across. In the quiet pastoral scene nothing else seemed to move except for the birds in the air and a yoke of oxen being driven before a plow in a distant field. Osbert was aware, as always, that out of sight there was continuous movement and teeming life: grass growing, trees drinking the water that had lately run deep into the earth, nestlings breaking out of their shells, ants building their hills, moles their tunnels, hedgehogs burrowing, bees busy in the cowslips, earthworms being turned up under the plow, foxes stirring in their coverts. It was as it had been for thousands of years, since the migrations of peoples had passed along the ridges of the downland, leaving on its scarps and in its folds the works of their hands: dolmens, tumuli, encampments, castles, mills, villages.

"I should not say it, I suppose," began Mr. Smallwood, preparatory to saying it, "but I never really liked Mr. Wrox-Hampden. I found it difficult to decide if he were a knave or a fool."

"One is as bad as the other," said Osbert. "They do equal damage. Whether it be done out of knavery or stupidity the result is the same."

Mr. Smallwood agreed. "Both are an offense against the Lord."

Mr. Reddle walked a distance in silence before he said, "Do we not pray to God that His will be done?"

"Certainly."

"Then was it God's will that the drunken Wrox-Hampden should offend Him by despoiling a virgin? If so, the sin is as much God's as the squire's."

"Nay," said the rector, "you must not lose your faith. If you allow this sorry affair to cause the loss of your faith, Wrox-Hampden will have won. Won, that is, in this battle of the continuing war between good and evil, in which we are all obliged to take sides."

In the lane leading past the paddocks to the Hall's lawn and shrubbery the two men saw approaching the children's pony cart. Marietta was leading Skittles, and Lottie sat in the cart holding baby Violet. "Today is Letty's birthday," Marietta told them, stopping to speak. "Is she not a bonny wee one? She is a year old today. It is too bad she does not know it so she can enjoy it, but she will enjoy the day anyway, and next year she will know, she is very quick."

She was indeed a bonny little lass, so well covered that nothing was visible of her but a rosy face with fat cheeks surrounded by the frills of her bonnet. Mr. Smallwood said, "God bless her, may she have many more happy returns of this day." Osbert Reddle thought, She looks just like the rest of them, they all look like their father, and he remembered the purpose of this return visit to the Hall. Could it have been only little more than twelve hours since he had stood in the rain and pounded on the door?

"The other will also mark his birthday today," Mr. Smallwood said as they approached the house. "The twin, the one they took away."

"Gave away," said Osbert.

"I hope he is as thrifty as this one," the rector remarked.

They arrived at the door with its knocker shaped like a lion's head. There was also a bell, which Mr. Smallwood pulled. Minutes passed. Osbert knocked. Mr. Smallwood pulled. Eventually the door was opened by the housemaid Maggie. She dropped a curtsy to the rector as she stood aside for the callers to enter.

"We should like to see Mr. Wrox-Hampden," said Mr. Smallwood.

"I believe he is not in, sir. He went out riding."

"When do you expect him? Mr. Reddle and I wish to see him."

"I do not know, sir."

"We shall wait."

"Yes, sir, this way, please."

"There is no need to show us the way about this house," said Mr. Reddle. "We shall wait here, in view of the staircase, where he is bound to pass."

It was nearly an hour later that the interview began. It was held in the first-floor sitting room that had been—still was—Maria's, adjoining her bedroom, because here there could be no possible interruption and no chance of being overheard. The dog, Caesar, had accompanied its master into the room and had been violently ejected, with kicks and oaths, by Osbert Reddle.

Mr. Smallwood summoned up courage to do his duty. It was made easier by the squire's unkempt appearance and odor of the stables that gave advantage to the neat and cleanly clergyman. "I shall mince no words," he said when all three men were seated. "It has become known to me that you are guilty of a very grave sin in the form of a crime committed against a young woman who was placed under your protection."

"What? What?" stammered Arthur Wrox-Hampden. "When was this? What was this?" He knew in the back of his mind to what the rector referred, but he had put it back there deliberately, hoping that if he forgot it himself, it would be forgotten. And so it had been until this moment.

The rector cleared his throat. "I refer, sir, to the rape of Miss Elsie Wetherby." He fixed the squire with a steady, accusing gaze. He was determined to stand firm. Osbert Reddle was sitting next to him, not looking at Wrox-Hampden for fear he would be tempted to kill; several possible weapons were at hand by the fireplace, on the mantelpiece, on tables, on Maria's escritoire a heavy inkwell and a paper cutter.

Arthur Wrox-Hampden leaned forward. "That is a strong word to use, an ugly word."

"It describes an ugly deed."

"Well, you need not call it by that name." The squire sought to find justification for not so describing what he had done to Miss Wetherby—

or, rather, he thought, what had occurred between them. She had come voluntarily to his room, at night, she had enticed him—yes, it was she who had approached him and made an overture by touching him. She had put temptation in the way of a lusty man whose wife had denied him his conjugal rights for months, who had left him and gone off to Italy. You could not place a tempting dish before a starving man and not expect him to fall upon it. As he remembered it, she had made no objection. Anyhow, it had been only once; the rector was making a mountain out of a molehill. "I did not seduce her," he declared.

"No, you did not. You raped her."

"Did she tell you that? She could not have! Everyone knows I am a good-natured fellow. I would not willingly hurt anyone!"

"The hurt you inflict unwillingly, then, must be all the greater." The rector rose to his feet that he might look down upon the huge man he had always disliked and now despised. "You have committed a terrible crime against a young woman who was under your roof and under your protection, just as much as were your own daughters. What if this crime had been committed against one of your daughters?"

A look of terror appeared on Wrox-Hampden's face. He began to sway back and forth like an animal at bay. "You will not tell my daughters?" he pleaded. "Not my daughters. You must not tell them!"

"We shall tell no one, sir, but it is to spare Miss Wetherby and your daughters—not to spare you."

"Miss Wetherby would not tell my daughters, would she?" pleaded the man. "I was always fond of little Miss Wetherby. And I love my daughters. If anyone was to rape one of my daughters, I would kill him. Yes, that is what I should do, kill him."

There was a moment of silence as these words sank in.

"Now we are getting somewhere," said Mr. Smallwood.

"Yes," said Osbert. "Perhaps you can now begin to understand why *I* would like to kill *you.*"

"Why on earth should you want to do that?" the squire asked. "What is Miss Wetherby to you? She is not your daughter."

"She is my intended wife," said Osbert. "You took what should have been mine, and mine alone. And you took from her the right, the duty, the joy of giving herself to a man for the first time in an act of love. You made what should have been an act of love into the most terrible experience of her life." Osbert's voice quivered, and his hands, clenched tight, were trembling.

"You are truly a wicked man," said the rector. "I hereby deny you the comforts and sacraments of the Church. You are never to enter the sanctuary until such time as I am satisfied that you have truly repented of your monstrous sin. You are driven out of the temple of the Lord. Your soul shall find no rest in purgatory. I suggest, sir, that you examine your conscience—if you have one."

He and Osbert Reddle left the room with the big man staring after them, openmouthed, a look of bewilderment on his face.

"A cup of tea will be most welcome," the clergyman said as they walked back to the rectory. "Not a word about this to the ladies, of course. I must say I believe stupidity might be the biggest sin of all; as you pointed out, it can do as much damage as any other."

Osbert was thinking over their earlier conversation. "You said, sir," he began, "that the squire is either a knave or a fool, and it matters not which, for they do equal damage. Wrox-Hampden is both, so the damage is compounded. The knave committed a crime, and the fool does not recognize it as such."

"He must be made to," said the rector.

Arthur Wrox-Hampden remained sitting, as they had left him, for a long time. Mr. Smallwood need not for a moment have feared the loss of his living, for the squire did not have in his nature any streak of meanness, nor had he any thoughts of retaliation or of seeking vengeance. In his view, people should do what they were paid and expected to do. Hence the vicar was not stepping out of line in accusing him of wickedness, for that was the province of a clergyman. It could not have been accepted coming from anyone else—Reddle, for example; it was none of Reddle's business what he, Arthur Wrox-Hampden, did, and had the tutor not already been dismissed, he would certainly have found himself today without employment. Mr. Smallwood, in line of duty, had told him to examine his conscience—if he had one. Of course he had one! Everybody had a conscience; it was part of the equipment that distinguished man from animals. But the examination of it required introspection, to which Arthur had never been given.

The rector had called him a wicked man, a sinner—a criminal, even. This opinion of him was so diametrically opposed to his own views of himself that on hearing it, he had been shaken. Smallwood was a good man, a good Christian, a man of the cloth; he would not lie; it must be that he truly thought his friend and parishioner Arthur Wrox-Hampden (whose bread he had broken, whose wife he had churched, whose children he had baptized) to be a wicked man. Smallwood had said he must repent his sins. Repentance meant realizing that he should not have done that of which the rector would have him repent. Until he realized and repented, he was not to be allowed to go to church; that was his punishment. He had never in the whole course of his life enjoyed going to church, so how could not being allowed in there be construed as punishment? It was more like a reward. He wished he had studied theology, like his brother Cuthbert, but he knew himself to be incapable of understanding the intricacies and mysteries of man's relation to God or even to other men. Arthur felt his thoughts wandering about in his head like lost sheep. He tried to herd them back into his conscience.

If Smallwood called him a wicked sinner, then it followed that Smallwood disliked him. He had not known himself to be disliked by anyone. He had always thought himself to be regarded as a good-natured fellow, ever ready for a good hunt or a good shoot, a splendid host, set a good table, only the best port and brandy, enjoyed a good laugh, wouldn't hurt a fly—willingly, that is. How could Smallwood dislike him? And the tutor chap, actually talking about killing him. Dangerous fellow. Good he was no longer let loose around the children. Look at the brutal way he had treated Caesar, for no reason beyond a desire to be cruel to an animal. Caesar had never done anything to *him*. If Reddle could treat a dog so, who was to say he had not so mistreated the children under his tutelage?

The children. Arthur's thoughts returned to his family. How was he to tell Maria and the children about his banishment from church services? Who would read the lessons in his place on Sunday mornings? It was all very well for Smallwood to tell him, Arthur, never to set foot in the church, but how was this prohibition to be explained to Maria and the children? Smallwood should have thought of that before he acted so high-handedly.

Hours passed. The life of the house went on without him. Dinner was served and eaten, dishes washed, dogs put out, doors locked, servants gone to the attics, the family to its beds, lights extinguished. At midnight Arthur called to Caesar and left the house with the dog. In pale moonlight the shapes of the trees stood about, and in the distance on Sheerwater Pond there lay a shimmering path of silver.

❧ 16 ❧

An Illegitimate Birth

During the past weeks alone together in Rome, Maria and her daughter Lucy had grown close. They had seen virtually no one else, and at home that would probably have resulted in their getting on each other's nerves. Here in exile they clung to the small unit of home they represented in the alien city with its foreign ways. The climate was unpleasantly hot, the food strange to their palates, the language spoken too rapidly ever to be understood. Had they not known it must soon end they could not have borne it. Lucy grew ever larger and ever more restless. She refused to stay confined to the house even in daylight and made the maid, Abigail, accompany her about at any and all hours. There was no danger of her being seen by anyone who mattered; the *haut monde* had long moved on from Italy to meet elsewhere, in cities with more agreeable climates or beside cool mountain lakes.

In England it was known that Mrs. Wrox-Hampden had taken her two elder daughters for a season in Rome, where their near relation Robert Fox had invited them. Miss Marietta had returned to England before her mother and sister, in company with Mr. Fox, in order to pay him a visit at Foxbridge Abbey. The other two ladies had remained in Rome to take advantage of the remaining month of the lease on their lodgings.

Maria had decided Lucy and the infant should remain somewhere in

Italy, where for all anyone knew Lucy might be a young widow of modest means who chose to live abroad for reasons of economy. If the child were to be brought home to Wrox, Maria told Arthur, it would forever bear the stigma of illegitimacy, which would not matter so much in Italy. She wrote:

> Italian society is not closed to non-Italians born on the wrong side of the blanket, provided they are *well* born on the other side of it. In fact, I met a man at a reception in the Villa Lambrosi who declared himself with pride to be a *bâtard* of the late Duke of Warminster, and he was made much of. Our esteemed friend Benjamin Share, as you know, claims to have royal blood by descent from Edward the First or Third—it matters not which. I am not sure that I believe him, he is such an accomplished storyteller, but the Italians have no way of knowing if it be true or not, and Mr. Share is made much of. He is gone now, in company with James Edge. Marietta was about with them a good deal while they were here. Lucy was, of course, kept out of sight, and James did not once inquire after her. It is very hard on Lucy. She is paying dearly for her sin, as we must all do.

Mother and daughter sat in the drawing room one morning when Maria brought up the subject of the baby's future. She had been making a layette, which had kept her pleasantly occupied. "Lucy," she said, "you can remain here in Italy with your child openly, rather than take it home to England to live somewhere unacknowledged."

"I will never live anywhere but Wrox, Mama. I would rather die than remain here. I wish to go home, and I would prefer to go with the child than without it."

"No one suggested that you go without it, Lucy, although that could make no difference to the child. It does not know one place from another. It is to be born in Italy, after all, and my father used to say that a person is always drawn back to the place where he was born, even though he may have removed far from it."

"It was your father who said also that the month in which a person was born is always his favorite month. Anyone born in February who liked it best would be an idiot."

"The Bellwood cousins who went out to the West Indies are drawn home to their birthplace in England," Maria continued; "they bring their children back home to school."

"They have to," said Lucy, "if they expect the children to be educated, as there are no schools in the Leeward Islands that I am aware of. Besides, it's a good way to get rid of them."

"What a way to talk, child! They do what is best for the children, not to get rid of them."

"Sometimes getting rid turns out best for them," said Lucy. "Ask your son Edward in twenty years." She had been feeling very uncomfortable since the day before, unable to keep still. She was walking about with her hands on her swollen belly. "I wish I could get rid of this thing right now," she said. "I want to get it *out* of me; then we can decide where it is to live." She stopped moving about and stood still, a look of concentration on her face. After a long moment she gave a gasp. "Mama, I felt a pain! It was as if someone were dragging at my insides, trying to pull them out. Wait—let's see if it does it again." A few minutes later she cried out excitedly, "It did! It did it again!"

Maria put down her sewing and ran to fetch the maid. "Run, Abigail, run to the midwife. Then come back quickly and help me. I shall put on water to boil. Go upstairs, Lucy, and get undressed, I shall be with you directly."

On her way out Abigail encountered the *postino*, who was about to knock at the door. "*Corriere dopopranzo*," he said, handing her two letters.

"It's the post, madam!" she called to her mistress.

"Put it on the table, Abby. I have no time for it now. And do hurry; stop dawdling to talk to the postman."

Lucy refused to lie down. She moved restlessly about her bedroom, back and forth, as if she expected to drop her cub like a wild animal, stopping to hang on to a bedpost during intervals between pains. Her mother at last persuaded her to change into a nightdress and lie on the bed, and it was thus the midwife found her nearly an hour after Abigail had left. The woman had been recommended, because she spoke a little English, by the Italian doctor who served Maria's landlady and other families in the neighborhood. She spoke enough to say what she needed as she went about her business. She told Maria she had stopped by the doctor's house to leave word of her whereabouts; she thought he would come by later if he got the message. She was not very clean, Maria noticed; her black dress showed the dust of the streets, but she put over it a large apron with many pockets and washed her hands and arms carefully, up to the elbows. From one bulging pocket she drew forth a large clock that she set on a table by the bed, from another a sheet of paper and a pencil. She made it known that she required hot water, a basin and a receiving blanket. She then sat to watch Lucy and record her progress.

"She looks flushed," Maria said anxiously, hovering at the other side of Lucy's bed. "Hot. *Caldo.*" She reached over to lay a hand on her daughter's forehead.

"Today *caldo*," said the midwife, pointing to the window that was open to the sights, sounds and squalor of the city. But she took Lucy's wrist and felt her pulse, looking at the clock and silently moving her lips. The clock moved on. The afternoon moved on. Lucy's pains were closer together. The doctor did not come. Lucy's pains became merged into one interminable one, as did her screams of rage. The *levatrice* rose and closed the window, under which in the street curious passersby had stopped. The child showed no sign of being about to emerge from the womb. The woman was reaching up inside Lucy, who lay on her back with her legs splayed and hands clutching her hair. Her eyes were rolled back in her head.

Watching helplessly, Maria could bear it no longer. A terrible cry burst from her throat. It was the anguished cry of all mothers through all time: If I could suffer in the place of my child, I would do it gladly! I had rather bear the agony myself than watch as my child goes through it.

Maria's suffering in giving Lucy birth, long forgotten, was as nothing to what she was now enduring. It was as if the body once sheltered inside the mother were there still, so deep inside herself did Maria suffer with her child. Every cry of Lucy's came from Maria's own heart. Frantic by now, she could bear no more. "I shall go for the doctor!" she declared. She picked up the paper on which were written some numbers and letters and made the woman dictate the doctor's name and address (*in-dinizzo nome dottore*). Then she ran down the stairs and out the door. The small crowd in the street fell back. *"Far presto, signora,"* someone called.

"Posso aiutare?" a man asked. She recognized the keeper of a nearby shop.

"Oh, please!" she said, and thrust the paper into his hand.

"Venire," he said, "I go with you." He took her by the elbow, and together they ran along the street and across the piazza.

When day broke, Lucy's terrible ordeal had come to an end. The doctor had been unable to save the mother. A baby boy lay squalling on the sofa across the foot of the bed where Marietta had slept.

In the morning Maria went around to the British consulate. The consul was a man she had met at various houses during the past winter. He was most kind and helpful. A wet nurse was found. Arrangements were made for Lucy to be laid to rest in a grave between cypress trees at the foot of the pyramid of Caius Quintus. A courier was about to leave the consulate for London; he could carry the sad news back to Wrox.

Two unopened letters had been lying all the while on the table in the curve of the staircase. Maria picked them up and carried them into the drawing room, where she sank into a chair by a window to read them. She was exhausted. She knew she must put forth the energy to make arrangements necessary for her return to England and the strength to undertake the journey. My poor Lucy, she prayed, who did not fit into this world, may she find a comfortable resting place in the next. And her baby. What of her baby?

Maria opened her eyes and held the letters toward the light. One was from Dr. Pipkin. Why would he write to her? It could not be for any happy purpose. Was one of the children ill? After what she had just been through, she could not face it. She set the doctor's letter on her lap and turned to the other. It was from Stoke-sub-Ham and addressed by Georgiana Hampden.

My dear Maria,

Today being the first birthday of my darling little Gift from God Edward, I am writing to give you an account of his first Year in this World that is so full of Temptations and Pitfalls, both of which he has thus far avoided. His health is excellent, as he has now recovered completely from an early tendency to suffer with the Colic, through which he was cared for by the excellent woman who is his Nurse, you need have no Concern on that Account. He weighs nearly 2 stone. His fontanel has closed completely. He cries very little, although he showed a Tendency and Aptitude for it, he soon learned he could not get his own Way by crying, and after many Attempts to get Attention in that Manner he realized the Futility of exhausting himself and subsided. At 7 months he cut his first tooth, the left middle one (bottom). His fifth Tooth has begun to appear, which he seems to wish to encourage with his Thumb, and as we cannot allow him to grow up sucking his Thumb it has been made fast to his little Hand by a clever device of Esther's that allows him to move his fingers but not to put them into his Mouth as the Device will not permit of their entry. You will be happy to know that the darling Boy is very attentive when his Uncle Cuthbert reads to him at bedtime, which does seem to help him fall Asleep. His nurse, Mary Roberts, is very fond of him, he is in Good Hands.

I hope his sister Violet is as happy as he and send kindest regards to all at Wrox from all here at Stoke Rectory.

Ever your loving sister,
Georgiana Hampden

How distant seemed the rectory of Stoke-sub-Ham, where an infant had just completed his first year of life! Thank Heaven he is in the care of Georgie Hampden, Maria thought, and is not my concern. This one lying upstairs on Lucy's old bed *is* my concern. What shall I do?

She turned to the letter from Dr. Pipkin. It had been posted at Bunbury on 29 June.

Madam,

It is my painful but necessary duty to inform you of the death of your husband, Arthur Wrox-Hampden. His body was discovered in Sheerwater Pond yesterday afternoon, 28 June. He had not to all appearances suffered, nor had he been ill, as he was in good health when visited during the afternoon of 27 June by Mr. Smallwood, the vicar. Mr. Wrox-Hampden is to be laid to rest on 3 July, at 11 A.M. in the churchyard of Wrox. Believe me, Madam, you have my most sincere condolences and my deepest sympathy in your great loss.

Respectfully yours,
W. Pipkin

During the following night a lady dressed in black, her face veiled, descended from a carriage before the door of the convent of the Villa Nante on the Via di San Giorgio. She was accompanied by a maid. Between them the two women carried a large basket in which lay, upon a silken cushion, an infant swathed in fine linen, surrounded by a delicately worked layette, the whole under a clean blanket. On the blanket was pinned an envelope containing a large sum of money and a letter written in English. The nuns of Nante were known to speak English, for the convent had been founded by the daughters of a rich Irish merchant, a pilgrim to Rome in the pontificate of Pius VI. The women laid the basket on the stone steps before the doors of the convent and rang the bell. They then returned to the carriage and were driven off.

Two days later Maria Wrox-Hampden and her maid left the house on the street off the Piazza Navona and began the journey back to England.

❧ 17 ❧

A BODY IS DISCOVERED

On the morning after Miss Wetherby's sudden romantic departure with her unlikely Prince Charming, Marietta and Lottie sat disconsolately in the common room that was between the schoolroom and nurseries. Time hung heavy. It was summer holidays, so they would have had no lessons in any case, but Miss Wetherby had always found some activity or other to fill the days. They were used to having occupations arranged for them: interesting walks with Mr. Reddle, the historian, botanist and connoisseur of all living things; sewing sessions with the fine needlewoman Mrs. Cluster; visits to county fairs or country house gardens; hours with Miss Theodora at the pianoforte. Now they had been left to their own devices, and they had none. They had been reading aloud Charles Dickens's latest novel, *Oliver Twist*, but could not continue until *Bentley's Miscellany* arrived with the next installment.

Lottie was in the window seat, looking out at the green and pleasant landscape, so familiar she had all but ceased to see it. In the distance the surface of Sheerwater Pond shone silver where the sun hit it. She noticed near the bank an unfamiliar object, no bigger than a small animal of some sort. Then she realized that it appeared to be small only because of its distance. Seen close, it could be a large animal. Or it could be a large rock. It was not moving. There was no big rock by the bank in Sheerwater. "Marietta," she said, "come here. Look at the pond—there—to the right of the willow tree. Do you see something?"

Marietta went to stand by her sister. "Where? Oh—yes, I see what you mean. What do you suppose it to be? It looks as if a rowboat had been turned over upside down. I don't think it is alive; it does not move. Perhaps it is a dead animal. If so, it is an uncommonly large one."

"Could it be a cow, do you suppose?" Lottie suggested. "Or a deer?"

"It is not large enough."

"It could be partly submerged."

"Let us fetch Papa's telescope."

"He would not like that."

"We can look through it where it is, we need not move it, he need not know."

"What if he were to come and catch us?"

"He will not be indoors on a day like this," said Marietta.

They went to the room below, on the first floor, where their father had positioned his telescope to cover an angle of fully 130 degrees. Seen through it, the object in the pond jumped to life size; it was apparently some large, dark, thick-skinned animal.

"It does not look like a cow or a deer," said Marietta. "Let us walk down there and see."

Without stopping to put on their bonnets, they left the house and started off in the direction of the pond. They walked rapidly, enjoying the fresh breeze fanning their faces and the sun warming their bare heads, bringing out highlights on their hair. Both had the thick, beautiful Hampden hair that was ginger-colored in their father and sister Lucy, auburn in Lottie and a rich chestnut in Marietta.

As they drew near the pond, the strange object became even more clear. When they arrived on the bank, they saw the body of their father, facedown in the shallow water. Lying flat with his head on his paws, staring fixedly at its master, was the dog Caesar.

"It is Papa!" cried Lottie. She began to scream.

"Oh, may Heaven help us!" exclaimed Marietta. She stood transfixed, staring down at the awful sight. "What shall we do? I must fetch help. Stay here, Lottie, do not leave, and I shall go for help." She lifted her skirts and ran back toward the Hall, then saw that the house of Nettle, the farmer, was closer and he was at work in a nearby field. Stumbling and panting, she headed toward him as fast as she could, calling out, "Help, please help." She arrived at his fence out of breath while he lifted his head from his monotonous work to look in her direction. "Please . . . help . . . please—"

Nettle touched his forehead, lifting his cap. "What is it, miss?"

"Fetch help—quickly!" pleaded Marietta. "It is Papa; he needs help. Fetch someone, please—"

Nettle dropped his hoe and went to the barn in search of his grown son, whom he sent for Mr. Spence. It was fully half an hour before the three men followed Marietta to the pond and found the corpse. Lottie was running back and forth along the bank, sobbing. The mastiff had not moved.

"Why, 'tis the squire himself!" said Spence.

Nettle crossed himself. Young Nettle stared with open mouth.

"Please!" cried Marietta. "Save him! Help him!"

"I am afraid he is past help, miss," Spence said, but he took charge effectively, ordering the Nettles into the water, where he followed them, careless of his boots and clothing. "We shall carry him to the Hall," he said. "Do you and your sister go straightway and send for the doctor and for the priest. Hurry, now." He waited until the young ladies were well away before bending to the heavy task that he thought it not fitting they should watch.

After the three men had lifted and dragged the corpse to the bank under the willow, Spence sent young Nettle for a wheelbarrow, and it was in this, with enormous limbs hanging out dripping over the sides, that the squire's body was brought into the well room at the Hall. The dog, Caesar, followed it.

The sensational news was quickly spread. There was no undertaker nearer than the cathedral town of Glanbury, distant by thirty miles. He was summoned immediately after Dr. Pipkin. He in turn got hold of Mr. Smallwood to make the necessary funeral arrangements. The authorities at Bunbury were notified of the death. Word was sent to the Hampdens at Stoke-sub-Ham and to young Arthur at Oxford. Augustus was already on his way home for the holidays. Dr. Pipkin undertook to notify the widow and daughter, who were still in Rome. Mrs. Bellwood at Hatche Castle was on her way to Wrox in her own carriage with her maid almost before the word had reached her that Cousin Arthur had been found dead in mysterious circumstances; knowing he had never been ill a day in his life, she was sped on her way by intense curiosity.

Marietta, although herself suffering from the shock, had found strength to do what must be done since many responsibilities were now on her shoulders. The house must be readied to receive the influx of relations and friends. Cook and the butler had to get in touch with tradespeople and suppliers; housemaids must make ready the bedrooms. The rector asked her if they should not notify Robert Fox at the Abbey. "He was stepson to the squire, was he not?"

"As far as I know, they never met," said Marietta, "and I do know he would not come." She was waiting to write to Lady Edge and the local gentry until the time and place for the funeral should be set. This depended upon determination by the police magistrate of the cause of death. He presumed it was by drowning. The squire could not swim.

"It is my belief Mr. Wrox-Hampden was already dead at the time his body was placed in the pond," said Dr. Pipkin. "It could not be an accidental drowning, for the water is not above four or five foot deep. There is no place in the pond there where he could not stand upright. He could not have drowned unless it were on purpose and he took his own life."

"If that be so," said the rector, "I cannot bury him in hallowed ground."

"Could he have suffered from sudden heart failure or a stroke?" asked the magistrate.

"In my opinion, that would be unlikely. Mr. Smallwood, you were, I believe, the last person to see the deceased alive. Was he not then in good health?"

"So it appeared to me. And to Osbert Reddle. Mr. Reddle was with us."

"What did you discuss at this meeting?" asked the magistrate. "For what purpose did you seek the interview?"

Mr. Smallwood reviewed in his memory the conversation of the previous afternoon. He regarded it as privileged information, as if held in a confessional. The subject of the meeting had been the deflowering of Elsie Wetherby, and he would never reveal that.

"Did he exhibit any signs," asked the magistrate, "that might lead you to think he contemplated taking his own life?"

The rector pondered this. "No, no, I cannot say he showed any tendency toward the idea of taking his life, no."

"Certainly not," said Dr. Pipkin with conviction. "Of all men I have ever known, he was the least likely to commit suicide. He positively relished life, enjoyed it."

"That is so, yes," said Mr. Smallwood, "as far as his own life is concerned. Yes, he did appreciate his own life."

"That rules out suicide," said the magistrate. "So now we come to who murdered him, and by what means, and how did the body come to be where it was found?"

"I cannot imagine," said Dr. Pipkin.

"I may proceed, then," the rector said, "to prepare for interment in the churchyard."

"And I," said the magistrate, "must try to determine who is responsible for this unfortunate death. I do not know where to begin. Did Mr. Wrox-Hampden have any enemies that you know of?"

"I would say," said Mr. Smallwood, "that he was, above all, his own enemy."

"But we have ruled out suicide," the magistrate said. "Now there must be an investigation, I suppose. I cannot avoid it."

Two peelers sent from London had been sworn in as local constables by the Bunbury police magistrate. They lodged in the village with the part-time parish constable. Although they wore plain clothes on their duties, they were conspicuous among the railway navvies, who wore velveteens and spotted neckcloths. The peelers held no sinecure. The navvies were a dangerous lot of brawny, insolent men who tormented the villagers, denuded the countryside of hares and pheasants, carried off farm girls to their encampment and on payday nights staged scenes of wild disorder around the public house. They not only preyed on locals but staged ferocious fights among themselves, on which they bet heavily, fights that the peelers were supposed to prevent or interrupt—a useless endeavor in view of the Bunbury workhouse's being already filled to capacity.

It was because these London police were experienced in dealing with crime that the local magistrate appointed one of them to investigate the murder of Arthur Wrox-Hampden. He was Police Sergeant S. Frakes, a native of Bethnal Green, and he had never before been farther from it than the Thames embankment. A village was new to him. He had found it little different from the city, with a few honest folk living together surrounded by teeming life in the shape of workmen, vagrants, peddlers, swindlers and the encampment dwellers in their makeshift rural slum that was as loathsome as any in London. When he was assigned to investigate the murder of Arthur Wrox-Hampden, he had been told that the criminal probably came from among their population, but if so, he would be long gone along the road, leaving no trace that could be followed. Hence to seek him out among the transients would be useless. Sergeant Frakes accordingly began his investigation among the Wrox tenantry and the inhabitants of the Hall and found himself in a world very different from that which he had heretofore known. He had never seen sheep or tasted mutton or been aware that the cloth on his back had originated on the back of a sheep. He had never looked at a view that contained no building or seen flowers anywhere but on a street barrow. He had never walked between hedgerows or sat under a tree. When he walked to Wrox Hall on the evening of the day the body was discovered, he found himself for the only time in his life inside a dwelling that contained, instead of many people to a room, many more rooms than people.

He entered the Hall from the back. The servants were finishing their evening meal, having served it earlier in the dining room to the two young ladies and Mrs. Smallwood, who was come to stay the night with them. The squire's body had been removed by the undertaker to lie awaiting burial in the church. He was in company there with one other, entombed beneath his effigy, a knight who had followed Richard Lion-Heart to the Holy Land and been the only one of three hundred to return. The rector had seen to it himself that the church door was secured by a padlock; its windows were barred. It was a comfortless resting place, so damp that moss grew in the cracks of the paving stones under the font. It was now made secure against invasion by body snatchers or rats.

Sergeant Frakes was made welcome by the Wrox servants, who recognized one of their own, although from so different and exalted a background. They stood in awe of him as being a Londoner and an officer of the law. This deference, too, was all new to Sergeant Frakes, who was accustomed to being avoided, reviled and used as the target of stones thrown from dark places of concealment. He accepted a nice cup of strong tea and a treacle tart, then brought out pad and pencil to take evidence.

The master had last been seen by any of them at breakfast on the day before. When the housemaid had gone up to do his room, he had already left. Tole, the coachman, or the stableboy would have seen him if he had called for his horse to be saddled. No one knew where he had been all day. In the afternoon Maggie had let in the rector, Mr. Smallwood, in company with the former tutor, who had spent the previous night in the house. Tole had brought him from the village in the middle of the night; they could not say for what purpose he was come. In the morning, at breakfast (the last occasion on which the master had been seen), Mr. Reddle had behaved very strangely to the master, rude he was, and he had left the place very suddenly, taking with him Miss Wetherby, the governess. They did not know where he had taken her.

Maggie, the housemaid, did not, for reasons well known to herself, mention the matter of the brooch, but she began now to put two and two together without knowing, as she would have said, that their sum was four. Mr. Reddle was in love with Miss Wetherby; he had been fondling her in the schoolroom when Maggie took up a breakfast tray. Then she had given him the brooch, and he had realized the governess was the squire's wench. In Maggie's opinion, it was Mr. Reddle who had done in the master. She did not say so.

However, all present thought that this was a strong likelihood, in view of the scene at the breakfast table, which had been witnessed by the manservant and by Cook, who had herself carried up to the dining room a second covered dish of kippers. Mr. Reddle was the Most Likely Suspect.

The butler suggested that Mr. Frakes might call upon Tole in his quarters over the stables to ascertain where it was he had driven Miss Wetherby and Mr. Reddle. It happened that Tole was not at home, but Mrs. Tole said that their destination had been the rectory.

The rector had also briefly held the opinion that Osbert Reddle might be guilty. Had he not several times said he would like to kill Mr. Wrox-Hampden, had even said it in front of the intended victim? "Perhaps you can now begin to understand why *I* would like to kill *you*," he had said.

Mr. Smallwood, in a terrible taking, had gone straight to the tutor when he first heard the news of the murder. "Did you kill Mr. Wrox-Hampden?" he had asked.

"I did not," said Osbert Reddle. "Had I done so, it would have left Elsie alone in the world when she most needed someone. I would not do that to her. I would have killed him and hanged for it gladly were it not that I must live for her."

Mr. Smallwood believed him. There was, furthermore, the incontrovertible evidence that from the moment he and Mr. Reddle had returned to the rectory yesterday afternoon Mr. Reddle had never left it. Mrs. Smallwood and Miss Theodora, not to mention Elsie Wetherby, had so testified.

Mrs. Bellwood of Hatche was the first to show up at Wrox on the heels of the rumor that Cousin Arthur had been done away with. She traveled throughout the night, stopping only once to change horses, lest someone should arrive before her, who, after a death, was always first on the scene. She would not for worlds have missed a funeral and went even to those of strangers in order to compare one with another and count the number of the mourners. For the death of Cousin Arthur—so unexpected—she had been quite unprepared. It was wrong that he should have heard the last call so suddenly and taken her by surprise. She had been given no hint of impending death. In fact, she had never known any person who took so much pleasure in being alive as had Arthur. No one had ever killed so many grouse on her moors, with so much enthusiasm, as had he.

She descended from her carriage at the Hall in the early hours of the morning, requiring rooms and immediate refreshment for herself, her maid, horses and coachman. She was received politely by Marietta Wrox-Hampden, who had so recently stopped at Hatche and whom she had just aroused from an uneasy rest.

"What can I do to help?" she asked after they had embraced.

Marietta smiled wanly. "It is kind of you to come, Cousin Bessie. I hope you have not been inconvenienced."

"Of course I came, my dear," said Mrs. Bellwood. "My own convenience is my last consideration. Do tell me what I can do to help. Jones shall help, too"—she indicated her maid—"and Hilton"—pointing to the coachman—"so soon as we are settled and rested. We shall all need to bathe and have some refreshment; we have been on the way all night; it is a long journey, as you know."

Hilton was almost asleep standing up. A stop had been made to change horses, but there had been no change of driver. He had known from the way his mistress had taken off from Hatche like a firehorse smelling smoke that their objective would be a funeral. He wished she would do her good works by means of a different hobby, one that could be followed at regular hours.

"Of course, Cousin Bessie, you must be spent. Have Hilton take the carriage around to the stables; I shall send someone to assist him with the horses. Do you come with me. I shall show you to your rooms, where I hope you and Jones will be comfortable. Cook can have some refreshment ready as soon as possible." Marietta was near tears. She longed for someone who could indeed help her—at this moment help her to deal with Cousin Bessie, who kept offering, all the way upstairs, to help "as soon as I have rested and changed my clothes, my dear, I have been sitting up in this all the night, Jones will require the use of a flatiron—"

Augustus arrived next, half a head taller than when last seen, his clothing outgrown, finding it strange that neither of his parents was at home and that his father never again would be. His first stop was at the small domestic zoo, assembled by himself and Mr. Reddle, to ascertain that the tortoise, guinea pig, rabbit and mole had been fed regularly by the stableboy. The mole had died. Next Augustus made straight for the pianoforte and spent hours at the keyboard with no one to stop him or say he should be playing sports outdoors rather than music in. "The pianoforte needs tuning," he told Lottie, and proceeded to tune it.

Next came the string of callers, neighbors from near and far, the landed gentry of the shire, expressing condolences and hoping to hear details about the squire's passage into the next world, undertaken so suddenly. From Bunbury came two retired colonels, with their wives, and the widows of two others; Dr. and Mrs. Pipkin; Mr. Weston, the attorney, and Mrs. Weston; Major Rollins; the Son of E. Hole and Son; the rector of Bunbury church; Mr. Maule, the banker; tradesmen of the town paying their respects. Now Mrs. Bellwood came into her own and really did help Marietta in receiving all these people and offering refreshment. "Oh, we shall find out who did it, never fear," she said over and over. "Scotland Yard has sent an inspector all the way from London," for so she elevated the station in life of Sergeant Frakes. He, meanwhile, was taking note of every individual as each came and went. Mr. Weston, the attorney, provided a golden nugget of information: The Deceased had been about to bring suit against his overseer, Mr. Spence, and charge him with defraudation; Mr. Wrox-Hampden had called on Mr. Weston about the matter several times. Mr. Spence therefore had a strong Motive. Moreover, it was he who had brought the body to the Hall, clearly showing he had been near the pond and knew his way around, knew the habits of his employer.

Marietta had been looking forward to the arrival of Lady Edge, that she might have word of James and Mr. Share, but the dowager did not call.

❧ 18 ❧

THE SQUIRE IS LAID TO REST

Wrox church was small and ancient, the nave Norman with the later addition of a Gothic apse, both bearing crosses at the peaks of steep, lichen-covered roofs. The approach to the church was through banks of shrubbery and passed the adjacent rectory, a handsome stone house, not large but of pleasing proportions, with Mrs. Smallwood's garden flowers brilliant against the gray stones. Beside and behind the church stretched the churchyard, all the way to the common at the back. Eight generations of Wroxes lay here in their graves. The gravediggers had finished the work begun before daylight, and Arthur Wrox-Hampden's last resting place lay open to receive his earthly remains.

At eleven o'clock a large congregation had gathered in front of the church when Mr. Smallwood, preceded by an acolyte carrying the cross, led in procession to the graveside the members of the immediate family. Archdeacon Hampden and his wife had just arrived, having traveled all day and night. Young Arthur was with them, and Augustus. The two girls followed. Mrs. Bellwood was accompanied by Miss Theodora. From a respectful distance, standing among the gravestones of centuries past, the tenants and laborers of Wrox watched. Neither Mr. Reddle nor Miss Wetherby had put in an appearance. On the common the Gypsies, lately arrived from only they knew where, took in the situation and determined how they might take advantage of it.

Mr. Smallwood, reading from the order for the Burial of the Dead, began, "I am the resurrection and the life, saith the Lord . . ." and he continued on through "The Lord gave, and the Lord hath taken away; blessed be the name of the Lord." He took his place at the head of the coffin. The family lined up on either side of the grave, Mrs. Smallwood between the two girls, facing the church so their tear-stained faces might not be seen by the onlookers. "Lord, let me know mine end," the rector read, "and the number of my days: that I may be certified how long I have to live. . . ."

The windows in the nave of the church had been placed high by the builders so as to make of the sanctuary a small fortress in time of siege. This had left bare walls the length of the nave and some ten feet high. Along the southern side, facing the churchyard, Mrs. Smallwood had had overshadowing trees removed and had planted espaliered plum trees. They stood there hand in hand against the length of the wall, sheltered from wind, with the warm stones of the old church holding the sun's heat for the benefit of their fruits. There was no other such planting, to anyone's knowledge, in all England. People came to see it from miles around. The plums were equally renowned. When fully ripe, they were of exceptionally large size, of a blue-purple color with silvery gray overtones, their skins stretched almost to bursting by the sweet, juicy pulp within. To pluck a ripe fruit and eat while it was still warm from the sun was to taste of Paradise. Mrs. Smallwood's sharp eye now noticed on her plums the first faint flush of ripening. It was time to have them netted against the birds, she thought.

"For as in Adam all die, even so in Christ shall all be made alive," the rector was saying. He was aware that his wife was not listening. He also knew that if he were to accuse her later of not paying attention, she would say she knew it all by heart. "But every man in his own order," he went on, "Christ the first fruits . . ."

Mrs. Smallwood saw in her mind's eye the beautiful ripe plums to come and began preparing herself for the annual Watch. She could outwit the birds, but the village boys were another thing altogether. This year, with the swarms of disreputable vagrants around and about, in whose midst the treasured fruits tempted, she foresaw a difficult time. The Plum Watch customarily began at dawn with the ripening of the first plum. She shared her vigil with the churchwarden, the beadle and her gardener, one of them being always on Watch. Mrs. Smallwood had devised a means of outwitting the boys very cleverly, by means of a ladder placed against the inside wall of the church under a window, from which she could survey the churchyard without being herself observed. The village boys had "caught on to her," as Mr. Smallwood drolly put it, but she felt certain she would be a match for the interlopers, who could not yet have "caught on" to her and who, by next summer's Watch, when they might have done so, would by God's mercy have moved on, following the tracks they had themselves laid, to some distant place.

"The grace of our Lord Jesus Christ, and the love of God, and the fellowship of the Holy Ghost, be with us all," said the rector.

"Amen," said the mourners.

Archdeacon Hampden could not allow them to have the last word. "So be it!" he shouted in ratification after his brother's departing spirit.

Throughout the burial service the rector had found it necessary to raise his voice in order to be heard above the noise from the nearby construction and its counterpoint of wagon wheels, barking dogs, shouts and the cries of peddlers. It all came as a shock to young Arthur, who had not been at home since Christmas. He had seen on the way between Hall and village how the railhead was creeping across the countryside, dragging its noisy trail over quiet farmlands. And these transient laborers, who went where the path of the tracks took them, whose muscles built bridges and borings, cuttings and embankments—they spread like a local disease of the earth, a kind of spurious eczema. It was perfectly possible to believe that a gang of them had murdered his father. The squire could have caught them in the act of poaching, or stealing from the traps of poachers, or ravishing the daughter of a tenant, or making off with a pig under cover of night.

Sergeant Frakes was lurking around near the grave, furtively taking notes on the circle of mourners, trying to determine if the murderer was among them and returning not to the scene of the crime but to the scene of its conclusion, hoping the evidence could be interred with the victim. No suspicious-looking person had appeared to Sergeant Frakes's eagle eye during the service, and he was the last to leave the graveyard, in case such a person might show up late to make sure his victim was safely interred. He was passing the church door when he heard a hue and cry raised within the edifice. The vicar, still wearing his surplice and followed by his wife and the acolyte, came hurrying out. "Oh, Sergeant, there you are, I was coming after you, thieves have been in the sanctuary, the chalice is missing—and the paten! Mrs. Smallwood failed to lock the door during the service—"

"You must have mislaid them, Jonathan," said his lady. "No one would be so depraved as to steal sacred vessels."

"How could I 'mislay' the communion vessels? I always place them with scrupulous care where they are kept."

"It is a good thing the cross was not in there as well. It is solid silver—of greater value than the vessels."

"No thief could walk off with the cross, Ada! Don't be ridiculous, he would be far too conspicuous."

"Tommy could walk out with it!" Tommy was the acolyte. "No one would think twice of it. He just did walk out with it."

"And he walked back in with it," said Mr. Smallwood. "He did not walk *away* with it."

After a while Sergeant Frakes was able to make out what had happened. He was shown the place where the chalice and paten were usually kept, and they were not there. A description told him what to look for: the silver chalice, a big cup like the Holy Grail that held wine, and a small silver dish or tray for the bread.

"Ten to one it's the Gypsies," the sergeant said.

"What use would they have for them?" asked Mrs. Smallwood. "Gypsies are not C of E."

"Madam, if they are made of silver, as you say, they are of great value and could be sold for a large sum."

"To whom? No one could use them except in church."

"It is the silver, Ada!" her husband said impatiently. "The silver is valuable apart from its sacred character. Sergeant, will you look to the Gypsies? I shall come as soon as I change my clothing, that I may identify the holy vessels."

The Gypsy encampment was alive with the usual men, women, children and dogs, all looking as suspiciously at the policeman as he did at them. A thorough search among their pots, utensils and other possessions uncovered nothing of any value or interest. The paten could have been easily concealed on a person, especially one of the women with their long, full skirts. The chalice would be more difficult of concealment, but the sergeant ordered each of the women to walk rapidly, break into a run and then roll upon the ground, until he was satisfied that no large silver cup such as the Holy Grail was in the Gypsies' possession.

"We shall have to look elsewhere," he said to the clergyman. "I shall, of course, report the theft to the magistrate. And next time, sir, lock up your valuables."

"How can there be a next time?" said poor Mr. Smallwood, more dreadfully distressed than he had ever been in his life.

Wrox Hall was a different place without its late master. His presence had been everywhere, in the sound of his loud voice, his heavy tread on the stair, the way he slammed doors in closing them, how he filled the big chair at the head of the dining table, where he had eaten and drunk so heartily, sometimes noisily. His great dog now lay on its side all day in front of the empty fireplace, lifting its head at the sound of approaching footsteps, then laying it back down when the steps were not those for which it listened.

Archdeacon Hampden immediately took over the master's place, to the annoyance of young Arthur. He sat at the head of the table without being asked. He announced hours for morning and evening prayers, at which he ordered the servants to appear. He instructed Cook to prepare dishes to his liking and Aunt Esther's. Young Arthur, who considered himself now to be the master of the house, was resentful of his uncle's taking over the place that should be his own. The takeover was done with the archdeacon's usual humility: He was unworthy of this great trust, he ventured to suggest, but he hoped to do a better job as surrogate father to his nieces and nephews than the real father had done because he would have the guidance of God, of which his brother had not had the benefit. When a letter came from Whitehall a few days after the funeral, he opened it before Arthur even knew of its arrival, so it was he who had the painful duty to perform of reading to the family the news from Rome of Lucy's death. It may be imagined with what reluctant relish he performed this duty, with Aunt Esther standing by, and followed the reading with a prayer asking the Lord to grant "to us, who are still in our pilgrimage, that we may be joined hereafter with the sister whose soul thou hast been pleased to take unto thyself in glory everlasting."

Young Arthur, whose rightful place was now at the head of the house of Wrox, was obliged to watch it usurped by Uncle Cuthbert, a Hampden—in fact, the quintessential Hampden: large, loud, overbearing, insensitive to the needs or feelings of others. Arthur had the Hampden ginger hair and large hands and feet, but he lacked the larger than life-size dimensions of his domineering father. He had always been overshadowed at home. He had been happy at Oxford, where he had emerged as an individual with a mind of his own, who chose his own friends, lived his own life. He had intended to take orders and had been directing his studies to that end—not that he was of a pious nature or spiritually inclined, but because it seemed the likeliest occupation for his admittedly meager talents. He was unsuited to naval or military service. He loved the home land and wished to settle eventually at Wrox. However, so vigorous was his father, and in such robust health, that he might be expected to be alive for another quarter century. The clergyman's living in the comfortable Wrox rectory seemed to young Arthur to be the best solution to passing the time until he should inherit.

Now he saw in Uncle Cuthbert—archdeacon, custodian of five parishes—a clergyman in action, and he disliked what he saw. He began to fear that his uncle would even go so far as to remove himself and his fearsome wife altogether to Wrox Hall, ostensibly for the good of his fatherless nephews and nieces. Maria Wrox-Hampden was a strong-minded woman, but it was certainly possible that in her double bereavement she might succumb to the force of the archdeacon's overweening humility. Who would dare tell him he could not do his duty as he conceived it to be?

To some young men the calling to the priesthood comes as a sudden, blinding light summoning them to labor in the Lord's vineyard. Young Arthur's conversion, just as sudden, came to him from the reverse direction. He would never, he saw in the revelation of this blinding light, enter the priesthood and thus become a colleague of Uncle Cuthbert's. He saw the light even as the archdeacon was launching himself onto the murky waters of another prayer, one that made less and less sense the longer it continued to flow. On and on it went, sentences whose predicates followed so long after the subject as to have been lost at sea, so to speak. Phrases like the "sting of death," "resurrection to glory everlasting," "falling peacefully asleep and waking up after the likeness of Christ" were thrown out like jetsam. After what seemed an eternity (another word that had often recurred) the archdeacon gave his blessing to his brother's children and freed them from bondage.

Young Arthur rose off his knees a convert. With the glorious feeling of having been saved he now faced his responsibilities. It was the archdeacon who must be driven from the temple, not the moneylenders; they would be necessary in the restoration of the Wrox properties that Arthur intended to effect. He would never preach from the pulpit to his tenants and laborers; old Smallwood did that well enough. He saw them as oppressed people who were already in the promised land, which must be kept for them, perhaps even by means of the railway now invading it to connect it with other, distant lands.

Young Arthur felt that his thoughts were beginning to ramble through his mind like the sentences of the archdeacon's prayers and that his metaphors were mixing themselves. But if his thoughts wandered, they did keep to the path that led to his eventual goal.

He did not even need to summon up courage when he spoke to his uncle. "Thank you, Uncle Cuthbert," he said. "You have done your duty, so it is now—well, it is done. My mother will be returning, and I think it would be better if you were not to be found here on her arrival. You see, you are so like my father, it would remind her too painfully of him she has lost."

The archdeacon was taken aback. "How can you say that?" he exclaimed. "Why, I am nothing like my brother, nothing at all! If anything, I am my brother's keeper. God gave him into my keeping, and I have tried not to be proved unworthy of the trust. Sister Maria, in her great double loss, would not wish me to turn my back. It would be to turn my back on my duty."

"Your duty," said his nephew boldly, "lies in Stoke-sub-Ham. There is your flock that is lost without its shepherd. The bishop would not like to hear that you neglect it for personal reasons, however well intentioned. You can pray for my mother at Stoke to just as good effect as here."

The archdeacon murmured something about his nephews and nieces and bringing them comfort.

"You have just made us all most *un*comfortable," said Arthur. "To kneel upon the floor without even a hassock is not a comfortable position. We are not here as penitents."

"Young man, you are treading upon the very verge of impudence," said his uncle. "If you cannot respect me—and I do not demand respect, it is not I who deserves it, it is due to the cloth—if you do not accord me the respect that is my due, you must at least accord it to the cloth I wear."

"I mean no disrespect to the cloth, Uncle," Arthur assured him. "Mr. Smallwood wears the same cloth, and we are Mr. Smallwood's parishioners."

"Ah, Smallwood wants to make himself indispensable, does he, for fear of losing the living? Just like him; all he thinks of is buttering his own nest."

"Mr. Smallwood's living is quite secure, Uncle, and it is not right that you should take on his duties, leaving your own flock untended."

There could be no answer to this without further denigration of Mr.

Smallwood, and even Uncle Cuthbert could not insist upon taking over the rector's duties on the ground that he was the more unworthy man. He was quite unaware that he had been the instrument of his nephew's salvation from a life of toil in the Lord's vineyard. He and Aunt Esther left for Stoke-sub-Ham on the following day.

"Arthur has rid us of En-wee Who!" exulted Lottie.

Maria Wrox-Hampden arrived from Rome in the afternoon.

∂ 19 ∞

MR. REDDLE HELPS AUGUSTUS

When Tole drove Mr. Reddle and Miss Wetherby to the vicarage, they were received with the utmost kindness by Mrs. Smallwood and Miss Theodora. Elsie was clearly in a nervous condition. They put her to bed and cosseted her, refraining from asking any question about her abrupt, unexplained arrival in their home. It seemed likely she had been dismissed from her post by the squire; she had been ill in the spring, they knew, so it was possible she had ceased to be useful at the Hall. Abrupt dismissal could certainly account for her suffering a relapse.

The two ladies were aware that the vicar and the tutor had been shut in the back room for some time, after which they had walked out together. Their destination could only have been the Hall. Mrs. Smallwood's curiosity was thoroughly aroused, but she had no doubt it would be satisfied as soon as she herself could be shut with her husband in their bedroom. Before that time, however, there was another private meeting of the two men after supper.

Mr. Reddle began by thanking the clergyman for his support, his courage and the hospitality shown in giving shelter to Miss Wetherby and himself.

"Nay, nay," said Mr. Smallwood, "it would have been quite unworthy on my part to have refused you. It gives me great pleasure to be able to prove that my usefulness as a Christian minister extends beyond preaching to the living and burying the dead."

"I am glad to hear you say that, sir," said Osbert, "for I am going to request that you perform another of your useful services—namely, Holy Matrimony."

"You wish to marry the unfortunate Miss Wetherby?" asked the rector. "That is noble of you, sir."

Osbert Reddle could scarcely believe his ears. Was Elsie, then, a fallen woman in the sight of God? "I beg your pardon, Vicar," he said. "There is no nobility in a desire to espouse the woman whom one loves. I have loved Elsie Wetherby for a long time. She has done nothing that would cause me to cease to do so. *She has done nothing*," he repeated. "What was done to *her* was monstrous. I must take her away from here as soon as possible, and it were better we should be married before we travel together."

"Yes, yes," said the rector apologetically, "I meant no reflection upon her. She is a fine woman. She will make you a wonderful wife but for—"

"But for what, sir?"

"Like Caesar's, a wife should be above reproach."

Mr. Reddle, who had been pacing the floor, stopped abruptly and fixed the rector with a cold stare. "She is above reproach, sir," he said.

"Of course, of course," Mr. Smallwood agreed. "I meant not that she *deserves* reproach, but that she will invite it. Her situation invites it; it is not her fault."

"Her situation is known to only four persons," said Osbert. "They are you, me, Mr. Wrox-Hampden and Miss Wetherby herself. I do not believe any one of us will betray the confidence." He remembered the maid Maggie, then told himself she was not a witness to anything. She had seen nothing and heard nothing. Still, rumors, however basely founded, could be spread abroad by ignorant persons, and the sooner he took Elsie far away from their source, the better.

"If you and she both wish it, if you consent together, I shall start to publish the banns next Sunday," said the rector.

"We must not wait for the banns," Osbert urged. "You know all the circumstances, sir, and do you not think the bishop will grant a special dispensation?"

"Under certain circumstances, of course," said Mr. Smallwood. He counted rapidly. The rape had occurred some time back; he did not know exactly when. Neither did Reddle. But he supposed it to be possible that a living consequence might result from that terrible crime. "I think we may dispense with the banns," he said. "Yes, yes, by all means. There will be no difficulty."

"I thank you, sir, and now I must ask you to grant a further favor. I need to inform Elsie of these arrangements, so I should like to be allowed to speak to her privately in her room."

"Very well, very well," Mr. Smallwood said, rising. "I shall tell Mrs. Smallwood and my daughter. Mrs. Smallwood will be very much surprised, I daresay. She likes to get to the bottom of things," he added.

"There are some things of which even she will never get to the bottom," Osbert said sternly.

"Yes, quite. Quite so. Come, Mr. Reddle, you shall be alone with your intended bride."

So it was that the Smallwood ladies were summoned from the room where Elsie lay and Mr. Reddle was admitted.

He closed the door and approached the bedside. Elsie looked up at him with an expression that pierced his heart. With a sob he went down on his knees by the bed and took her thin white hand between his two. "My own darling," he said, "my Elsie, my beloved—"

When he could speak calmly, he told her that Mr. Smallwood had agreed to marry them immediately, and he would take her away forever from this place.

Elsie did not withdraw her hand, but she said in a surprisingly firm tone, "But I cannot marry you, Osbert. You know that."

"Do you not love me?" he pleaded. "Do you not wish to be my wife and to go away from here under my protection?" She was silent. "Do you love me? Elsie, tell me, do you?"

"Yes," she whispered, "you know that I do. You only cannot imagine how much. It is not you. It is . . . that I cannot marry anyone."

"But *why?*" he insisted.

She hesitated long before daring to speak to her lover on the painful subject that she knew was never to be mentioned between men and women, certainly not unmarried men and women. At last she said, turning away her head, "You see, because of what he did, I might someday find myself with child."

It was some time before Osbert realized that she knew nothing at all about the reproductive process contained in her own body. Still holding her hand, he addressed the back of her head, sparing her the embarrassment of having to face him. "My dear one," he said, "how long is it since the crime against you?"

"I am not sure—"

"It is many weeks, is it not? Months, even?"

"Yes."

"And have you since then had menstrual flow? Have you had regular monthly bleeding?"

"Yes, two or three—"

Osbert thought his heart would burst. It was evident Elsie believed that if she ever had a child in all the rest of her life, it would be the squire's. Very gently but explicitly he told her what her mother—or someone—should have. "So you see," he finished, "it is not possible that you could have such a child."

"It is a great relief to me," Elsie said. "You cannot think what a relief."

"Then it is settled," he said, and began caressing her hair, her forehead, her dear face. He lifted her hand to his own face and used it to wipe the tears from his cheek. They remained quiet for several moments.

There came a knock at the door. Mrs. Smallwood was doubting the propriety of a closed bedroom door with a long silence behind it. "May I bring you some tea?" she inquired.

Osbert drew a long sigh. He wanted to shout, Go away, you foolish old woman! Then he realized that the deep feeling of the shared moment was too intense to have lasted. He shrugged and gave Elsie a smile that said, We need not be impatient now; we have all the years of the world ahead of us. To Mrs. Smallwood he called out, "A few minutes more, madam, if you please, we have pressing business to discuss."

Elsie agreed to be married as soon as she was a bit stronger and felt ready to face the journey to Exeter, where, Osbert assured her, his parents would be happy to receive a daughter-in-law. Before leaving Bunbury, they would stop at Mr. Maule's bank and withdraw Elsie's savings. "My dowry!" she said proudly.

Kind Mrs. Smallwood gave her a sleeping draft followed by a glass of warm milk, and next morning she slept long and peacefully for the first time in many weeks. When she awakened, the day was already half spent, and the rector gone from the rectory. He had been summoned to the Hall because the squire's dead body had been found in Sheerwater Pond.

Arrangements were made for the marriage of Mr. Reddle with Miss Wetherby to take place on Monday afternoon in Wrox church and for their departure next day from Bunbury by the Taunton coach. The day dawned clear, promising well. Mrs. Smallwood busied herself cutting and arranging flowers for the altar and for decoration of her house, where a modest wedding feast was to be held. Miss Theodora was helping Elsie Wetherby take in a dress suitable for wearing at the ceremony, while yet keeping an eye on the cook, who was baking and icing a cake.

Osbert Reddle got out of their way by setting off for a long walk across the country he had grown to love while living at the Hall. As he was leaving, Mrs. Smallwood came hurrying out of the church. "If you run into anyone from the Hall," she said, "please ask them to keep the squire's old dog at home. It has been hanging around its master's grave; the diggers had to come back twice. Nasty great creature, I am afraid of it."

Osbert said he did not intend to go near the Hall, but if he saw the mastiff, he would head it in that direction. He went on with his walk.

It was a farewell tour of those familiar places where he had observed Nature going about her work in all her wondrous ways. Here he had felt the wind on his cheek and the sun on his back. Along this lane he caught the scent of hawthorn and bluebells. On that bank he heard the sweet melody of the skylark. In that hollow he smelled the pungent odor of the byres and stopped to talk with the byremen, whose speech he had been attempting to translate—another of his many hobbies. In the sky a vulture circled ever lower over a pasture where some small rodent lay dying.

On the south down he caught sight of a familiar figure approaching and waved to Augustus. The boy came running to meet him. It warmed the heart of the tutor to see the gladness with which the boy greeted him and shook his hand. Augustus was carrying a small cage. He explained that the mole had died and he sought to replace it. "There used to be mole runs behind Nettle's cottage," Mr. Reddle said. "Come, let us walk in that direction, and we can stop by to see if the tanager nested again this year in the orchard."

The two had met briefly in the past winter, when Osbert Reddle had stopped by Mr. Plumptre's school. He had gone there to observe it and seek the advice of the headmaster about founding his own school, and naturally while there he had seen Augustus and discussed him with the schoolmaster. Mr. Plumptre quite agreed with Mr. Reddle that trying to teach Augustus anything was a waste of time for both teacher and pupil. "The boy can never hope to go to university," Mr. Plumptre had said. "He wastes his time at every opportunity playing at Mrs. Plumptre's pianoforte. If I forbid him, he takes revenge by an absolute refusal to open any book. It is a kind of blackmail. Only if I permit him access to the keyboard will he oblige me by studying his Latin."

Mr. Reddle had spoken to Mr. Plumptre about the school at Blitchley that made a specialty of music lessons for the boys, and the headmaster had concurred in thinking it might be the better school for Augustus. "I am naturally most happy to have the fees that Mr. Wrox-Hampden pays for Augustus. My expenses here are not small. But a headmaster should look to the good of the child rather than to the lining of his own pockets, and I do believe Augustus to be wasting his time here, not to mention my own."

This conversation had not been reported to the boy, and without referring to it, Mr. Reddle now asked Augustus how he was getting on at Plumptre's.

"Oh, it is not so bad," said the boy. "Mrs. Plumptre lets me play on her pianoforte sometimes. It is an old square thing, out of date, but better than nothing. But her selection of music is frightful; she has only hymns and some nursery rhymes set to tunes fit for little children. Do you suppose, sir, that you could send me some music? Mr. Chopin visited England last year and had some of his music published in London. I should dearly like to see it."

Osbert began to understand that the piano was to Augustus what books were to a scholar, paints to an artist or the countryside to a naturalist like himself. The boy was starved. To deprive him of the means by which to express his talent was to let his soul perish. The talent he possessed—perhaps even genius—must be given its outlet lest it starve to death. The tutor looked at the boy, standing there in his worn, outgrown clothing, holding his mole trap with a large red hand at the end of three inches of bare arm and looking up from under the ginger hair with an expression of forlorn hope like that of a mendicant. Mr. Reddle remembered a previous attempt on his part to secure music lessons for Augustus. He resolved to make one more appeal to the boy's parents—parent, he amended hastily in his mind. "Is your mother at home?" he asked.

"Yes, sir. She was not here for my father's funeral, but she arrived soon after. She had been in Rome with Lucy. Lucy died, sir—did you know?"

"Mr. Smallwood so informed me. I am very sorry. I should like to call upon your mother." Mr. Reddle realized there was no time when he could do this except following his wedding. "Please tell her to expect me in the late afternoon."

Augustus's attention, childlike, had been distracted by a strange sight approaching across the open country. It looked like a misshapen beast moving along the railway track with a regular, jerky motion—now up, now down. It moved rapidly as if bent on some definite purpose. Osbert followed Augustus's gaze and stared as the creature came closer. It was a sort of platform being propelled by two men standing upon it, facing each other and pumping their arms up and down, up and down, on two large crossbars. They looked neither to right nor to left. One was looking forward in the direction they were going, the other back the way they had come. The thing came closer to them, passed before them across the field and seemed to slow down as it approached the village.

"What was *that?*" asked Augustus.

"I do not know," said Mr. Reddle. "It is most ingenious. It allows men to move themselves about as if in a horseless carriage."

"But they are the horses," Augustus said. "Is that how the railway is to be run? If so, why would the men wish to do the work of horses?"

Mr. Reddle would not for a moment admit ignorance, the Achilles' heel of the teacher, on any subject. In the natural sciences he was thoroughly at home; a knowledge of physics was not in his repertoire of accomplishments. "The railway will have an engine," he said. "It will be propelled by steam, not by horses or men. The engine will pull the cars."

"And who will pull the steam engine, sir?"

"It will be fed coal by a man to make it run."

"As horses are fed oats," said Augustus. "Those two men, just now, they were pulling themselves, doing the work of horses. I hope their wives fed them well with oats before they started on their journey."

"It is a means of getting rapidly from one place to another," said Mr. Reddle. "Very convenient."

"Excuse me, sir, it is not a bit convenient, since they can go only along the tracks of the railway to and from the places where the tracks run. What if they wish to go to Bunbury? They would have to walk or get horses."

"It is not very different from rowing a boat," Mr. Reddle observed. "A rower is conveying himself from one place to another and can go only along the riverbed."

The man and boy turned to continue their walk toward the orchard and Nettle's barn. Augustus could not stop thinking about the men moving themselves along the railway tracks. "They are doing the work of horses," he insisted.

The teacher in Mr. Reddle, in abeyance since he had left Wrox ten months before, now came happily forward as he told Augustus about how in the Orient men pulled between shafts a passenger vehicle called a ricksha (short for jinricksha) and were paid by the mile, just like London cabbies.

"Well, I am glad they get paid," said Augustus. "It is more than the cab horses do. Some cabbies are cruel to their horses. The ricksha puller would not be cruel to himself. And think of the money he would save by being both the horse and the cabby."

They both laughed, enjoying the schoolroom sort of talk.

"Only one mouth to feed," said Mr. Reddle.

"And no need for a stable," Augustus said. "It would save a lot on rent. And they would have no crossing sweepers or street cleaners—that is, unless . . . ?"

"Oh, I do not think the ricksha man would do *that* like a horse," said Osbert. "In the Orient *that* is saved, it is highly prized, it is used for fertilization in the fields, where they have no horses."

❧ 20 ❧

A COUNTRY WEDDING

The marriage ceremony was performed by Mr. Smallwood at two o'clock, in the cryptlike old church dimly lit by candles. Rays of bright sunlight slanting in through the high windows served to intensify the darkness in the nave below, where the beautiful old font held masses of Mrs. Smallwood's tall perennials: heliotrope, larkspur, delphinium, Canterbury bells, iris and stock. The churchwarden had been pressed into service to give the bride to be married. Miss Theodora stood up with her. Elsie wore her best black silk with a kind of collar fashioned from garden flowers that removed from her dress any suggestion of mourning. The brooch with her mother's hair was present at the ceremony, half hidden at the bride's throat between two tea roses. A few friends and neighbors, such as the Pipkins and the Bunbury schoolmaster with his wife, were in the front pews.

Mr. Smallwood's deep, mellifluous voice began, "Dearly beloved, we are gathered together here in the sight of God . . ."

Mrs. Smallwood might often let her attention wander during church services, for it was true she knew them all by heart. However, the Form of Solemnization of Matrimony always had her full attention. She waited hopefully for any man to step forward if he knew why the man and woman should not be joined together, but this had never happened. She now heard her husband say, "If any man can show just cause, why they may not lawfully be joined together, let him now speak, or else hereafter for ever hold his peace."

In the pause that followed came Mrs. Smallwood's voice, correcting him. "Any cause or just impediment," she said. Again there was silence. Everyone turned to stare at her. Miss Theodora bowed her head in mortification. "*I* can show none," said Mrs. Smallwood, "but perhaps there is someone present who can?" Everybody present held his peace.

The rector's voice, its sound of confident assurance replaced by a quaver, turned back to the persons who were to be married and continued, "I require and charge you both, as ye will answer at the dreadful day of judgment—" and on, without further interruption, to the benediction with its concluding prayer: "That ye may so live together in this life, that in the world to come ye may have life everlasting. Amen."

Following the brief, moving service, Mr. Smallwood did not even wait until he had removed his surplice before he said to his wife, "How could you do that, Ada?"

"You had left out 'just impediment,' Jonathan."

"I had done no such thing. Just impediment is not in the form; it occurs in the wording of the banns of marriage."

"But no banns had been published. There had been no previous opportunity to hear of an impediment."

"I cannot rewrite the Book of Common Prayer to suit you," said the rector, "and in any case, it is none of your concern."

"I beg to point out, Jonathan, that the question was addressed to the whole congregation, of which I am a member in good standing—in fact, of the very best standing. Sometimes you accuse me of not paying attention to you; then you complain when I do."

"Paying attention to the service is one thing. Taking it over is quite another. It is unseemly. As far as I know, you have never been ordained. You must never do it again."

"I doubt I shall ever have *just cause* to do so," said the lady, "for it is unprecedented in my experience to have a Christian marriage without the banns having first been published. However, my dear, let us not dispute. ' "There is much to be said on both sides," said Sir Roger.' I would not for worlds have poor Miss Wetherby and good Mr. Reddle think that there is a just impediment to their having been joined. And now come, Jonathan, the wedding feast awaits us, as in Cana of Galilee."

The small company that was gathered in the rectory garden under the grape arbor sat down to a feast indeed. Mrs. Smallwood's table, dressed with her good linens, offered larded turkey poults, jellied tongue, a ham ornamented with candied fruits, various pies, Chantilly biscuits and bowls of trifle flavored with the best sherry. Mr. Smallwood said grace, giving thanks to God for His great bounty and a warm acknowledgment to the agent—namely, Mrs. Smallwood—who had labored to make it so bounteous.

The bride could not believe she had so recently walked through the Valley of the Shadow of Death. Osbert Reddle wondered if perhaps God had come to realize the terrible injustice He had wrought in the crime against her and if He was now trying to make up for it. During the service the husband had heard for the first time his wife's baptismal name, Elizabeth, and realized Elsie was the pet name by which her mother had called her. He held Elsie's left hand on his knee under the tablecloth, feeling the wedding ring (a loan from Mrs. Smallwood), and looked into her beautiful face, which he was now going to see daily for the rest of his life.

By five o'clock all was over but the clearing away. The bride went upstairs to rest. The beadle locked the church, leaving the fragrant flowers to the recumbent crusader. Miss Theodora carried covered baskets of uneaten festal foods to the poor families of the village, despite her father's warning that with so many moochers about it was dangerous to do so. She did not fear danger, yet in setting forth, she was performing an act of immense courage. Over the years the villagers and neighbors had grown used to her appearance, but with the influx of strangers into the countryside she had found herself stared at when she went about and sometimes avoided, as if her affliction were contagious. She had heard a vagabond woman, as she walked by, call her little girl back into the caravan, saying, "Mind ye be careful and don't ye stare at 'er face, ye'll catch the pox, 'tis catching."

The bridegroom walked back to Wrox Hall.

Mrs. Wrox-Hampden was in the drawing room, with her elder son and daughter, awaiting the visit from the former tutor. She was thin to the point of being gaunt, with blue shadows under her deep-set dark eyes. Much had been required of her. She had had to make critical decisions. Every last bit of strength she possessed had been called for, and she had given it. And now, instead of being able to rest, she found she must face one disaster after another. To begin with, Miss Wetherby was gone—just like that, no notice given. Reddle, the tutor, had come and fetched her; apparently he had realized Lucy was beyond his reach, Marietta would never have him and Lottie was too young. Then Arthur had taken her to visit his father's grave, and they had found it to have been disturbed; some unknown hands had been digging in the fresh earth covering the coffin and had evidently been frightened off before the coffin had been exposed. Today, when she rang for tea, she had noticed it was Abigail who brought it and remarked that she had not seen the butler since her return. Arthur had been obliged to tell her he had left, that he was now in partnership at Wrox with the publican, whose business had grown too much for him to handle, and the two men were now intending to expand the public house into an inn, with several rooms to let, facing the railway station—a prime location. Marietta was now running the household. And then there was that policeman hanging around, saying someone murdered her husband. It was all too much. Maria sat with her head against the back of her chair and her hands on its arms. Her eyes were closed.

While growing up, Marietta had felt many conflicting emotions in regard to her mother: love, resentment, admiration, dislike, envy, respect, affection—but never pity. Now she was sorry for her. Mama felt the loss of Lucy and Papa, of course she did, that was not the reason for pitying her; it was that she had *never loved those she had lost*—or been loved by them. Papa had married her because she was the heiress of Wrox, and she had known that. Marietta resolved to make it up to her and love her. She hoped her mother would not make it difficult to do so just because she was not accustomed to it. She must have been loved by her first husband, Mr. Fox. She was not then an heiress, her older brother still lived, she had possessed no fortune beyond a dowry that Mr. Fox did not need, for he was extremely rich. He must have been in love, and Mama must have been his beloved.

"Mama," Marietta asked, "was your heart broken when Mr. Fox died?"

Tonelessly Maria said, "So that is how you see it. I was not married to Mr. Fox for love, on his part or mine. He was a gentleman who had been twice married with no issue. He sought a healthy young wife who would give him an heir. I am told he looked far and wide before he settled on me. I was quite attractive then, when I was young. I was just sixteen, I had spirit and Heaven knows I was not barren." Maria gave a long sigh. Then, "I did what was expected of me," she said in a flat tone.

Abigail came to the door to announce Mr. Reddle. Maria opened her eyes as Arthur went forward, extending his hand. "Come in, sir," he said warmly.

"Good evening, Mr. Reddle," Marietta said, rising. "I am happy to see you. I feared that on the day you took Miss Wetherby away we should never see you again. You did not go far then."

Mr. Reddle shook hands with her, then crossed the carpet to stand in front of Mrs. Wrox-Hampden, to whom he extended his hand in turn. "Madam, I extend my deepest sympathy to you in your great double bereavement. Please accept my condolences."

Maria opened her eyes. She ignored the proffered handshake. "You took Miss Wetherby away," she said. "Then she did not leave of her own free will. Where is she now?"

Mr. Reddle took great pleasure in speaking for the first time the name of his wife. "Mrs. Osbert Reddle is staying at the rectory with the Smallwoods," he said. "Mr. Smallwood married us this very afternoon."

Marietta clapped her hands. "I knew it!" she exclaimed. "It is so romantic! Miss Wetherby pined away for love of you, and you came to get her as in a fairy tale!"

"What nonsense," said Maria. Was this marriage not very sudden? So that was how the land lay, she thought: The tutor and the governess had been carrying on an illicit love affair all these years under her very roof, in full view of the children! It was well that her late husband had not suspected it, else he would have thrashed Reddle within an inch of his life before throwing him out. And what an example for that mealy-mouthed Miss Wetherby to have set for the girls, the little hypocrite! "What brings you here now, Reddle?" she asked discourteously. "It will do you no good to ask for your old position back, you know."

Mr. Reddle in his new role of hero and married man found it difficult to maintain a deferential tone, but he knew he must do so lest he antago-nize the woman and lose Augustus's cause. He declined a cup of tea (he had but just risen from the wedding feast) and announced the purpose of his call: to plead that Augustus be allowed to study music.

It became apparent that young Arthur, as his former tutor had always thought of him, was now the head of the house and lord of the manor. "My brother," he said, "will be obliged to earn his living. He cannot do so while playing upon a pianoforte."

"We have had all this out once before," said Maria. "This is a waste of time."

"Since then," said Osbert, "I have talked with Mr. Plumptre."

"Going behind our backs," said Maria.

"Ah, yes," Arthur said, "Mr. Plumptre wrote to my father to say that Augustus will never be a scholar but that if he would but apply himself to his studies, he might do well enough. He is not stupid, according to Mr.

Plumptre, just lazy and disinclined to exert himself. He needs to spend more time at his studies, not at the pianoforte, which can only serve as a distraction from them."

"Leading nowhere," said Maria. "It will never help him to earn a living. He would be fit for nothing but to teach music, like that poor Theodora Smallwood."

Mr. Reddle drew himself upright, and a flush spread over his face. He swallowed hard before speaking, sending his Adam's apple on a sudden, rapid journey. "Teaching is the noblest of professions," he declared. "It is how all man's knowledge is passed along from generation to generation. We do not inherit Latin and mathematics and the love of Shakespeare; we must learn them, as did your son Arthur. I am proud to have been his teacher."

"And a very good teacher you are," Arthur said warmly. "Splendid. I should never have gone up to Oxford were it not for you. But—" He paused, coughed and pressed the tutor to take tea, which was again refused. "Lessons on the pianoforte are different from Latin or mathematics or history. They are useless; they are a mere end in themselves, leading nowhere. They are well enough for young ladies. My sister Marietta plays very well indeed; everyone sings her praises—"

"*Not* very well, Arthur," Marietta corrected him. "I do not perform very well. Augustus does far better."

Mr. Reddle took her up. "It is unfair to Augustus. He has had to listen to his sisters tinkling away at the instrument and asked why they should be given the music lessons that were denied him."

"Because music lessons are for ladies," said Arthur.

"There has never been a female composer," Osbert pointed out. "Where is the lady Bach, Beethoven or Liszt? You cannot tell me it is because they have been denied opportunity because of their sex, since it was always they who were given the music lessons."

"They are not expected to compose," said Arthur; "it is the performance that is their role."

"Has there ever been a reputable lady performer?" Osbert asked.

Maria, who had been silent during the discussion, brought up the Swedish songstress whose name she could never pronounce, even had she remembered it. "Aunt Sophia Cheycester used to go all the way to London just to hear her perform."

"Her instrument is contained in herself," said Osbert. "No woman has ever performed with distinction on any other. Neither has a female distinguished herself as an artist, although 'twas ever the girls who were taught to paint watercolors and china plates, not the boys. They cannot say they were held back on account of their sex."

"Ah!" was Arthur's comment, for he could not refute the tutor's statements. "But now that we have a Queen, now that our monarch is a woman, I'll wager that a hundred years hence 'twill be a different story."

Mr. Reddle, who a short time ago would never have asserted himself to argue with his presumed betters, now said boldly, "Then you have only a century in which to produce a female Shakespeare, a Milton in petticoats or a Rembrandt belonging to the fairer sex. They had best be getting busy with their paints and pianos."

Marietta intervened. "We females may not be geniuses," she said stoutly, "but we are their mothers. We are like those carriers of the bleeding disease who do not catch it themselves but bear it within them to pass on to their male children. However, you gentlemen have lost sight of the subject. We were discussing Augustus and his desire for a musical education."

"Do not think of it as merely a recreation, as it is with the ladies," said Mr. Reddle. "The organist and choirmaster at Glanbury Cathedral is a man, a well-known interpreter of Bach and Handel."

Out of a long silence Maria spoke. "Very well. Let him have his music lessons. It does no good to forbid them anything; they will have their own way in the end, even if it leads to their own ruin. It was no use telling Henrietta to stop dancing, or Lucy to cease riding all over the county by herself, or Robert to help his sister with all that money he does not need. It was no use asking all the little boys not to die. Dr. Pipkin tried to save them, but they would die in spite of it."

"Mother!" cried Marietta. "Oh, my dear Mother—"

"I must go," said Mr. Reddle, rising hastily to his feet. "Thank you for hearing me out. God bless you." He left Maria alone with her children and let himself out of Wrox Hall for the last time.

In the lane he met Sergeant Frakes, headed in the opposite direction. The nursemaid, Nancy, had caught the policeman's eye, and he had been spending his evenings in the servants' hall, where he expected to be a guest at supper. It was the only way he could spend time with Nancy, who was allowed but one afternoon off a month in order to visit her parents. Sergeant Frakes had once or twice joined Nancy while she pushed Letty around the park in her pram, but he dared not be seen again there, as it was not logical that he should be investigating Squire Wrox-Hampden's murder by constantly interviewing his child's nursemaid.

"How are you coming with your investigation, Sergeant?" asked Mr. Reddle, stopping to chat.

"Slowly, sir, slowly. I has my suspects, but I has to interview everyone who might know something. I am glad you come out in the clear yourself, sir. Not that you had a Motive."

If you but knew, Osbert thought. Aloud he said, "I do have a suggestion, Sergeant. There is a witness to the crime; only unfortunately he cannot speak. I refer to the squire's dog, Caesar. There can be no doubt Caesar knows who killed his master. That might give you a clue."

"The *dog*, sir?"

"Yes, the dog. If you could confront the culprit with the dog, I am certain it would attack. Perhaps if you were to follow the animal, it might even lead to the murderer. Well, good night, Sergeant. Good-bye, I should say, for I am leaving here tomorrow."

"Good-bye, sir. I am glad I do not have to prevent you leaving; you are free to go for all of me."

❧ 21 ❧

THE SCANDAL IN BUNBURY

Next day at the rectory the newlyweds were making ready for their departure by the Taunton coach, due to leave Bunbury in mid-morning. Breakfast had been served early; Miss Theodora was helping the bride to pack; the rector was watching the road for the hired barouche to arrive from town. Mrs. Smallwood, who abhorred an idle moment as Nature abhors a vacuum, was filling time by helping her gardener in netting her plums against the birds when she saw approaching through the churchyard the Misses Marietta and Charlotte Wrox-Hampden. They were carrying between them a large, flat package loosely wrapped in tissue paper. It was obviously very heavy.

"Are we in time?" Marietta asked. "Lottie and I want to say good-bye."

"Let Hawkins carry that for you," Mrs. Smallwood offered.

"Oh, no, thank you," Lottie said. "We have managed so far. Luke brought us in the pony cart as far as the churchyard wall."

"We shall miss Miss Wetherby dreadfully," said Marietta.

"Mrs. Reddle," corrected Mrs. Smallwood. "And so shall my daughter. I do not know how Theodora will manage without Miss Elsie; it will not be the same. Come along, let us go to the house. Hawkins, do not pull it tight there; the branches need to be kept straight along the wall but not flattened *against* it. Come, young ladies, I shall tell Miss Elsie you are here to see them off. More's the pity."

"Your garden is the prettiest I know of anywhere, Mrs. Smallwood," said Marietta as they passed it. "You must put in many hours of work. Mama never cared much for flowers."

"She does other things," Mrs. Smallwood said kindly. "She is a far finer needlewoman than I. When Lottie was a baby, I remember the coverlet your mother made for her pram; it was of the finest embroidery, with drawn hems, lovely it was. Does the baby Violet have it now?"

"Yes, she does," Lottie said. "She is the sweetest little thing in the world, she is so pretty."

"And what of her brother?" asked Mrs. Smallwood. "What do you hear of him?"

"He is well, I believe."

"Poor little souls," Mrs. Smallwood remarked. "They should be together. But that is not any of my business, is it? And here is Miss Elsie, so you can say your good-byes."

The governess and the music teacher were at the rectory gate. Elsie wore a pretty new straw bonnet with green ribbons that Osbert had selected at the Bunbury milliner's.

"What in the world have you there?" asked Miss Theodora.

"It is a wedding present for Miss Wetherby," Lottie said.

"Mrs. Reddle," Marietta corrected her. The present was set down before the bride. "It is something to make you think of us whenever you look at it."

"I shall think of you constantly," Mrs. Reddle said, not trying to hide her tears. "I do not need a reminder."

"Unwrap it!" urged Lottie.

It was an engraving of the Sistine Madonna that had hung in the common room for so many years it had ceased to be noticed. Originally it had been Aunt Augusta Pounceby's wedding present to the Wrox-Hampdens. "Oh, should you give it away?" Elsie Reddle asked. "Did it not belong to your parents?"

"Everybody had forgotten about it," said Lottie. "No one has looked at it for years. It will be more noticed now. We shall all see it again when we look at the bare place where it hung and recall it to memory. Then we shall think of you."

"Why, I thank you; it is beautiful," Elsie said, trying to sound enthusiastic while wondering how in the world the ungainly object was to be transported to Exeter, via Taunton. Her bridegroom had come up to the little group at the gate and taken in the situation. Speechless, he stared at the picture. "It is a wedding present," his wife told him.

Mrs. Smallwood turned on the sisters. "Never," she said sternly, "not *ever*, give a present that will be a trouble to the receiver. A gift that the recipient neither needs nor wants is no gift at all; indeed, it is worse than no gift, for that could not possibly be of trouble."

"Mama, *please*—" begged Miss Theodora, going red with shame. Lottie had begun to cry. The Reddles looked uncomfortable, as if it were they who had criticized the Sistine Madonna.

"Oh," said Elsie into the awkward silence, "but we want this above everything, do we not, Osbert? I have long admired it. I never dreamed I should be so fortunate as to possess it. Do not cry, Lottie, for you will make me unhappy, when I am the happiest person in the world to think that you would part with the Madonna for my wedding present."

The job carriage arrived. Elsie's few belongings and her husband's valise were stowed inside. Under the direction of Mrs. Smallwood the wedding present was hoisted up to the seat beside the driver. "Perhaps it will be stolen," said she hopefully.

Promises were made to keep in touch through correspondence. Embraces, thanks and farewells made the rounds. Then Mr. and Mrs. Osbert Reddle climbed into the equipage, and the sisters watched again as the tutor bore the governess off into their future.

"Good riddance," Mrs. Smallwood remarked.

The Wrox-Hampden sisters looked at her aghast. "Mother, how could you!" exclaimed her daughter.

Her husband said, "For shame, Ada—"

"Oh, I did not refer to our guests!" Mrs. Smallwood said hastily. "They were always more than welcome, you know that. It was my great pleasure to have them here. I shall miss them sorely. I was referring to that useless albatross of a wedding present."

Lottie's tears flowed anew. Marietta laid an arm across her sister's shoulders. "Mrs. Smallwood," she said, "I beg to contradict you. It is a most useful object. Has it not already been twice used as a wedding present? And there is no reason it may not be so used many more times. Indeed, it leads a most useful life, for how many objects can be used over and over without wearing out?"

Lottie laughed in spite of herself. Miss Theodora clapped her hands. The rector said, "Yes, I see it has a life of its own. When you marry, Miss Marietta, Mrs. Reddle might send it back to you."

"Well, let us hope it does not get stolen," said Mrs. Smallwood. "I should have insisted it travel inside the carriage."

The old Roman road led to Bunbury and the West Country as it had through the centuries, now bearing so heavy a load of traffic that Osbert remarked it would soon need a new surface for the first time since its building by the legions of Constantius. The barouche entered the town and the market square, where it was turned toward the Bird & Bottle. Across the square, at the corner of the High Street, was gathered a small crowd of people, more than the pavement could hold, blocking the street.

"What could that be?" Osbert wondered. "It is not market day. Usually the strolling players and itinerant merchants come around only on market day. Perhaps there has been an accident."

They were driven into the innyard where the Taunton coach would stop. Osbert paid the driver, made disposition of the luggage and conducted Elsie into the inn, where he left her in the snug. "Do you wait here, my dear," he said. "I shall do the errands and determine what is going on across there." He had her bankbook, now in his charge, and intended to fetch her savings. He walked over the big, irregular cobbles of the square, and when he arrived at the far side, he saw that the crowd was gathered in front of the bank, surging up to its very doors, which were closed. The police constable was stationed in front of them, bracing himself against the advances of the angry citizens, who were mostly men of all ages with a few women standing by.

Osbert recognized the dressmaker Mrs. Cluster. "What is going on?" he asked her without preliminary greeting.

" 'Tis the banker," said she. "He has gone off with all the money. Maule it is. He has skipped the country and taken it all with him. He has me money, he has, what I worked for so hard and saved up. 'Tis a terrible thing." And then, before Osbert's astonished gaze, she opened her mouth wide, threw back her head and uttered a piercing, long-drawn-out noise, something between a wail and a shriek.

Osbert's heart stopped, then began a furious thumping as if to make up the lost time. He thought he might be going to faint. He walked away unsteadily to where he could lean against a wall, beyond the crowd. He saw the police magistrate come out through the bank door, lock it behind him and move away through the clutching hands and threatening fists of the people gathered in the street. Had their number been any greater, they could have formed a mob.

Osbert Reddle suddenly felt utterly helpless. Of late he had been feeling exactly the opposite, assertive and competent, protective of Elsie, taking charge of her life and his own. Now, on a sudden, the very earth was sliding out from under his feet. What should he do? This news would surely cause his dear wife to collapse entirely and to retreat back into the slough of despond from which he had so carefully brought her. He leaned against the wall and stared across the square toward the inn where she waited for him. He saw the stagecoach come along from the direction of Salisbury and turn in at the innyard. He straightened himself and started slowly walking back across the market square. It struck him that Elsie might well hear the devastating news at the inn before he could get to her. He increased his pace to a run.

Miss Wetherby had been paid thirty pounds a year, of which she had managed to save twenty. Twice yearly she had taken ten pounds to Mr. Maule for investment, and it was her belief that she brought to her marriage as dowry the large sum of nearly two hundred pounds. Her gratitude to Osbert for marrying her despite her degradation was boundless, but she could at least be glad she did not come to him empty-handed. She had been robbed of her pride and self-respect, along with her maidenhood, but not, she believed, of the money she had saved at such terrible cost.

❧ 22 ❧

YOUNG ARTHUR TAKES CHARGE

All summer little was talked about but the absconded banker. Two police inspectors from London had arrived at Bunbury within forty-eight hours of his defection. The investigation into Maule's disappearance took precedence over that of Sergeant Frakes into the squire's murder, about which the countryside had been losing interest in any case, so long had Sergeant Frakes dawdled. It appeared that Maule had been plotting his dastardly crime for months, if not years. Many funds were unaccounted for. He had left Mrs. Maule destitute, but it was conceded that one main reason for his decampment had been a desire to leave her, for she was a woman generally disliked. The London police detectives had traced the absconder to the Liverpool docks and there lost all trace. His name was on no passenger list at Liverpool, or at the port of Bristol, which had also been checked just in case. It was believed Maule was on the high seas en route to North America and would never be heard from again, nor the money. He had cut the painter.

Opinion concerning the departed banker was mixed. Some had always mistrusted him (although none sufficiently to say so) on account of his fawning manner and criminally small ears, too close to his head. Others were caught by surprise, would never have taken him for a thief and said he had always given to each customer's account, large or small, his personal attention. As to his ears, it had never been proven that size or prominence of the ears was related to character. Eyes, yes; small and shifty eyes were invariably the mark of a person to be mistrusted. Ears revealed nothing, unless it be that if pointed at the top, they were shaped like the devil's. Maule's every feature, every remark, every habit were gone over in minutest detail, and the general conclusion was that most people are too innocent and too trusting, that henceforth they would be more careful with their money and keep it hidden at home. For at least four months after the money had disappeared along with Mr. Maule, the shipping news was followed in the heart of rural England in the hope that a packet out of Liverpool bound for North America had been lost at sea.

Mr. Weston, the lawyer, was put to work day and night. Among other things, Spence, the Wrox overseer, had secured a loan from Maule's bank with the land agent when he bought Wrox lands. The loan no longer existed; the land lease was a worthless piece of paper. To whom did the railway right-of-way belong? All Bunbury businesses had had accounts with Maule, from the ironmonger, innkeeper and grocer on the square to the old church on the hill, whose funds were managed by the churchwarden. Many individuals, like old Colonel Glimpse, Major Rollins and even the dressmaker Mrs. Cluster, had lost all their savings.

An exception was E. Hole & Son. They were lucky. Young Hole, whose Christian name was Samuel, had begun to pay court to Miss Marietta Wrox-Hampden. He called upon her regularly, sitting in the drawing room while she played on the pianoforte or walking with her in the park, always accompanied by her younger sister Lottie. The young ladies were still in mourning and did not go about in society, but they did receive callers. To Marietta, Samuel told the plans that were to make him a fortune: The Holes had entered into an agreement with a concern in Manchester to construct a mill near the Wrox railway station. The down wool would be manufactured in quantity on the banks of the river Sheer, using modern machinery, and the finished cloth shipped by rail all over the country, perhaps even abroad if the proposed new trade laws were passed. Lord Melbourne's government was favorably inclined toward the merchant class. Samuel Hole's sons would go to a university or into one of the services, and his well-dowered daughters marry into the gentry.

The bright future Samuel Hole saw for himself he did not discuss with Marietta, but his self-assurance (based on the certainty of such a future) gave him the confidence needed to pay her court. He was a well-set-up young man of twenty-six, of medium height, with pleasing features and good manners. He knew every facet of his business, from the birth of a lamb to the merino cloak Lady Edge wore to church. His ledgers were meticulously kept. He saw the land around Wrox as one vast sheep pasture serving his factory. He described to Marietta and Lottie the various breeds of sheep and his plans to phase out the flocks that produced the best mutton in favor of those whose wool was superior. They all grazed on the same downland, and bigger profits were to be made from what people wore than from what they ate. A sheep can be eaten only once, but a crop of wool is gathered year after year. Samuel Hole saw the wool as being a crop to be harvested, and therefore, the flocks should be husbanded with the greatest care. He intended to bring into the county a Glasgow-trained veterinarian; they were known to be the best. Hole woolens from Wrox would be world-renowned. Young Hole was enthusiastic, intelligent, capable and energetic. He had never read a book.

Maria Wrox-Hampden watched young Hole's courtship of Marietta listlessly, as she did everything else in these months following the two latest deaths in the family. Since Lucy's behavior had made it impossible that Marietta could ever marry James Edge, her daughter could do worse than take Samuel Hole. Maria discussed it with Arthur, now the head of the family, who was attempting to restore the estate to some sort of order.

"With this factory being built by the Holes," she said to him, "it is possible they will become merchants, as distinguished from shopkeepers." It was perfectly respectable to be in trade if the goods traded originated on or in the ground. The Bellwoods' large fortune had come from tea via the East India Company, Aunt Augusta Pounceby's from coal mines via her late husband. Cane, silver, rubber, lumber all were legitimate sources of a gentleman's wealth, whereas the man who sold the coal and the grocer who purveyed the tea were tradesmen. Hole the draper was in trade; Hole the owner of his source of supply was not. He could suitably call on Miss Marietta Wrox-Hampden.

Young Arthur Wrox-Hampden had never heretofore given any thought to the manor and farms that would one day be his. They existed, as solidly permanent as the earth itself. Now he came to see that the very earth of Wrox, as well as the Hall, was not as it was in the beginning, is now and ever shall be. His father had not understood that the possession of anything of value—be it land, house, money, brains, a talent, a wife, a Sir Joshua Reynolds—mandated taking good care of it, else it would become valueless. Long-neglected farmlands had been sold cheaply to buyers, who restored them to valuable property worth twice what they had paid. Money squandered rather than invested was gone. Wrox Hall, not properly maintained, now needed not only a new roof but new everything under the roof, for nothing had been kept in repair.

Neglect of valuable possessions was not considered to be a crime, or a vice, or a sin, but a name as wicked must be found for it, since surely any of these three could be the direct result of neglect. Old Arthur had simply not known—not cared—what was happening to his property while he was hunting across the fields of Wrox Hall, sleeping under its leaking roof or betaking himself far from it on some chase after grouse, salmon, fox, deer or women.

There was no question, now, of young Arthur's leaving the place to return to the tranquillity of Oxford life. It was absolutely necessary that he try to salvage something of his inheritance and provide for the support of his mother and sisters. Money must be found first for the restoration of the Hall itself. This money must perforce come from the sale of land and of any valuable contents of the house.

Old Arthur would have denied responsibility for any disasters caused by neglect, saying it was the fault of his overseer, Spence, who was paid to look after the estate. Spence had proven to be untrustworthy. He had allowed things to go to seed, so that the land and tenant cottages were in a bad way; then, when the squire had been obliged to sell property, Spence it was who had bought it—with money stolen from the squire by Spence's own mismanagement. The truth was that Spence, Tole and a dozen other incompetents or miscreants would have to be dismissed. Old Arthur would never have done it, for to send an employee packing requires courage. The squire always avoided controversy. Everyone must like him, think him a good fellow, not hold him to blame. For example, he had avoided all responsibility for bringing Spence to book by making it the responsibility of Lawyer Weston. Young Arthur now had to face up to the unpleasant duties his father had avoided.

He started upon this formidable task by calling on the overseer.

Albert Spence was a man of middle years, son of a yeoman, who had learned estate management under the Duke's bailiff and was thereby highly qualified for his occupation. His appearance bespoke trustworthiness, for he was prematurely white-haired. There was nothing deferential or even respectful in his manner toward his employer that might have aroused the suspicion that he had something to hide.

The overseer's house had been the principal dwelling on a farm belonging to the estate. Standing on a slight rise, it was a large farmhouse or small manor, three-storied, with walls and gables of rubblestone and mullioned windows. It looked snug and well cared for, the windows glittering clean and clear in the morning light, a low wall in front surrounding flower beds, with a freshly painted gate at the head of a path leading to the front door. The whole of one side wall was covered by an espaliered copper beech whose topmost branch reached the chimney stack. Behind the house a small barn faced the stables across a cobbled courtyard. The whole presented a picture of an ideal English rural home that Benjamin Share would have been delighted to sketch; he would not have had to omit one stray animal or unsightly object, for there was none. One of the front rooms, with an extensive view over the land all the way to Sheerwater, had been put to use as the overseer's office, with a window through which he paid the laborers their wages, and here Spence received Arthur Wrox-Hampden.

The younger man was the one ill at ease, for he had a long way to go before he could learn to deal with subordinates. Uncle Cuthbert he had found the courage to dismiss from his house, but Uncle Cuthbert was a known quantity, so to speak, whose intentions to take matters into his own hands had been evident. He was not an employee suspected of criminal activity that had not yet been proven in court.

Arthur thought to begin from a point distant to that at which he intended circuitously to arrive. "The condition of my property is not such as I had hoped to find it," he began. "The Hall is in a shocking state of neglect."

"So it is," said Spence agreeably. "I am of the same mind."

"As are other buildings on the estate."

"It requires money to keep barns and stables in good condition," said Spence. "As for the Hall, that is not my concern. I was never required to account for the Hall, only the farm buildings, not the houses."

"This house appears to be in excellent condition," Arthur said.

"Thank you," said the overseer. "I think so myself."

Arthur was dumbfounded. "But is not this one of the houses?"

"No, it is not. This house is my property. I bought it from the estate. I have the deed at hand here; I can fetch it to show you. The squire knew all about it. Oh, on the other hand, I forgot for the moment. The deed is with the other papers at the attorney's."

Arthur knew not what to say. Leaving the subject of buildings, he returned to the land, how some had lain fallow too long, some left unplowed and unplanted, some undergrazed that could have supported more sheep or cattle.

Spence quite agreed. "I tried time after time to point out these matters to the squire, but he never would give me his attention. It requires hired hands to plow the fields and money to buy flocks, and there never was the money."

There was not the money, Arthur thought, because there were not the crops or the flocks that produce the money. It was a vicious circle. The overseer's neglect was the result of the squire's neglect. Was his crime, worse than mere neglect, likewise caused indirectly by the squire? Spence did not look like a dishonest man. Perhaps he would not have become one if it were not that the squire's behavior had given him opportunity. The commission of a crime certainly requires the opportunity to do it. A born criminal would not have chosen to become an estate overseer, for he could never have foreseen an opportunity to commit crime. Responsibility for the sad state of affairs at Wrox must be borne by Arthur's late father.

Nevertheless, Spence was guilty, no matter who was initially responsible, and Arthur had to deal with him. He asked to see the overseer's books and was told they, too, were in the hands of Mr. Weston, the lawyer, who had been preparing a case on the squire's behalf.

"I shall have to pursue it," said Arthur.

"I suppose so," Spence agreed, "but it will be costly. Attorneys do not work for nothing."

Arthur felt his hackles rising. "One expense I shall no longer bear," he said, "is that of having you in my employ."

"Oh, Mr. Wrox-Hampden and I agreed on that before he entered eternal life," said Spence. "It is some time since I have been overseer here. That is one reason you find things in such poor condition. It has distressed me to see the farms neglected and I no longer having the overseeing of them."

Arthur tried to take this in and could find no words with which to make any comment.

"Pray do not ask me to resume my responsibilities here," Spence went on. "There is no recompense you could offer me sufficient to induce me to return. I am to be Wrox stationmaster as soon as the railway is completed beyond the village."

Arthur left in defeat, vowing to himself that the defeat would be only temporary, no matter how large Mr. Weston's fee. He would get back what was rightfully his; Spence would never be stationmaster; he would be put out of his comfortable home and into jail. His former house would make an ideal dower house for Maria Wrox-Hampden to live in with her daughters until they married. He himself knew nothing of husbandry or agriculture, but he was resolved to learn, and he would almost certainly never be found guilty of neglect.

Toward the end of September, Sergeant Frakes presented himself to Mrs. Wrox-Hampden to report that he had determined the cause of her husband's death, and he wished to inform the family before filing his official report with the magistrate at Bunbury.

The work gang had laid the rails beyond Wrox far enough to warrant moving their encampment to the west, beyond Bunbury, which would be only temporarily disturbed by their descent upon it since it was to have no station. Sergeant Frakes could postpone no longer making some sort of disposition of the Wrox-Hampden murder case. He wished to remain at Wrox permanently as police constable. He wished neither to return to duty in Bethnal Green, where he was despised, nor to be moved on with his colleague to the village nearest the next encampment of the navvies, who reviled him and endangered his life. He had turned up no evidence in the murder investigation sufficient to indict anyone, but for the good of his career he could not afford to admit failure.

At his request Mrs. Wrox-Hampden and her three oldest children received the sergeant in the dining room, where he could spread out his papers upon the table while the family sat around it. He had lists of suspected persons and copious notes taken at interviews with each one. There were other lists, with headings such as "Last Seen Alive By," "Has Possible Motive" and "Had Opportunity." One list contained the names of all servants connected with the house, grounds and stables; another the names of all tenants and farm workers; another the names of the squire's friends and associates, from the Smallwoods at the vicarage to the tradespeople of Bunbury. The sergeant made it clear that he had been assiduous in the performance of his duty and had left No Stone Unturned.

"Miss Marietta Wrox-Hampden informed me," he began, "that she knew in advance her father was to die. A certain ghost that abides in Wrox Park is known to put in an appearance before the death of any member of the family. I therefore started my investigation with the family members themselves, of which there were only three in residence on the night of the murder—namely, the three daughters of the victim, the Misses Marietta and Charlotte and a baby. Miss Marietta informed me that the appearance of the ghost—which was corroborated by the coachman, Mr. Tole, who had likewise seen the phenomenon—merely presaged a death but could not say when the death would occur, whose it would be or what would be its cause. There were no means by which I could personally secure an interview with the phantom, since I was not— am not—a member of the family. I therefore temporarily abandoned this line of investigation and turned to the living persons who might be able to shed some more light. In all, I conducted interviews with one hundred and three individuals, ranging in age from eight years to ninety-two. I have here the detailed reports of those interviews, which as you can see comprise some two hundred and thirty pages."

"You need not read them all to us," said Arthur hastily into a pause made ominous by the sergeant's shuffling of papers. "We know you did your work thoroughly. I would appreciate your sparing my mother and sisters any further details that might distress them."

The sergeant put aside one pile of documents. "Very good, sir. I was going to tell you of the dog. The squire's dog, that is. It occurred to me that the dog, who was always with its master, must have been a witness to the crime and might lead me to the criminal."

"Do not say," cried Lottie, "that it was Caesar killed Papa!"

"I do not think so, miss," said the sergeant. "There would have been marks on the body, and in any case it would lack a Motive. No, I think the dog saw who killed its master and is not telling, so to speak, because it cannot Bear Witness. But I collared the dog and took it with me to confront me prime suspects, and it showed no especial reaction. I then gave it its head, while still on leash, and went with it wherever it led, to see if it would give me some clue."

"That was most ingenious of you, Sergeant," said Arthur.

"Thank you, sir. Well, sir—and ladies—it first led me a chase all over the old ruin in the park. It went sniffing all about, up and down. That was where Mr. Tole said he seen the ghost from time to time. Then off we went to the big pond, where the corpse was found—beg pardon, madam, where we found the deceased. The dog went crazy there, sniffing and barking, almost like there was an invisible person there what the dog could smell and I couldn't see."

"The ghost has been known to appear at Sheerwater," said Arthur. "The sighting was followed by the death of my sister Henrietta."

"Is that so?" said the policeman. "I must add that fact to my notes." He made as if to do so.

"Not now," said Arthur. "Let us get on with it."

"Well, sir, next place the dog led me was to the grave of the deceased in the churchyard. It made as if to dig up the corpse, it did, or at least to let out of the grave the ghost of the deceased. So that is how I know who did away with Mr. Wrox-Hampden."

The little group around the table was silent. Each member looked expectantly at the police sergeant from London.

"It was the ghost done it," said Sergeant Frakes. "The malign apparition appeared to its victim in the night at the edge of the pond, and the squire was dead of fright before he fell into the water. That accounts for being no sign of violence nor no murder weapon, nor was he drowned because the water was too shallow."

"Then this closes the investigation, Sergeant," said Arthur, rising. "Thank you for all your trouble. You can go back to your regular assignment, which I am sure will be a welcome change for all of us. It has been a difficult time for everybody."

"Some good has come of it," said the policeman. "Speaking personally of myself, this is. I expect to be married to a local and settle in the village."

"And who is the lucky young lady?" Arthur asked. "Someone we know of?"

"Yes, indeed, sir, someone you know well; 'tis the baby's nursemaid, Nancy Skaggs." Sergeant Frakes turned to address Mrs. Wrox-Hampden. "You will be after finding another girl now, madam, since Nancy will soon be minding her own wee one, not the late lamented squire's."

It was a relief to Maria to have the cause of her husband's death determined at last. Now Arthur would rest undisturbed, a suitable inscription for his tombstone could be composed, and the heavy rectangular stone laid over the grave like a lid that no agent, human or animal, could lift. She went to her desk to write the epitaph to be incised on the slab by the stonemason.

Sacred to the Memory of
Arthur-Wrox Hampden, Esq., of Wrox Hall
Who in the Fifty-fourth Year of his Age
and in the Full Vigor of Life
Overwhelmed by the sudden Appearance of a
Disembodied Spirit Expired in a Moment
on the Twenty-eighth Day of June 1838

Mrs. Wrox-Hampden was relieved to have had Sergeant Frakes's solution to the mystery of her husband's murder, but although he had been paid for his services by the government, she too had paid a dear price: the departure of Nancy Skaggs. Not only was she losing one after another of her family, but she was being robbed, one after another, of her household staff. The governess had been abducted, the butler turned traitor, the water boy corrupted by the high wages connected to the railway. Now the nursery maid, with little Violet barely fifteen months old, had succumbed to the seduction of Sergeant Frakes.

Even Nurse was behaving badly. She would not assume the sole care of Letty: She was too old, and in any case no one can be expected to stay on twenty-four-hour duty with no time off. A replacement must be found for Nancy Skaggs—but where? Such local girls as had not gone off after the navvies (and those who had we were well rid of) were expecting to have jobs in the new mill; they could live at home and make good wages. A search was begun for a Welsh or Irish girl who might be willing to escape from rural poverty to the backwater of Wrox rather than to the lights of Liverpool or Birmingham. Maria thanked Providence that Georgie Hampden had taken the boy twin, else the situation would have been impossible. Even with a nursery maid, *two* infants to look after— she could not bear even to think of it.

Meanwhile, Lottie was called upon to help with the baby. The situation was as in poor families, in which the older children look after the younger. Arthur and Marietta were already giving Lottie her lessons. Their mother could not comprehend how things had come to this pass. The railway was supposed to bring goods and people and various benefits to the country; instead, it was taking them all away.

One afternoon, for the first time in years, Mrs. Wrox-Hampden set foot in her children's nursery. She went through the schoolroom and common room as if on a tour in a foreign country. She had never seen the butterfly collection. She noticed the rectangle conspicuous on the dusty wall where the color was several shades lighter but had no remembrance of what picture had hung there. She did remark how shabby were the furnishings in the common room and how the window curtains were frayed along their edges, and her conscience prodded her with a small pang. Something must be done inside the house as well as out, where, her son Arthur had told her, an entire new roof was necessary.

In the day nursery little Letty was pulling herself up off the floor by a chair seat and taking a few awkward steps before falling down, crawling back to the chair and trying again. She was talking to herself—or perhaps to the world—in gurgling sounds. When the tall woman dressed all in black came into the room, the baby stopped crawling, pushed herself up to a sitting position and looked up at her mother. Then she lifted her arms and smiled broadly, as if showing off her pretty little pearls of teeth. Maria's heart was unlocked. Tears came to her eyes. She ran across the floor, knelt by the baby and enveloped her in a yard of black veiling. Nurse, who had risen from a corner when her mistress entered, said, "I'll be going down to have me tea now, ma'am." Had there been a nursery maid, Nurse's tea would have been brought up. She left mother and infant alone.

Maria took Letty up and sat with the baby on her lap. There was no one to observe her as she fondled it, kissed it and cooed at it in imitation of its own attempts at language. How could she ever have thought the little girl unwelcome in the world? She reproached herself bitterly. Because she had lost so many, she had thought she wanted to bear no more children only to lose them. She should have been thankful that God had given her five living ones (seven if you counted Robert Fox and the twin boy) and that He had taken only five. From now on she would deserve this little treasure. She stroked the peach-soft skin and kissed the back of the neck where a lock of auburn hair curled upward. Letty kicked her stout legs, waved her arms about, gurgled and smiled.

The lovely emotional moments passed. They had been just that—passing moments. Letty now strained and struggled to leave the maternal embrace and return to the floor. She wet her nappy in Maria's lap and began howling with rage, calling for Nanny between howls. The mother was helpless to bring back the docile, smiling baby of a few moments before. Nurse would not return for at least half an hour—an eternity. Maria thought, I must not resent Letty's preferring Nurse to me, it is only natural she should do so, she loves the person who feeds and tends her, when she grows older, she will love me, I will make her love me, she shall be the comfort of my old age, I am old enough to be her grandmother.

A flying fist caught the mother a blow square on the mouth, which she had formed into an O as she was saying "Sh-sh-sh-h!" It hurt. She could feel dampness seeping through her skirt.

Letty howled on; the color in her face was now a good match for her hair. The little pearls of teeth were veiled in saliva that was dribbling down the sides of her chin. Her mother's ears rang with the noise.

* * *

A nursery maid was found, fortunately, in the form of a young house-maid from the castle. When the Duke was not in residence, the staff was reduced to a minimum necessary for maintenance; the upper servants went with the family to whichever of its other seats it had removed. The young maid, Norah, an orphan, wanted steady work and a home, and although she had not had nursery experience (none of the Duke's six daughters was yet married), she thought she would like the work, and Nurse could train her. She fitted in well enough in the servants' hall, where they were happy to hear about life in a ducal castle. It was, of course, vastly above that at Wrox Hall, and Norah was seen to have come down in the world. At the castle there was a whole staff to wait on the staff. The housekeeper had an assistant housekeeper. The butler had a first and a second underbutler. The head footman had subordinates in a descending order of importance. The servants' hall had its own cook, and *he* waited on the Duke's cook what was called a chef—a French gentleman—and *his* two what was called sous-chefs. "We always had the best of everything," said Norah.

When the Duke removed from one seat to another, he was accompanied by all the higher servants and by his chaplain, two secretaries, a companion, a chess player, a librarian and half a dozen hangers-on. Only the curator remained at the castle, in charge of its enormous collections of art and furnishings that included ceilings and doorways painted by Angelica Kauffmann, gildings, antique statuary in the orangerie and all the contents of rooms that together formed a vast private museum. In the absence of the ducal family certain saloons and halls were opened to the public one day a week for a threepenny charge, the proceeds going to the Bunbury poorhouse.

Cook, who was sister to the laundress Annie Clegg and aunt to the lately departed Adam, decided she was happier in service at a country gentleman's house where she served the master than she would be at a ducal castle serving the servants. Norah had never seen the Duke; his apartments were cleaned only in his absence. "I had rather look out for a baby and dust a nursery," said Norah, "than to dust all them statues and busts in the halls. You can't talk to 'em. You *could*, of course, but what's the use when they don't answer, and I think Letty understands what I say, she's a clever little thing, she is."

As the cold weather took over the country, Norah admitted that the servants' hall at Wrox was cozy, more like somebody's home, and she herself had a more important position, as assistant to Nurse, than she had enjoyed at the castle. In time she became devotedly fond of baby

Violet, as one does of a wholly dependent pet. She took pleasure in bathing the wee thing, and feeding her, and taking her out in the park when the weather permitted. "I declare I come to love her like she was me own," said Norah.

❧ 23 ❧

Chance Meeting in the Taunton Coach

M r. Reddle had contrived to keep his wife secluded at the inn in the
snug until the departure of the Taunton coach. She had not
witnessed the arrival of the Bunbury passengers, who were immediately
informed of Mr. Maule's crime. Two of them were depositors, who
rushed across the market square immediately and joined the crowd in
front of the bank. A local man, also a bank depositor, who had been
booked to depart for Taunton, did not even show up. So Elsie Reddle left
Bunbury without having heard the devastating news. Her husband
handed her into the coach and settled beside her with a sigh of relief. A
place was found for the Sistine Madonna on the empty seat of the passenger who had failed to appear. There were only four other passengers,
a couple with a child and an elderly gentleman with white hair and a
benign countenance, dressed soberly in gray with a clean white stock,
wearing gaiters, buckled shoes and a broad-brimmed hat.

The coach was turned out of the innyard toward the west. Elsie, being
subject to motion sickness, leaned back and closed her eyes; she was
looking very drawn and pale.

"Excuse me, madam," said the elderly gentleman, leaning toward her.

He was seated opposite, facing forward. "May I have the pleasure of exchanging seats with thee? I am not at all affected by riding backward."

The offer was gladly accepted. Elsie now sat by a window facing the direction in which the coach was traveling. She leaned back again, gratefully, closing her eyes. Osbert reached over to close the window, for the wind that had been behind her back was now blowing directly upon her.

"Excuse me, madam," the gentleman said again, "but may I give thee some helpful advice? If thee will sit erect and look out at the horizon, thee will not feel the effects of the motion. And the window should remain opened, as the circulation of fresh air is important. Breathe deeply. Keeping the eye on the horizon, which remains stable, will obliterate the sensation that it is moving. I am sure thee will soon feel comfortable."

It was so. During the remainder of the journey to Taunton an acquaintanceship was formed between the Reddles and Mr. William West, as he proved to be. He was a member of the Society of Friends—commonly called Quakers—a native of Pennsylvania in the United States. He had been in England visiting his first cousin, Raphael West, son of George III's court painter, Benjamin West. He told them his ancestors had gone to the American colonies with William Penn and had prospered there. He was a large landholder, member of the state legislature, elder of the Friends' Meeting. He was on his way now to Liverpool to board a packet for the return voyage to America. When he learned that Osbert Reddle was a teacher, he became much interested. Before the coach had arrived at Taunton, he knew the situation of the newlywed couple and began urgent appeals.

"I am a director of the Friends Central School in Philadelphia," he said. "The need for experienced teachers in America is very great. We need doctors, attorneys, leaders of the community, and they cannot be produced without skilled instruction first in the fundamental subjects of study, the three Rs, as someone has called them—reading, writing and arithmetic. Thee says thee would like to start thy own school. I can promise thee that if thee were to emigrate, I would see that thy dream would be realized."

Leave England? The possibility had never entered Osbert's mind. Only men who were dissatisfied here at home went to the colonies (as he still thought of them). Mr. West's own forebears had gone because of religious persecution. Young men with no dependents went to find employment, to start new lives, to seek their fortunes—or perhaps to escape the law. Soldiers who had been sent there to fight had stayed on after the fighting was over. Osbert had so deep an attachment to the soil of England and to her long history that he knew he would suffer dreadfully from being transplanted.

Mr. West was obviously sincere in his desire to recruit teachers for the American former colonies. "It is most kind of, er, of you," said Osbert, "to suggest my removal to what is called the New World, although it is as old as any other part of the globe. But I am a married man and cannot just pull up stakes to go hither or yon. Even if I wished to leave England. My wife is also a teacher," he added. "She was governess in the—" He started to mention the Wrox-Hampdens, then thought better of it and finished, "She has had years of experience in teaching young ladies."

"Then thee and she would be doubly welcome in a Friends' school," said Mr. West, "even in a school for boys. A tenet of our faith is the equality of all men and women."

"Do not think me out of order, sir," said Osbert earnestly, "but the faith of the Church of England also holds all men and women to be equal in the sight of God."

"We believe them to be equal in the sight of man," said Mr. West.

They spoke some more of schooling, and Osbert told about Mr. Plumptre's constructive punishment. Mr. West nodded approval. "We do not strike children," he said, "for they cannot strike back. At Friends Central School no teacher would rap a boy's knuckles or hit the palm of his hand with a ruler or slap his face. His hands and his head are his dignities as a human being; they are what make him a man and not a dumb animal. If we respect them he will respect himself."

At Taunton the Reddles were to stop overnight and take the Exeter coach the next day. Mr. West was continuing on to Liverpool. The Reddles wished him a safe voyage home, and he parted from them with earnest injunctions that they should emigrate. He gave them his address in Philadelphia and begged them to correspond with him.

In their room Osbert remarked to Elsie, "What a pleasant gentleman. I think I never before met a Quaker."

"What exactly is a Quaker?" asked she. "Are they heathens? Do they not believe in the Lord Jesus Christ?"

"Oh, they are Christians," said Osbert. "I feel sure they are. Some are called Shakers. I am not sure of the difference between them. I think Quakers do not approve of music and dancing, whereas Shakers are very fond of dancing; they dance during their religious services."

"That sounds to me like heathens in Africa," said Elsie. "It is no wonder they were forced to flee to America, where there are wild Indians."

"There are no wild Indians in Philadelphia," said Osbert. "You heard Mr. West say it is a very up-to-date city. It was the first capital of the Republic; it was where those men met who formed the new nation."

"Revolutionaries," Elsie said. "A city founded by revolutionists and inhabited by heathens. If that makes it up-to-date, as Mr. West says, all I can say is whatever is the world coming to."

"We shall soon know, my dear," said her husband, "as whatever it is coming to, it is bringing us with it, willy-nilly."

They went downstairs to supper. The public room was noisy and crowded but sufficiently far from Bunbury for Osbert to feel safe from the fear of anyone's mentioning its bank. Elsie was very tired and ate little. Osbert, on the other hand, was feeling, in his relief, full of vigor and love. He was hungry. He had a cut of beef with Yorkshire pudding and some boiled cabbage. He ordered a tankard of stout. He forgot he was without employment and without Elsie's savings that she thought he had procured from Mr. Maule. This was his wedding night, the first he and Elsie had been in the same bedroom alone together—really alone. He looked at her dear face and was struck simultaneously with the thought that he had not yet given her a wedding present and the realization of exactly what that present should be. He would take her to be fitted with a pair of spectacles! She would truly be entering a new life in a new world where she would see things she had never seen before. Small things, like smiles and frowns. Smaller things, like the ants that had walked unnoticed across the hem of her skirt when they picnicked with the children on the verge at Sheerwater and the ladybug she had not seen against the red of a garden rose. Suddenly he leaned over and said to her, very seriously, "There are a hundred and eighty thousand species of beetles—did you know that? Is it not amazing?"

Elsie put back her head and laughed and laughed. Color came into her cheeks. When she could stop laughing and speak, she said, "I had thought you were thinking of me—of us. And all the while you were thinking about *beetles*—" She could not go on for laughing.

"But I *was* thinking of you," he protested. His train of thought had been perfectly logical. He tried to explain it, ending where he had started, with the wedding present he intended to give her but was not going to tell her now what it was because he wanted it—them—to be a surprise for as long as they could be, which was until he could take her to a certain shop in Exeter where it—they—would be fitted to her.

"This has been a long day," Elsie said when she was composed. "I am quite tired, Osbert."

"Naturally," said he. "Let us go up to bed. We are to make an early start tomorrow."

Tired though she was, Elsie did not sleep at all that night. Osbert murmured words of endearment between the kisses that rained down upon the face and bosom of his beloved. He had loved her for so long, and had wanted so desperately to possess her, that he could not control the torrents of his passion. When he was spent, he realized she had been lying mute and trembling, enduring rather than receiving his love. He fell back in despair. He almost felt he should apologize to her—but no, he had only taken what was his by right. An unknown hand had killed Arthur Wrox-Hampden, but he had not died; he was in the bridal bed at this moment. The bridegroom turned from his wife and lay awake, staring into the darkness.

Elsie felt tears sliding down her cheeks to the pillow. She had not realized it would be like that—that awful night on Maria Wrox-Hampden's bed. Her dearest mother had told her never to forget that she was a lady and must always behave accordingly. She had never behaved otherwise. She now found herself in a situation in which she had no idea how to behave at all, let alone in a ladylike manner. She put a hand to her throat in the familiar gesture that invoked her dearest mother's guidance. She vowed that if it should happen again, she would behave *comme il faut*—that is, resign herself to the humiliation out of gratitude to Osbert, whom she loved with all her heart. It was the least—it was the most—she could do to repay him. She, too, stared into the night, and after a while she sensed that he was asleep, and she was content.

The senior Reddles welcomed with loving warmth their son and his wife, whom they had not been expecting. They were a happy couple, enjoying a good income from the wholesale trade in wine and spirits, living in a comfortable town house, surrounded by congenial neighbors and the families of two married daughters. They were immensely proud of Osbert, an educated man, and proud that his bride was the daughter of a Church of England clergyman. At first they were disappointed in her appearance—so pale and sickly-looking—but Osbert explained she had recently been ill, that normally her health was excellent, and Mrs. Reddle set to work to cosset her and fatten her with special stews and puddings.

Elsie came to feel she was the luckiest woman in all England—if only it were not for that. Osbert was very patient with her, but he began to think he had been patient for so long, it was long enough, why should he have to continue being patient, why should he be paying over and over for the crime of Arthur Wrox-Hampden?

After a few days of rest and meeting with the Reddle family and friends, Elsie was given her wedding present from Osbert. The lens grinder who kept a shop in the town near the cathedral, being a friend of the older Reddles, made Osbert a very fair price for Elsie's new spectacles, and the day she first wore them marked the real beginning of her new life. She saw things she had never before seen. Trees that had appeared as large green objects were revealed to be composed of a myriad of small, individual leaves. The sky was not vacant; it was filled with birds flying and clouds traveling. The walls of the great Exeter Cathedral with its massive Roman towers were not built of solid masonry but were interrupted and ornamented by countless details. The face of her mother-in-law, Mrs. Reddle, was observed to have a kind, sweet expression. Osbert's head, seen in profile, was quite sharp in outline, not at all blurred. He was a handsome man! Elsie began putting on weight; her cheeks showed color; her new relations began to appreciate "what Osbert had seen in her," as Mrs. Reddle put it.

When they left Wrox, Osbert had heard the promises exchanged between his wife and Miss Theodora Smallwood to write often, so on first reaching Exeter, he had sent word to Miss Theodora instructing her never to mention the failure of the Bunbury bank. When a letter arrived for Elsie, he watched without trepidation as she opened it. She did so eagerly, hoping for word of her dear former charges. Did Lottie have a governess to take her place? Could Marietta be going to marry Lord Edge? Perhaps Augustus was to be allowed to study music, as opposed to merely taking lessons on the pianoforte.

The letter was composed of many sheets of thin notepaper, with writing on both sides of every page. Miss Theodora wrote in a very fine hand, in lines very close together, across the paper from left to right and then, to economize, gave the page a quarter turn and continued her letter again across the paper from left to right. To decipher it was as good as doing a puzzle. Anyone who could make sense of it could have deciphered the Rosetta stone. Elsie removed her spectacles and held the letter to the window, close to her face.

"Let me, my dear," said her husband. "You must not strain your eyes." He took the sheets and placed himself in the chair by the window. Elsie sat opposite on a sofa, prepared to listen.

Nothing that went on in the county escaped the attention or the pen of Miss Theodora. There had been a wedding in the Chapel (a temporary, makeshift one, the former home of Penrose, the thatcher) between Miss Nancy Skaggs and Police Constable Frakes, and none too soon according to Mr. Smallwood. "Mr. Arthur Wrox-Hampden," Osbert read, "has bought for his baby sister Violet a most unusual kind of pony basket. It holds only the infant, the pony pulls it, she enjoys holding the reins while the pony walks about and the nursemaid walks alongside." Osbert was proceeding confidently with the reading when a word he was approaching leaped up at him off the page. The word was "murderer." He stopped.

"What is it, Osbert?" Elsie asked.

"I am afraid I cannot make it out."

"Let me try."

"No! No, my dear. I shall manage somehow." He saw the sentence ahead was "The murderer of the squire has been identified." The following page was obviously devoted to this subject, so although he would have preferred not to mention the name of Arthur Wrox-Hampden, Osbert saw he could not escape again. He was forced to read on. He avoided looking at his wife.

The murderer of the squire has been identified. It was thought all along that the villain would prove to be Spence, the overseer, but he would have had to have several accomplices, and there were no marks on the body nor any sign that it had been carried or dragged to the pond. Sergeant Frakes, as he was—he is now our local Police Constable—very cleverly used the squire's dog to lead him to the ghost of the hermit, which had pursued the squire to the pond when he was out walking with the dog at night, and the squire had dropped dead on the spot. The ghost has not been seen or heard from since. It is a great relief to all, as we can now sleep safe at night. . . .

Elsie said nothing, and Osbert read on as best he could to the bottom of the last page, where the letter ended, fortunately not cross-written, with sentiments of undying friendship and dearest love always.

The name of Arthur Wrox-Hampden was not heard again, but his presence was there between man and wife. His children's names were often mentioned. He could not be avoided in Osbert's unspoken thoughts. Mr. Smallwood had as good as said Wrox-Hampden would go to Hell if he did not repent, whereas in repentance he would be saved. Had it transpired that his death was by his own hand—a suicide—it would have meant he had repented. So it was well that a cause had been determined which ensured the dead man's exclusion from a life everlasting in Heaven. Elsie would never have to encounter him again in this world or the next. But he remained. He would not go away. "The evil that men do lives after them," Osbert said into his pillow one night, and for the first time in his adult life he shed tears.

The summer wore to its end. The tracks of the Great Western Railway were laid into Somerset as far as Yeovil. A new school year had begun, and still Osbert had not found employment. His lack of a degree made it impossible that he should apply to one of the public schools. He wrote to Mr. Plumptre, asking the favor of a recommendation. Responses to his inquiries were discouraging. A Mr. Rompe, who ran an Academy for Young Gentlemen in Birmingham, offered to Mr. Reddle a suitable position, beginning after Christmas, and that of housekeeper to Mrs. Reddle, who would live in a separate wing of the school next to the female servants under her supervision.

The senior Mr. Reddle urged his son to come into his own trade. It was prosperous. He could find an agreeable house within a walk of the warehouse where the offices were located. Advancement to the eventual ownership of the business was certain.

Osbert was tempted. He went for long walks alone while he pondered every aspect of his situation and his wife's. At last he went to see his father at the warehouse, where drays were being loaded and unloaded while clerks took inventory and directed consignments. His father's office was small and dark, furnished with an enormous desk and two hard chairs. The view from the single window was of a livery stable opposite.

"Please do not think, Father, that I am unappreciative of your generosity," he began, "but I have no inclination toward making wholesale trade my career. The only talent I possess is for teaching, and were I not to exercise it, I should lead a miserable life. Every bird sings its own note and must do so or remain silent. I believe I am called upon to pass along our common heritage of knowledge to the next generation, as the bishop is called to serve God and Her Majesty the Queen to rule the Empire. I could not sit here in this room all day by myself doing accounts and issuing orders. I should feel useless."

The senior Reddle's feelings were hurt. "I do not consider myself to be useless," he declared. "I provide purveyors of wine and spirits, and innkeepers who serve them to the public, with the necessities of their trade. Were it not for me, where would all their customers be, including you? Is it useless to provide the public with necessities, and my family with a comfortable life?"

"No, Father. What I meant to say was that *I* should be useless here because I should fail at it. Whereas I can be a successful teacher. I know a great deal about a great many things, having a retentive memory, and I know how to tell it all to children. It is a talent not to be despised. It is not remunerative—as is your own talent for business—but it will support Elsie and myself if I am given the opportunity."

"What became of your wish to establish a school near Wrox?" asked Mr. Reddle.

Osbert could never tell his father about the two heinous crimes against Elsie that had been committed there, but he began to think that word of them would sooner or later inevitably be spread as far as Exeter. He made up his mind that the best chance for Elsie's happiness and his own lay in their removal altogether from the beloved homeland. He recounted to his father the story of their encounter in the stagecoach with the Quaker Mr. West. "I am considering Mr. West's offer," said Osbert. "It appears that both Elsie and I could perform a greatly needed service in Pennsylvania."

"I did not mean to drive you to that!" exclaimed poor Mr. Reddle. "Do not, I beg you, take such a step. It would be irrevocable. Your mother and sisters and I would never see you again! It is unthinkable. I cannot face it."

"It must be faced, Father," said Osbert.

His father broke down. "Would that you had never set foot in that coach and never met the Quaker man," he said, nearly in tears. "It was an ill chance. I would he had stayed in America where he belongs and left us alone and not come interfering with our lives. Who will tell your mother? I shall not do it; you will have to do it yourself."

"I shall have to tell Elsie first, and that will be equally difficult."

"God help us!" Mr. Reddle ejaculated. "I wish those d——d colonies had never been discovered. They are so far distant. Perhaps you will be lost at sea! It is all too terrible to contemplate. It is such a drastic decision to take."

"I quite agree," said his son. "But there are times in one's life when a decision must be taken, and that time is now for Elsie and me."

❧ 24 ❧

James Returns to Edge Park

James Edge returned home in time for Christmas a man of the world. While in Rome he had become interested in Italian politics, as explained by Benjamin Share, and had endeavored to understand its intricacies. As far as he could make out, there were several squabbling parties united only in a common desire to be rid of Austria, a distant place of which James had barely heard and which seemed to have no reasonable connection with Italy. For the first time his mind had been directed away from England toward the Continent and the great diversity of its various governments. They had visited France, Germany and Switzerland. Everywhere the doors of the *crème de la crème* had been opened to the young lord, and marriageable girls put in his way. Some of these young ladies were even English, brought to a European capital in the hope they could make a better matrimonial catch there than was likely in Northumberland or Yorkshire.

Europe in the aftermath of the Napoleonic era served to interest James in the politics of his homeland. Politics took hold of his imagination. He saw that national conditions and international relations were constantly changing, and politics could be the instrument of change. He remarked to Mr. Share that he would have liked to stand for Parliament after reaching his majority, but of course he could not do so.

"Be glad you need not," said Benjamin. "It is a rough game. Avoidance of it is one of the privileges of being a peer. You will take your seat in the Lords without its being contested, and you can work there equally well for the good of the country and for any changes you deem desirable."

"As far as I know," said James, "the business of the Lords is to block, or at least to slow, the process of change."

"A useful service," Benjamin said. "Change brought about too fast is revolution. Let us thank Heaven for our young Queen, she will have many years on the throne, very stabilizing for the country; no one will overthrow her, we shall have no Buonaparte to wreck havoc in our beloved isles as he did throughout Europe. In introducing you to the *haut monde*, our tour has had the corollary effect of making you appreciate our own dear land, 'This precious stone set in a silver sea,' as Shakespeare put it. I am sure your mother will be well pleased."

Lady Edge was more than pleased with the results of James's having met the wide world beyond his home and considered she had made the right decision in choosing Benjamin Share to perform the introduction. An interest in politics she had not foreseen as a result of the grand tour. The Edges had always been Tories. At dinner parties in the home shire, after the ladies had withdrawn and the port been handed around, the gentlemen, Whig and Tory alike, enjoyed amicable political discussions. They seldom became heated, as every man participating was aware that the county in which they had their various properties was remote from the seat of power. It contained no large industrial city. Everyone knew everyone's business. They went to the hustings and voted each for his chosen parliamentary candidate. After dinner they all together, since Victoria's accession, gave a toast to Her Majesty the Queen. One notable who never raised his glass to her was the Duke. The Duke was a Jacobite; he did not recognize the rights of the Hanoverians to the throne of England. The very thought of these stout, gouty, whoring Germans, who could not even speak English, caused the Duke's daughters to fear he might have an apoplectic fit. Following the departure of the ladies at castle dinners, a toast was proposed to the King over the Water, when the gentlemen would pass their glasses of spirits over the water goblets before drinking. The Duke alone took this rite seriously; his guests saw no harm in humoring his harmless eccentricity. He was a living fossil.

*   *   *

In three months James would attain his majority and make his maiden speech before the Lords, when it would become apparent whether he was Liberal or Conservative. Having been out of the country, he had not followed the reforms introduced by Lord Melbourne and was keen to catch up on domestic affairs. So full was he of European customs and ideas that he entertained thoughts of the diplomatic service. He said nothing of this to his mother for the time being, as he knew she expected him to take up residence at Edge Park. A great celebration there was planned for his coming-of-age. The young peer now would occupy a town house in Piccadilly when Parliament was sitting.

Thus it was not only Christmas to which James had come home. He had returned to a New Year, to his coming-of-age, to the assumption of inherited responsibilities and to the brilliant future for which his mother had so well prepared him.

Mr. Share was to stay over at Edge for a fortnight to acquaint her ladyship with the details of the past year's travels. What with all the holiday festivities, caroling, wassail bowls, assemblies, balls, feastings, midnight mass in the castle chapel and Christmas morning service in the parish church, every day was filled with activity.

Benjamin Share was overjoyed to find himself on Christmas Eve at last inside the ducal castle, even if only in the chapel along with tenants and servants. It was a bitter winter's night, and the ancient stone walls of the chapel held its cold and the cold of centuries past. The congregation was muffled to the ears and thickly gloved, making it impossible to turn the pages of the Book of Common Prayer. When the Duke's chaplain opened the service with the Collect of the Day, his breath was visible on the frigid air. Gradually, as he proceeded, the heat of assembled human bodies created a modicum of warmth. A place had been found for Mr. Share in the loft, overlooking the nave that contained the family, the nobility and the Duke's sarcophagus. This had belonged to an Egyptian queen. The Duke had had it brought from Thebes and had never lain down in it to see if it fitted him, although he had instructed his daughters that he was to be buried therein. The Duke was not a tall man, but he was considerably taller than any ancient Egyptian, man or woman, and his daughters dreaded the day when they would have either to disobey their father and risk his eternal displeasure or to cut off his feet.

It may be imagined with what relish Mr. Share measured the mummy case with his eye, trying to determine if it might be possible of alteration, but it was made of Egyptian syenite, the hardest of all stone. He wondered if the Duke should be somehow fitted in, what disposition would be made of the royal mummy. He could dine out on this discovery for at least a twelvemonth, and he added it to his repertoire. He had certainly seen and measured the Duke's final resting place with his own eyes, so his listeners would know he had himself been within the ducal walls. They need not know the walls were only those of the chapel during a service, when he had been squeezed into the loft with the estate agent's family.

It had come almost to the New Year when Mr. Share remarked to his hostess that he had not seen about any of his old friends from Wrox Hall.

"The family is in mourning," said she. "They do not go out in society. You must have heard of the squire's having passed on to a better world and the manner of his passage."

"Mrs. Wrox-Hampden wrote me of it," Mr. Share said. "Most extraordinary. I know, of course, the story of the Wrox spirit—that of the hermit who was starved to death because it was believed he was his own ghost—but I had not thought it malevolent; I had thought it more to be pitied than feared. If it wished to avenge itself, why should it have waited so long?"

The phenomenon was discussed in much detail, leading Mr. Share to give an account of similar cases of appearances that heralded deaths. The Bavarian royal family had a Black Lady who appeared to them before a death, and the Prussian royal family a White Lady. Every appearance of either lady had always been followed within hours by a royal death. In the case of Queen Teresa of Bavaria she was immediately seized with cholera on seeing in her antechamber an unknown, mysterious lady dressed in black, and three hours later she was dead.

"I do not suppose the Bunbury doctor could have failed to diagnose the cholera," said Lady Edge. "And the Wrox ghost is a man. And the family is far from being royal. I cannot see any connection."

Mr. Share's feelings were hurt. His stories were always told for their own sake, not for the sake of any necessary connections, relevant or not. "I should like to call upon the Wrox-Hampdens to express my condolences," he said, "if it could be arranged without inconvenience."

"I suppose you may take the fly this afternoon if you must," said his hostess.

"May I go with you?" asked James eagerly.

"I am afraid not," said his mother. "We have an engagement with Mr. Hamper, the bailiff. It has already been put off too long, as we are so soon to go to London."

"I should like to see Miss Marietta again," said Mr. Share innocently.

"She was most appreciative of all I was able to do for her when in Rome."

Lady Edge, who could not have sat up any straighter than she habitually did, now gave the impression of having done so. "What is it you say?" she demanded. "How could you have seen that girl in Rome?"

"Oh, she and her mother were there last winter, with Robert Fox, Mrs. Wrox-Hampden's son, Fox of Foxbridge Abbey, you know. He has quite the most delightful villa in the city and is well known for his entertainments."

Lady Edge could scarcely credit the evidence of her ears. How could Maria Wrox-Hampden have been so impudent as to have followed James to Rome with her unfortunate daughters? Would the woman stop at nothing to throw them in his way? "I suppose," she said icily, "she had with her also the elder girl, Lucy."

"No," said James, "Lucy was not there. Only Marietta. She had a great success in society, she is so pretty and clever. She is quite grown-up now."

"I do not understand why the girl was never mentioned in your letters," said his mother. "Oh"—she remembered one letter containing an allusion—"you did say something of having met an attractive young lady. I assumed her to be some person unknown to me. I did not send you to Rome in order to meet clandestinely with Marietta Wrox-Hampden."

"There was nothing clandestine about it," said James. "Mr. Share was present at all times when we were not at some entertainment or ball. And I did meet many other young ladies, as I did tell you in my letters. But it was pleasant when so far away to find someone from home. I should so like to see her again."

Lady Edge scented danger. Like a she-wolf defending her cub, she moved quickly between it and the threat to its life. "I am sure you will see her. We shall not be in London above two months."

Mr. Share realized that he had blundered in first mentioning the young lady's name. He was puzzled. Last time he had been either at Wrox or Edge relations between the two houses had been more than cordial, more than friendly; they had been even intimate. Something had happened, something nameless, a breach of some sort. If it were to come down to his having to take sides, he must, of course, ally himself with the higher-ranking of the two. "Never mind," said he, "it is of little importance. Mrs. Wrox-Hampden will understand if I fail to call upon her. I would not wish to intrude on her grief. Not to mention the inconvenience about the fly." He desired at any cost to be relieved of having to drive himself over to Wrox, as he was terrified by the thought of a runaway horse. He knew many stories of accidents involving drivers far more experienced than himself. The late Lord Canterton had been carried several miles over a Scottish heath in a fly behind a runaway horse and been dumped from a bridge into the river Wold. His body had never been seen; it had simply vanished. Only his riding crop was found, caught in a bramble on the riverbank. The horse was unhurt and, when approached, was docility itself, standing patiently, waiting to be led away from the scene. It was supposed that some evil spirit had entered it for the purpose of doing away with Canterton, the horse being merely its instrument. The horse had, of course, been destroyed, and the spirit exorcised. Mr. Share knew of no reason why anyone should use a horse and fly as a means of murdering him, but presumably neither had the late Lord Canterton.

"I intend to call upon Maria Wrox-Hampden myself," said Lady Edge. "I shall ride over to Wrox with Mr. Share this afternoon while you are with Hamper. There is no further need now for me to have dealings with him. You will find him to be a splendid fellow; your affairs have prospered in his keeping."

Benjamin Share's heart jumped into his throat, as they say. He pictured a runaway horse with himself at the reins and Lady Edge hanging on to the side of the fly in fear of her life. "Please do not feel you must call at Wrox on my account," he pleaded. "There is no need to undertake the journey."

"I shall order the carriage around for us at four o'clock," said Lady Edge, who was just as fearful of being driven by her guest as he was.

Mr. Share's relief was visible on his face.

James could not neglect his plain duty to confer with Hamper. He resolved to find some free time before leaving for London when he would ride over to Wrox and see Marietta. They would have much to talk about. He would tease her with favorable descriptions of all the young ladies in the *haut monde* who had been presented to him for his inspection like prize cattle at the county fair. The mention of Lucy's name had reminded him of those weeks at the close of summer when he had been so happy in her company; such a strange lass she was, more like a lad in some ways, so unlike her younger sister.

Mr. Share's sense of relief had been succeeded by one of curiosity. He could hardly wait to call at Wrox so he could spy out the lay of the land.

On arrival at the Hall, Lady Edge and her guest were received by Mrs.

Wrox-Hampden, her son Arthur and her daughter Marietta. The greeting between the two ladies was formal. No embrace was exchanged, or term of endearment. The caller expressed sympathy in the loss of Maria's husband, from which Mr. Share drew the conclusion that this was their first meeting since that unhappy event some six months previous. He himself was warmly received, as was his due as the premier guest of England. He was chagrined when Lady Edge, without even being seated, demanded to see Mrs. Wrox-Hampden alone in her sitting room, and he was left to entertain the young people.

Upstairs, behind closed doors, the two old friends faced each other.

"I have just learned, Maria," said Emma Edge, "that you followed James to Rome last winter."

"I had no idea James was to go to Rome, else I should certainly not have gone there. To avoid him was a large part of my reason for going. When he walked into Robert's house there, I was quite taken aback by surprise."

"Why did you leave Lucy here, then? Was the story not true that you told me in your attempt to marry her to James?"

"Lucy was with me in Rome," said Maria.

"James says she was not, that there was only Marietta."

"Lucy did not go about in society," said her mother. "You know very well why she could not. We removed to Rome for her confinement, that it should not be known of here, and that her child not be born here. I have some pride left, Emma, despite all that I have been forced to swallow."

"And what of the—" Emma hesitated, on the verge of using a word for an illegitimate child that she had heard applied only to those of kings.

"The child was born on the second day of last July," said Maria. "It was—it is—a boy."

So it was living. "And where is it now?" Emma persisted.

"He is in Rome. He is well taken care of. I have seen to that."

There was a catch in Maria's voice and a glint in her eyes that touched her old friend. Emma put out a hand. "Oh, my dear," she said, "how very brave of you, to give up a grandchild, a boy, even though it was—well, it was for the best, of course, but still—"

The kindness affected Maria as no ill treatment could have done, and she allowed the tears to gather and then flow unchecked.

Emma took Maria's hand in both her own and pressed it. She felt horribly guilty because her main sentiment had been that of relief, not sympathy. The bastard was safely far away in Italy, no false charges were to be brought against James, the whole wretched episode was going to be forgotten, all would be as before, before that dreadful girl Lucy had tried to drag the name of James into the mud in which she had wallowed.

While the ladies were in retirement, Samuel Hole had been shown into the drawing room. It was evident that he was an habitué; he spoke of having been there only the day before. He and Arthur had some scheme going involving sheep and a wool factory near the railway station—excessively dull conversation, but Mr. Share was able to report it on the way back to the Park to Lady Edge and to say that if he was any judge of which way the wind was blowing, it was blowing in the direction of an engagement between Miss Marietta and this Whole fellow, whoever he might be.

"He is the son of the draper at Bunbury," said Lady Edge, and she felt a genuine sympathy for poor Maria, her girlhood friend, who had held such high matrimonial hopes for her daughters and would be obliged to settle for so much less. Maria faced a further diet of pride to swallow.

Later, with their after-dinner brandy, James asked Benjamin for news of Marietta and the household at Wrox. Now that their relationship was no longer that of cicerone and pupil James was allowed to address Benjamin by his Christian name, which permitted of more personal conversation. As always, Benjamin's answer was colorful and delivered without any disparaging remarks. "Miss Marietta was her usual self, which is to say quite incomparable. It appears she has a suitor, a nice-looking young man. If she should accept him, that would be satisfactory proof that she considers him to be good enough for her."

"I always observed," said James, "that you never say anything disparaging or uncomplimentary about anyone."

"I cannot afford to," Benjamin said. "It is so easy to be misunderstood. One must be careful lest one be misquoted. I learned my lesson early. There was a very rich lady, the widow of a brewer, who built a beautiful seaside villa at Wythe, which is near Angnor Regis but not nearly so fashionable. I remarked to a friend that Mrs. X., as I shall call her, quite possibly built at Wythe because she was too *nouveau* (or should I say *nouvelle?*) to be received at Angnor. I had no reason to know if that were so; it was purely speculative. To my horror I later overheard my friend telling another, 'Mr. Share said that Mrs. X. tried to build at Angnor but was rebuffed by society there and forced to settle for Wythe.'

"On another occasion, still painful in my memory, I said something quite innocently only to hear it completely turned about. A gentleman and a lady introduced me to their daughter. He was a most handsome man, in a very manly way, with prominent features and a strong chin. His wife was as pretty a woman as he was handsome a man. The daughter unfortunately took after the father, not the mother, and the handsome man did not make a pretty woman. I remarked to my friend that it was a pity the girl resembled her father rather than her mother, whereupon he said to me, 'How can you say that? Why, I think Mr.———to be very good-looking. It is odd you do not think him so.' Which is not at all what I had said. So you see, James, why I am careful not to say anything that might be misconstrued."

"I should find it difficult to watch my tongue so carefully," said James. "It must be a considerable strain."

"In time it becomes a habit," said Benjamin. "Good habits are as readily acquired as bad."

James understood that every career to be successful required the observance of certain rules and strictures, the profession of Welcome Guest being no exception. To begin with, the Welcome Guest must never overstay his Welcome. Benjamin Share had never done so. He invariably left while he was still Welcome.

"Let me hasten to add a remark or two," he said now to James. "Never saying anything unpleasant about someone is very far removed from always saying something flattering. I never do that. I try not to make any remark that might make me disliked. I would never pay a meaningless compliment in the hope of being liked."

"As do some we know," said James meaningfully.

Mr. Share knew very well to whom he alluded but would, of course, not say so, for that would have been to say something unpleasant about James's aunt, his father's maiden sister, who was also spending Christmas at Edge Park.

The Honorable Madge Edge's entire conversation consisted of a long string of compliments. "Prettiest frock ever I saw," she would say to a lady by way of greeting, causing the lady to believe her dress—which she had put on and forgotten—was a more welcome sight than herself and calling attention to the fact that the garment was perforce either a new or worn one. "Such a droll fellow, he has a wonderful sense of humor," Aunt Madge would say of a man who had never in his life made a witty remark but who had a good memory for repeating the tiresome jokes of others. "Oh, you are—or he, she or it is—wonderful," was one of the

Honorable Madge's constant refrains, without any mention of whatever wonderful qualities had produced such a wonderful result. It went without saying that her own possessions and attributes were so much less wonderful that she almost seemed to be asking for pity. Her own new frock was "this old rag, I should have given it to the church bazaar." Her sense of humor was lacking because "I have such a poor memory, I can never remember a droll story." As for being wonderful, she declared she was wonderful only for "getting in people's way, I don't know why my friends put up with me, they are wonderful."

James, who found his aunt to be tiresome almost beyond toleration, had not realized until now that what she was asking, quite desperately, was simply to be liked.

As they were on the way upstairs to bed, the last of the large house party to say their good-nights, Benjamin said to James, "Miss Marietta is now the daughter of the house of Wrox. The elder girl has died."

"Oh!" James exclaimed. He felt a pang of genuine sorrow. Lucy's was the first death among those of his own generation. "How did it happen?" he asked. "She was so full of life—"

"I believe it was Roman fever. She died in Rome and was laid to rest there."

"In *Rome?*" James inquired, incredulous. "But that is odd, is it not? She must have gone to join her mother and sister there after we had left."

"It was very hard on Mrs. Wrox-Hampden," Benjamin said, "because it was within a week, I believe, that her husband was murdered. It was always said of poor Lucy that she should have been a boy."

"I do not agree," said James, "and I knew her better than anyone."

The two men parted, and James went down the hall to his own rooms. Everything had been made ready for the night. The bedcover had been removed, his nightshift laid out, the lamps lighted. His manservant was waiting up for him.

"No need to stay, Henry," James said. "I shall manage very well. Good night."

"Good night, my lord." Henry withdrew and closed the heavy oaken door without making a sound.

James lay awake and thought of Lucy. She had once done a remarkable thing for him. It had been done out of friendship. She had been with him in one of life's great moments, sharing an experience that his fellow undergraduates had sought in dark alleys with women of dubious background. James's introduction to manhood had not been carried out furtively, with shame, in fear of a dreaded infection. It had been done simply, spontaneously, joyfully, naturally. He had learned from it what it was he wanted to do later with the woman he would love and cherish as his wife, and until he should be married to her, he would wait for her. He felt toward Lucy an immense gratitude. Later he was ashamed to realize that he also felt a sense of relief. No one now would ever know what Lucy and he had done on that golden afternoon at the end of summer-time. He need not fear she would tell Marietta.

So his thoughts turned easily from Lucy to Marietta, and he slept with Marietta's smiling face looking on in his dreams, where she came and went as she had in his life. He watched her coming toward him with her characteristic walk, one of her great charms. Marietta did not stroll, or amble, or hang back. She walked as if she were going to something of immense interest and was impatient to arrive at it. She came toward James in his dream, smiled and walked past him and away, going he knew not where.

❧ 25 ❧

THE YOUNG LORD COMES OF AGE

Within the next five years there were more changes in the life of the neighborhood than had occurred in the preceding five hundred. A woolen factory was opened at Wrox, now served regularly by the railway. Rows of cottages for the workers were built facing the common. The proprietors of the public house bought two adjoining houses and offered overnight accommodations for up to twenty travelers. The grocery was joined by a merchant who sold building supplies and by a butcher's shop. The farmers now sold their pigs, sheep and calves to the butcher and bought back meat from him according to their needs. Itinerants such as tinkers and knife grinders, who used to pass through the village once a year, now came oftener, as did mendicants and drifters seeking employment. One of the young doctors, Jenkyn, whose practice in Bunbury consisted of those who were not patients of Dr. Pipkin, moved to Wrox, as did E. Hole, the draper, who went to live in the house formerly occupied by the overseer Spence, which he held on a yearly lease from the Wrox estate while preparing to build his own impressive mansion near the factory. Albert Spence went to jail.

Among the long-established families also there were changes. Augustus Wrox-Hampden removed from Mr. Plumptre's school to Blitchley. Two of the Duke's daughters were married off and never returned to the castle: one went to live in Wales; the other eloped with a groom and was shipped out with him to Canada, where he found employment with the Hudson's Bay Company and prospered. A third, Lady Amelia, was long rumored to be engaged to a wealthy young peer whose seat was in the neighborhood; certainly she had her cap set for him, and who would turn down a duke's daughter, even one as desperately plain and plainly desperate as she?

A dramatic change occurred in the life of young Viscount Edge, who came of age in March of 1839. With his mother James left Edge Park for London right after the New Year, and there he found himself in the highest society that Benjamin Share would have described as the *beau monde*. He was introduced to the Prime Minister and invited to dine at Holland House. He sat through twelve-course dinners in great houses. He spent mornings with the tailor who fashioned him an entire new wardrobe, and in the afternoons he sat for his portrait to Sir George Hayter. He was bidden to Brooks's Club, where the favorable impression he made assured him of an invitation to join. Ahead was his maiden speech to the Lords and his first London season. By the end of it every marriageable young woman in the United Kingdom would have been introduced to young Lord Edge, and he could take his pick or wait for the next year's crop.

James was thoroughly enjoying himself. His every moment was occupied in an interesting manner. The future stretched before him full of promise, the promise of a life of happiness and usefulness. He was being courted not only by the women who were the important hostesses but as well by their husbands, influential men who sought his support on one side or the other in the House. If ever he felt homesick for the countryside of his birth, why, Edge was always there; it was his home and his heritage, at no great distance from anywhere in the world now that the railway had eliminated time and space. One would be able to take luncheon in London and dine the same day at Edge Park.

The young lord's luck held, against all odds, even through the twenty-first birthday ball at Edge, for bad weather might well have spoiled it. Lady Edge had been urged to postpone it until June, but she refused to consider that. Her son had been born on the first day of spring, and she superstitiously regarded the date as portentous. There had once been snow on that date heavy enough to blanket the county under eight inches, but this year the sun shone, the temperature was mild, the March wind blew but did not howl, and James Edge attained his majority.

Every tenant on the estates was at the celebration, every farmer and his wife wearing their Sunday best, every tradesman who supplied the Park, every gardener and all the gentry and nobility of the county. The bishop and his lady (who stayed in the house), the clergy, the family solicitor and doctor, all were in attendance. The Duke was not in residence, but his four unmarried daughters had come to stay at the castle for the occasion, and it was noticed that young Lord Edge, while courteously receiving them all, had paid particular attention to Lady Amelia. There was music and dancing in the saloon and portrait gallery, both alight with thousands of candles that shone on the arrangements of hothouse flowers brought from London. Young ladies and gentlemen danced the quadrille under the chandeliers of the Adam room. Tables of whist were set up for their elders in the library. The honored young man was toasted in champagne. At midnight there was spread a feast prepared by cooks imported from Paris: turtle punch, plovers' eggs, turbot in jelly, prawns, lobster salad, decorated hams and tongues, ornamental pies and Genoese pastries that were towering works of art, surrounded by Swiss meringues and Italian creams.

Mr. Benjamin Share, ceding his accustomed place of precedence as First Guest, busily made sketches of people and pastries as mementos for James. The Hon. Madge Edge declared the party the finest she had ever seen, and in this case she did not exaggerate.

It was not until the next afternoon that James, having slept until two o'clock, remembered he had not seen at the ball Marietta Wrox-Hampden or anyone else from Wrox Hall. Surely, he thought, had they been there he would have noticed them, especially Marietta. When he asked his mother why they had been absent, she admitted it was because they had not been invited. "The family is in mourning," she explained. "It is not yet a year since the squire's death."

"Surely it was up to them to decline!" James exclaimed. He was now twenty-one years of age. He faced his mother angrily. "Not to invite them was worse than discourteous, Mother, it was an insult! How could you have done that?"

Poor Lady Edge. She knew that because of the unfortunate Lucy business, James could never marry any of the Wrox girls, and she had thought that if he did not see them, the mere idea would not have a chance to enter his head. She had made a great mistake, as she now realized, when James ordered his horse to be saddled and brought around that he might ride over to Wrox to apologize for the slight. "I shall tell them the reason you gave, that the omission was not an oversight but a decision deliberately taken," he said. "They must now be thinking they were overlooked, and their feelings must be wounded."

His mother watched James ride off in the direction of Wrox Hall and realized how foolish she had been. Had the Wrox-Hampdens been invited to the ball with all the rest of the county, they could either have come or not, and neither Marietta's presence nor her absence would have been especially remarked. Now it had come to have such importance that James had left her, and a houseful of his guests, to go over and make apologies! He was apologizing for her, his own mother's behavior!

The whole Edge party was invited to dine at the castle this night. Lady Amelia had blushed sheepishly when thanking James's mother for the coming-of-age party and had added words of praise for the son being honored. "You must be very proud of him, your ladyship," Lady Amelia had said, "he is so distinguished." Then she had ducked her head, giggled nervously and followed her sisters out.

Since his father's funeral young Arthur, now squire of Wrox, had devoted all his time and energies to the restoration and management of the demesne. It was a formidable undertaking. He was gone from the Hall all day, returning only to dine and sleep. The results of many years' negligence that kept coming to light were increasingly discouraging. All the farm buildings and fences needed repair; fields needed clearing, flocks replenishing. Farmers in need of money had received a few shillings at the market for lambs or calves that had later fetched pounds, after having been fattened by others in transactions with Spence as go-between. The land marked out for the railway right-of-way had been sold for twenty pounds an acre to a purchaser who had resold it six weeks later to the Great Western Railway for fifty. It had transpired before his father's death that the purchaser and profiteer both had been Spence. Mr. Weston, the attorney, had at first denied the existence of a deed showing the squire to have sold the overseer's house to Mr. Spence, in lieu of money owed to him, but such a document had been turned up in the records of the land agent, and in the opinion of Mr. Weston, the squire's signature thereon might be a forgery. It had been compared with genuine examples of Wrox-Hampden's careless, sprawling, illegible hand, and Mr. Weston determined that he would have to engage an expert from London to testify as to its falsity or genuineness. All this time the young squire was negotiating with Samuel Hole and his father about downland and flocks that were to be a source of supply for the woolen factory. Young Arthur had also to assume all the duties of an overseer until he could afford to hire one.

He had been aware when James Edge's coming-of-age was to take place—not a soul in the shire was unaware of it—but he had not realized that he, his mother and his sister Marietta had not been invited to the ball. All the county had been bidden—even the Smallwoods, whose parish was not the Edges' but merely adjoined one of theirs. Maria could not understand it, for her dear friend Emma was not a mean or vengeful person; in fact, hers was a warm and affectionate character. Moreover, she was in every sense a lady, who would never have behaved in a manner unbecoming such a one. On the day of the ball Maria hoped until the last minute that a message would be brought from Edge Park to say they were expected, but it had not come.

When Arthur got home at the end of the day, he found his mother in bed with a headache and his younger sister Lottie trying to comfort Marietta. Lottie had suggested playing duets upon the pianoforte and had found some music that Augustus had arranged for four hands.

"I'm sorry Mother is not well," said Arthur. "Will she not then be going to Edge?"

"No," said Marietta, who had obviously been crying. "Neither shall you, nor shall I."

"Why, what has happened?"

"Nothing has happened, Arthur, that is the trouble, and nothing is going to happen." Marietta got up from the piano bench and walked across to the door. Before her brother could ask anything more, she left the room.

"Is Marietta also not well?" Arthur asked Lottie.

"She is in low spirits." Closing the music pages, Lottie told him the reason. The Wrox-Hampdens had not any of them been invited to Edge Park to celebrate the heir's coming-of-age.

"But that is unthinkable!" Arthur exclaimed. "What has gone wrong? There must be a mistake. It is surely an oversight."

"Mama does not think it a mistake," said Lottie. "She says it is a deliberate snub."

"But *why?*" Arthur asked, bewildered. "What earthly reason have the Edges to snub us?"

"I do not know," said Lottie. "But I dislike to see Marietta so unhappy."

"I think we should go to the ball," said her brother, "for certainly we must be expected first of anybody in the neighborhood. Their feelings will be hurt if we do not. Because Lucy and Papa have heard their last calls, it is all the more reason why we should make an exception for the Edges and go to congratulate James. He would not understand our staying away."

"Mama will not go," said Lottie, "lacking an invitation. Nor will Marietta."

Arthur gave in. He would have liked to go to the ball, being young and naturally gregarious. It was long since he had had an enjoyable time or danced with any pretty girls. But if he were to go by himself, how could he explain his own unbidden presence and the absence of his mother and sister? He went up to the nursery to say good-night to Letty, dined with Marietta and Lottie and went early to bed with a sheaf of papers relating to the estates.

The young Scottish vet whom the Holes had induced to settle in the neighborhood had announced himself horrified by the local practices in regard to farm animals. Mr. MacTavish was difficult to understand—he did not speak proper English—but his opinions came out loudly and clearly. To Mr. MacTavish each creature was an individual, with personal health problems and medical needs. In his view a good, healthy cow was worth three of Nettle's bairns who were dependent on its milk. The wool-producing sheep he saw as valuable employees of the Holes. The ways of the local shearers were an abomination, nothing less than cruelty to animals, and those of them who would not learn his better ways would be out of employment come shearing time. It was torture for a sheep to give up its wool to these inept wielders of the clippers. Being paid by the number of ewes shorn, they worked at cruel speed, injuring the skin with nicks and cuts, getting skin and blood mixed in with the wool, which they ripped and cut unevenly, making it good for no better use than to make Army blankets. Mr. MacTavish was not only in favor of raising healthy sheep but also for keeping them happy, and those sheared under his supervision produced for the Hole looms clean wool from unblemished skins. It was with Mr. MacTavish and a shearer that Arthur and Samuel Hole had an early appointment on the morrow, so it was as well to go early to bed tonight and leave the dancing to young men with no responsibilities.

Next day Arthur was gone after an early breakfast and was again away all day. Maria kept to her bed except for a brief visit to the nursery, where she enjoyed petting her baby while Norah saw to the changing of nappies and hushing of cries. Letty never gave Norah one moment's trouble, and the little nursemaid exhibited incoming teeth and interpreted unintelligible sounds for the benefit of the doting mother. Letty had been sent to her, Maria decided, to make up for the loss of Henrietta, and she found it in her heart to forgive her late husband for the manner of Letty's conception. She even wished that he, who had adored Henrietta, could have been spared to see Henrietta's restoration taking place in the form of this beautiful child.

In the late afternoon, when James Edge came riding up to the Hall, he found no one to receive him except Marietta and Miss Theodora Smallwood, who had walked from the vicarage in order to hear all about the ball. The Smallwoods had regretted their invitation to attend, Mrs. Smallwood saying they had no means of getting to and from Edge at night, and even had they had such means, she and her daughter possessed no suitable ball gowns. Miss Theodora knew the real reason was her own disfigurement, which made it painful for her to enter a room full of strangers, and she knew her mother, of all people in the countryside, would have enjoyed herself there the most. So her poor face became yet more painful to her than had it spoiled only her own pleasure.

She could scarcely credit her ears when Marietta said that no one from the Hall had attended the party, nor believe her eyes when Lord Edge was announced and was shown into her presence.

James and Marietta had not met since they had said good-bye in Rome so long ago. And just as they had been overset with joy to see in the papal city a familiar face from home, so now each was equally joyful to see the face familiar from those happy days abroad. James thought he had forgotten just how pretty Marietta was and how exactly the dark amber shade of her hair matched her eyes. Marietta thought, He is now a man! How handsome he is! She remembered how she had stared to her heart's content at that patrician profile while Mr. Share was drawing it. Now she dropped her gaze and asked James pray to be seated.

James did not wish to mention in front of Miss Theodora the reason for his call. He knew he had not seen her at the ball—he would, alas, have remembered it had he done so—but he had no way of knowing that an invitation had been issued and declined, so he could not bring up in her presence the subject of balls or invitations thereto. The three sat making uninteresting talk about the weather, which had been singularly uninteresting in itself of late, until the vicar's daughter rose and declared she must take her leave. She had hesitated because she thought it might be her duty to remain as chaperone, but she decided that if her presence in that capacity were needed, Marietta would urge her to remain. Marietta making no such request, Miss Theodora left the two young people alone.

Immediately James explained why no invitation to his party had been received at Wrox. "It was wrong of my mother," he said. "She meant it kindly, I feel sure, she acted out of consideration for your feelings as being so recently bereaved, but I believe it to have been wrong of her. It should have been for you and your mother and brother to decide if one or all of you should come to wish me well."

"I *did* so much wish to go!" Marietta assured him. "No one wishes you well more than I." She blushed and lowered her eyes, hoping she had not spoken too boldly. "But perhaps it would not have been seemly, since we are still in mourning for my father and sister, and as we were not invited, we were not offered a temptation we ought perhaps to have resisted."

"All the same," said James, "you should have had the offer, to resist or not, as you thought best. I should have enjoyed it myself much more had you been there." He had not noticed her absence from the ball until this very hour, but he was certain that what he had just said was true. Had he seen Marietta walk into his house last night, his heart would have jumped for joy, as it had just now done when he had walked into hers.

He had so much to tell her. "I thought Miss Smallwood would never leave," he said, crossing the carpet to take a seat near Marietta. "Benjamin Share sends you his affectionate greetings."

"Dear Signor Partay," said Marietta. "How is he?"

James laughed and settled back in his chair comfortably, tapping his whip against a boot. "As always, he is *sui generis*. Do you know, I believe him to be the only example in the world of an absolutely happy man! He has no family responsibilities—nor any other, except to himself. He has never done anything he did not choose to do, nor has he gone to any place where he did not want to go. He pays his passage in the world in a coin of which he has an endless supply; however much he spends, it is never diminished."

"Perhaps he is happy because, unlike most of us, he sees no shortcomings in himself," said Marietta. "He even admired his dreadful likeness of you he made that day in Rome. Or I should call it an *un*likeness, should I not?"

"You see?" said James delightedly. "Signor Partay is perfectly happy not knowing that he has never captured a facial likeness; no one has ever told him. So he makes admirable likenesses of coats and coat buttons, as he does of scenery and ruins. Should he ever perceive the difference, I think it would ruin his happiness, which would be a great pity."

"Indeed, it would," Marietta agreed. "He is a self-made man. He should be knighted for his creation of himself. And if he could not believe himself to be the ever-welcome guest, he would cease to be so."

"What a loss that would be to society," James said. "Most of us, don't you know, are dull dogs."

"Not you, surely," said Marietta. "It cannot have been dull to stay in London and be received at court and hear the opera."

This was the opening James needed to recount the story of his sojourn in the capital, of the statesmen he had met, of the fitting for the bottle green velvet coat he wore last night ("it was most tedious"), of sitting to Sit George Hayter, who had only recently painted a three-quarter-length portrait of Lord Melbourne, standing. He, James, had been worth only the time to make a head and shoulders, seated. "Its most prominent feature is the high, stiff collar and enormous cravat. Mr. Share would have done it as well as Sir George."

"But the face?" Marietta asked. "Is it a good likeness?" The inquiry gave her an excuse to stare at the subject, as if appraisingly.

"It is well enough," said James modestly. "A necessary part of turning twenty-one is sitting to an artist. It is a tedious business. My father was done by Raeburn. The first Edge portrait was by Sir Peter Lely. So I am to hang with them and shall not have to bother with that anymore."

"Oh, you shall have to pose again when you are in your prime as Governor-General of India or Ambassador to Siam. By then you will be accustomed to various kinds of tedium."

"I shall have to get used to sitting still in the House, certainly, but not to a painter of portraits. We shall be sitting for likenesses to a machine." James went on to describe how, when in Paris the year before in company with Mr. Share, he had seen a demonstration of the invention of M. Louis Daguerre, a process that developed images on a metal plate. "One will not be required to sit still as long for the machines as for Sir George. It is a miraculous discovery."

Marietta, not at all interested in the method by which this miracle was worked, was much impressed by the miracle itself. "An inanimate object making the likeness of a person?" she inquired, unbelieving. "Well, I never could imagine such a thing! A machine that could do that could also read and write, I suppose, and create a true 'speaking likeness.' You will need no little plate on your picture frame saying 'James Almeric, seventh Viscount Edge.' The picture will speak: 'I am the seventh Viscount Edge on my twenty-first birthday.' This invention will surely put the Hayters and Raeburns out of work."

James laughed. "You are as clever an inventor as M. Daguerre himself."

"Oh, no, not I. I could never invent a talking portrait."

"Then you are a great prophetess, like Mother Shipton, for someone will invent it. Did she not say, three hundred years ago, 'Carriages without horses shall go,/ And accidents fill the world with woe'? And now look at the railway carriage that brought me from London!"

"What else did she prophesy?"

"Some things that came true. Many that did not. She said, 'Around the world thoughts shall fly/ In the twinkling of an eye.' That, of course, is impossible of proof, although Mr. Share told of a remarkable coincidence when a dying man in the Indian civil service spoke to his wife in England telling her he was about to depart this life, and she woke their children to pray for him. So he recovered."

"Perhaps he would have done so anyway."

"That is probable, I should think. Still, it cannot be proven. Mother Shipton also prophesied that men would walk, ride and talk underwater and in the air. And that iron shall float in the water. And other unlikely happenings. Mother Marietta Wrox-Hampden prophesies that portraits made by machine will move their lips and talk."

"If I am to be a Mother Shipton, I must prophesy in a verse," said Marietta. "Did she not always speak in rhyme?"

"To be sure," said James. "She was as good a poetess as prophetess. Let me see—what rhymes with 'picture' or 'wall'?"

"Can one have a conversation with the picture? Does it answer questions? Or does it merely state who it is and how old?"

"That is for you to prophesy."

"Perhaps it speaks to the other portraits: 'I am your great-great-great-grandfather by Sir Peter Lely.' "

"That is silly," said James.

"You have made my rhyme for me right there."

The happy laughter of their delight in each other was filling the room when Lottie came in to join them. She had the baby Violet by the hand. "See who has come to call," she said. She set the baby down upon the carpet. "It saves a step," she explained. "It is useless to put her in a chair, she will climb down immediately. But if I leave her on the floor to begin with, she will insist upon climbing up on the chair. See? I told you so! I believe she understands everything I say. Don't you, precious?"

The baby made a comment of some sort that Lottie was certain was addressed to her and contained her name. She was glad to see her older sister looking so happy; the miserable business about the ball must have been straightened out. Marietta was positively aglow, she had never looked prettier.

When James said he must reluctantly return home, Marietta asked if he would not stay to dine. "You need not mind about changing; we are only the family here now."

"How I wish I could!" said James. "But my mother expects me at home. We have a houseful of guests come for the ball. As a matter of fact, I believe we are expected for dinner at the castle. I really must go now."

After he had taken his leave, Marietta ran to the window to see him mount at the horse block and ride away. His chestnut colt was a beautiful animal and James a born horseman. He looked so handsome in the saddle, Marietta thought, Sir George Hayter should have painted him astride. She watched him walk his mount to the edge of the park, start him at a trot that moved on to a canter and broke into a gallop as they disappeared in the direction of home and all those ducal daughters who were expecting him.

The happiness that Marietta had been wearing like a shining garment fell away like one discarded. She looked woebegone.

"Don't cry," said Lottie. "He will come back. I know he will."

Mr. Share was, of course, delighted to be at last dining at the castle and took extra pains with his appearance while he dressed. He gave considerable thought as to how he should refer to the occasion in future conversation and correspondence. It was not as if His Grace himself were to be present, so he could not say he had dined with the Duke. "When I dined at the castle" sounded too much as if it were a one-time occasion and he not a guest staying in the house. "When I dine at the castle" implied doing so on a regular basis and would certainly be found out by any person who did frequently sit at the ducal table and drink to the King over the Water. He decided in the end that he would say either "The first time I dined at the castle"—for that was strictly true—or "The last time I dined there," which was equally true. Neither locution could possibly be taken to mean "the only time," which was just as true but did not have the same satisfactory ring to it.

If James Edge were to marry the Lady Amelia or one of her sisters, then Benjamin Share would assuredly even become an habitué of the castle and be able to say he dined there often *with* the Duke.

❧ 26 ❧

MARIETTA HAS A SUITOR

Excerpt: Letter to Maria Wrox-Hampden
at Wrox from Georgiana Hampden at Stoke-sub-Ham

My dearest sister,

Baby is two years old today, so I know you are thinking of him and wish to hear how he is getting on, for indeed he is Getting On, dear little soul that he is. He has all his milk teeth now and walks around a great deal, holding on to his Nurse or on to various objects of furniture. He has taken to pulling things off tables, so Esther cannot allow him in the drawing room or in the dining room, but she and Cuthbert faithfully visit him daily or oftener in his Nursery to see how he is getting on. Cuthbert often reads Baby to sleep, and although Baby does not yet understand the Scriptures, he evidently is soothed by the sound of his uncle's voice. When he grows up, he is going to look like Cuthbert and my dearest Charles, for he has the Hampden coloring and the head that is large, perhaps a bit too large for his body, but that is better than the other way around, and the Hampden head has always been considered to be out of the ordinary. I regret to say he has shown a tendency to disobedience, and only yesterday refused positively to eat his supper, but Esther has devised a way to force him to take nourishment by holding his nose with one hand and putting food down his throat with the other, for all the world as if he were a little bird! Of course he is too young to realize she is doing him a kindness for his own good, so he starts to cry the minute she comes into his nursery, not caring that her feelings may be hurt. But Esther is very good about it and says he is too young to know what is for his own good, and we must not spoil him. . . .

When Maria showed the letter to Arthur, he surprised her by becoming upset. Arthur had taken on responsibility for her and for all his younger sisters and brothers. He made his mother account for every penny she asked for, and she had had to lie about what had become of a sum she had recently sent to the convent of the Villa Nante in Rome. Now he declared she had made a mistake in allowing Aunt Georgie to adopt little Edward. "It is no place for a child," he said, remembering his own visits to the Cuthbert Hampdens. "It is sickening the way in which she refers to him as 'Baby.' He is two years old."

"Georgie needs him," said Maria, "and they are company for Cuthbert and Esther."

"That pair are not fit company for a child," said Arthur. "Uncle Cuthbert is a pompous bore, and boredom can slowly kill a boy's spirit as readily as a slow poison could his body. Uncle Cuthbert is merely a pompous bore, as I said, but Aunt Esther is cruel. I believe she takes pleasure in force-feeding an infant and calling it for his own good. If Aunt Georgie were a fit mother, she would not allow it."

"Oh, Georgie cannot possibly stand up to Esther," said Maria, "any more than can anyone else."

"I do not like it," Arthur repeated. "It does not appear they love Edward as we love Letty. It is well known that an infant must be loved in order to develop properly."

"Of course they love him!" Maria exclaimed. "Why else should they have him? All Georgie's love is lavished upon him, for there is no one else with whom he must share it. In that he is fortunate. I think I know better than you," she added, "what is best for Edward."

Arthur argued no more. He thought he would like to go and see for himself how Edward was Getting On, as Aunt Georgie put it, but he was far too busy to leave Wrox and had far too many responsibilities. Mr. Weston was preparing a lawsuit against Spence, and midsummer was no time for a landowner to absent himself from the land now coming into full productivity. His mother and sisters needed him, as did all the dependents who worked for a living on the land and at the Hall.

It happened that on the very morning of the twins' second birthday the stolen chalice and paten were restored to Wrox church. At dawn a gamekeeper crossing a field next to the railway track, who thought himself the only human creature astir at that hour, caught sight of movement under a beech tree at the far side of the field. Thinking it was a large animal up to some unknown purpose, the gamekeeper ran over to see what it was doing and found, to his astonishment, that it was a Gypsy man. He was digging up from under the tree's roots Mr. Smallwood's lost communion vessels! The gamekeeper had a gun, so it was easy work to march the man across the common to P. C. Frakes's house, rouse the policeman and turn in the thief.

The year before, with the attention of the whole village focused on the squire's funeral service in the churchyard, the Gypsies had entered the unlocked church unobserved, made off with the silver and buried it nearby. No sacred vessels had been found in their possession—as they in fact had not been—and they had gone their way rejoicing, with song and laughter, a lot of the latter no doubt up their sleeves. They had returned this year, as was their custom, to retrieve the loot from the year before, and for the first time in generations had been caught in the act.

What could Constable Frakes do? Nothing whatsoever beyond ordering the Romanies to move on immediately, as they did, cursing the gamekeeper and all his ancestors and descendants. The communion vessels were returned to the church, and the vicar advised, unnecessarily, to keep them locked up. Mr. Smallwood summoned his wife, daughter, cook, housemaid and gardener and conducted a short service consisting of prayers of thanks for the safe return, with additional prayers beseeching the thieves to repent of their misdoings, go and sin no more. They had already gone.

All summer Samuel Hole had worked as hard as Arthur, and of necessity he had been much away from the county. The woolen factory now under construction would require the services of skilled artisans—carders, spinners, dyers, weavers—who could train local workers. Samuel sought master craftsmen throughout the Midlands. He had even traveled to Germany on the track of a rumor that artificial dyes were being introduced there, but these had proven unsatisfactory, and he contracted to obtain indigo from the West Indian island of St. Kitts, cochineal from Central America, ocher from France and other products to make dyes from Egypt and the Mediterranean. Meanwhile, Hole Father was supervising construction of his new house, taking advantage of the presence on the spot of contractors and workmen. It was to be a "gentleman's residence," built from the plans of an architect in three stories, containing parlors on either side of a wide hall, both front and back staircases, and a wing large enough to accommodate a staff. Mrs. Cluster still maintained her workrooms at Bunbury and employed three seamstresses, but she foresaw a move to Wrox in the near future, when her customers should find it easier to travel by rail than by coach.

Until the factory should be running profitably, young Hole was in no position to engage himself to be married. But he saw Marietta going about in society with the end of mourning and other young gentlemen beginning to pay her court. He had heard that the viscount, briefly at Edge between visits to the Continent and sojourns in London, had called several times at Wrox, and so Hole determined to declare himself. After seeing Arthur Wrox-Hampden one morning on a matter of business, he asked to speak to him in private and brought up the subject close to his heart.

"I must tell you my sister has no fortune," said Arthur. "You cannot count on that."

"I do not expect it," said Samuel. He did sincerely admire Miss Marietta Wrox-Hampden, but even had he not, marriage to her would have advanced him in a way worth more than money.

"I shall speak to my mother," said Arthur, "and let you know."

The Wrox family had been landed gentry for four hundred years. Ownership of the property could be traced back to the Domesday Book. There were no peers in the ancestral tree, but there were an admiral or two, a lord chief justice, several high sheriffs of the county, a knight and the daughter of a baronet. The Hampdens on their side could be found to include a seventeenth-century archbishop, by way of barristers, fellows of Oxford colleges, men of the cloth and, in the person of Georgiana Hampden, an earl's granddaughter. Cousin Julius Cheycester was an Elder Brother of Trinity, currently Harbormaster of Singapore. Sir George Hatche, Bart., in dire want of money, had sold Hatche Castle to Cousin Paul Bellwood, a rich Hampden by marriage, who could afford to keep it up and who thus acquired an impressive address. The two families were not of the aristocracy but were certainly wellborn and well connected.

"I shall not pretend the draper's son is a suitable husband for Marietta," Arthur's mother said when he told her of his conversation with Samuel. "He is not out of the top drawer. On the other hand, he is at least respectable and looks to being eventually well off. We know we cannot provide any portion for Marietta, unless we are to sell another one of the farms. I suppose he will expect a marriage settlement?"

"I have told him he cannot expect it. However, were we in a position to offer it, I should not be inclined to do so. It seems to me as if the offer of a settlement were like offering a bribe, paying a man to marry one's daughter and take her off his hands. As if without a dowry a woman were of no value to him. It is to treat a young woman as if she were a chattel."

"To the contrary," said Maria, "were *he* to offer *us* money for the girl, and we to sell her, that would be to treat her as a chattel."

"It would at least be to set a value upon her, Mother. Now Hole is all very well, I daresay; he is not a fortune hunter. But Marietta is an exceptional young woman; the man who marries her will be lucky indeed. She does not need a portion in order to make a suitable marriage. I believe James Edge has taken a fancy to her."

"No, no—that is not possible!"

"Why not? A portion to him would be of no importance."

"He is to marry one of the Duke's daughters," said Maria positively, intending to close the door on the subject. "And if young Hole is serious and is of good character—why, I suppose Marietta could do worse."

Marietta was sent for and told that Samuel Hole had asked for her hand. She sat facing her mother and the brother who was now head of the family. "I am not surprised," said she.

"Then you have been encouraging him," said Maria.

"No, Mama, I have never done that."

"Well, daughter, he has been sufficiently encouraged by some means to have spoken to your brother."

Marietta turned to Arthur. "And what did you tell him?"

"I shall make no objection. If you wish to marry him, you may."

"Is that what you wish?" asked her mother.

Marietta looked from brother to parent. They appeared neither to encourage nor to discourage a decision one way or the other. They had not asked if she loved Samuel Hole.

"He is sincerely attached to you," Maria said, "for Arthur has told him he cannot expect a settlement."

There was a silence. The first fire of autumn glowed in the grate, each coal making its small contribution to the comfort of the room and to the swelling of Aunt Augusta Pounceby's coffers. It was one of those days when the temperature was warmer outdoors in the sun than inside under the high ceilings of the Hall.

"Well?" said Arthur. "Shall I tell him he may call?"

Marietta rose and went to the long window to look out on the park. The early-autumn afternoon scene was one of peaceful beauty. Norah had baby Violet out for a pony ride. Skittles was walking in front of the big basket on runners, pulling it across the smooth turf while the nurse-maid and Luke, the stableboy, held his head and Letty the reins. The infant was yelling with delight, her little head thrown back. Her bonnet had fallen off, and the sun was shining on bright copper curls.

"Well, child?" Maria asked. "Will you have him?"

Marietta turned back to the room. She lifted her head proudly.

"I would rather never marry at all," she said with deliberation.

"Come," said her mother, "he may not be a lord, but he is not to be despised."

"What shall I tell him?" asked Arthur, taken aback. "I cannot tell him you said that."

"Tell him I think he should have spoken to me on the matter before he brought it up with my brother. We are not living in the Middle Ages."

Then she left her mother and brother to go up to her own room. She lay down on the bed, without even removing her shoes, and stared long at the canopy overhead. She would never be married, she vowed, if it were not to James.

Maria Wrox-Hampden appeared to have recovered from the depressed condition—melancholia, as Dr. Pipkin termed it—from which she had suffered since the return from Rome. She had begun to take pride in her appearance (she was a strikingly handsome woman), and she had taken up her old habit of fine needlework while receiving guests or callers, wearing the little gold thimble that had been her grandmother's, the rapid movements of her fingers among the brightly colored threads drawing attention to their beauty; they were slender and delicate, with shell-like nails. Her dark hair was now streaked with white wings on either side of the brow in a manner that accentuated her fine eyes.

Wrox Hall was getting a new roof and up-to-date plumbing. There was no more hunting across the fields, leaving the foxes to multiply undisturbed in their coverts and stalk those creatures the gamekeepers used to protect. Of the horses, the hunters and the squire's mare had been sold. Marietta was supervising the renovation of the Hall's interior as Arthur was of its surroundings. Visitors marked the improvements, as did those guests who once more filled its rooms for long stays.

Mrs. Bellwood and Mrs. Warnfield came for a fortnight. Cousin Julius

Cheycester, on home leave from Singapore, stayed with his wife and two daughters for a week. At Christmas Arthur had two of his Oxford classmates, who escorted Marietta to the assemblies and played charades and dumb crambo in the common room with Augustus and Lottie. Augustus's voice was undergoing changes in register and volume that caused people to turn and stare when he joined in the singing of the Christmas hymns and carols. Happy at Blitchley, he was growing apace and looked to be every inch a Hampden. His hair was the color of carrots, so that he was known in school as Rufus.

When Robert Fox left Rome for Foxbridge Abbey in the early spring, he stopped off at Wrox, to Maria's great pleasure. The longer Robert stayed unmarried, the higher rose her hopes that he would "do something handsome" for his half brothers and sisters. He was invited everywhere in the county and dined at Edge Park, where Lady Edge told him James was settling in beautifully in his new life, his maiden speech had been well received, he was a rising star in the party of the PM.

"He is so young," Cousin Bessie Bellwood said of James to Maria. "His head will be turned, he will be ruined. So much money and so high a position at so young an age! He will be quite spoiled; it will be the ruination of him."

"I should think the opposite," said Maria. "The responsibilities and duties will be the making of him."

"What a catch!" Mrs. Bellwood exclaimed.

"It is said he is caught. One of the Duke's daughters, the Lady Amelia, has been seen riding with him in London."

Robert Fox confirmed this. He had seen them together; at any rate he had seen Edge with one of the Duke's daughters, it made no difference. He remembered how in Rome two years before the young viscount had been seen about with Marietta, but there had been no rumors of or speculations about a possible match in that quarter. Robert was one of the very few who knew what had happened in Rome, and he kept his mouth shut for obvious reasons. He did interfere in the affairs of his Wrox relations to give some advice to his half brother Arthur.

"It is apparent," said he, "that Wrox is by way of becoming a factory town and a marketing center. Do not, for Heaven's sake, sell any properties in the village or near the common. They can only increase in value and bring ever higher rents."

This advice was the opposite of that offered by Uncle Cuthbert Hampden, who came with Aunt Esther at the beginning of Lent, prepared to stay during the penitential season and return to his parochial duties in time to celebrate Easter. On ecclesiastical matters, about which he might be supposed to be an authority, his opinions were delivered with hypocritical disclaimers to omniscience; on matters pertaining to practical business, about which his ignorance was abysmal, he invariably spoke with unqualified authority. "As I feared," he declared, "the railway is the ruination of the place; it is no longer the quiet little corner of God's good earth that its Maker intended it should be. Get rid of any property you may still have in or near the village, my boy, for it is well on the way to being ruined."

The archdeacon and his wife pointedly abstained from eating certain foods of which they were fond, emphasizing their self-sacrifice by watching in disapproval as others ate their customary fare. Uncle Cuthbert instigated regular morning prayers at which the servants were required to be in attendance. Forbidding any dancing in his sight or the sound of any music in his hearing, he locked the pianoforte and ordered Miss Theodora Smallwood to stay away from the Hall until after Good Friday.

This last was the move that was his great mistake. Arthur and Marietta had not always attended the morning prayers. They had controlled laughter at the dinner table when they had noticed the reverential expression, an almost spiritual longing, on their uncle's face as he ostentatiously refused a sherry cream trifle. They had watched the locking of the pianoforte with shrugs; Uncle Cuthbert was denying himself the pleasure of listening to Marietta play, just as he was depriving himself of the pleasures of the table. But when he forbade Miss Theodora to give the lessons that were her livelihood, they protested.

"It is my belief we must forsake secular pleasures in this season," said the archdeacon.

"The greatest of music was written for the Church," Arthur pointed out. "Bach and Handel—"

"And there are Lenten hymns, Uncle Cuthbert," said Marietta. " 'Awake My Soul' and 'I Am a Soldier of the Cross.' "

"There is roast beef in the larder, but it may not be eaten on Friday," the archdeacon said. "Only on Sundays. Sundays are not counted among the forty days and forty nights; there are forty of each without the Sundays. In my opinion, I suppose Miss Theodora can give her music lessons on Sundays; there is no theological reason why she should not."

"The reason she should not is that she plays for the hymns in church on Sundays; she does not teach. Teaching music is her profession, and she does not work at it on Sundays, nor do we, her pupils, have lessons on that day."

Aunt Esther backed her husband; they invariably acted as one—which one it was impossible to tell, so like-minded were they. "Maria," said Aunt Esther to her sister-in-law, "you cannot allow your children to speak so impertinently to their uncle."

"They are of age," Maria replied mildly, without looking up from her work. "I can no longer tell Arthur how to behave."

"Then you should have taught him better when you could," said Aunt Esther.

"Nor can *you* tell *me* how to behave," Maria said. She lifted her eyes and confronted her in-laws. "Theodora Smallwood is to continue coming here twice weekly to give music lessons, whether the church calendar says it be Advent or Epiphany or Lent. Cuthbert may absent himself from the house on those days if he wishes not to hear the sound." She slipped off her thimble, gathered up her work and placed it on the sofa next to where she had been sitting. As she rose to leave the room, she said, "Arthur is now the master in this house, and you—Cuthbert and Esther—are his guests."

The archdeacon and his wife were perforce silenced. Later, in their room, Cuthbert said to her, "Hetty, it was a sad day in this house when my brother died."

"Maria could not wait to take it over," said Hetty, the unlikely bearer of this pet form of her Christian name. "I do not believe it was the hermit's ghost that killed Arthur; I believe it was Maria. She wore him down."

"I would be inclined to agree with you were it not that she was in Rome when he was called above, and had been for some time before that."

"Oh, yes, there can be no proof one way or another. Any more than a disembodied spirit can be hauled into court and accused of murder." Esther, who was making ready for bed, paused in the arranging of the thin gray hair that she was plaiting from her nape down into a rattail. "Cuthbert, I have been thinking."

"What is it, my dear?"

"If one finds oneself during Lent in a house where it is not strictly observed, is one obliged to observe it strictly?"

"I shall give that thought," said the archdeacon, and went to bed with Lent-connected thoughts, like roast beef and sherry trifle, running through his head.

Aunt Esther climbed in beside him and lay in her customary posture, flat on her back with bony arms crossed on her chest outside the covers, legs together, feet pointed straight up. Marietta, who had once seen her aunt lying so when in bed with a cold, had remarked to Lottie that Mrs. En-wee Who looked like a recumbent figure on the top of a Gothic tomb. "More like one inside it, I should think," Lottie had said.

Since Arthur Wrox-Hampden, the head of the house, did not regularly attend the morning prayers, the servants saw no reason why they should be obliged to do so, and gradually the archdeacon's congregation dwindled to include only his wife, Nurse and Mrs. Tole, who came to pray for her husband's restoration to sanity from a series of dreadful nightmares in which he imagined the rats from the stables below were invading their apartments. So the prayers were discontinued, nobody missed them, and on Maundy Thursday the Cuthbert Hampdens left for Stoke-sub-Ham in order to be there for the joyous Easter celebration.

Arthur said to his mother, "We cannot allow those people to be in charge of Edward's upbringing."

"It is Georgie who is his mother," Maria said. "She is not at all the same as they; she is of a very sweet and gentle nature."

"Which means she would not dare stand up to them, as we did."

"Cuthbert is an archdeacon, Arthur, and Esther is his helpmeet in every way. They do what they conceive to be their duty. They do not intend to be unkind."

"I think they do intend it," said Arthur. "But what difference does it make what their intention is? They are unkind."

❧ 27 ❧

THE GYPSIES STEAL SOMETHING PRECIOUS

O ne day in mid-June Miss Theodora Smallwood arrived at the Hall to give a music lesson out of breath and a full quarter of an hour early. She had tidings that could not wait. "The Gypsies are back on the common," she announced, "so be sure you keep everything of value under lock and key. And tell the farmers to watch for poaching."

"I am sure Arthur knows," said Marietta. "But thank you for hastening to tell us."

"Oh, it is not that." The music teacher waved aside consideration of Gypsy thieveries. She sat down nowhere near the pianoforte, as if she had not come for the purpose of playing upon it. "You will never guess the news I bring. All the county is talking of it."

"The Queen is expecting a child," Marietta guessed.

"Oh, is that so?" said Miss Theodora. "Well, I'm sure I wish Her Majesty a safe delivery. My news is of someone not quite so highly placed—although very nearly. You will never guess what happened at the castle! The Duke's second daughter, the Lady Eleanor Stuart, has eloped!"

Marietta felt color rush to her face. The green-eyed monster nudged her. She and Lottie, who was also to have her lesson this morning, had never set eyes on any of the Duke's daughters, but they were as sure of their existence as of that of the angels in Heaven. "Are you sure it was Lady Eleanor?"

"I believe so. It was the second. I think the Lady Anne is the eldest. One would have thought the eldest would be the first to wed, but then the whole thing was done out of order."

If the bridegroom were James, Marietta told herself, there would have been no need to elope, yet still she sighed in relief when Miss Theodora said, "She ran away with one of the grooms!"

"The Duke must be furious," said Marietta. "Will he disown her?"

"I think it romantic," Lottie said. "They must be in love."

"My father says the Duke is not as angry as you might think. My father is a great friend of the Duke's chaplain, who told my father that the Duke merely gave Lady Eleanor a lump sum to pay for their passage to Canada and told them not to come back. She has forfeited her inheritance, which is a great saving to the Duke. My father says that the longer His Grace's daughters remain unmarried, the less they will cost him in the long run. He would have to settle a very large sum on a daughter who married a man of rank, but so long as she remains unmarried, she is of no expense to him beyond what it costs to support her. No, the Duke is not too much disappointed. I imagine the person most disappointed is the groom."

"Is she pretty, the Lady Eleanor?" asked Lottie.

"The chaplain told my father that none of the ladies is a beauty. Which is odd, as they were born of three different mothers, who had two apiece before dying. One would think at least one of three would have produced a beauty. My mother is sorry for them."

Marietta could not imagine why the vicar's wife, mother of poor disfigured Miss Theodora, should feel sorry for young women who were merely plain, who were daughters of a duke and who rode and danced and flirted with James Edge. "I cannot see they are to be pitied," she said.

"They all know they were born only because a son was hoped for," Miss Theodora explained. "That is why my mother feels pity for them. A cat can look at a king, and a clergyman's wife may pity a highborn lady. I," she added, preparing to start the lesson, "was and am very much wanted by my dear parents. No one need feel sorry for *me*."

It was that evening that Nettle and his eldest boy discovered the body of the old squire's mastiff. Drawn to the bank of Sheerwater by the swarms of buzzing flies, they found the bloated corpse, crawling with maggots, in the exact spot where it had kept vigil beside its dead master. Not knowing what else to do, Nettle and his boy between them got the animal's remains into a rowboat and took it to the deepest part of the pond, where they threw it overboard along with the maggots. The flies went elsewhere. Nettle walked up to the Hall and told Luke, the stable-boy, to tell Master Arthur what had happened. Arthur in turn told his womenfolk that Caesar had died and been disposed of. They all expressed no regret. It was as if their period of mourning were indeed over for good; the last, true mourner was gone.

On the third anniversary of the Queen's accession, third birthday of the twins, Georgiana Hampden sat down to write her annual letter to her precious Baby's natural mother, describing his progress and accomplishments. She regarded this as an act of generosity, assuring her sister-in-law that the right decision had been made in giving away her son to be brought up in a Christian household that would otherwise have been childless. The letter read in part:

> My dearest boy is regrettably still subject to fits of violence, altho' not of as long duration. After his dinner had been put before him yesterday, on being told to thank God for his good dinner, he would not do it. Esther would not let him get out of his chair until he had done so, which enraged him. I tried to bring him to obedience, but he resisted all efforts and screamed as loud as he could. At last Cuthbert was obliged to administer a spanking, and by this means extracting from him the thanks for his good dinner, which had remained uneaten. He has promised to be good henceforth, so now all is smiles and he as merry as ever, dear little soul that he is.

Maria Wrox-Hampden never read Georgie's effusion. The birthday was a beautiful June day that lay over the whole country like a blessing. In the early afternoon Maria was sitting in her room by an open window reading a new story, *The Paris Sketch Book*, by Mr. Titmarsh. It had been lent to her by Major Rollins, who had said it was of interest because Titmarsh was rumored to be the pseudonym of a well-known popular author. Major Rollins, who had lost his money in Maule's bank and now lived on a small pension, was himself the subject of a rumor: that he was courting the widow Wrox-Hampden.

Maria had embroidered with yellow daisies a little blue poplin jacket for Violet's birthday present; it was to be given to the child later, with the specially baked cake that would have three candles stuck in its icing. She neither saw nor heard anything of what happened that afternoon on the other side of the house.

Luke had harnessed Skittles to Letty's basket, which the little girl had nearly outgrown, that she might have one last outing in it. He and the nursemaid, Norah, had agreed that Miss Letty was now old enough to ride the pony's back, if both of them walked alongside. Letty loved the pony, and her way of saying "Skittles" made everyone laugh, it sounded something like "squirrels." "Oh, squirrels?" Lottie would say, teasing her. "No, *squiwwels*," Letty would reply, exasperated, "I said *squiwwels*."

Luke was watching from astride the paddock fence when he saw Norah stop the pony at the lane, preparatory to turning him and the basket around and heading back for the stable. Luke jumped down from the fence to go ahead of them and was walking away with his back turned when he heard the screams.

As Norah told it later, in a state of hysteria, it was a wasp, a big nasty black and yellow thing, they must have brushed against it in the shrubbery, something had aroused it, it had headed for the baby girl's unprotected little head, Norah had brushed it away, it had stung her in the hand, it had moved on to the pony's rump, it must have stung the pony, Skittles had simply kicked wildly and taken off, galloping down the lane out of sight, dragging the basket with Letty in it, after knocking Norah down on the ground.

Luke told how he had heard Norah's screams, had turned to see Skittles taking off with Letty in the basket, how he had gone to help Norah and together they had set off after Skittles and the baby, now out of sight around a bend in the lane. It must have been a half mile or more before he came on the pony stopped by a gate. The basket had been overturned. It was empty. Miss Letty was gone. Luke and Norah had run up and down along the hedgerows and looked into the fields, calling Letty's name. She was nowhere to be seen. She had simply vanished. Two people they encountered and asked had not seen her. One was a carter who was bringing home a cart horse; the other was a stranger, a lad who looked to be a vagrant, a Gypsy even. He must have been poaching, for he had a hare by him that must have been bagged. He was of no help because he could barely understand them, and when they did succeed in asking if he had seen a little girl, he had pointed them toward a spinney some distance off, and when they reached it, they had searched and called out, and it was in vain. Letty had simply vanished.

So it was that nearly an hour passed from the time the wasp stung until the effect of its attack was reported back at the Hall. Of course, all hands were dispatched to search every inch of land and buildings. Arthur Wrox-Hampden rode to the village to tell PC Frakes and then on to Bunbury to the police magistrate, who would have the search extended to cover the county and all its roads. It was Marietta who faced the awful duty of telling her mother.

The Gypsy lad had indeed been seeing what he could cadge by scrounging in the countryside. The Gypsies were about to break camp and move on toward the north, having enjoyed a profitable stay in the neighborhood. The boy, whose name was Tony, had freed the hare from a trap at the expense of its left foreleg and had put it in a gunnysack, where it struggled briefly and bled to an early death. Tony was heading back to the village green with the Gypsies' supper when he saw the pony Skittles, dragging the basket, go smashing against the gate. The basket was bounced high in the air over a hummock; its passenger—a little girl— was thrown out against the fence and lay still upon the ground. Tony recognized the pony. He knew it belonged to the family at the Hall. He ran to the unconscious child and made a quick search for any valuables. There were none, aside from a gold bracelet that he had off her arm in the twinkling of an eye. Just as quickly he decided that she herself, dead or alive, was an object of value, and he had the hare out of the gunnysack and the child in it in under a minute. He even had the presence of mind to tear off the bottom of her dress and stuff it into her mouth so that if she were not dead, she could not cry out. All his movements were unobserved and unobservable because of the hedgerows that lined the lane to a height over his head. The gunnysack was under a bank in a field when the two people came running along and discovered the pony by the gate. Tony understood very well their desperate inquiries about a little girl; he was a consummate actor who could assume a look of puzzled innocence as well as any. He could see that they cared nothing about the dead hare, so he pretended to think it was because of the hare they were questioning him. Then he allowed understanding to dawn and pointed them off into a spinney in the direction opposite to the one he himself intended to take.

The sack was heavy. The child was squirming and attempting to cry out. In fear that she might be smothered to death, he hurried as fast as he could back to the Gypsy caravan, bent nearly doubled with the weight of the sack on his back. Anyone who saw him would have thought his catch to be at least a small calf or a large sheep, but he got back with it unobserved.

His father's reactions were as quick as his own. The tent, fortunately, had not yet been struck, and into it the women and children were herded. Letty was given a sleeping potion, her face and neck were smeared with pitch and she was laid in the arms of Tony's mother. When the police arrived at the encampment, they first searched the van thoroughly (so they thought), and then, when they moved to the door of the tent to continue the search, the child was moved just as quickly under a back flap over to the van. Inside the van at the far end, under a false floor, was the hiding place of all the loot. If necessary, it could be used to hold a small child (it had often held a goat), and so that evening, without appearing to be in any hurry, the Gypsy caravan left Wrox common and before dark was well beyond Bunbury on the road north.

Had Tony's father been familiar with the Bible, he might have said, "This is my son, with whom I am well pleased." He removed from around his neck a chain with a gold locket that had been in his possession for three years and hung it around the neck of the little girl from Wrox Hall; it would, he told his son, identify her when they asked the ransom. And so Aunt Augusta Pounceby's likeness went traveling with the Gypsies the length and breadth of England as far north as Hadrian's Wall.

Mr. Smallwood hurried immediately to Maria's bedside, carrying his prayer book and a sincere desire to be of comfort to her in this her latest calvary. He found her lying fully dressed upon her bed with her eyes sunken like deep dark pools between cheeks and forehead. Her face was deadly pale.

"My dear friend," said the vicar, "I came as soon as I heard of your terrible loss. We must pray together for the little one's safe return. First I shall offer a prayer for you, that God may give you strength to bear your affliction." He knelt by the bedside and opened the Book of Common Prayer and in his melodious, well-modulated voice began reading with great sincerity and conviction. "O Merciful God, and Heavenly Father, who hast taught us in thy holy Word that thou dost not willingly afflict or grieve the children of man: Look with pity, we beseech thee, upon the sorrows of thy servant Maria, for whom our prayers are desired. In thy wisdom thou hast seen to visit her with trouble, and to bring distress upon her. Remember her, O Lord, in mercy; sanctify thy fatherly connection to her; endue her soul with patience under her affliction, and with resignation to thy blessed will; comfort her with a sense of thy goodness; lift up thy countenance upon her, and give her peace; through Jesus Christ our Lord."

As he said "Amen," the rector made the sign of the cross in the air between himself and the woman lying on the bed. He lifted his well-used book and turned a few pages. "Let us pray for the safe return of the child."

"No more praying, I beg you," said Maria in a surprisingly firm voice. "If this is according to God's blessed will, as you say, it makes no sense whatsoever. Was it God's will to take her in order that it might be His will to return her? Why should she, a helpless innocent, be the instrument by which this will was carried out?"

"He moves in mysterious ways," Mr. Smallwood said, at a loss for an answer.

"His ways are indeed mysterious," said Maria, "and I think He owes us an explanation. When my little boys died one after another, they were baptized that they might go straight to Heaven. I was told God had taken them according to His will. I was the instrument through which His will was carried out." Maria looked straight at Mr. Smallwood and asked him a direct question. "Why must I have suffered so dreadfully in order that a stillborn infant should go straight to Heaven?"

The rector bowed his head. "In time all things will be revealed to us," he said, "if we do not lose faith."

Maria continued to gaze at him steadily from under the straight black line of her brows. "I was taught," she said, "that Heaven must be earned by living a Christian life here on earth. Why should the souls of those who have not lived any kind of life on earth go automatically to Heaven? Had the babies been given the choice, they might not have lived good Christian lives at all."

"There was no possibility of that, you see," said Mr. Smallwood. "You may rest assured that none lived an evil life. That must be of comfort."

In a tone of voice that sent a chill along his spine the woman responded, "That is nonsense, and you must know it. It makes no sense at all. If you wish to know what I think of God's will, I shall tell you: God's will is exactly the same thing as pure chance. Was it God's will that the pony should run off with Letty? If so, then her abduction is as much His fault as the nursemaid's. What good would it do if we were to pray for Letty's return? Are we to beg Him? Did God cause my little girl to be snatched away in order that we should importune Him for her return? Is He insatiable in His wish to be pleaded with and praised? Does He enjoy this?"

Mr. Smallwood's eyes filled with tears. "My dear Maria," he said, weeping, "you must not speak so of Our Lord. It is sacrilege. In His infinite Wisdom He knows what He is doing."

"Well, I do not," said Maria. "And until He gives me an explanation, I shall not get down on my knees and beg. She will be found by some happy chance—or she will not be—" Maria broke off, and the voice that had been so strong began to quaver as she cried brokenly, "If she be not returned to us, I wish she may die, for what her life would be . . . I—I can . . . not . . . contemplate."

Mr. Smallwood knew not what to say or do. Nothing in his years of labor in the service of the Lord had prepared him for this. Still on his knees, he began to murmur, "Our Father, which art in Heaven, Hallowed by thy Name—"

Maria interrupted. "No more praying, I beg you. If it be God's will to punish me, He has accomplished His purpose. But why did He choose, as His means of making me suffer, the destruction of a helpless child?" She closed her eyes and turned away her head upon the pillow.

Mr. Smallwood gave up. "Try to sleep," he said, "and you will see things differently in the morning. Until then may our blessed Lord keep you, may the light of His countenance shine upon you and give you peace." Still in tears, he rose from his knees and left the room. In the sitting room Maria's children looked to him. "She needs help," he said, "beyond what I can give her. Do you see what you can do. I do not think she should be left alone."

On his way down the stairs the vicar was met by Nurse, on her way up with a sherry negus intended for Mrs. Wrox-Hampden, who had refused food. "Please, sir," Nurse said, "before you go, would you please look in on the nursemaid? She is in a terrible way, says it's all her fault and talks of taking her own life if Letty is not soon found. She is Chapel, sir, but we all have the same God—don't we?—in time of trouble."

Mr. Smallwood, deeply distressed after his inability to help Maria, hurried with his prayer book to the night nursery, where he found Norah on her knees beside her narrow cot in the corner, wailing at the top of her voice and beating her head with both fists. By sheer physical force he made her stop, and it was not easy, for he was an elderly man without vigor and she a strong young woman. At last he got her up and made her lie still, said a prayer over her and went to tell Nurse to send for the new young doctor at Wrox, who could come from there much faster than Pipkin from Bunbury. Both mistress and maid, said Mr. Smallwood, needed bodily as well as spiritual help.

The detective who was sent from London to assist the local police was as much baffled as PC Frakes. He examined carefully the gate that had stopped the pony and all the ground around it. Since the accident there had been much passing along the lane and through the gate. Rains had obliterated any tracks of men, beasts or wheels. One of Violet's little shoes, sodden with rain, was found under a bank in the field. The London detective was at first of the opinion that she was hidden somewhere near, but a search of every possible hiding place in the countryside turned up nothing. The carter was closely questioned again. He could not have had anything to do with a kidnapping, nor, it seemed, could the Gypsy lad who had been frightened by Luke and Norah into leaving his hare, in fear of being caught with it and arrested for poaching. The police had made a thorough search of the Gypsy camp before the Roma-nies' departure. They were carrying away nothing, not so much as a chicken or pig. "They're the same tribe as allus comes by here this time of year," the detective was told. "When they left, they had no child with 'em but their own filthy brood." They were first thought to have Mrs. Smallwood's spectacles, which she had left on a table under an open window, but "it turned out it was a magpie took 'em; they was found in the magpie nest along with two silver teaspoons what the Gypsies would surely have preferred to Mrs. Smallwood's spectacles."

The police all over England were notified to be on the lookout for Violet, and her description was published in newspapers.

The neighborhood and the county called at Wrox to express sympathy, as if there had been a death in the family, but Maria would see no one. Her indomitable spirit had been broken at last. She left her room only to go to the nursery, from which she could look out over the shrubbery to the lane along which the little girl had been dragged. When she caught sight of Skittles in the paddock, rubbing his neck against the fence as if nothing had happened, she cried out and ordered that he be somehow disposed of and never seen again.

Lottie was inconsolable. Her little sister had grown into being her companion. They talked together a lot and played hide-and-seek indoors and out. Letty spoke in whole sentences, very precisely; the only letters she had trouble with were *l* and *r*, both of which sounded like *w*. She called herself Wetty, Lottie was Wotty and Norah Nowah, just like the man who built the Ark. Lottie was certain that Letty would be able to tell any policeman her name and address, for although "Wrox" was pronounced "Rox," it did begin with a *w* and "Wox" would be perfectly intelligible.

❧ 28 ❧

Samuel Hole Proposes Marriage

When Lady Edge, who was in London, heard the awful news, she left directly for the country and was driven over to Wrox to pay a call of condolence on her old friend. The disappearance of little Violet, because of its uncertainty, was in a way worse than a death. After all Maria had endured, she had now lost her *benjamine*, her youngest and last child. She was in need. "If only I could *do* something," the dowager said. "Perhaps my men could drag Sheerwater."

"That has been done," said Maria, "and nothing found but the carcass of Arthur's wretched mastiff. The boaters and fishermen on the river have been alerted to watch out for—" She could not go on.

Lady Edge's heart was wrung. The two women were of an age, but Maria looked older by ten years. She was gaunt; her hair, now becoming quite white, had not been dressed. Those great dark eyes appeared to be framed in bone. "My dear," said Lady Edge, "will you not come to stay with me? It might be well if you were to get away from Wrox, which must hold so many sad memories."

"Thank you, Emma, but I cannot leave. They might bring Letty back as suddenly as they took her. I must be here when they bring her back."

Emma Edge was moved to tears, which enabled Maria in turn to weep long and uncontrollably, as she had not yet done. The two women clung together. Lady Edge did not leave until Maria, quite exhausted, had wept herself out and lain down on her bed. Downstairs, young Arthur waited to thank Lady Edge for coming. "It was most kind of you," he said. "I am sure my mother appreciates it."

"If she should be able and wish it, I hope she will come to stay with me," the dowager told him. "It might do her good to come away."

But Maria would not hear of it. Mrs. Bellwood urged a visit to Hatche; Aunt Augusta Pounceby suggested that the famous waters of Chipping might be restorative; Esther Hampden and the archdeacon invited her to stay at Stoke-sub-Ham that they might jointly offer prayers for Violet's return and where the sight of Violet's twin brother might be of solace; even Robert Fox, in town for the season, proposed that she should come to Foxbridge Abbey as soon as the season was over. Benjamin Share, who could not offer the hospitality he was so expert in receiving, did offer to cut short a stay in Scotland and visit Wrox on his way to the Swiss Alps. Arthur proposed that Marietta and Lottie accompany their mother to the mineral springs at Baden-Baden, where the change of scene and regimen would be total. To all such suggestions Maria turned a deaf ear and withdrew to her own rooms. Occasionally she walked in the park and once asked Marietta to show her the very spot in the lane where the empty basket had been found. She forgave Luke and Norah, declaring they were but instruments of God's will, as she herself had been so many times. Norah stayed on as a parlormaid, awaiting the return of her little charge.

Time passed. Rumors were heard that a child answering Letty's description had been seen near the docks in Liverpool or in the putrid slums of Glasgow, but investigations led nowhere. Marietta became her mother's nurse and companion, Maria depending on her more and more as she continued to withdraw from the outside world. Young Arthur worried about his sister as well as his mother; Wrox Hall became a wretched excuse for a home.

In the spring Maria summoned Police Constable Frakes to the Hall and asked him to be on the lookout for the annual return of the Gypsies to the common. She had taken it into her head that they would have Letty hidden somewhere nearby, and they would either demand money for her return or—if they had decided not to return her yet—they would not let her near her home lest she recognize it. PC Frakes promised to keep an eye out for the tribe and watch their movements like a hawk. But that year the Gypsies did not show up.

On the thirtieth day of June, soon after the twins' fourth birthday, there arrived from Georgiana Hampden a large packet that contained, besides her usual letter about little Edward's progress, a photograph of Archdeacon Hampden. It was the first photograph of a person—as distinct from a landscape—ever seen at Wrox, so it had to be looked at with interest. "I wish the photographer had chosen a different subject," said Maria, "since to look at it, it is necessary to see Cuthbert."

Georgiana had written, in part:

I feel sure you will be interested to have this remarkable photograph actually *in color*, taken at Bath by a process called daguerrotypy. I should have wished to send you a likeness of Baby Edward ["Baby!" exclaimed Arthur. "He is four years old!"], but in order to capture a likeness the subject must remain still for a full half hour, and although Esther and I tried for some time to induce Baby to remain still long enough for the Exposure, he refused to do so and had quite a Tantrum of temper, so I suggested we send you instead this picture of Cuthbert, who was very good about remaining still for the necessary length of time. One cannot see in the picture the Clamp that held his head in place, and I think you will agree that it is very successful. In the background is a Tropical Forest, which is said by persons who have visited the tropics to be very like. It is painted upon a moveable screen. Cuthbert chose it from a selection that included a battle at sea, the Royal Pavilion at Brighton and St. James's Park, London. Cuthbert very drolly said it was as close as he was ever likely to come to visiting the tropics. . . .

Uncle Cuthbert in the forest was seated on a chair that would probably never have been found there, next to a table upon which lay under his hand an open Bible. He might conceivably have been a missionary and thus more likely to be seen in a jungle than in St. James's Park, at a sea battle or in front of the Royal Pavilion. Cuthbert was wearing his black frock coat, the hand not on the Bible was inside the front of the coat in the style of Bonaparte, and his always high forehead looked more prominent than ever because of the retreat from it of his once ginger-colored hair.

The daguerreotype was placed facedown on a table in the drawing room, where it could be turned over for inspection by curious visitors but need not be looked at unless one wished to see the archdeacon in his chosen jungle. "I do not see why I should be forced to look at Cuthbert," said Maria, "simply because he is able to sit still for half an hour with his head in a clamp."

On the land Arthur's efforts were being rewarded. Wrox woolens were to be shipped around the world; a paper manufactory was being built upriver from the village, now rapidly becoming a town. Spence was in durance for cheating, thieving and forgery, his wife and children were in the poorhouse and his former home was leased to a paper manufacturer since the Holes had moved into their grand new mansion.

The Holes were determined to be exemplary employers. Model housing, with indoor plumbing, was built in neat rows for their workers and brought interested planners and architects to look from other parts of the country. Streets were being paved. The last coach had left the Bunbury inn, and all long-distance journeys were now made on the railway.

Samuel Hole's feelings had been deeply hurt when Arthur told him Marietta's decision. He believed that he was not considered good enough for her despite Arthur's assurance that both he and Maria had given their consent to the match. Instead of being discouraged, Samuel's was the opposite reaction; he was angry. He would show them! If the elder daughter would not have him, he would have the younger! So he set about deliberately to court Lottie. Samuel called upon her instead of upon Marietta. He talked to her endlessly about the mill, its products, the model housing, the flocks that produced the wool and on and on. The rest of the family became as familiar with it all as Lottie herself and, unlike Lottie, grew heartily tired of it. Lottie would repeat at the dinner table every word of what Samuel had told her. "The veterinary, Mr. MacTavish, says the animals are superior to us, that we are more dependent upon them than they upon us. Without them we should have no meat, no milk, nor eggs, nor woolen clothing and no sport to hounds. Whereas if we did not pen them in and feed them, they would revert to a feral state and survive very well, for they know how to look after themselves. Feral means wild, the way they were to begin with. The people with the best animals are the best fed and therefore the best-looking. Mr. MacTavish says he can tell by looking at an animal what its master will look like. We are what we eat, for it becomes part of us."

"How disgusting," said Maria, who had begun to emerge oftener from her own rooms and now joined her children at the dinner table. "I shall lose my taste for mutton."

"Perhaps that is not exactly what Mr. MacTavish said, for he does not speak English. It is what Samuel *thinks* he said."

"How can Samuel even *think* he knows what the man says if he does not understand it?"

"Samuel knows what Mr. MacTavish is talking about even when he does not comprehend what he says."

"Samuel should be in the diplomatic service," said Arthur.

On Lottie's seventeenth birthday, in September, Samuel called upon her, bringing a beautiful dark blue pelisse, made to her measure from the finest wool by Mrs. Cluster, who now supervised a shop near the rectory where garments fashioned from Wrox woolens were sold. There was to be a garment factory built near the mill, and eventually a big shop, with different departments selling various sorts of clothing for men and women, from hats to shoes. Samuel further envisioned a chain of such shops throughout the south and west of England.

"This is a birthday present," he told Lottie, "that your mother might not approve, for I believe an article of clothing is not considered to be an acceptable present from a man to a lady who is not his wife. However, if you will do me the honor of promising to become my wife, perhaps your mother will say you may accept it, along with my hand." This speech had been carefully prepared, written and rewritten, memorized and now delivered like a line in a play as Samuel shook out the garment and placed it across Lottie's shoulders.

Mr. Smallwood published the banns, the entire Hole family—heretofore nonconformist—was baptized and received into the Church of England and the wedding date was set for a day in early December, far enough ahead of Christmas to be convenient for the Cuthbert Hampdens to come from Stoke-sub-Ham, Mrs. Bellwood from Hatche, Robert Fox from the Abbey—even Benjamin Share, who was to spend Christmas at Edge Park. The Chipping aunts, of course, declined to make the journey away from the waters, but Aunt Augusta Pounceby sent a wedding present. She could well have afforded a Paul Storr or Bateman tea service, but she was one of those very rich persons who think valuable presents are expected of them because they can afford them, and Mrs. Pounceby believed that if she did give expensive presents, she would soon enough find herself unable to afford them. It was agreed that the covered vegetable dishes that arrived with her card were plate. "Just like Augusta," said Maria. "I am not surprised. She must have been delighted when she heard of this new process. It does look like silver, but one can see and feel the difference. Augusta cannot fool me."

"Perhaps she is not trying to fool you, Mama," said Marietta, "any more than she surprised you."

"What would have surprised me," said her mother, "would be a valuable present of real silver. She gave your father and me when we married an engraving of some sort by Raphael—or so she said. I do not believe the process of engraving had even been invented in Raphael's day; it was patently an imposture. I wonder what became of it. No one would wish to steal it."

Marietta, who at the time would never have dared tell her mother about the Reddles' wedding present, now related the whole story, including Mrs. Smallwood's observations and the departure of the job carriage with Raphael on the seat beside the driver. Maria threw back her head and laughed until her sides ached. It was a wonderful laugh, girlish and merry, even infectious, so that Marietta joined in after getting over her surprise; she had not heard her mother laugh in years. "How I should love to tell Augusta!" Maria said when she could speak. For the first time the daughter saw that her mother must in youth have possessed great charm. How sad it was that neither of her husbands had loved her; she must have thought herself not lovable.

❧ 29 ❧

JAMES AND MARIETTA MEET AGAIN

The young Viscount Edge was as highly placed in the *haut monde* as anyone not of royal blood. He had chosen to ally himself with the Liberal party, so he was taken up by the Prime Minister and introduced at court. The Ambassador to France invited him to Paris to observe the duties of a liaison officer with the possibility of future advancement to the ranks of diplomacy. Whenever he was in London, he conscientiously occupied his seat in the Lords and kept his ears open. As an eligible unmarried peer he received more invitations into society than he could accept. He attended the balls at Devonshire House and Lansdowne House. He enjoyed every moment of it all. He did not yet feel the want of a wife or any need to assume familial responsibilities. He saw the Duke's daughters in town, quite often taking one or another of them in to dinner when the order of precedence placed them naturally together. He knew the scandal of Lady Eleanor and the groom. He was at the wedding in St. Margaret's Westminster when Lady Anne (now a woman of nearly forty) was given in marriage by her father to a Welsh small landowner (or a small Welsh landowner, for the bride towered over him). The Duke was known to take no sides in political matters, so James was surprised to find himself summoned to the castle when it chanced he was at Edge for two days when the Duke was in residence.

As James told it later to his mother, the interview began with the Duke's mentioning matters common to Edge Park and the castle, some of whose extensive holdings adjoined those of Edge. It then became apparent that another common interest had entered the Duke's mind when he spoke of the possibility of families being joined which already had adjoining properties. "I do believe he was matchmaking," James told his mother. "He spoke of four daughters as if offering me a choice of goods. Lady Mary was very musical, he said, and asked if I cared for music. Lady Amelia was not as pretty as her older sister but was equally amiable and would possess a larger fortune, as her mother had been an heiress. I was vastly embarrassed, I knew not where to look. I said that if and when I came to marry, I need not do it for money. If you did not have a fortune, said he, would you marry for money in order to keep up your title and estate? If that were the only way to do it?"

"What said you to that?" asked Lady Edge.

"I said it was a hypothetical question, and I did not think it pertinent. Then His Grace said some more about families and various properties, and we parted. He asked me to dine tomorrow, so I suppose I must. No doubt the ladies will be displayed for inspection: The Lady Mary will play music, and the Lady Amelia be amiable, if not pretty. But, Mother, I did think afterward about what he said—that is, would I marry for money if it were the only means of keeping up Edge and my position in the world?"

"Yes?" said his mother.

"And I decided I would. I think the name and the place to be more important than the temporary holder of them. And if I did not possess the requisite amount of money, I am sure I have no other means of procuring it."

"Could you not find *one* of the four remaining girls to appeal to you?" Lady Edge asked. "I confess I should like it if my grandchildren were also grandchildren of a duke. Edge would make them a very suitable background."

"As to that," said James, "I believe Edge to be as much as the Duke can hope for now that he has seen one daughter off for Canada and another for Glamorgan. It might make him quite happy to see a third here, close by. The Lady Amelia is not so bad, although she does have an irritating laugh, and there is nothing more irritating than laughter when there is nothing to laugh at."

"It is done from self-consciousness," said Lady Edge, "not mirth. She is not aware that she does it. I should pay no attention to it if I were you."

"You would not have to live with it," James said. "I would, and it would be hard to live with."

"You would get used to it. Your dear father had a habit of grinding his teeth while asleep to which I found it most difficult to accustom myself."

"You were the only one who had to put up with it. It is not as though he did it in public, as Lady Amelia Stuart laughs."

"When you see more of her, you will find you notice it less, as I did with your father," said Lady Edge. She told her son His Grace was paying him the highest compliment, believing as he did that, like royalty, his children should marry within their own rank, and in his view, this rank was yet higher than that of the upstart occupants of the throne. A marquess or an earl might better have suited him, but a seventh viscount was by no means to be snubbed.

It was soon known in the country that James had gone to call on the Duke and been closeted with him for some time, then that he had dined at the castle with only the family present. Marietta heard it all and was miserably aware that no call had been paid at Wrox. But why should he come here? she asked herself. No one would choose to dine here when he might be at the castle, dining off gold and porcelain upon fare prepared by a French chef, and seated on velvet with a white-gloved footman behind his chair. The castle was like a small court. An invitation to dine there was a command, and attendance obligatory.

At the end of November the Edge bailiff, Mr. Hamper, journeyed to London to confer with Lord Edge on estate business. He carried the books and records for the year's transactions and spent an entire day at the Piccadilly house making a strict accounting. He was as conscientious as he was trustworthy, and just as capable. The year at Edge was winding down with everything in perfect order and large profits showing from rents and harvests. Hamper spent the night in the town house and saw the young lord again at breakfast before going back to the country.

"And what is the news of the neighborhood?" asked James. "Is your family all well? What of the new rector at Edge Corner?"

Hamper's wife had given birth to their third son. A large acacia tree had been blown down in a storm onto Edge Corner church and had knocked down the steeple, which the bishop's steward had come to see and had promised to have repaired. The Wrox-Hampden girl was to be married next week to the son of Hole, who used to be the draper in Bunbury and now owned woolen mills and had built himself over at Wrox a house fit for a lord. Wrox was now getting to be more important than Bunbury, said Hamper; it was the railway that was responsible—

James interrupted. "When does your train leave?"

"Half past ten o'clock, my lord."

"I am coming with you." James threw down his napkin and got up, leaving a plate of stewed kidneys half eaten. He bounded up the stair, calling for Henry to pack his portmanteau and make ready to leave immediately for Edge.

That afternoon Marietta was in her mother's room, reading aloud from the *Monthly Review* while Maria embroidered Lottie's new initials on a fine linen face towel, when there came a knock at the door. Marietta stopped in mid-sentence to say, "What is it?"

"Please, ma'am," said Maggie as she opened the door, "there is a gentleman downstairs to see Miss Marietta. He said he is in a great hurry. I showed him into the small sitting room."

"Very good," Marietta said, "I shall come down. Excuse me, Mama, it must have something to do with the wedding. I shall be back straight away."

She went through the drafty hall, pulling a shawl across her shoulders, down the great stair and opened the door of the small sitting room, used now for visitors because to heat it was possible. There facing her, with his back to the fire, stood James Edge.

"Marietta," he cried out, coming toward her with arms outstretched, "you cannot possible marry anyone but me!"

Before she quite realized what was happening to her, she was swept off her feet in a great hug. Then she was put down, and James was kissing her first on the forehead, then on the cheek, then on the lips, a kiss that sent a message through her whole body down to her very toes. When he stopped kissing, he held her so tightly against him that she could feel his heart next to her own—*thump, thump, thump*—

"How could you *think* of marrying somebody else?" asked James. "When I love you so much. I love you more than anything in the world. I would not want to stay in the world if you were not here, too. You are the whole world, Marietta, Marietta, I do love you so much!"

"I would never marry anyone else, James," she said. "I had already determined that. I was not intending ever to marry at all."

He held her by the arms as he stood back to look at her face. "How beautiful you are," he said simply, and meant it with all his heart. Then:

"Hamper said you were to be married within a week, to the son of the draper at Wrox." She was staring at him, eyes wide in incredulity. "Hamper—he's my bailiff, you know, absolutely reliable chap, he told me—"

"Oh," Marietta said. "Now I see! No, it is not I who am to marry; it is my sister Lottie."

"Lottie! But she is a child."

"She is past seventeen."

When at last he understood that the Wrox girl who was to be married was not Marietta, James went limp with relief. Still holding her, he led his love to a sofa and sat beside her, looking in wonderment at her face as if he could not take it in. "You are so beautiful," he repeated. "When I heard you were to be married, I realized you could not marry anyone but me. Is that not so, Marietta?"

"Oh, yes, to marry another would be quite impossible. For me, that is, but not for you."

"I? Why, I never for one moment even considered marrying anyone but you, my darling," said James, believing sincerely in his heart every word he uttered with his lips. "You must know that I have always loved you and never anybody else."

"I, too, James." She smiled as she said it, and her parted lips were so sweet, with pretty teeth just showing between them, that he had to lean forward and kiss them again.

The door was opened, and Maggie showed in Miss Theodora Smallwood, come to discuss with the bride the music for the wedding ceremony. It appeared evident to her that her advent on the scene was unwelcome. She backed away, sought an excuse to retreat, blushed all over her poor face and said the wedding music was of no importance. Marietta, feeling sorry for her (as she now did for every other woman in the world, even the daughters of dukes), very politely put the vicar's daughter at her ease and, followed by James, left the room to go in search of the bride and groom. In the great hall, under the stair, she and James hugged and kissed for a full five minutes, enjoying it the more because they were the only persons in the house, or in all England, who knew where they were, what they were doing and how much they loved each other.

James lifted her hair to kiss her ear and whispered into it, "Have you any irritating habits or mannerisms? I hope not."

Suppressing the desire to laugh aloud in her surprise, Marietta said in almost a whisper, "That is for you to discover. I daresay I have, but if they are the same as yours, we should get along very well."

"I shall look forward to making their discovery," he murmured as they both smothered laughter lest it be overheard. He wanted to laugh aloud and even shout out his joy as he thought of his narrow escape; then he went away, saying that he must of necessity return immediately to London and that he would write as soon as he arrived there.

Composing herself, Marietta returned to her mother's room and the *Monthly Review*, wondering if Maria would notice the difference in her since she had left half an hour before.

"What was it?" asked Maria.

"It was only Miss Theodora, come to talk about wedding music."

"The Mozart, I suppose," said Maria. "One does get tired of the same old thing."

"Every part of the marriage service is the same old thing, Mama, but it will all be new to Lottie." Marietta felt that her happiness must sound in her voice like music, must shine from her face like a beam of sunlight, filling the room. Her mother seemed not to notice it, and that made Marietta laugh softly.

Maria looked up from her work, her fingers holding the needle, with cotton and thimble poised for the next stitch. "What is amusing?"

"Nothing, Mama. Everything. Lottie's going to be married within the week is the most wonderful thing that has ever happened. It is a miracle."

"I would hardly put it so extravagantly. She is very young. Had she waited, she might have done better. I should not choose to be called Hole; the name has no distinction."

"I think it remarkably distinctive."

"I never heard of a girl's being so overjoyed because a younger sister is being married first."

Marietta took up the periodical and turned pages. "Now, let's see, where were we—"

The wedding was well attended despite the notable absence of the Cuthbert Hampdens. Uncle Cuthbert had refused to travel from Stoke-sub-Ham to see his niece married because the bride's older brother had given him offense. The archdeacon had assumed he would be called upon to officiate, and he had been rebuffed by Arthur, who said that if Uncle Cuthbert were to perform the ceremony, it would unfairly do Mr.

Smallwood out of his fee. The archdeacon wrote back, pointing out with satisfaction that Arthur was the one to be out of pocket, as Uncle Cuthbert would magnanimously have waived a fee in view of his close relationship to the bride.

The bride looked pretty in a dress made over by Mrs. Cluster from the ball gown her mother had never worn, and when she left with her husband on the railway for a wedding journey to Brighton, she appeared to be happy. But it was remarked by some persons that Marietta seemed to be more radiant by far than the bride. She radiated a happiness that shone out from her smiling face, that expressed itself in her walk, as if she trod on air, and in her speech that sounded as if the words had been set to music. When still, she seemed pensive, as if daydreaming, and she looked a great deal out of windows that faced in the direction of Edge Park, in the distance across the river. She watched for the postman as if awaiting an important communication, and after he had left, she was often closeted in her room for hours. She was inattentive to conversation, even to direct questioning, and had constantly to be begging people's pardon and requesting that they repeat themselves. She had no appetite. Even the servants, who now had so much to do, noticed and remarked upon her strange behavior.

"She's by way of taking it all very hard," Maggie said to Norah. " 'Tis well known young Mr. 'Ole courted 'er first, then changed suddenlike to Miss Charlotte. Miss M's nose is out of joint."

"To my mind," said Abigail, "the wind's blowin' from another direction altogether." Abigail had been with the mistress and the young ladies in Rome. "A young gentleman came callin' on her not long ago, and you wouldna guess who. Luke recognized his 'orse—and it was the lord's from over to Edge Park, it was."

❧ 30 ❧

The Course of True Love Does Not Run Smooth

The introduction of the postage stamp, coming as the railway was linking all parts of the country to the land's end, made it possible for letters to travel from one place to another as rapidly as their writers. The lovers had agreed, in the constant stream of correspondence that flowed between Piccadilly and Wrox, that they would tell their respective mothers at Christmastime of their intent to marry. James was back at Edge by the twentieth of the month and drove himself over to Wrox next morning. Both houses were full of guests and relations come for the holidays, but James managed to see Marietta alone by arrangement in the small sitting room. He appeared at the front door at ten o'clock, having left the horse and fly out of sight, and was let in by Marietta, who had been waiting for him since nine. The secrecy was part of the immense fun of being in love and being alone together. Murmuring and whispering and smothering laughter, lest they be caught out, added to the pleasure of shared embraces and confidences. But the time had come to move on to the next step in the ritual of courtship—the announcement to the world. Being openly seen to be in love, receiving congratulations, planning the wedding would be even more delightful than clandestine meetings and love letters.

"Let us each tell our mothers on Christmas Eve," James suggested, "and on Christmas morning they will announce it to everyone."

"What a wonderful Christmas present!" said Marietta. "You will come over here in the morning, and we shall all go to church at Wrox."

"Then I shall fetch you back for dinner at Edge." James caressed his love's hair, stroked her soft cheek, kissed the pale eyelids, fringed with amber lashes, that were closed over her amber-colored eyes. They both sighed blissfully. James did not ask himself if or why he deserved to have such effortless good fortune. It was all part of himself. There had been no bad fairy at his christening; none would have dared put in an appearance, it would have been so out of place. If James had done nothing to deserve having all the best of everything, he had certainly done nothing *not* to deserve it.

It was difficult to find his mother alone on Christmas Eve, so James sent word by Henry to Lady Edge's maid saying he would come to see her before retiring. The Yule log had been brought in; roast suckling pig, goose and plum puddings were served at dinner, after which the carolers had been around and been invited in to the saloon to feast on cakes, nuts and wine punch. It was late before James, carrying a candle, went along the upper hall to his mother's particular rooms. She was waiting for him, ready for the night in the big bed with its high canopy in which he had been conceived and born. It was midnight.

"Happy Christmas, Mother," said James as he leaned over to kiss her cheek.

"Happy Christmas, my son," she replied, taking his hand. "And you indeed look happy. You have been smiling all day."

"I am happy." He sat on the side of the bed. "I am come to tell you why, that you may share my joy."

The mother waited. She knew, of course, what was coming.

"I am engaged to be married to the person I love most in all the world. Marietta Wrox-Hampden has consented to be my wife." James looked at his mother in happy anticipation, waiting for her expressions of joy and congratulation. Instead she went quite pale, a look of horrified amazement appeared on her face, she leaned back against the pillows and closed her eyes.

"Mother? Did you understand me?"

"Oh, no—no, no, no! It is not possible!"

"How can it be not possible? It is all settled. We love each other and are to be married."

Lady Edge, still with her eyes closed, tightened the pressure of her hand on his. "You and Marietta can never marry. It is not possible," she repeated.

"But *why*, Mother? What conceivable reason is there to prevent it? She has no fortune, but were she a great heiress, it would add nothing to what she is without it. She is so sweet, so beautiful, so gentle and loving—"

"Stop!" ordered Lady Edge. She opened her eyes and looked at her son with an expression as if the features were carved out of stone. "You can never marry that girl, and there is an end to it. We shall talk no more of it."

"Yes, we shall!" James exclaimed, rising to walk about the room. "You cannot object to the marriage and give no good reason. You have known Marietta all her life, as her mother before her. You know she is unexceptionable in every way; there can be nothing against her. What have you to say against her?"

"Not against her as such," said his mother miserably. "It is . . . that —that there are circumstances you know nothing of. You must trust me when I say it is impossible."

"Again you will not say why!" shouted James. "Well, madam, I do not need your permission to marry anyone I choose! I cannot think what has got into you. I assumed you would be happy in my happiness. Why do I deserve this treatment?"

"I cannot tell you tonight," said his mother in tears. "I shall have to speak to Maria Wrox-Hampden first."

James stood at the foot of the bed, trembling with rage. "Marietta is speaking to her mother tonight, as I to you. And I shall see her tomorrow and bring her here, which is to be her future home. Do you understand?" And he turned away, left the room and went along the passage to his own part of the house, forgetting his candle. There was someone coming toward him with a lighted candle, shielding the flame with his hand. It was only Benjamin Share, returning from the water closet at the end of the corridor.

"Merry Christmas to you, James," said Benjamin.

James did not answer.

At Wrox, Marietta asked her mother and older brother to stay behind in the drawing room after the rest of the household had retired. There had been a large party, several guests stopping overnight, others come from Bunbury for dinner and caroling. Augustus accompanied hymns on the new piano that was his Christmas present. They all joined in singing "Adeste Fideles, "While Shepherds Watched Their Flocks" and "The First Nowell." The three Smallwoods were, of course, present, and the vicar said grace with a moving invocation that included, among those on whom God's blessing was asked, "the dear ones who are unable to be present among us but are with us in our thoughts and in our hearts." The senior Holes, being Dissenters no longer, had of necessity been included in the company and came with the Samuel Holes, who stayed over and occupied the haunted bedchamber. Samuel had not known beforehand about the ghost but, when told of it, declared stoutly that he did not believe in it and would believe in it when he saw it. "It is not a thing that needs to be seen to be believed," said his wife. "As far as I know, it has never been seen. Hearing is believing just as surely as seeing."

Marietta, who had been pacing the floor in her impatience, shut the drawing-room door behind her sister and brother-in-law and came back across the room to where her near relations waited by the chimney. Arthur remarked what James had always noted in Marietta, that she walked as if her feet were carrying her toward some wonderful future. She stopped beside them. "Mother, Arthur! James has asked me to marry him!" Her face was aglow.

Arthur was taken by surprise. He had not noticed anything "going on" either under his very nose or behind his back. But he immediately said, "How splendid! It is marvelous news indeed." And he went to his sister to take her hand and kiss her on the cheek.

"Yes, is it not?" said Marietta, squeezing the hand in hers. "Mama?" She looked over to see her mother, grown pale and trembling, fall back into an armchair at the side of the fireplace. "Mama?"

"Oh, no," said Maria, laying a hand upon the black bombazine directly over her heart. "Do not say so—not this!"

"What is the matter, Mama?" asked her daughter, incredulous.

"Yes, Mother," Arthur said, "what is wrong with you?"

"It cannot be," said Maria faintly.

"What cannot be?"

"Marietta and James cannot marry."

"I should like to know why not," Arthur demanded.

"We have promised each other," said Marietta, deflated and bewildered.

Arthur was equally bewildered. "What has got into you, Mother?

Why should you spoil their happiness? I do not understand you. What possible objection have you to offer?"

"I shall have to speak to Emma Edge," Maria said at last. "This can never be. It would not do."

"James is coming here tomorrow—today—Christmas—that we may announce it to everyone here. Then I am to go back with him to Edge and tell them there."

"No—no," Maria repeated, over and over, "no, no, no, no—"

"But *why?*" Arthur insisted, truly fearing for his mother's sanity. "You cannot simply continue to say no without offering rhyme or reason. What is the matter with you?"

"Does Emma know of this?" said Maria.

"James is telling her now, tonight," Marietta said. "It is to be announced tomorrow, for Christmas—" She could not go on but turned to cling to her brother, who put an arm around her.

"It is for me to make the announcement," said he, "not for my mother. And it shall be done as Marietta and James wish it."

"It can never be," Maria said flatly. "Nothing must be done until I have seen Lady Edge."

Arthur went to stand before her. "Now, listen to me, madam. Is there some reason why you have taken this stand?"

"Yes," she whispered.

"Then I demand to know it."

"I cannot tell you. You must believe me."

"Mama!" cried Marietta. "Is there some reason why I can never marry? Is something wrong with me that I do not know about?"

"No, no," said her mother, "it is not that. You are perfect."

"Is it money, then? James does not mind that I have no money."

"You have more than money," Arthur put in. "You are worth your weight in gold."

This kindness unlocked the flow of Marietta's tears. She cast herself down on a sofa and sobbed, in a state of shock and utter bewilderment. "I do not understand," she murmured through her tears. "I do not understand."

Maria felt as if she could not herself bear the sorrow she had been obliged to inflict on her child. She trembled, and she, too, wept uncontrollably. Arthur stood between the two women, looking from one to the other, utterly at a loss. "I shall wait on Lady Edge directly Christmas is over," he said at last. "Until then let us retire and say no more."

* * *

James Edge was at Wrox on Christmas morning before anyone was up, knocking the lion's head against the big front door until the sound of it echoed around among the stables and outbuildings, setting dogs to barking and sending pigeons aloft to beat the frosty air with their wings. A cock crowed somewhere on the home farm, then another farther distant, like an echo. James had not retired all night or changed his clothing; he still wore his bottle green velvet coat. The sun was barely up, giving just light enough to see his breath. Quite unconscious of the bitter cold and sharp-toothed wind, he continued to pound on the door, until at last it was pulled open by Marietta herself, who had not slept. He went in, and she closed the door behind him, leaning against it as he turned to her. The entry was dark and cold.

"Did you speak to your mother?" he demanded.

"Yes."

"What said she?"

"I—I cannot bring myself to tell you. She is not rational."

"Nor mine," said James. "She refused to listen to me. She seems to think there is some reason why we cannot marry. Do you know of any reason?"

"No, James, indeed I do not. I cannot understand why they do not wish us to be happy."

"We shall be happy, dearest, despite them. They are not necessary to our happiness. I am come to take you with me back to Edge."

"But I cannot do that! I cannot go where I am not welcome. It is your mother's house."

"It is *my* house! I can put out my mother if I so wish."

"No, let us be sensible. It is Christmas Day. We have no right to spoil Christmas for everyone else."

"They have no right to spoil our whole lives."

"They must be made to give an explanation."

The sound of approaching footsteps was preceded by the appearance of a sleepy footman in nightclothes, carrying a light. He held it up toward the two young people clinging to one another by the door. "Is that you, miss?"

"Yes, it is all right. Leave us alone."

"I am Lord Edge," said James, who knew perfectly when to use the name to which he was entitled. "Leave us alone."

"Yes, my lord," the servant said doubtfully, not daring to disobey.

Footsteps and light went off to be swallowed into the silence and darkness of the house.

"They cannot forbid us to marry without giving a reason," James pursued. "I shall come directly Christmas is past to speak to your mother. You understand that nothing she may have to say—or refuses to say—will make any difference. We do not need permission to marry, for we are both of age."

They parted, each to spend a miserable Christmas but more than ever determined to marry despite mysterious obstacles put in the way for no known or apparent reason.

❧ 31 ❧

An Unhappy Christmas

On Christmas Day the postman was late on his rounds because he was held up at each house to drink a hot buttered rum or eat a slice of plum cake and to accept a shilling for each of his five children. He did not stop by the vicarage until afternoon. The Smallwoods had been out at midday dinner following church and found him just leaving the vicarage. "I put a letter for you in the slot, mum," he said, "for Miss Theodora from America."

"Oh, dear Elsie!" exclaimed Miss Theodora. "She is writing to me for Christmas, I feel sure. What remarkable timing!"

"Thank you, Jenkins," her mother said. "Won't you come in and share a little Christmas cheer?"

"Thank you kindly, mum, but no." Jenkins would have been glad of a glass, but he feared a sermon, prayer or hymn might be its price. "I'm keen to get home to the missis and the young ones, it bein' Christmas Day. There's five of them, you know; they expect their dad to bring 'em somethin', even if it be only old Dad's company at supper." Thus reminded, Mr. Smallwood produced five shillings and wished all the little Jenkinses a blessed Christmas.

Ever since Jenkins had been appointed postman, he had been obliged to miss church services, a deprivation he regarded as one of the perquisites of his job. He could not know that he had played a small role that morning in the drama of Mr. Smallwood's Christmas message to his flock.

As a general rule in his sermons the vicar relied heavily on sporting terms and similes: the game of life, the race for the crown, vaulting over obstacles, keeping in the swim of things and so on. Mountains were climbed (figuratively) to reach the pinnacle of life everlasting. When he tried temptation, the devil had met his match in Christ. Life was like the game of hockey, played on a slippery field, full of falls—and with goals. On this Christmas morning the congregation had been bidden to go forth and spread the glad tidings of the Savior's birth from door to door, even as Jenkins, the postman, carried the news of less important happenings.

Mr. Smallwood unlocked his front door that Theodora might retrieve her letter from the floor inside. Until the removal from the church of the communion silver the vicarage door had never been kept locked, but following the theft Mrs. Smallwood had won the argument against this custom of being too trusting. ("The Bible itself tells us thieves break through and steal," said she; "it does not say they walk in and help themselves. The least we can do is to make it more difficult for them; it is surely wrong to abet them. Anyone who would steal silver from the house of the Lord would certainly not think twice of stealing it from mine.")

Mr. Smallwood and his wife had been going over the attendance at church (she made the number fifty-nine) and remarked the absence of Mrs. Wrox-Hampden and Miss Marietta. The young squire had put in an appearance to do his duty in reading the lessons, but he had departed abruptly before the communion service. "I cannot understand it," said the rector, "as all were in good health and good spirits only last night."

"And on Christmas Day when, as at Easter, attendance is obligatory," said his wife. "It is thanks to them we now have the Holes," she added. "The Holes can be counted on when the alms basin is passed, and for that we must be grateful."

"Quite so," Mr. Smallwood agreed. "Like many converts, they are holier than the Archbishop of Canterbury."

"Why, Papa, you made a pun," said his daughter.

"So I did," he agreed, laughing heartily as he took the meaning.

"Do you not think, Jonathan," Mrs. Smallwood pursued, "you should go to the Hall to inquire?"

"It would seem to be a chastisement," said he.

"But if they abstained from the service for any reason other than illness they merit chastisement. If they are indeed ill, they might wish H C to be taken to them at home."

"In that case they would send for me."

Mrs. Reddle's letter had been posted early in December at Philadelphia. As she had written previously to Miss Theodora Smallwood, the Reddles were settled in rooms on Chestnut Street, in the house of a widowed relation of Mr. William West who, like them, taught at the Friends' school, her subjects being mathematics and astronomy. The house was in the middle of a row, built of red brick with white stone steps at the front door. The Reddles had a sitting room at the front, with the engraving of the Sistine Madonna above the fireplace, and a bedroom at the back. They took their meals with the widow Fraser, their landlady. Osbert Reddle, because of his eclectic learning and inspired teaching, was making a name for himself. Mr. West had declared that the chance meeting in the Taunton coach had been the luckiest of his life. Osbert inspired his colleagues and pupils to reach for high standards of scholarship. Elsie Reddle taught English composition and literature and even had a few students in French. They both were leading useful lives in a great modern city—so different from rural England.

There were drawbacks, to be sure. Both Osbert and Elsie had been dreadfully homesick. He hated living in the city and found walking along the banks of the Schuylkill with his butterfly net not at all the same as roaming the downland around Wrox. Then there was the dreadful climate. One would have supposed that sailing due west from England in the same latitude, one would have encountered the same climate, but not at all: Pennsylvania was, unaccountably, directly across from Spain! The past summer, Elsie wrote to Theodora, had been very nearly unbearable for the terrible, suffocating heat that was so humid one was perpetually wet. There was no relief, except occasionally following a thunderstorm that brought even more moisture. She and Osbert had suffered greatly, but fortunately the school was closed during all the worst of the summer months, and with autumn had come relief and renewed activity; indeed, wrote Elsie, they were so busy she had had to make the time to write to her dearest Theodora, sending her warmest love, kind regards from Osbert and assurances of undying friendship.

After posting this letter, Elsie went on household errands for which Osbert had no time, including a call at the Garrard Bank to draw out some cash. While in there she had had a quite extraordinary experience, which she recounted to Osbert at the end of the day.

"My love," she began (the Quakers, who did not show affection in public or use endearments, were often discomfited by the Reddles' openly expressed devotion to each other), "do you believe in doubles? I mean, do you think that for everyone on earth there is another somewhere in the world who is exactly like him?"

"No, I do not," said Osbert, "for some people are black, some brown, some Chinese and some red Indian. If you or I had a double, he or she would have to be here in the white part of the world, and if everybody had one, they would be running into each other in the streets."

"If there be no such thing as a double, then today in the Garrard I saw Mr. Maule, the Bunbury banker."

Had Osbert not been seated, he would have fallen to the floor. He grasped the chair's arms to steady himself and said, "No, that could not be! Are you sure?"

"Yes, he was behind the counter. I was as close to him as I am now to you. It was indeed he."

"I must have been wrong about the double," said Osbert, breathing hard. "For Maule could not be at once in Bunbury and Philadelphia."

"He looked straight at me, Osbert, and when I said, 'Why, it is Mr. Maule, is it not?' he turned and hurried away and went out a door at the back. I was about to explain to him why you had withdrawn all my money so suddenly, which I hoped had not inconvenienced him. Another clerk waited upon me. Here is the cash." She handed him an envelope. "Why should Mr. Maule have business in Philadelphia? Could the Garrard have some connection with the bank in Bunbury?"

"I intend to find out," said her husband.

Next day he excused himself from attendance at his morning class in biology and went to the Garrard Bank. He knew Maule only by sight, would never have remarked him but for Elsie's having recognized him, and he was sure Maule did not know him at all, for he—fortunately—had had his savings at Exeter with his father. He walked into the bank and approached the nearest clerk. "Have you a gentleman employed here who is lately come from England? I believe his name is Maule."

"No, sir. The only English gentleman here is Mr. Morris; he has been with us now upwards of three years. May I be of assistance?"

"I wish to see Mr. Morris. It is with him I have business."

"If you will wait a moment, sir, I shall see if he is free."

Mr. Morris regretted he was not free. Mr. Reddle sat down to wait until he should be free. At lunchtime Mr. Morris perforce came out of hiding, as Mr. Reddle rose to confront him. "Mr. Maule, I believe?"

"You are mistaken, sir. My name is Morris."

Mr. Reddle bowed. "As you wish. At one time it may have been Maule."

"Who are you?" demanded the banker.

"I am the husband of the lady you knew as Miss Elizabeth Wetherby of Wrox Hall, England."

Morris, trapped, looked about the room and said, "Not here, not now. Let us walk out together as if going to lunch, by prearrangement."

The two men walked out and into Market Street, where they strolled along in the winter sunshine as if enjoying the fresh air. "It was by unhappy chance that she ran into me yesterday," said the banker. "I had never seen her in the bank before."

"As she does not usually attend to such business, I must consider it to be by very happy chance she did so yesterday." Osbert had determined exactly his plan of action and now carried it out. To denounce Maule and expose him would be sweet revenge and cause his extradition to face charges at Bunbury and a life in prison, but it would not restore to Elsie one penny of her money. So he now told Maule that two hundred pounds, plus three years' interest—in the equivalent American currency —were to be deposited to his account at the Garrard, whereupon nothing would be said concerning the bank failure at Bunbury.

"But that is blackmail," Mr. Morris protested.

"No doubt it is."

"That in itself is a crime, sir," said the banker, grasping at a straw.

"I suppose it is, and if you report it, I shall be arrested, whereupon I shall be obliged to give the reason for my crime."

"How do I know it will not be repeated over and over?" asked Mr. Morris in a wail.

"Because, sir, I give you my word that it will not. The day the sum mentioned is deposited in my account I shall withdraw the account and place it elsewhere, and you will never hear from me again."

Maule cringed. "Very well, very well," he muttered.

Osbert stopped walking, turned to face the other and grasped him by the shoulders. "Would to God I could denounce you," he said in a low, intense tone. "Look at me, sir! What you stole from Miss Wetherby was more than money to line your pockets. You took her self-respect, her years of sacrifice, her security, her dignity and pride—"

Maule was slobbering, trying to speak.

"Do you understand me?" Osbert shouted. "Do you realize the extent of your crime?"

"Please—" Maule begged. Passersby were stopping to stare. Osbert pushed him backward so hard he fell to the pavement, then turned away and walked off.

That night, after they were in bed, he told his wife the whole story. He would not have been human had he been able to keep it longer to himself, and there was no one else in whom he could confide without exposing Mr. Morris.

Fortunately Elsie was strong enough now to withstand the shock. She even showed a healthy desire for revenge. "Could you not write to the magistrate at Bunbury and tell him where to find Maule? You did not promise him not to do that, but merely that you would not blackmail him further."

"No, my love, I could not do that. You do not understand the principle of blackmail, which is that in repaying your money, he has bought my silence."

Elsie turned into his arms. "Oh, my dear love," she murmured, "I do think you are the most wonderful man who ever lived on earth. You could never have a double; there could not be another like you." And she gave herself to him with her whole heart, forgetful of anyone or anything else.

Osbert Reddle, the obscure teacher, uprooted from his homeland and cast by fate upon an alien shore, felt himself to be the happiest man on earth, because of his criminal act against a fellow criminal.

❧ 32 ❧

AN OBSTACLE OVERCOME

On the morning after Christmas, Arthur Wrox-Hampden, on his way to Edge Park, was passed on the road by James Edge going in the opposite direction. He was received in the morning room by Lady Edge.

"Madam," said Arthur, bowing over her hand, "I am come on behalf of my sister, who informed me that she had been asked in marriage by Lord Edge and had consented to an engagement."

Lady Edge inclined her head. She did not invite the young squire to be seated, and they remained standing throughout the interview.

"My mother, for no discernible reason, informed my sister and me that their marriage was impossible. She said that your ladyship should be consulted, as you would know of such a reason."

Lady Edge turned away to gaze into the fire. She drew herself erect, lifted her head and, still avoiding the eyes of her visitor, said, "Your sister Lucy gave birth in Rome in July of 'thirty-eight to an illegitimate child, and she died in childbirth."

Arthur took hold of a high-backed chair to steady himself. "You must be mistaken, ma'am," he said.

"No," said Lady Edge, "you have but to ask your mother." She turned now to face him. "Lucy told your parents that its father was James, hoping James would feel obliged to marry her. She lied, of course."

Arthur thought about this. Then he said, "Was there any possibility she was not lying?"

"Certainly not. James was at Oxford, he was but nineteen years old. Lucy was well known to be morally loose; she had lain behind every haystack in the country—"

"I see," said Arthur at last. "But this accusation by Lucy, if false, why should it now prevent a marriage between James and Marietta? It was long ago; Lucy is dead and buried."

"The child lives," said Lady Edge.

Arthur was again silent, taking it in. His mother had deceived him cruelly. He had a living niece or nephew, whoever its father, an illegitimate child! "Who else knows of its existence?" he asked.

"No one. Your mother and I. Dr. Pipkin. Some persons then in Rome, where the birth must have been registered."

"If James be not the father, what is to prevent his marriage to Marietta? Her sister's sins should not be visited upon her."

"Do you not see? James does not know of Lucy's accusation against him."

"If it be not true," said Arthur, "why need he or anyone else ever know of it? If neither he nor Marietta be in any way at fault, why may they not marry?"

"It would ruin James's life."

"Accusations are not proofs. Especially made long ago by one who is dead. If they were to be brought against him, James would have only to deny them."

"The child lives," Lady Edge repeated.

"That will remain so, madam, whomever James marries."

Lady Edge approached him and looked directly up into his face. "Do you not see," she said, "the impossibility of Lucy's sister coming into this house as its mistress and into this family as wife and mother?"

Arthur could not but acknowledge that he did see why that would be regarded as impossible by Lady Edge, as well as by his mother, who had been concealing all this time the whole dreadful business and even the existence of Lucy's child. He took his departure from Edge Park and returned home with a heavy heart that ached with sympathy for his innocent sister.

* * *

"I beg you not to press me," Maria said to James. He and Marietta were with her in the drawing room, behind the closed door. The lovers sat side by side on a small sofa, holding hands. "It should be enough that your mother and I both oppose the match."

"It is not enough, ma'am," James said. "If you refuse to give us your blessing, we shall marry in spite of it, and you will never see Marietta again."

One more child lost to her! Maria closed her eyes, leaned back and thought hard. There was a long silence. "If Marietta will leave the room, I shall give you my reason," she said at last.

James kissed the hand he held and let it go. Marietta left, closing the door behind her departure. Her lover had risen with her and now did not resume his seat but stood facing the pale woman in black.

"In January of 'thirty-eight," Maria began, "our daughter Lucy informed her father and me that she was expecting a child. She was unmarried. When we pressed her to name the father, she named you. Her father and I called on Lady Edge, your mother, and informed her of this. You were absent from home. Your mother said it was impossible that you could be the father, much less was it possible that you should marry Lucy, who was disgraced. I therefore took Lucy to Rome that her child might be born there and no one at home know anything of it. Lucy was delivered of a male infant on the second of July of that year. She died in giving it birth."

James walked about in a daze, not seeing the room around him, stumbling over a footstool, catching himself, then falling into a chair.

"You can understand," Maria continued, "why it were better this should never come to light. It can only be hurtful to you and to Lucy— and to Marietta. If by any chance you might be the father—"

James was forcing himself to remember that golden September afternoon in the beech wood. It had been only once. There had been no assignation, no seduction, no lusting—but there had been no love either, just a mating of two young creatures who happened upon each other when alone. He could now see why it was wrong that the opportunity had presented itself, why a boy and a girl should not have been going about the countryside alone and Nature been allowed to take its course.

"It is known you and Lucy were together a good deal before you went up," said Maria.

James thought long and hard. He need admit nothing, for the only witness was the dead Lucy. He came to a stopping place in his circling thoughts. "What about the child?"

"He is in Rome. He is three and a half years old by now."

Again James was silent. Then, "It happened once," he forced himself to say. "Only once."

"I am obliged," said Maria, "to ask you a question, though it gives me great pain to do so. A man can tell if a young woman is . . . inexperienced. There is the hymen, the penetration of which causes pain to the woman, the rupture, and bleeding—" She did not after all pose the question.

James flushed scarlet from his throat to the roots of his hair; he was in an agony of embarrassment. "I was not aware," he stammered, "of such —of that—of those—"

"Then there is no way of knowing anything for certain, is there? You can understand, James, why we did not wish Marietta to hear of this and why marriage between you is not to be thought of. I could not tell her."

"Then I shall," said James, "for she has a right to know. And my having to tell her will be punishment far beyond the crime." He could not think of that one act in the beech grove as being a crime; he had not forced himself upon Lucy, nor had she seduced him. Had it been a crime, then the birds of the air and the beasts of the fields were criminals. Yet he had no excuse to offer Lucy's mother, especially since that single act, or a similar one elsewhere, had resulted in Lucy's death. "I shall tell Marietta," he said to her mother, and left the room in search of her.

He found her upstairs in the common room, where so many hours of her girlhood had been passed—happily, she now thought, for she had then been without a care and with no unpleasant feature in her life except for the bullying of Lucy. Now it all seemed long ago: Not only was Lucy gone, but so was that whole part of her life—one-third of it— along with Papa and Lottie and Augustus, baby Violet, Miss Wetherby and Mr. Reddle. She wondered what Mama was telling James that she did not wish her daughter to hear.

Since Lucy was dead, James could very well have denied her whole story or at least have said that she had initiated him into manhood by deliberate seduction, but he was an honorable man, and he told Marietta exactly what had happened and how. He did not believe himself to be the child's father, but he could not absolutely deny the possibility. It seemed unlikely; in novels and myths a single encounter invariably resulted in a birth nine months later, but in real life that was known to be rare.

"Lucy was my friend," said James, "but I did not love her, nor she me.

It was not done from love. You are the only one I have ever loved or ever shall."

Marietta heard him out, saying nothing. She had given no thought to the thing that had been inside Lucy's body and made her so grotesquely malformed. Marietta had assumed it was still inside Lucy, a part of her, lying in the Roman cemetery, forgotten along with its mother, and now it seemed Lucy, who had tormented Marietta in childhood, was come back from the dead to ruin her life, and James's. She felt hatred of Lucy rising from her stomach until she could taste it like bile.

James was looking at her with an expression that tore her apart. His beloved face was drawn and haggard, his hair disheveled, the beautiful eyes pleading for understanding, for mercy even. She could not bear it. Lucy was not going to be allowed to win; she was not to ruin both their lives.

"Had I had Lucy's opportunity," she told him, "I should have done the same, only it would have been done from love." She went to him and put her arms around his neck, lifting her face to be kissed.

"Oh, my dearest one," he murmured as he embraced her, "will you forgive me? Will you marry me after all?"

"I am glad you asked me," said Marietta, "else I should have been obliged to ask you—and I should have been terrified for fear you would say no."

The lovers sat together a long time without speaking, holding each other. Silence filled the house. Arthur, returning home, was struck by it as he went quietly up the great staircase. He paused at the top and listened to the silence; it had something to tell. He thought, There are so many kinds of silence. There is silence of those who have nothing to say; the silence of one who is at a loss for words and that which speaks louder than words; that of an unhappy couple who have quarreled and that of a happy couple who have loved. Some persons keep silent rather than hurt another, or rather than falsely praise or agree with him. There are silences of acceptance and rejection, of friends who need not speak and of enemies who dare not. There is the silence that all the earth must keep before the Lord and that of the captive in bondage to Uncle Cuthbert during an interminable sermon. Silence is never empty.

The silence throughout Wrox Hall this afternoon was that of people whose hearts were too full for words.

❧ 33 ❧

A RETURN TO ROME

Lady Edge took over the wedding, which was to be a very grand one, fixed for late May, with the ceremony at St. Martin-in-the-Fields and a reception afterward at the Piccadilly house. A special train was to be run from Wrox station up to London, carrying all the Edge tenantry, along with the county gentry, and returning in the late evening. The estate people were invited to the church and afterward to a sumptuous feast at the Wyndham Hotel, at which the bride and groom would put in a brief appearance. Mrs. Cluster, although without any real claim to inclusion, was invited out of courtesy as creator of the bride's beautiful gown.

Lady Edge accepted Marietta with warmth; she had never objected to the girl herself, only to the awful connection with Lucy, and as long as those waters were not further troubled, she made herself content. Many families, great and obscure, had buried scandals and seen them after the passage of time lie forgotten.

Marietta had wished to be married from Wrox and leave for her new life from her old home. Arthur, who was to give her away, had pointed out the impossibility of that. "There is no room in the church or the Hall. Half the House of Lords is to be there. James says an invitation will even be sent to the Palace. No, you must take each other for better or for worse at the height of the season in front of the fashionable world."

"The *haut monde*," murmured Marietta.

"What was that?"

"Nothing, Arthur. It is just that London means nothing to me. I have never even seen it, and I suppose you might say Wrox is in my blood."

"It *is* your blood," said Arthur. "Wrox is your blood, your sinew and your very bone. They were formed of the soil of Wrox, from food that either grew in it or grazed upon it." He looked at the pretty green shawl across her shoulders. "You are even wearing Wrox wool as surely as the sheep that first wore it. From the Sheer we take our waters, and the air we breathe is borne on the wind that blew over our downs and meadows."

"You sound like Mr. Reddle," said Marietta. "He was always talking of natural things."

"Yes, I suppose he is talking of them now in America. I should like to go someday to America. They are building a ship made of iron—have you heard? We shall cross the ocean in under a fortnight."

"An *iron* ship?" Marietta exclaimed. "Well, I never! Whoever heard of such a thing?" She laughed with delighted recognition. "Why, I know who heard of it. I did! Mother Shipton prophesied that 'iron on the water shall float as easy as a wooden boat.' Oh, I *must* tell James!"

Arthur had been wondering when his sister would bring James back into the conversation; he had already been absent from it for some time —longer than Marietta had ever before neglected to mention his name. Arthur liked and admired his prospective brother-in-law, but he had grown exceedingly tired of hearing "James this and James that." Now he could not imagine why James should be obliged to listen to a bit of doggerel of doubtful authenticity. People in love are downright tiresome, he decided, but in the back of his mind there lurked a little wish that he might find someone about whom to wax tiresome.

Archdeacon Hampden, when apprized of the forthcoming wedding, had declared his intention to perform the ceremony at St. Martin-in-the-Fields. He had even journeyed up to London to confront the rector of that parish with his unalterable decision. It was useless to attempt to get him to change his mind. The bridegroom's mother had taken over all the bride's traditional prerogatives, and he, the bride's uncle, *in loco parentis*, was going to be included in her nuptials. He needed no permission from Lady Edge. He did not say so much as "by your leave" to the rector. He was like the car of Juggernaut, crushing all opposition, and in the end he stood in St. Martin's beside the rector, towering over him and joining with him in eliciting vows and asking the blessing.

This performance constituted his and Aunt Esther's wedding present to the bridal couple. Aunt Augusta Pounceby sent a complete Chawner silver service, with dinner plates, soup dishes, sauceboats, salt cellars, covered meat platters and vegetable dishes, etc., etc., sufficient to set a table for twenty-four. The bride's mother said that was just like Augusta: she gave lavishly to the rich who already had a surplus, and to her poor relations who owned little of value she gave a piece of plate or a spurious engraving. Robert Fox made a present to the bride of a handsome emerald lavaliere. Maria parted with the Wrox pearls, saying she would never again have occasion to wear them, whereas Marietta could now put them to frequent use.

Benjamin Share's wedding present was the sketch he had made of James on the wall near San Gregorio in Rome. He had gone to the expense of having it framed in the Italian taste, as being appropriate to its setting. The frame attracted the eye away from the picture within it, which, as James said to Marietta, was all to the good. He told her at the same time that Benjamin had actually offered to accompany them on their *lune de miel*, having heard they were going to Greece. Mr. Share had never been to Greece, and he proposed to make a study, before the wedding, of its art, architecture and mythology—as James would not have time to do—so that he might conduct the young couple about Athens as he had done in Rome. "I told him," said James, "that he could teach me how to behave in the *haut monde* but he cannot show me what to do on my *lune de miel*."

When she saw him at a prewedding dinner, Marietta thanked Mr. Share for the picture. "I am glad you like it," he told her, although she had not said she did. "It is to hang in what will certainly become one of London's great houses. You and James will be known for your entertainments."

"I shall try my best, Mr. Share, though I know it will not be easy."

"Nonsense, my dear Marietta, of course it will be easy! Anyone can be a good host; it is more difficult to be a good guest. All a good host needs is a good cook. If I am to sing for my supper, the supper must be as good as the song."

The Honorable Madge Edge declared the bride to be the prettiest ever she saw and the groom handsomest. "It is like a fairy tale," she told her sister-in-law, Lady Edge, who smiled and said nothing.

The wedding journey was to take three months, the first fortnight spent in Greece, where James carried a letter of introduction to the court of the Hellenes, this by virtue of a granduncle's having been an author of

the treaty that put Otto on the throne. From Athens the wedding journey was to take the young Lord and Lady Edge north by ship to Trieste
and thence into Austria, Germany and France. Italy was not on the
itinerary. As their ship carried them up the Adriatic, both James and
Marietta were conscious that the Italian coast lay off her port side, and
when she called at Ancona and the passengers went ashore to see the
Arch of Trajan, they looked westward and knew that over the spine of
the peninsula was Rome.

At Trieste they left the ship for a private *vetturino* hired to take them
on the rest of their travels, with James's man Henry and the lady's maid.
When the vessel left port to head north again, James said to Marietta,
"We are going every mile farther away."

"Yes, I was mindful of that."

"Do you think, as I do, that we ought to go there?"

"As you wish, my dearest."

"If I could see the child, I would be certain one way or the other."

"He must now be four or five years old."

"It is only in books, for the sake of the plot, that children bear no
resemblance to their true fathers in order that both may be surprised
when the relationship is discovered. In real life there can be few mistaken
identities."

"I am sure that is so. There is not a Hampden who does not resemble
the clan in coloring."

"All men in the Edge line as far back as records go have had Greek
toes, as on the feet of Greek statues. You may have noticed mine."

"Oh, yes, there is not a bit of you from top to toe that I have not
noticed," said Marietta, blushing furiously.

"The first and third are of equal length," James continued, "and the
second is longer than either. They are a characteristic of all Edge men.
My bootmaker tells me they are quite rare."

"As are the Edge men," said Marietta, leaning over to kiss him. "If
you wish your remarkable feet to carry you back to Rome now, I am
willing to go along on my commonplace ones."

They disembarked at Trieste and four days later arrived unheralded at
a Roman hotel. There were plenty of empty apartments, the *haut monde*
as well as the tourists being elsewhere at this season. The heat was
abominable. They spent a night recovering from the journey; then on
the following morning they set out to see Lucy's child in the convent of
the Villa Nante, on the Via di San Georgio. As they descended from the
carrozza at the convent steps a cardinal-bishop passed by, headed for the

church, in a crimson sash, gloves and stockings, followed by two strutting footmen in cocked hats. "How can he stand to wear those clothes in this heat?" asked Marietta.

"The church is never hot," said James.

There were no windows in the convent walls, but in the door a small shutter behind a grille, closed from within, covered an opening. Beneath it was a slot for letters. James pulled on a chain that rang a bell within the wall and waited. After a long silence he rang again, and the shutter was pulled open. "*Chi è la?*" asked a soft voice.

"My name is Edge, Lord Edge. I should like to see the Abbess."

The face of a sister appeared, framed in nun's headdress. "These are not visiting hours," she said in English.

"Oh!" James was quite taken aback. He had assumed that since the nuns never left the convent, they would perforce be always At Home to visitors. "When may we see her?" he inquired, offering his visiting card at the grille. It was ignored, so he dropped it through the slot.

The sister said, "If you will put your request in writing to the Abbess, she will decide if and when to receive you." The shutters were closed.

James was not accustomed to having doors closed in his face; rather, they were everywhere opened to him before he had even knocked. "I had not expected the Papists to be rude," he said to his wife. "It was my understanding that they are so keen on making converts they go out of their way to rope one in."

They went back to their hotel and composed a letter for Henry to take around and drop into the convent door. The wording of it required considerable thought. It was customary with Edge to end correspondence with the phrase "Faithfully yours," but in this case he feared the meaning of the adverb might be misconstrued, so he simply signed it with his title, as he would have done a letter to the *Times*.

Reverend Madam,

My wife Lady Edge and I request the favour of an audience with you in order to discuss a certain infant boy of English descent who was left to your care in the night of 1 or 2 July 1838. I feel sure you wish to do whatever is in his best interests, as do we, and to this end we have journeyed to Rome for this express purpose.

Edge

It was two days before a reply came, by regular post. It was a brief note saying they would be received at the convent if they presented themselves at four o'clock on the following day.

When they rang the bell, they were examined through the aperture in the heavy door. Then a bolt was withdrawn, and a portress opened the door just wide enough to admit them. They found themselves in a little room barred with iron, in the company of a very fat old woman wearing layers of petticoats, with a crucifix hanging from her waist. James had removed his hat and now inclined his head courteously, saying, "I am Lord Edge. I think we are expected by the Abbess."

"Yes. This way, please." They were led along a stone passage into a small sitting area containing a wooden bench, two chairs and a lace-covered altar with a prie-dieu before it. It was a comfortless place, but at least it was blessedly cool, for it had never known any form of man-made heat and no ray of sunlight had ever entered. A small red lamp flickered in a globe hung from the ceiling. "Be seated, please," said the old woman. Her English speech gave no sign of its not being native to her.

"Will you tell the Abbess we are here?" James asked her.

"I am the Mother Abbess," said she, sitting down upon the bench and spreading her bulk along it. After a pause she asked, "What is it you wish me to do?"

The husband and wife looked at each other; each started to speak, stopped, started again and at last got out the reason for their visit. They wished to see the child.

"For what purpose?" asked the old woman.

"To be sure it is he, the English child left here five years ago."

"There was no English child. There was a boy, Benito, found on our steps four years ago."

"May we see him?"

"He is not here, signor."

"Then will you tell us where we may find him?"

"No, that I cannot do."

James tried to explain the advantages and benefits that might accrue to the child if he proved to be who he might be.

"What benefits?" asked the old woman.

"We shall be honest with you," Marietta said. "There is a possibility that Lord Edge is the child's father. If we could see him, we would be certain, one way or the other. And of course, he might stand to be well off; we would see to it he had every advantage."

The old woman's small, sharp eyes looked shrewdly out from above the fat white cheeks. "But you are Protestants!" she exclaimed. "The boy, Benito—if he is the boy you seek—is a baptized Roman Catholic. He was adopted when two months old by a good Italian family who wanted a son. What advantage could you possibly have to give him? And you not even sure he *is* your son," she added scornfully. "We regard a human life as being sacred, a child should be loved by his earthly father as he is by his Father who is in Heaven. A child is not to be given away when unwanted and later bought back when it is found convenient." The old Abbess rose, lifting her great bulk with difficulty to her tiny feet. "If you make any further attempt to see him," she said, "I shall inform the *polizia*. Follow me, please." And she led them back along the passage to the big front door that soon closed behind them. They heard the bolt pulled across.

The carriage awaited them by the convent steps. On the way back to the hotel they said little, just held hands tightly. Neither suggested that before leaving Rome, they visit Lucy's grave. Next morning they started back north again toward the cool Vienna woods and the northern cities where all the good things of the world waited to be spread before the young English lord and his lady. For the first time James wondered if it might be possible that he did not deserve them.

James took the Roman episode very hard. He felt it as his first failure in a life that had been one success after another. He was a nobleman, and he had not behaved with nobility. His self-esteem had been wounded. Marietta knew that she must restore it. She sympathized; she allowed him time for self-flagellation and repentance, certain he would emerge from Gethsemane purged and with self-esteem restored. She herself had been very much afraid the boy would prove to be James's, for if so, she would have hated the child. If James were to father any red-haired Hampden, it must be her own, not Lucy's.

When they returned to England at summer's end, James was eager to get back to his responsibilities and duties. They were followed by crates and cases of Louis XV furniture, Flemish tapestries, Belgian linens, French silks and a Bernardo Bellotto of the Fortress of Königstein—among other important canvases. It was seven weeks since Marietta had had a "period."

❧ 34 ❧

THE GYPSY SELLS A TRINKET

Benjamin Share was a nomad not, in a way, unlike the Gypsies. He moved from one place to another, picking up bright bits of information and conversation, moving on when he had collected what was to be had, which he paid for with the baubles he had acquired at previous stops. On the road he must often have passed the Gypsy caravans traveling over the same countryside and given them little thought; it was not his land on which they pitched their tents, his goose they stole or his back door through which they sneaked to pick up a cup or a spoon. Strange people! They had lived on English land for generations, yet were not English. Did they even know they had a queen? They used her roads but paid no taxes. It was known they had incantations and curses and spells; they could tell fortunes and predict the future. What gave them the right or power to do such things? Sometimes they sang—their own songs, of course, and the very musical scale was their own. What did they do if one died? No doctor had ever seen a Gypsy in his waiting room; no churchyard contained a Gypsy grave. They belong nowhere. Or could it be they are at home everywhere, like Benjamin Share? He must more than once have passed, unsuspecting, a barrow in which was a girl who had once been Violet Wrox-Hampden.

She was called Betty, for so they understood the name she gave when they picked her up. At first she had been terrified, even frantic, and cried so loudly they had silenced her in various ways when passing near a village or farmstead. Then she had become subdued, miserable, beyond tears. The Gypsies were patient with her, for she was potentially more valuable than any other of their possessions. She was in fact their possession, and it must sooner or later be decided how best to realize her value in terms of cash.

The decision was Calladine's. He was Tony's father and the leader of the family group, the one who decided where to make a pitch and when to move on. He spoke passable English, so he was able to talk to Betty, while the others conversed around her in a mysterious tongue. She listened to them in the tent that was sour with filth and acrid with smoke. Tony's mother was the one who looked after her, fed her and picked the lice off her dress. Betty watched the woman, moving about with supple strides in swirling skirts, silver earrings flashing like fireflies against her dark skin as she bent to poke the fire.

Betty was treated differently from the Gypsy children. She wore always the gold locket that was her identification. She was never allowed to wander far from the van or go unaccompanied into the woods. She slept in a cupboard under the bed at the rear of the barrow. She was well kept, lest her value be diminished, and she grew well, among the Gypsies but not of them, although it took more than a passing glance to notice her difference. She was taller for her age than they, her hair and eyes a different color, not black. She was not naturally light-fingered, like the Gypsy children who could not keep their hands from picking and stealing, and as she grew older, she could not be taught those inborn skills, for which she had no aptitude. However, she did very well at begging with her soft voice, large amber eyes and shapely little hands extended with appealing diffidence.

It was understood that Betty was to be treated with care. She was never molested or teased. She had the best part of the chicken to eat and the top of the milk to drink. She grew up as illiterate as the Gypsy children, but she learned certain skills besides beggary. She knew how to treat the animals, for in the tribe were clever horse dealers and other swindlers. She was taught to make herbal medicines and how to weave the osier baskets that were hawked to the gajos.

It was Calladine's decision what was to be done with Betty. It had been his intention at first to demand a ransom from the family at Wrox, sending the locket as proof that the Romanies had the child. But the risks were enormous. There would have to be a go-between and a locus determined where an exchange would be made. How could this be done without the police being alerted and put on watch?

As time passed, Betty proved to be worth her keep. When she was about thirteen years old, the Calladines acquired a fine new living wagon, drawn by two donkeys, with heat inside and a chimney through the roof. It even had rugs and curtains to form partitions. It was like a town house by comparison with the old vans. In it the Romanies even ventured for the winter near the big cities, where pickings were varied and infinite. And it was there that Calladine sold Betty to Mr. and Mrs. Sleepe.

His decision to do so was easily taken. In his whole life he had never made a moral decision; he did not ask himself—or anyone else —if there was anything wrong with selling a girl as if she were a piece of goods. There was no risk to himself in the sale to the Sleepes, for that couple was no more anxious than he to attract the attention of the police.

That winter the families of the Calladine tribe were living in the wagons on the Stepney embankment near the London docks, a convenient place for swindling homecoming sailors who had accumulated pay, and not far from the Haymarket, St. Paul's, the Inns of Court and those parts of the city frequented by the more prosperous classes of the citizenry. Most of the dogs had been abandoned in the country, leaving one to guard each wagon. Calladine had kept only his ugly yellow cur, whose bite was worse than its bark. The Gypsies had multiple opportunities to beg, cheat, pilfer, sell their handiwork and tell fortunes without having to keep moving on.

The tribe of Calladine prospered. The men wore real silver buttons on their coats and on the caps that covered their oily hair; the women sparkled with the bright stones hung from their ears and on their fingers. The skirts of the women and girl children were dyed all the hues of the rainbow. They brought color to the mean streets of Whitechapel and Holborn.

Betty was set apart from the Gypsy children. She was dressed in drab rags, her hair kept dirty and matted, her face and hands soiled. All the other children were hung with baubles, but Betty's only ornament was the dull gold locket out of sight under her dress. Her costume was that of a beggar girl, whose pitiful appearance could wheedle pennies out of the poorest people of the streets no less than from the swells in the Haymarket. Her pathetic mien also served well as a disguise, in case the police might still be on the lookout for a fair-skinned girl child with bright amber hair and eyes. Betty did not look like a Gypsy—or like a Hampden of Wrox.

But the time had come when Betty's usefulness was at an end. Calladine realized it the day he saw her approached in Seven Dials by two young gentlemen who obviously thought she was offering something more than a blessing in return for their pennies. "Thank you, no," said one, while the other held his nose and said, "Have a bath first, girlie."

So Calladine went to call upon Mr. and Mrs. Sleepe. They owned, and occupied, a fairly large house near Waterloo Bridge, on a respectable street, behind which was a warren of horrible slums. In and from this house they ran a business of accommodation, provided in the persons of young ladies who were known to be sober, genteelly dressed, often elegant. These ladies never solicited business. They had no expenses, being well fed, well housed and well clothed by the Sleepes. They were also well paid and thus able to accumulate for themselves considerable money. Mr. and Mrs. Sleepe were scrupulous in the keeping of accounts, for the goodwill of the ladies was as necessary to their own prosperity as was the satisfaction of the gentlemen who visited them. Most of these were in fact gentlemen, who returned again and again, bringing their friends, often seeing the same girl exclusively. Some had even fallen in love and taken a girl away, leaving a vacancy that Mr. Sleepe filled with conscientious care.

Two rooms on the street floor at the back of the house were kept for a special use; here dwelled what might be called apprentices. Mr. Sleepe described them as being "fresh"—that is, untouched. They were of great value, sometimes fetching as much as a hundred pounds for the ultimate loss of their freshness. Before this they would be cleaned up, dressed appropriately and given a course of instruction by Mrs. Sleepe. She herself seldom left the house; it was Mr. Sleepe who made all outside contacts, solicited trade, arranged terms and collected revenues. He was a good businessman and looked it; stout, well dressed, prosperous, a man of his word, he sold nothing but what was of top quality.

Calladine told Mr. Sleepe all about Betty, except where and how she had come to be with the Gypsies. He assured the man of business that Betty was gently born, healthy, not feebleminded, well favored when cleaned up, and unquestionably fresh. Gypsy men had nothing to do in that way with *gorgio* women; it was a matter of the purity of the Romany race, plus a distaste for consorting with the enemy. Betty was now, in womanhood—she must be about sixteen or seventeen—a liability to the tribe. The time of year was coming when the Romanies must take to the road, and they did not want to take her along. Rather than simply abandon her to her fate in the London streets, Calladine offered her to Mr. Sleepe for a reasonable sum. He was told to bring her to the house next morning early, before anyone was astir, that Mr. Sleepe might look her over and possibly make an offer.

So it was that Betty found herself, bathed and scrubbed from head to toe, hair brushed until it shone, fingernails cleaned and wearing a spotless dress, presented as "a fresh country girl" to Mr. Sleepe in the parlor of the house near the Waterloo Bridge. She had never before, that she could remember, been inside a house. She looked at the high ceiling, the walls hung with mirrors in ornate molding, the globed gas brackets and pendant lusters, at the upholstered chairs, gilt side tables, flowered carpeting, big fireplace with glowing coals, and she thought she was in a palace. She became aware, now that she had been cleaned up, that Calladine smelled bad; he stank. It was the smell of the barrow, concentrated in his person, and heretofore she had not remarked it, its being a natural component of the air. Mr. Sleepe did not smell foul like that. He did not smell at all, nor did his house smell like the inside of the living wagon.

Mr. Sleepe looked Betty over like a judge at a cattle fair. He asked her to show him her tongue and mouth. She was missing a few teeth, which brought a frown to his pink brow, but the remaining ones were not discolored, and her breath, which she was told to expel for his sniffing, appeared not to offend. No, he was not offended; he was even pleased. Compared with girls of the same age who had spent their lives in city slums, she was obviously superior in health and complexion. A sickly, undernourished young woman would be of no value to him. He thought Betty could be broken in as a maidservant while she learned London ways, after which she might suit him very well.

Drawing Calladine aside, Mr. Sleepe whispered into his ear a sum of money. There followed a few minutes of haggling, incomprehensible to the girl, before some bank notes went from Mr. Sleepe's pocket to the Gypsy's. Calladine walked over to Betty and tugged at the chain with the locket around her neck. "Extra," he said. "The trinket—two pound extra."

"Very well," Mr. Sleepe agreed, handing over the money. Calladine snatched it and left the room by himself. He did not say good-bye to Betty.

❧ 35 ❧

EDWARD GROWS TOO OLD FOR FLOGGING

Augustus had not gone from Blitchley to the university. Arthur wanted him to study at Oxford toward the degree of Doctor of Music. Instead, Augustus begged to study piano in London under the great German pianist Glückstein. The maestro's fees were large, but Arthur provided the money to meet them, and Augustus avoided other expenses by living with the Edges in Piccadilly. Besides keyboard he studied harmony and composition and set to music two of Blake's *Songs of Innocence*, acceptably enough to be allowed to play them in recital. None of his teachers told him he could never be better than second-rate, for had they been so frank with their pupils, they would soon have had none. So Augustus rarely came home to Wrox. Lottie and her three little girls—Lydia, Sophie and Agnes Hole—were often at the Hall, especially when Samuel, the husband and father, was away on the long voyages that spread ever-widening demand for Wrox woolens. The Edges had three little boys—James, Almeric and Mountjoy—who were brought to visit their Wrox relations whenever their parents were in residence at Edge Park.

Arthur was the prize matrimonial catch of the county, and many a cap had been set for him. Serious and conscientious, he had paid off his father's debts and then, ridding himself at last of the incubus, had gone to court to have the Hampden erased from his name; henceforth he was Arthur Wrox of Wrox Hall. All the properties near the station and in the village had been sold at a good price for housing and commercial purposes. The sheepfolds, under Mr. MacTavish's supervision, continued to provide the raw materials for the Hole factories. The Hall itself had a new roof, new plumbing and coal gas illumination. Nurse was now the housekeeper, and the household was running smoothly. There was a rebuilt carriage house in the stableyard containing a splendid new carriage and pair driven by the young coachman Luke. Tole had lost his mind and been put in the asylum at Glanbury, where he died in delirium.

Mrs. Smallwood passed into the real life soon afterward in a lamentable accident, the fault of PC Frakes's ten-year-old boy. It happened early on a July morning. Mrs. Smallwood's plums were ripe almost to the point of harvesting, and she had risen early to take her turn at the Plum Watch. Kenny Frakes had risen even earlier, intending to harvest a few of the luscious fruits for himself. Mrs. Smallwood, mounted on the ladder inside the church, under her lookout window, had seen the boy approaching, running from behind one gravestone to another, crouched over, arriving stealthily ever nearer to the prize. Mrs. Smallwood leaned through the aperture and cried out in a terrible voice, "Thou shalt not steal!" whereupon the terrified lad, hearing a Commandment from on high coming out of the church itself, instead of turning tail and retreating, became confused and ran forward toward the plum trees. Righteously indignant, Mrs. Smallwood made haste to climb down and prevent the theft; the ladder slipped under her; she was thrown from its height down into the sanctuary, where her head hit a corner of the altar. The boy heard the woman scream as she fell and the clatter of the wooden ladder against the stones. He was so frightened he cowered on the ground under the row of plum trees until he was found there by Hawkins, the gardener, who had come running on hearing the bloodcurdling scream. So it became known who had caused the dreadful accident and the death of Mrs. Smallwood. No one can trespass in a churchyard, as it is not private property but belongs in God's name to all those already laid to rest and those who will be in years to come. Even had the boy succeeded in stealing a plum or two, there would have been a question as to whom it belonged. The vicar's wife had been buried within sight of her plum trees, and the prize fruits had rotted in the sun, uneaten.

Mr. Smallwood missed her cruelly. Without her he was incomplete. His daughter did her best to fill the void left at the vicarage by her mother's passing, but to do so was quite beyond her ability. "Mama never did a mean thing in her life," Theodora wrote to Elsie Reddle in telling her the sad news. "She could have been consort to a king—or better, a co-ruler herself, like William and Mary—but she settled for a country vicarage and running the whole parish. Papa is inconsolable. When Mama was alive, there was always something going on, even if it was an argument. It is all so dull without her."

Mr. Smallwood took to calling at the Hall oftener than parochial duties required, and he often encountered there Major Rollins, who waited upon Maria any time he could find a means of transportation from Bunbury. Both gentlemen were at tea with her one day when the afternoon post brought a letter from New Zealand. Cousin Bessie Bellwood was there, staying in the house. She had come for Mrs. Smallwood's funeral and not had reason to leave since, no other one of her acquaintance having died elsewhere.

Mr. Smallwood had brought news of interest from the great world via his friend, the Duke's chaplain. Two years before, the Lady Amelia Stuart had married a German princeling, Alexander Gottfried Friedrich Ernst Viktor Hans August Heinrich Waldemar Albrecht, eldest son of His Highness Hermann Karl Maximilian, Duke of Württemberg-Hohenlohe, of Schloss Amorbach, Prussia. Recently Lady Amelia's (the Princess's) younger sister Mary had gone to visit at the schloss and done even better: she married the widowed father of Amelia's husband, thereby outranking him and becoming her older sister's stepmother-in-law. So a goodly portion of the Duke's English fortune was transferred from his estate to a provincial Hanoverian court. The Duke was satisfied with his daughters' rank but outraged that it should be German. He permitted the exiles to visit him in England, while refusing to return the visits and set his own foot in Prussia.

"Well!" exclaimed Major Rollins. "I would not be the daughter of a duke for all the world! Imagine having to go to live in Germany with a man who has a dozen names. What would one call him?"

"There is a choice," said Mrs. Bellwood. "She could have a different name for him every day for a fortnight without repeating herself."

"How could she be sure the same person would come? In a schloss of that size there must be other Hanses and Waldemars."

"It would depend which took precedence."

There followed a discussion about precedence, and whether a Prussian prince outranks an English duke, or if it depends upon whether they are in Prussia or in England.

Maria was always glad to hear news from beyond Wrox, as she never left it herself, except to go occasionally as far as Edge. She had taken it into her head not to leave home until Violet came back. She would not go to Foxbridge Abbey, or to the Chipping aunts, or to Hatche, or to stay at the seaside for reasons of health. Her hair was quite white, and she now wore a cap at all times; with her severe black dress it made her look distinguished, as Major Rollins made so bold as to tell her. He was assiduous in his attentions, hoping ever that the widow would suggest he make it easier to pay the attentions by moving to the Hall. Without some such encouragement he dared not make an outright proposal of marriage.

Major Rollins was the epicenter of his universe. Nothing happened anywhere to anyone that he did not relate directly to himself. When Arthur was telling the company about a trip taken to visit the bishop at Glanbury and remarked that on the way to the palace he had stopped at the Boar's Head for luncheon and eaten a game pie, Major Rollins had broken in with "I detest game pie, I do not see how anyone can eat it, especially if the game be hare, such as I was served at a London club where I was the guest of General Wolford . . ." and on and on, until no one ever got to hear about the visit to the bishop. Major Rollins could not afford to belong to the general's club, and he was of the opinion that the club should change its membership rules so he could afford it. The failure of the Maule bank had been deliberately engineered in order to rob the Major of his savings, and the losses sustained by others were an unfortunate side effect thereof. No Bunbury shopkeeper was to be trusted, because a waitress at Theobald's had once served Major Rollins the wrong brand of tea—by mistake, she said, but he knew better; he knew Theobald was out to discourage his patronage by reason of his having once complained that his tart was not as fresh as his neighbor's. "They all think they can get the better of me," said the Major proudly, and in fact, the Bunbury tradespeople were all now making it a game to see if they could.

Nothing apart from himself was of any interest to Major Rollins. In the widow Wrox-Hampden he saw a means of making his life more comfortable; to that end he waited upon her, paid her compliments, read aloud to her and endeavored to win her favor. Anything he did not know or understand was worthless. He had, for example, never heard an opera. Lack of any opportunity to do so was turned into a matter of choice: "I do not care for fat foreigners shouting and screaming in a language I do not understand."

Arthur Wrox found his mother's suitor unbearably tiresome, and once, when he could stand it no longer, he said, "Sir, can you not see anything from another's point of view?"

Major Rollins looked astonished. He was a small man with a weak chin that disappeared into two folds of fat on his neck. "Why, no, sir, how could I?" he replied. "That is an impossibility inherent in the very question."

When the letter from New Zealand was brought in to Maria, the Major, Mr. Smallwood and Mrs. Bellwood were all naturally inquisitive and hopeful that its contents would be divulged to them. Maria laid it at one side of the tea table, just to whet their curiosity, then after a while said, "Will you excuse me if I glance at my letter? It may be of importance."

The three guests pretended lack of the curiosity that consumed them by rattling cups in saucers, as if to drown out a letter being read aloud. Soon they were rewarded by Maria's exclamation, "Well, I never did—"

"What is it?" the three asked simultaneously, silencing the teacups.

"It is from Cousin Wilfrid Wrox in New Zealand. My first cousin, you know. He went out in 'twenty-four with some missionaries. It is he who would have come into Wrox had I not—oh, never mind that. He married some native woman there—a savage, for all we know—in 'twenty-five or 'six. He writes that he is coming to England next year to bring his son to Cambridge—his old college, Caius. He proposes to pay us a visit, he says he can put up at a local inn, but that, of course, is impossible; they will stay here. It might have been his own home to stay in anyhow had things been different."

"Why should he wish to come back?" asked Mr. Smallwood. "Have the missionaries no schools?"

"*I* should certainly wish to come back," said Major Rollins. "I should never have gone in the first place, halfway around the world to a land of savages. I should have known better."

"Do you mean to say they now take savages at Cambridge?" Mrs. Bellwood inquired. "The Liberals are going too far; a Tory government would never have allowed it."

"There was that American Indian savage," Mr. Smallwood offered, "fellow called Pocahontas, came over here and was actually presented to the King and Queen."

"I wouldn't have received him at court," said Major Rollins.

"He came only as far as America," said Mrs. Bellwood. "New Zealand is another thing altogether."

"Yes," the vicar agreed, "can't do that in a canoe."

"Kayak," the Major corrected him.

Everyone made a contribution to the interesting conversation that followed regarding New Zealand. Maria thought it was part of Australia. Mr. Smallwood hoped the missionaries were C of E. Cousin Bessie Bellwood knew for a fact that the natives were cannibals and ate missionaries on feast days of the Church such as Pentecost, Easter and, most particularly, All Saints. Major Rollins declared he had no wish to hear any more about New Zealand, as he never expected to go there and further knowledge of it than he already possessed would be of no possible use to him.

"It is . . . exotic, is it not?" remarked Mr. Smallwood. "Visitors from another world, almost another planet."

"I would rather have visitors from another planet than from this one," said Maria pointedly. "It may be a more interesting place."

"You will never find out," Mrs. Bellwood told her, "as you refuse to leave this house, and we must come here in order to see you."

"I would gladly go all the way to another world to see Mrs. W-H," said Major Rollins gallantly.

"You may say that with safety," said Mrs. Bellwood, "for you will never be put to the test; the journey there must be a vastly expensive undertaking."

Stung, Major Rollins launched into a diatribe against Maule, the absconded banker (whom he called an "abscoundrel"), but for whom, he declared, he would have been able to travel around the world as many times as he desired—which he did not desire, since he realized true happiness was to be found here at home.

There was another letter, and as soon as Maria saw the handwriting and the postmark, she knew it was Georgiana Hampden's annual reminder that her (Georgie's) darling boy was one year older. So was his twin. Fifteen. This year there was enclosed a photograph, for a photographer from Bath had come to Chipping for a month, during which time the whole town had turned out to have likenesses made. Aunt Georgie herself was in the photograph with Edward; her head, in a lace cap with dewlaps, rested against his shoulder, and her hand on his knee was clasped in Edward's. He was a thin boy with a sad expression. He was unquestionably a Hampden, for although the coloring did not show, it seemed the pale skin must be freckled and the hair what was called titian.

Maria showed letter and photograph to Arthur when they were alone. "He looks unhappy," she said. "I suppose it is impossible to hold a smile long enough for the photographer to do his work."

"He looks unhappy because he has to live with Aunt Esther and Uncle Cuthbert."

"It is fortunate he is so placed. I knew what was best for him. Had we kept him here, look what would have happened to him: He would be gone God alone knows where . . . lost. . . . As it is, we know where he is and that he is well cared for."

"That is not logical, Mother. I could as well argue that had he been kept here with us, he and Violet both would still be here, on the ground that the donkey basket could not hold two infants, and therefore, the accident would not have happened."

The letter upset Arthur more even than it had usually done. It began, "Had my dearest husband been spared to us, he would have been fifty-four years of age on Palm Sunday last, and our own Precious Baby would now be nearly sixteen. . . ."

"When will she stop this nonsense?" Arthur demanded. "If he had been spared . . . were he still living . . . he would be—how old? Will she keep it up until he would have been seventy, eighty? Or perhaps one hundred? How will she know when to stop? She does not know when he would have died had he not already done so. Our Lord Jesus Christ would have been eighteen hundred and fifty-two years old last Christmas had He lived—"

"But He did!" Maria interrupted.

"Yes," Arthur said apologetically. "I'm sorry, Mother, I did not intend to be sacrilegious. It is that I dislike to think of my little brother with those people, no one of his own generation to talk to or play with. I do not trust Uncle Cuthbert."

Farther along in the letter, he stopped reading again and said in a loud voice, "That is it! It will not do! Listen to this:

. . . when my dearest boy needs to be punished, Cuthbert no longer uses the rod, as he thinks Edward too old for flogging. This is a great relief to Cuthbert, who always said that punishing Edward was more painful for him than for the child. It is easier for both of them—and much less hard on me—to have Cuthbert "spare the rod" and be content to make himself unpleasant with his tongue. Edward will in time become accustomed to that, so while it may be less effective as punishment it will make life more tranquil for all of us. . . .

"I will not have my little brother so treated!" Arthur exclaimed, crushing the letter in his hand. "It is cruel!"

"They do not mean to be cruel."

"If they inflict wounds without intention, then they are at best stupid."

"Cuthbert is anything but stupid! He is a highly educated man, an archdeacon—"

"I shall go to see Edward," Arthur declared, "as soon as I can get away. It is a busy time of the year, but I must go."

"What can you do, Arthur, that is not already done?"

"I must find out. I feel if I do not, it may be too late. And while I am away, pray do not let yourself get into any entangling alliance that comes knocking at the door, so to speak."

"Oh—you mean in the person of Major Rollins."

"He is a nobody, Mother."

"Not in his own eyes. If he were not someone in his own eyes, he would indeed be nobody."

"Even in his own eyes he cannot be seen as a person of any importance."

"You are mistaken, Arthur. He is important to himself, and if that were not so, he would be of no importance at all. Do not rob him of his self-esteem; it is all he has."

The photograph enclosed with the letter had disturbed Arthur as much as the letter's contents. The sad expression on the boy Edward's face haunted him, as did the total lack of any expression on the face of

Aunt Georgie. Their relationship to each other seemed to be caught by the camera and fixed forever, as if it were permanent and unchangeable. It was astounding and upsetting that a machine could do what had always been done by the hand and eye of man. "The painters of portraits will find themselves without employment," Arthur said to his mother. "As will all the artists who paint landscapes and houses. We shall not need them to show us what persons and objects look like. They will no longer be necessary or even useful. They will be out of work."

Maria thought of the tremendous significance of this fact: artists becoming as unnecessary as gladiators or coach drivers. "They will have to paint from their imaginations," she said, "as did Botticelli with Venus and Benjamin West in the death of Wolfe. The machine cannot do that. It has no imagination, and it has no hands."

"It has the hands of those who operate it," said Arthur. "Hole tells me the Bunbury cottage weavers are without employment since one man with a machine can do in an hour what used to take many hands many weeks."

"Then there will be more people out of work," said Maria, "and they will not be able to buy what the machine produces."

"Mother, you are an unsung Adam Smith."

"Who is Adam Smith?" asked Maria. "I am not acquainted with him. It is a very common name."

❧ 36 ☙

THE CHIPPING AUNTS

Georgiana Hampden was a miserably ill-educated woman; she could not even sew. She had, however, been taught to read and write, to the end that she read a chapter of the Bible daily and wrote seemingly interminable lists and letters. The lists were ineffectual reminders of things to be done and persons to see that after a time became lists of things undone and persons neglected, but the mere fact that she had written a list of her obligations satisfied her that they had been met. As to the letters, they occupied all the time that would have been taken up by the activities on her lists had she done them. Edward's earliest memory of his Motherdear was of a small, round woman dressed in black, seated at her writing desk, sending out pages and pages of correspondence in all directions of the compass: to England, Scotland, Ireland and Wales, to Antigua, India, Australia, Canada, even to the United States, where the stepdaughter of a half sister had emigrated to Virginia, a place named after Queen Elizabeth.

All Georgiana's correspondents were greatly in her debt, for each needed to write only once to her, giving the news, whereas Georgiana wrote to all, telling each the news of all the others. This occupation made demands on her time but none on her intelligence, since it consisted of copying, at which she was accomplished. She had been taught writing as a child by being sat down in a chair to copy words and phrases set before her. These had no meaning in themselves, but Georgiana was clever at calligraphy; every word she copied was legible. Had she been forced to earn her living, she would have made an acceptable clerk.

Much of Georgiana's income was spent on writing paper and postage. She paid the wages of Edward's nurse, of course, as well as her own and little Edward's share of household expenses. These were considerable, as the Cuthbert Hampdens lived in a manner befitting his station as an archdeacon with five parishes in his cure. The rectory at Stoke-sub-Ham was a delightful country house, approached through an avenue of lime trees between well-kept gardens and shrubberies. Archdeacon Hampden and his wife were expected to entertain all the diocesan clergy—often the bishop himself—as well as the county families.

Aunt Esther deplored the plight of the parish poor, distributing to them after church on Sundays worn clothing and surplus produce (eggs and root vegetables). She never called on them at their homes, out of kindness: she knew they would be embarrassed and ashamed to receive the archdeacon's lady inside their humble dwellings. She did, however, pay sympathy calls upon those parishioners she was "sorry for," and those were invariably the rich, who, being unaccustomed to adversities, felt the more keenly a death or other misfortune.

Among Edward's other memories of childhood were Sundays—dreaded days of wretched misery. Aunt Esther was constantly trying new ways to serve the Lord, and at the time when Edward was a small child she held with Sabbatarianism: absolutely nothing was to be done on the Sabbath Day except serve the Lord. It was forbidden to travel or to cook food. No secular reading matter was permitted. Worst of all, most of the day was spent in church. Between services Edward was on occasion (when he had been naughty) locked in there by himself; in winter he suffered from chilblains and was often ill. Motherdear's letters described him as having "sickly inclinations, sometimes requiring the administration of a physic or other remedy."

Georgiana's means were adequate, but at her death little she possessed could be passed on to her adopted son. Edward would be obliged to support himself; the necessity of choosing a profession was impressed upon him from earliest childhood. Uncle Cuthbert decided he was to take holy orders, and to that end the archdeacon undertook supervision of Edward's religious education; his secular lessons were given by a curate from St. Simeon's.

This young man's duties were made more difficult from the beginning when it was discovered that Edward was left-handed. After all other efforts had failed to make him use his right hand instead of his left, that tool was tied behind his back whenever his slate was put before him. He was precocious in reading, but the result of the unfortunate left-handedness was an incapacity to learn writing. "Perhaps if he were permitted to write with the left hand," his teacher suggested, "it would be better than not at all."

"No Hampden is left-handed," the archdeacon replied. "It is unnatural. Edward is being stubborn."

The curate thought, Like his uncle, but he kept his thoughts to himself, and Edward wrote secretly, using his left hand, on paper taken from Motherdear's desk. Being intelligent as well as stubborn, he soon became skillful with the pen, and he wrote amazing stories for himself in the long summer twilights after Mary had put him to bed.

Edward had been born a perfectly normal boy, except for being a twin and small at birth. He soon caught up with his age and grew into a child of great potential. He was handsome, full of curiosity, eager for the love he heard talked about constantly but had never experienced. Motherdear smothered him with caresses and endearments one day and withheld them the next if he had done something to displease Aunt Esther or Uncle Cuthbert. This formidable couple spoke of their affection for the boy and cited it as their reason for punishing or ignoring him. The only person he loved was his nurse, Mary Roberts, a kind, affectionate woman whose position in the household made it impossible for her to intervene in Edward's behalf.

"I l-love you, M-Mary," the little boy said one day when the nurse had him out in the garden. She had brought from her own home a ball and a skipping rope. No one else ever played games with him. On the road near the rectory gate lived a respectable poor widow with a boy Edward's age whom he longed to have as a playmate, but it was forbidden that he should associate with one so inferior. "It would not do," Aunt Esther had said to Motherdear, "it would be the ruination of Edward."

"Might it not be the making of the other child?" Georgiana ventured.

"Unfortunately, human nature forbids such association. It is well known that attempts to raise people like that to our level have the opposite effect of dragging us down to theirs. Human nature, like water, seeks the lowest level."

So Edward played hide-and-seek and threw the ball with Mary. "I l-love you," he said to her.

"And I love you, Master Edward."

"You are the only p-person I love, Mary."

"Oh, you must not say that. You love your mother."

"N-not really. Not much."

"Shame on you, Master Edward. It is your duty to love her. And your Aunt Esther and Uncle Hampden."

"Why?" asked Edward. "They d-do not love me."

"They do their best for you," Mary said dutifully, while thinking that their best would not have had passing marks from her.

The three adults did, however, have many discussions about what was best for the boy. His tendency to stutter alarmed his uncle, who saw this habit as being an impediment to a clerical career. Aunt Esther was of the opinion that Edward's dismal prospects might possibly be remedied by way of childless Aunt Augusta Pounceby at nearby Chipping. "She is as rich as Croesus," Aunt Esther said, "or the wife of Croesus, if he had one —the Bible does not say."

"Certainly it does not," agreed the archdeacon, "since the man is not to my knowledge mentioned in the Bible."

"Perhaps it is the Apocrypha," conceded his wife. "Anyhow, wherever he was, Aunt Augusta is as rich—and she has no heir."

"It is useless to present Edward to her as a candidate for the role," said Cuthbert. "If you take him to Chipping with that end in view, you will be going on a blind-goose chase. However, it will be a summer holiday for the boy."

Thus began the years of annual visits to the Chipping aunts, at which Edward was presented hopefully to Aunt Augusta as a possible candidate for mention in her will.

The Chipping aunts were Augusta (Mrs. Thomas Pounceby) and her maiden sister, Catherine Hampden, known as Aunt Tass from her infant attempts to pronounce her name. Augusta was the oldest of all the Hampdens, and Tass the middle one. They lived together in Mrs. Pounceby's house in Chipping. Aunt Augusta was very rich, Tass equally poor. The elder was enormously fat. Their nephew Arthur, who had stayed at Chipping on holidays (as briefly as he dared), told his parents that Aunt Augusta's mind was as fat as her body; it required as long for a thought to travel through her head as for her body to move itself from one room to another of her vast house. The house was at the end of a crescent, so it had the advantage of windows along the south side as well as at front and back, but as those windows were kept covered for fear of peeping Toms, the house was dark inside.

Augusta was as torpid as a hibernating bear and, when aroused, could be as mean. Her sister, Tass, waited upon her hand and foot, fetched and carried, always at her beck and call, and was treated by Augusta like the servant she had become. Augusta was convinced that her sister—and all her other relations—were "after her money," and she took satisfaction in concealing her intentions as to the eventual disposition of her fortune. This fortune increased daily in value, as Augusta did not begin to spend all her income. She never went anywhere. Edward, hearing the grown-ups mention the ever-increasing fortune, pictured small black hills of Welsh coal growing ever bigger until they were as high as Mount Snowdon and hid it from view.

Miss Catherine Hampden (Aunt Tass) was a spinster in her sixties during Edward's boyhood, when Motherdear and Aunt Esther took him every summer to stay at Chipping. She had always been considered rather plain, but she wore a fixed smile as unvarying as if it had been painted upon her face. She was never seen without it. She had never been heard to utter a word of disparagement of any person or any thing. She agreed with every statement made and opinion propounded, even if they were diametrically opposed; it was a habit originally formed to avoid taking sides in family disputes, where she was always in the middle. By extension it had come to her never taking sides with anybody or expressing an opinion of her own about anything. She liked equally well all persons, all sorts of food, all colors of the spectrum, all flowers, every poem ever written or piece of music ever composed. She said never a word in disparagement of Augusta's nasty, yapping little pugs, whose care and feeding were part of her duties. Her cloying sweetness was as irritating to live with as was her sister Augusta's mean temper.

Edward's yearly holiday at Chipping was considered to be as beneficial to his health as a visit to the seaside, for the baths at Chipping, dating to Roman times, were nationally renowned. Twice weekly Aunt Tass maneuvered Aunt Augusta out to take the waters, and Edward was allowed to accompany them. The boy was perfectly well aware of the motives of his elders. He was to make himself agreeable to Aunt Augusta because she was very rich and had no children of her own. The way to make himself agreeable was to arouse her pity. He knew this because of an overheard conversation between Motherdear and Aunt Esther. "She may see her way to doing something for him if she feels sorry for him," said his aunt.

"One cannot help but pity a boy who is backward," Motherdear said, "who has difficulty writing and who stammers."

"The stammer may prove to his advantage after all," said Aunt Esther, "although it is tiresome to listen to; he takes twice as long to say something as anybody else."

"Augusta has twice as much time for listening as anybody else," Motherdear said.

Uncle Cuthbert forwent the visits to Chipping, and what he did with himself during the month of August was never fully known. He sometimes alluded to a "retreat," and he called often at the episcopal palace, inquiring after the health of its occupant and offering to stand in for the lord bishop anytime when he could be of use. He could not—not yet—confirm or ordain, but he was not unworthy of being called to deliver theologically sound sermons. He had had published a collection of these, which he dedicated to the Archbishop of Canterbury, and once he traveled up to London for the express purpose of delivering a copy at Lambeth Palace. It being August, the lord archbishop was not in residence, but his chaplain later acknowledged the gift with a graceful note. At the time, "I do not wish to appear to put myself forward," the archdeacon told the chaplain, "or to suggest that my sermons merit his lordship's attention. I hope his lordship will realize that there are humble toilers in the vineyard in even the more remote of his sees."

For Edward the only favorable aspect of the visits to Chipping was the absence therefrom of Uncle Cuthbert. Apart from that, all Augusts were merged in his memory into one long state of boredom. Once a year there was a treat: an excursion to view the White Horse on the chalk downs at Westbury. Twice he was taken by Mary to a fair at Bath, but after he became old enough to go away without Mary, there were no more such outings. Aunt Esther would take him for walks in Chipping, during which they passed the window of a tea shop and stopped to look at the mouth-watering display of pastries. They then turned away and continued walking, "by way of a wholesome and moral lesson of self-control and self-denial."

Aunt Esther was accustomed to say she did not "care for worldly pleasures"; it was one of her great virtues. But what pleasure she took, Edward came to realize, in spoiling the pleasure of others!

Without Mary the boy had no one in whom to confide and no one to love. Motherdear was kind and wished only good for him, and he felt guilty because he could not love her as she did him. She had been so cowed by the Cuthbert Hampdens as to be herself like a child at their hands—an obedient child, who did not always agree with her elders but dared not defy them. She often cried when Edward was punished, but she never protested that she saw no necessity for the punishment. "An only child in a household of adults," Cuthbert declared, "is in danger of becoming spoiled by so much attention. He must not come to think of himself as the center of the universe." But each person surely *is* the center of his own universe, Edward thought, and none more so than Uncle Cuthbert.

It became apparent to Aunt Esther that Edward was failing to ingratiate himself with Aunt Augusta; he could not be cowed, frightened or intimidated into showing any affection for the monstrous old woman. He grew taller; his voice changed; his fair skin showed uncomely blemishes. More even than he had in childhood, he suffered from the awful loneliness of his situation.

Aunt Augusta's house was filled with rare and beautiful things acquired in the early years of her marriage when she and Uncle Thomas Pounceby traveled a great deal. In the front hall an ebony long-case clock ("by Tompion") kept track of the interminable hours Edward spent within sound of its chimes. In the drawing room Florentine damask curtains were drawn across the windows on bright days to keep the sun from fading the Turkish carpet. Against one wall stood a bureau cabinet made of pollarded olive wood, with cut silvered glasses in the doors. Petit point needlework covered the seats and backs of the Queen Anne walnut chairs. Over the carved and gilded Adam mantel hung a Venetian mirror in the Chinese taste, reflecting the light of candles on a seventeenth-century Waterford chandelier. The enormous Pounceby meals were eaten off Meissen porcelain on a Sheraton dining table.

Aunt Augusta loved these things. She pointed them out to visitors, sometimes even telling them the cost. She "dropped" their names in the way some people mention important or titled persons of their acquaintance. Edward decided visitors called on these things, to see them rather than their owner—for who would want voluntarily to see Aunt Augusta?

The things were tended by the servants—dusted, waxed, polished, washed, wound—with greater care than most mothers give their children. Once when a large gentleman guest sat down too hard in the dining room and came crashing to the floor (to the delight of Edward), Aunt Augusta showed her concern. "Have you broken my Hepplewhite ladder-back chair?" she cried out accusingly. That was when Edward made a great discovery about his grand-aunt: Whereas one is supposed to love people and use things, Aunt Augusta did just the opposite; she used people and loved things.

Edward turned to Aunt Tass. He tried as hard as he could to entrap her into giving an opinion.

"D-did you enjoy the trip to the White Horse, Aunt Tass?"

"As much as anyone, Edward."

"What d-did you think of the p-picnic lunch?"

"It consisted of assorted sandwiches, peaches and a poke-cherry."

"Well, were—were they g-good?"

"Every last bite was eaten."

And so it would go. She could not be made to commit herself. Even on matters of known fact Edward could not persuade her to express an opinion.

"Aunt Tass, did you know the moon is distant from the earth by a million miles?"

"So you say."

"The circumference of the ear-earth is about twenty-four thousand, eight hundred and thirty m-miles at the equator."

"That may be."

"But it is!" cried Edward in exasperation, stamping his foot.

"It may be so."

"She has never measured the equator for herself," said Aunt Esther. "Why should she take your word for it?"

As it happened, it was Aunt Tass who told Edward that he was adopted. After a lifetime of desperate caution she let the cat out of the bag with a vengeance. Edward was trying to persuade Tass to smuggle books for him from the circulating library. Neither he nor she had any money. Tass was obliged to submit written accounts to Augusta of all her purchases. "I am not allowed to take a book," she told Edward, "unless it is to be read to Augusta. Ask Georgie."

"She would g-get Aunt Esther to choose it. I w-want to read *The B-book of Snobs*, and she would never p-permit it, being one herself. M-Motherdear is afraid of Aunt Esther. Everyone is."

"She is not your real relation," said Tass; "she is your aunt-in-law, as is Georgiana."

"Aunt Esther is M-Motherdear's s-sister-in-law."

"Yes."

"She was my f-father's sister-in-law."

"Yes, the same relation to you as Motherdear."

"No one can be the same r-relation as my mother," Edward said impatiently; then he happened to look over at Tass and saw that her face was scarlet and her mouth open behind a hand. Her eyes were rolling. "Wh-what did you s-say?" he asked her.

"I said nothing at all. Nothing. You know I have never said anything anyone ever paid any attention to." She fled the room in distress.

Edward sought out Motherdear, who was disseminating news in the form of letters copied out on her portable writing desk, without which she never left home. He drew up a chair and sat down close to her. "Motherdear!"

"Yes, dear boy?" Georgiana lifted her face, blank as a sheet of paper on which nothing had been inscribed. "I am busy."

"Are you my real mother?" Each word came out distinctly, without a stammer.

Georgiana began to tremble. Her china blue eyes filled with tears, her lips quivered. "Dearest boy, who has upset you?" she said in a quavering voice.

"Are you my real mother? If you are not, then who is?"

Georgiana started to cry. She was, of course, his real mother, she protested; he had been given into her keeping when but a few weeks old. She rushed on, telling him of the child she had lost, the twin sister who was left with his parents, they already had enough children, whereas she had none, having lost her dearest husband, Charles, as well as her precious baby. In every way that mattered she was his true mother, she needed him as much as he needed her, they were all each other had—

"And is my father dead?" Edward interrupted.

"My dearest husband is your father in every way that signifies. He is not dead; he lives above; we shall meet again on the Day of Judgment." By now Motherdear was crying piteously.

Edward left her to her tears and her letters. He let himself out of the big house at the end of the crescent and went walking about the town. Beyond the minster, the road led into open country, stretching out to the horizon under the hot August sun. He felt less resentment toward Motherdear than he felt hatred for the unknown parents who had not wanted him, who had rejected him, given him away, got rid of him once and for all. He hated those unknown persons even more than he hated Uncle Cuthbert and Aunt Esther, the wolves to whom he had been thrown. He had walked halfway to Calne before he decided what he would do. Nothing rash or hasty, but a carefully plotted escape. It would require that money be stolen from the adults at Stoke rectory, as well as that he should have a well-laid plan. It would all be futile if he were to be caught and returned to Stoke-sub-Ham. He would make sure before running away that he could never be traced and found. He turned around and walked back to Chipping.

❧ 37 ❧

EDWARD GETS AWAY

Edward returned to Stoke with Motherdear and Aunt Esther, giving no sign of his intention to run away. Georgiana was more affectionate than ever, wordlessly asking his forgiveness and understanding in countless humble acts, like asking for his opinion, offering favorite foods and making him, for the first time, an allowance—a shilling a week. On one of her lists of things to be done she had written "Remind Edward" and had failed to remember of what he was to be reminded. Aunt Esther, unknowingly, gave Edward the reminder in the form of an order. "Before you do anything else," she said to him, "write to your Aunt Augusta and thank her for your stay at Chipping."

"Oh, yes, by all means," Georgiana chimed in. "She was so kind to you. She must not be allowed to forget you between now and next summer. Now that you have an allowance, you can save some toward a Christmas present for Aunt Augusta."

"Aunt T-Tass is more in n-need of one," said Edward. "Were I to g-give anyone a Christmas p-present, I should rather it b-be her."

"Aunt Tass needs nothing," Aunt Esther said. "Thanks to Augusta's generosity, she has all that anyone in her position could possibly need."

"Yes," Georgiana agreed, "Tass is well taken care of. Augusta has

showered Tass with kindness. She will be looking elsewhere for a benefi-
ciary of her charity."

"Do not call it charity," Aunt Esther ordered. "That smacks of the
public weal, of giving money to persons who have no claim to it beyond
being pitiable. Augusta is fortunate to have blood relations who will need
money quite as much as any stranger in the poorhouse."

"You may use my writing paper, dear boy," Georgiana offered.

"And show me what you have written," added Aunt Esther.

"I sh-shall write to her," Edward said, "only pro-provided I do not sh-
show it to you. Or t-to anybody," he added.

"Very well, dearest child, I am sure you are old enough now to compose a suitable letter of gratitude. You need not show it to us."

"Provided it is written with your *right* hand," said Aunt Esther. "Do
not slide back into the lazy habit of not using your *right* hand, like all
sensible people."

Edward was well aware that he was expected to provide for his own
future by "sucking up," as he thought of it, to Aunt Augusta, which he
had no need to do now that he intended to make his own way in the
world.

Soon after the return to Stoke the bishop heard the last call, responded to it and, after a well-attended burial service in the cathedral,
was laid to rest in the close near his predecessors. Cuthbert Hampden
spent many hours on his knees praying—silently, for a change; as a
general rule he could be heard all over the house. It was the same with
his sermons, which were rehearsed *à haut voix* during the week before
their delivery. One Sunday afternoon after church he accused Edward of
not having paid attention to the sermon.

"I h-had already heard it, Uncle."

"One cannot hear too much of a good thing," said the archdeacon.

"One may ch-choose not to listen," Edward said boldly. He did not
care now what Uncle Cuthbert might do; even if the floggings were to be
resumed, that would only increase his resolve to escape.

Cuthbert flushed, lending an unpleasant mottled tone to his complexion. "Not to listen is a form of criticism, as if a sermon were not worth
the listening or as if you thought you could do better yourself. Could you
do better?"

"Of c-course not, Uncle Cuthbert." To himself Edward said, That is a
silly question.

"Then you have no right to criticize."

To himself Edward said, That is a silly conclusion. Aloud he said,

"D-does that mean, Uncle, that if I do not l-like a n-novel by Mr. D-Dickens, I may not s-say so because I could not do better? Or if I found a h-hymn tune dull, I am n-not allowed to call it so on the g-ground that I could not c-compose a b-better one?"

"Exactly!" said his uncle. "You have hit the nose on the head! Until you can replace me in the pulpit, you are obliged to listen to me! Quite so. Precisely. I have not preached in vain. Now you understand the importance of paying attention: it is in order that you may someday do better. First, of course, you must overcome your unfortunate stammer. We shall continue the recitations and the reading aloud. Let us begin with the Nicene Creed." He took Edward by the shoulders and moved him to the center of the room, which happened to be his study, then sat himself down facing his nephew. "Now, my boy: 'I believe in one God, the Father Almighty—' "

Edward began. Every time he stumbled his uncle made him go back to the beginning and start over. He never got beyond the first few words. Once he said, despairingly, "Uncle C-Cuthbert, w-would it not b-be b-better to f-finish it, even if im-imperfectly?"

"No, no, my boy. We must be patient. If I have the patience to listen, you can do no less than have patience to persevere. No, begin again—"

Edward began again, not caring if he finished or not, knowing that in a few months he would be gone, far away, where no one would know him and return him to Stoke-sub-Ham. He had been covertly stealing money in ingenious ways—a penny here, tuppence there—from the offertory, the poor box, the grocer, Mr. Dredge, his aunt's purse and his uncle's locked desk drawer. The words of the creed had become meaningless now; he did not hear himself saying them; he even got through three sentences before he held himself up on the difficulty of "only-begotten," which came out as "gebotten."

Uncle Cuthbert's ruler was rapped on the corner of his desk for the hundredth time. "Once more, my boy—"

He was interrupted by two happenings. First, the parlormaid brought a letter that had been delivered by the afternoon post. Secondly, the Reverend Mr. Dredge stopped by, as he was accustomed to do only on weekdays for the purpose of tutoring Edward. "My news cannot wait until tomorrow," he said. "I am come from the cathedral. Word has been received from Lambeth."

With the Nicene Creed forgotten, the archdeacon leaped from his chair. "Yes, yes, my dear Dredge, what is it?"

"Our new bishop—"

Cuthbert wondered fleetingly why Dredge should have been chosen to bring him the news. Surely it would have been more fitting for the archbishop to have sent an emissary from London—

"Our new bishop is to be Dean Wicker. I felt sure you would like to know. We are all delighted, he being already at the cathedral and familiar with all the work of the diocese. He need but move his household from the deanery to the palace. It is a very popular choice."

As Edward looked at his uncle's stricken face, it dawned on him that the archdeacon had hoped—even expected—the miter and crozier were to be passed to himself. Had it been possible for Edward to feel sorry for anyone else, he might at this moment have pitied Uncle Cuthbert; even that terrifying tyrant did not always get his own way.

"I am sure Mr. Wicker well deserves the honor," the archdeacon managed to say. "He was ever assiduous in his attentions to the late lord bishop. *I* would never bowtow like that to anyone. It is not everyone who gets what he deserves here on earth. I have always held that it is in the afterlife we get what we deserve, which is why we must do our best in this one."

"A sound philosophy," said Mr. Dredge. "Keeps us on the straight and narrow path, eh?, lest we stray in search of greener pastures and lose our way."

"I believe Dean Wicker to be my junior by at least a decade?" asked the archdeacon.

"Oh, quite, sir," agreed Mr. Dredge. "We shall not have to worry for at least ten years for fear of our new bishop's showing signs of—of getting perhaps a bit too old—with all due respect, Archdeacon."

"I must acknowledge I am a decade closer than Wicker to getting what I deserve." Cuthbert smiled weakly. "A bishopric is a great responsibility; one must travel a great deal to cover all the diocesan duties. Even I, who have but five parishes in my care, must keep an eye on them all and visit them periodically. Had the lord archbishop's choice happened to fall on me, I should have had to think twice about accepting the honor."

"Doubtless his lordship of Canterbury took that into account," said Mr. Dredge, and Edward was astonished to see his tutor look over at him and give what might have been described as almost a wink. There was no need, Edward thought, to be afraid of Uncle Cuthbert, and from now until he ran away, he would not fear the wrath of his terrible uncle, any more than had the Archbishop of Canterbury. He would not go so far as to feel sorry for the archdeacon, nor would he pity him, but he need no longer be afraid of him.

It was next morning before the archdeacon bethought him of the letter that had arrived on the previous afternoon and gave it his attention. It was from his nephew Arthur Wrox (as he now called himself, having abandoned his patronymic) and announced an intended visit to the rectory. "No 'if you please' or 'by your leave,' " Cuthbert said to his wife, after reading her the letter. "What do you suppose he is after?"

"He is up to no good," Esther said, "we may be sure of that. As it is many years now that we have not been invited to Wrox, I find it strange Arthur should come here. If he wished to apologize, he need only have invited us to stay."

They had not seen Arthur since Marietta's wedding to Viscount Edge at St. Martin-in-the-Fields, on which occasion the Wroxes had been rude to them and treated them like poor relations, giving themselves airs just because one of the girls had married a peer. The girl was born a Hampden, after all; her father had been Cuthbert's younger brother, the brother whose keeper Cuthbert had considered himself to be. Since the wedding there had been no invitation to stay at Wrox, much less to be guests at Edge Park, one of the finest seats in all of southern England.

"I suppose we must receive him," said Esther.

"It is too late to stop him. He is due tomorrow."

"Does he come by railway or by land?"

"On the railway. I shall send the carriage to the station. We need not go ourselves."

At dinner Cuthbert told Georgiana, "Arthur Wrox-Hampden is coming here to stay tomorrow. He now styles himself simply Wrox, as if he were ashamed of us. The Hampdens are as good a family as the Wroxes in anybody's book."

"Wh-who is he?" Edward asked.

"He is the son of my younger brother, Arthur, who married a Wrox. He is our nephew."

"He used to stay with us sometimes in the holidays," said Aunt Esther, "long ago when he was an undergraduate. He was inclined to keep to himself. I remember one day when the young people in the neighborhood were having a picnic, or an all-day outing of some sort, he stayed locked up in his room and refused to join them—very unsociable."

"I always rather liked Arthur," said Georgiana timidly. "He was nothing like his father—nothing at all." She caught Cuthbert's eye regarding her with indignation and blushed. "Perhaps he has changed and is more like his father now, since he has come into the inheritance."

"And that's not what it used to be in old Squire Wrox's day," Cuthbert pointed out. "I hope young Arthur does not expect us to help him out, put his chestnuts on the fire—"

"If so, he comes in vain," said Esther.

Arthur had been at the rectory for nearly a week before the reason for his visit was revealed. He had dreaded meeting his little brother, knowing nothing of the boy beyond what was told in the annual letters of his adoptive mother. The situation was even worse than Arthur feared. To begin with, he found a gangling adolescent who was awkward and sullen, with a sly look, as if he were hiding a secret. The youth spoke rarely, and when he did, it was with a lamentable stammer. His teacher, Mr. Dredge, was well-meaning but had no experience of boys or how to teach them. Much of his time was taken up with an effort to make his pupil do everything with his right hand. It was Mary Roberts, Edward's old nurse, who told him that there were hidden in Edward's room, under the drugget, pages of stories and compositions written secretly by the boy, using his left hand.

Arthur learned a lot from Mary. Being no longer in the employ of the Hampdens, she dared pour out her feelings concerning the treatment Edward had received at their hands. She told him of the Sundays when the child was locked in the church, of his being deprived of playthings ("frivolous, they call 'em"), of the floggings that the archdeacon considered it his duty to administer ("and, sir, it is my belief that Mr. Hampden *enjoyed* doing his duty").

Mr. Dredge likewise confided in Arthur Wrox. "Edward's mother is under the archdeacon's thumb. She has been told that to treat the boy too kindly would be to spoil him." The tutor also unburdened himself of his own opinion regarding Cuthbert. "His maundering on about his great humility does not, even to a child, seem humble. In strictest confidence, sir, I venture to tell you that Mr. Hampden talked himself out of the bishopric by declaring to the dean and chapter that he was unworthy of the high office. I could not help but be amused. Mr. Hampden boasts that at dinner parties he is always seated at the side of his hostess; my mother tells me it is because the hostess is loath to inflict him on her other guests, whom she wishes to have enjoy themselves. I hope no one ever tells him that; it would be a cruelty."

"I do not understand," said Arthur, "why those who inflict cruelty should themselves be spared from experiencing it."

On the first Sunday Arthur was at Stoke he sat with Edward through a morning service that lasted for three hours, followed by a break for midday dinner, then an afternoon service that might go on until dark and often did so in winter, when darkness fell early. This sleety November Sunday was unusually cold; there had been freezing rain for days. Stoke church was shut tight, and braziers lit throughout the nave and chancel. Aunt Esther and Motherdear brought foot warmers and carried muffs. Every pew was filled, which helped create additional warmth.

Archdeacon Hampden's sermon went on even longer than usual, making up in length for what it lacked of substance. His tone of voice, rising and falling, now shouting, now whispering, was a soporific that soon caused eyes to glaze and heads to nod. An ever-increasing lack of oxygen added to the irresistible desire for sleep. Arthur was pinching his wrists, jerking his head back and widening his eyes in an effort to stay awake when he noticed a gradual change in the rhythm of Uncle Cuthbert's speech. He was slowing down. Arthur heard, as from a great distance, an allusion to Jonah in the den of whales, spoken with decreasing volume and lessening speed. Through half-closed lids Arthur saw Uncle Cuthbert's big, bare head drop forward onto his chest. The voice faded away. There was a moment of silence during which, from a back pew, came a vehement snore. Arthur Wrox laughed aloud. So did Edward, seated next to him. Arthur tried unsuccessfully to smother the sound in his handkerchief, and after a few moments nothing remained of his faux pas but an uncontrollable shaking of his shoulders. Edward was gasping for breath, looking toward the pulpit with terrified eyes. Uncle Cuthbert's leonine head was jerked upward; he searched mentally for his place in the train of his thought, could not find it and turned to face the altar, saying, "And now to God the Father, God the Son and God the Holy Ghost. . . ."

Out in the fresh, cold air after the service, Arthur said to Edward, laughing without restraint, "En-wee Who put himself to sleep! How splendid! Wait until the others hear this. They won't believe it; it is too good to be true."

"What will he do to us?" asked Edward fearfully.

"We shall see. We must give him time to think up something suitably evil. Come along, Edward, let us walk about a bit; it seems to have stopped raining. I have to talk to you."

The talk began with the simple statement, "I am your brother. We are both sons of Maria Wrox and Arthur Hampden, now deceased."

Over an hour later, arriving in the dark back at the rectory, the brothers found Uncle Cuthbert, as expected, awaiting their return. He was furious. "How dared you?" he shouted. "Where have you been? How dared you laugh in church—and when I was speaking!"

Edward stepped defensively behind Arthur to stare over his brother's shoulder at the almost purple face of their uncle. "Oh, come on, Uncle Cuthbert," said Arthur easily, "no harm was done. You fell asleep, that's all. It was lack of oxygen, of fresh air; we all needed it."

"Lack of fresh air is no laughing matter, Arthur."

"Indeed not, sir. It puts people to sleep. You were not the only one. Look at it from the point of view of the congregation."

"I look at it from the point of view of Almighty God," Uncle Cuthbert declared, "and He knows better than any congregation."

"I am sure He sees the humor of it," said Arthur. "He sees everything, does He not? And surely humor is a part of life."

"Do not blaspheme, Arthur. God is not a humorist. The Bible says Jesus wept. Nowhere does it say Jesus laughed. Come into my study, please."

They followed him, Edward with trepidation, into the book-lined room with its ponderous furniture, and the archdeacon closed the door. "I think it is high time you returned to Wrox," he said to Arthur.

"I quite agree, Uncle."

"You are a bad influence on Edward. He has never before laughed. It would not occur to him to laugh."

"I shall leave tomorrow, sir," said Arthur. "And Edward is coming with me—home to Wrox."

After the first shock occasioned by this announcement, all three Hampdens accepted it. Poor, submissive Motherdear was overcome with grief until she was persuaded to believe that the parting would be only temporary, that her dearest boy was simply going to pay a visit to his Wrox relations. The Cuthbert Hampdens, after a dreadful scene in which Arthur stood up to them, became reconciled to Edward's departure, and in no time they came to see it as having been taken at their own instigation.

"He had become too difficult for us to cope with," said Aunt Esther. "He was without gratitude for all that was done for him. It is not easy to order the life of a large household around a child. We have been freed to do God's work."

Uncle Cuthbert said, "The boy would never have fitted into life in an episcopal palace; we should not have known what to do with him there. Well, it matters not now; it is all water under the dam."

Having rescued his young brother, Arthur knew not what to do with him. On the journey home he tried to explain to Edward the boy's peculiar situation. "Our mother regrets that she impulsively gave you into Aunt Georgie's keeping when you were a baby," he said. "Mother was sorry for Aunt Georgie, who had lost a child, and she thought you might take his place."

"I-I suppose I d-did so," said Edward sullenly. "M-Motherdear at least wanted me; she did not g-give me away. Until now."

"It was her mistake to take you to live with Aunt Esther and Uncle Cuthbert, but she thought he would take the place of a father."

"And wh-what did my own f-father think?"

"He never wished you to be given away from the beginning."

"Why d-did he permit it? He could not have loved me either. Uncle Cuthbert did not love me."

Arthur's heart sank. Edward sat opposite him in the railway carriage but did not look at him directly; he stared out of the window as the fields and villages passed across his vision, as if it were they moving and not he. "I do not think he loved you," said Arthur, "because I do not think Uncle Cuthbert loves anyone, except possibly Aunt Esther, because she carries out his will. I—that is, we, your mother and mine—we did not want you to remain with them."

"I d-did not intend to. I am g-going to run away. I have s-saved almost enough m-money."

"You do not need to run away now. I am taking you home."

"W-why?"

"Why? Why—because we want you, we love you."

"You c-cannot love me, for you d-do not know me. And those who d-do know me do *not* love me. Th-they say I did n-nothing to merit it."

"Oh, Edward!" cried his brother. "Love does not have to be earned; it is freely given!" He put out a hand, but Edward did not move either of his, which were loosely clasped, hanging between his knees.

"I love Mary Roberts," the boy said, and closed his eyes over gathering tears as he remembered his old nurse's kind face from which the train was taking him ever farther away toward he knew not what.

When they arrived at Wrox station, Arthur saw, to his surprise, Maria waiting on the platform with Lottie. They had come in the carriage with Luke to meet the train. Maria put up her arms to embrace the tall boy Edward, who looked so much like his father. "I wished to be the one to take you home," she said.

❧ 38 ❧

THE NEW ZEALAND COUSINS

On a mild, sunny afternoon in early summer James Edge rode home with Hamper from an inspection tour of the remoter parts of his estate. Parliament was not sitting, and he had joined Marietta and the three boys at Edge Park. James's ambitions to serve Queen and country in the foreign or diplomatic service had been postponed, for the sake of family and home. Meanwhile, he seldom missed a session of the House, and he served many causes patronized by Prince Albert, such as the Society for the Improvement of the Condition of the Laboring Classes. He made speeches in favor of Free Trade. He advocated the building of housing for artisans in order to encourage stable and happy family life. The Prime Minister dined at the Piccadilly house. Edge had been mentioned as a possible successor to Lord Palmerston as Home Secretary.

On this pleasant day James rode his chestnut mare into the stableyard at Edge, dismounted and walked toward the enormous stone-built house where he had spent so many almost solitary years as a boy. His heart lifted in joy as he saw on the lawn Marietta, playing croquet with the children. "Oh, I cannot hurt you, Mounty, can I?" he heard her call to the youngest. "I am dead on you, am I not? What shall I do?" He watched her move across the smooth green sward in her pale yellow dress, making a lovely picture with the blue sky above and the brightly colored mallets and balls. He never failed to take pleasure in seeing her walk with that graceful, swinging gait that made one want to go with her wherever she was going. She saw him standing there and waved. "Come and partner me, Jamie," she called. "I am getting badly beaten."

They played happily until lengthening shadows on the lawn sent two nursemaids out to fetch in the young gentlemen. Their parents walked to the front of the house hand in hand.

"Do you believe we get what we deserve in life?" James asked his wife.

"Some of us get much more," she said, "like me."

He raised her hand to his lips. "It is *I* who do not deserve *you*."

"Then we are a perfect match, Jamie—two persons getting what neither deserves. It is the first time ever I heard of two wrongs making a right. By the way, Mama sent to ask us to spend the day tomorrow. The New Zealand cousins are come to stay. We are all expected, the boys to play with Lottie's girls."

"I must work in the day. Do you go with Mother and Aunt Madge and Benjamin. I shall come later."

A most wonderful piece of good fortune—richly deserved—had come to Benjamin Share. He was stopping now at Edge Park en route to London for the purpose of seeing his publishers. Two volumes containing his sketches of English country houses had already been issued, with accompanying descriptions and little personal touches in the form of memoirs, anecdotes and letters that made the books of much greater interest than mere guidebooks. On the cover of the first volume was a photograph of the Duke's castle with his standard affixed rigidly to a flagpole over the battlements. The standard had been painted by Mr. Share onto the original photograph taken without it, since on a still day the flag would have hung limply or, on a breezy one, have flapped too much. Very cleverly the original had been rephotographed with the painted-on standard, so that it looked for all the world to be exactly what it was: the photograph of a real castle with a bogus standard superimposed on it. The cover was much admired and accounted for many sales of the book to persons who hoped to be taken—figuratively speaking—inside the castle in the pages within. They were not disappointed. Inside the book was a sketch of the castle chapel with the Duke's sarcophagus in a place of prominence and in the text the "inside information" about its provenance as the mummy case of an Egyptian queen.

Mr. Share's book had met with much success, assuring him of a nice income which, since he had no living expenses, he had been able to save. Now it was proposed that he should publish similar volumes covering the countries of eastern Europe as well as Wales and Scotland. The owners of such country houses and castles as Benjamin had not yet visited were eager to have him stay with them long enough to make their acquaintance and sketch their seats. Mr. Share was now the person whose company was sought by the elite. He need no longer name titled persons to prove acquaintance with them; they now boasted to their friends that *they* knew *him*. It was gratifying to see his profession actually paying him in pounds and guineas, over and above board and lodging. This was particularly pleasant since he had not been feeling good of late, and he knew of no health spa in England or on the Continent where he would be a welcome (nonpaying) guest.

In the morning two carriages left Edge for Wrox, one containing three boys, a governess, a nanny and a nursemaid, the other Lady Edge, the dowager Lady Edge, the Honorable Madge Edge and Mr. Benjamin Share. The dowager, for want of a dower house on the estate, had withdrawn into a wing of Edge Park, where she lived independently of her son and his family with her own household, comprising a domestic staff, coachman, carriage and pair, and an unpaid companion in the person of her sister-in-law. The Honorable Madge was cut out for the role; she did as she was bidden, praised all things not her own possessions and deprecated no one except herself.

In the great hall at Wrox a considerable company was gathered. Augustus Wrox-Hampden had come from London to ask his older brother for money to emigrate to Philadelphia; he was awaiting an opportunity to approach Arthur with his request. Young Edward Hampden was there, sitting alone in a dark corner, as was his habit; he had just come home from a winter of tutoring at Mr. Plumptre's school.

Soon after their return from Stoke, Edward had confessed to his older brother how he had stolen money for the purpose of running away. "It w-would have saved them m-money in the end," he justified himself, "as they w-would not have had to k-keep or f-feed me any l-longer." Arthur had returned to Uncle Cuthbert the amount taken, saying only that he wished to make a contribution to the poor of Stoke parish.

Lottie and her husband were present, Samuel eager to meet a man from New Zealand, where, he had heard, there were a lot of sheep. Maria sat on a big sofa, her hands busy with needlework. Beside her was her oldest son, Robert Fox, who claimed credit for making the match between his half sister Marietta and Viscount Edge; they had discovered each other at Villa Brozzi.

Arthur was standing before the hearth, now empty and with its yawning cavern concealed behind a five-foot-high folding screen. Facing Maria in two armchairs were Cousin Wilfrid Wrox and his son, Cecil. Major Rollins, Mr. Smallwood and Miss Theodora were seated on less important chairs on the outskirts, as it were, they not being members of the family.

For years the Reddles had been writing to Miss Theodora from Philadelphia urging that she join them there. Piano lessons were much in demand—not among the Quakers, but with the other prominent residents of the city, who even talked of some day forming an orchestra; the Quakers did not believe in music. (When Miss Theodora read this aloud, Augustus exclaimed, "What do you mean, they do not believe in music? It is possible not to believe in fairies, or in Father Christmas, or not to believe in the devil, but how does one not believe in music?")

Theodora had been obliged to reject all suggestions by the Reddles that she emigrate, on the ground that she could not leave her father alone. Mr. Smallwood, at the same time, had been desirous of moving into a home for elderly clergymen at Glanbury but felt he could not leave alone his poor, afflicted daughter. Arthur Wrox had straightened out this misunderstanding: the vicar was soon to retire, and Arthur had promised to advance Theodora her passage money to America.

The party from Edge arrived and introductions were made. Cousin Wilfrid proved to be a respectable-looking man of middle years, perfectly presentable, wearing no war paint, and his son Cecil fair-haired and quite handsome, not at all giving the appearance of having savage blood. When Lottie had met him, she had blurted out, "Why, Mama said we all know your mother was a savage—"

"That is not what Mama said," Arthur corrected her. "What she said was '*For all we know*, Cousin Wilfrid married a savage.' Not the same thing at all. Do watch your tongue."

Cousin Wilfrid proved to be one of those persons with whom it is impossible to carry on a conversation or even a discussion; all intercourse with him took the form, sooner or later, of either an argument or a lecture. His first lecture was in reply to a polite question from the dowager Lady Edge, who welcomed him home to England and asked if he found it much changed since his youth. "Yes, indeed, madam," he replied, and took up five minutes in describing the changes since the year 1824, which were perfectly well known to those present who had either lived through them or been born since. "I did not expect to find things as they were thirty years ago. Time brings change, and one cannot escape the times in which one lives."

"Unless by entering a monastery," said Mr. Smallwood.

"Even there one would not escape change," said Lady Edge, "merely have no control over it." As she spoke, the sound of the train's whistle could be heard as it approached the station at Wrox. The windows in the room were open, and into the silence following the passing of the train came the shouts and laughter of grandchildren playing blindman's-buff in the park.

"The invasion of the countryside by the railway was as unavoidable as was that of Caesar's legions or the Norman conquest," said Mr. Smallwood, who still—six years after losing Ada—looked around following his statement as if expecting it to be contradicted. "And the face of the land will never be the same."

"We expected the steam engine to make it easy for people to come here," said Marietta, "but of course it also makes it easier for them to leave."

"Like the steamship," Lottie observed, "that will carry Miss Theodora away where we shall never see her again."

"Of course you will!" said Augustus. "If she can cross the ocean in ten days, so can you."

"Very different from the long voyage when Cousin Wilfrid went out to New Zealand as a missionary," said Maria.

"*With* the missionaries, Maria," Cousin Wilfrid corrected her, "not *as* a missionary. I wish you would get things straight."

"New Zealand is an island, is it not?" asked Samuel Hole.

"New Zealand is two islands," said Cousin Wilfrid, and he proceeded to describe both: beautiful, fertile, with exotic plants and animals, with the sea visible almost everywhere and snowcapped mountains in the south as spectacular as the Alps. Sheep? Oh, yes, prize sheep, delicious mutton, incomparable wool. The natives? Oh—the Maoris, Polynesians, they keep to themselves, we keep them where they belong, there is no intermarriage, New Zealanders are Britons, Cousin Wilfrid himself had gone out with emigrating missionaries, had married the daughter of a missionary, they had had two daughters and then this son, Cecil.

Cousin Wilfrid Wrox was a very important person in New Zealand. Not only was he a landowner, with property on both islands, but he had founded the colony's newspapers and now published the *Auckland Gazette* and the *Christchurch Chronicle*. As Cecil would inherit these successful enterprises, it was desirable he should be a well-educated man; hence his enrollment at Cambridge. "He could be *educated* in Auckland, like the girls, it is all very well for them, but he would not become *cultivated;* there is a difference."

"Tell us about the voyage from New Zealand, Wilfrid," said Maria. "Did you come by way of Cape Horn or the Cape of Good Hope?"

Neither. The voyage had been made across the Pacific to California, then overland in America to New York and thence across the Atlantic to Liverpool. It had been six weeks of tedium, not to say danger. Cousin Wilfrid made the voyage sound as tedious and dangerous as possible in order, he said, to discourage immigration to New Zealand. "We welcome those who have something to offer, such as teachers, doctors and engineers. We do not wish to be sent any of your criminals and convicts, such as was done to Australia. I'm glad the Aussies have put a stop to that. But we likewise have no welcome for starving peasants and beggars, those poor superfluous souls like the Irish who complain there is not enough land for the people. Why don't they put it straight? That there are too many people for the land!"

The talk went on through a four-course meal served at three o'clock, with everyone participating except Major Rollins and Edward, whose opinions were neither sought nor volunteered. The major had been sitting silent, a bit out at elbows and quite out of sorts, of no importance except in his own eyes, thoroughly bored by New Zealand, a place to which he intended never to go. He had been courting the widow Wrox-Hampden for years now, as boldly as he dared, to no avail; a permanent move on his part from Bunbury to Wrox was never suggested, and it became ever more difficult for him to arrange the temporary transportation back and forth necessary to his courtship. He pondered the advisability of calling to Maria's attention the difficulties he faced and overcame for her sake, and then into the back of his mind there stole the thought that she might suggest a way of avoiding those difficulties different from the one he had in mind. He ceased to listen to Wilfrid Wrox and the others, concentrating on the ample and delicious food being passed around the long table, where he had come to feel almost at home. When he had first started to call on the widow, bringing books to lend or Bunbury tarts (he did not in the beginning come empty-handed), he had lingered long enough to force an invitation to a meal, and gradually the invitation had become implicit in his failure to depart before tea, or lunch, or dinner, as it might be. Now a place was automatically set for him, and he was fed by the servants like an unwelcome household pet allowed in the dining room.

As they were returning to the drawing room, the dowager Lady Edge remarked to Maria how silent young Edward was, even withdrawn. "it was a mistake to separate the twins."

"I wish you would stop saying that, Emma. You keep harping on it."

"It is not as if I were wrong," Lady Edge said huffily. "If you had listened to me in the first place—"

"You always want to tell other people what to do."

"It would be well for them to listen. But do not let us quarrel, Maria; it is not my intent to reproach you, merely to point out that you were mistaken in thinking it was for the best to separate Violet and Edward."

"It just happens you were right about that," said Maria, "but you need not keep on reminding me. I am perfectly capable of self-reproach."

"Oh, my poor friend," Lady Edge said sympathetically, "you know no one grieves for you more than I." It was true. She extended a hand. Maria took it in both hers, and the two ladies mourned together silently for a minute.

Later in the day, after James had ridden over from Edge, the talk turned to politics and government. There was no hereditary peerage in New Zealand, of course, although its ruler was Queen Victoria. The middle classes had been enfranchised, but not the Maoris. "It would not do," said Cousin Wilfrid, "to have a Maori man voting and not the white women. The women would not like it, and I shouldn't blame them. They'd want the vote for themselves."

"If women had the vote," said Marietta, "there would be no more wars. I should not have to worry about my boys being killed in battle."

"That is where you are mistaken, Cousin," said Wilfrid Wrox. "If women could vote, they would turn into Amazons and embrace war; they would rush to enlist in the services."

Miss Theodora Smallwood had been in constant correspondence with Elsie Reddle in Philadelphia and had made a habit of bringing her letters over to the Hall to be read aloud. "Perhaps Mr. Wilfrid Wrox and Mr. Cecil will be interested in a letter from America," she now said, "since they traveled here by way of that country."

Cousin Wilfrid's only interest in that continent had been to cross it as soon as possible, but good manners required him to listen politely to this poor disfigured woman; he need not look at her.

"Excerpt: Letter to
Miss Theodora Smallwood from
Mrs. Osbert Reddle

"The Society of Friends—plain people, as they say of themselves—take great pride in being absolutely truthful. It is said of Mr. William West that he has never told a lie. Our landlady, the widow Fraser, who is related to him, told us a story about an attempt by a neighbor of his to catch him in a lie, with the connivance of Mrs. West. One evening, when the Wests were seated in their parlor, the neighbor came to the door and rang the bell. When Mr. West went to answer it, Mrs. West slipped out of the room and left the house by the back door.

" 'Is thy wife at home?' asked the neighbor.

" 'She was a minute ago,' said Mr. West."

Miss Theodora looked up from the letter and laughed. "Elsie tells it well, does she not?"

"I did not know the Quakers were an amusing people," said Cousin Wilfrid.

"They do not have that reputation here," the dowager Lady Edge told him.

"Perhaps they behave differently in America, where things are more lax," Mr. Smallwood suggested. "It may be one reason they emigrate in the first place, to enjoy more freedom of speech."

"I am glad I am C of E," said Major Rollins. "I can say what I please without leaving home."

The New Zealand cousins stayed for a month. Cecil passed his examinations and was accepted at Caius. It was understood that Wrox Hall would be his home during his undergraduate years and that he would be invited to stay during the holidays at Hatche, Edge Park and Chipping, among other family places. Cousin Wilfrid went to London and arranged with Fleet Street editors an exchange of dispatches, destined eventually to become a worldwide press service. He spent days with Samuel Hole, talking about the possibilities for trade in woolens and if it would be more profitable to ship raw New Zealand wool to the English factory or if a Hole factory should be built at Wellington, a town on the South Island near the sheep farms.

Before leaving England, Wilfrid Wrox thanked Maria from the bottom of his heart for having spared him from inheriting the estate, being saddled with it and forced to remain there.

❧ 39 ❧

A Meeting in London

Augustus had come to realize what his music teachers should have told him from the beginning: he could never be a first-rate performer or a composer of better than the second rank. He had applied for work in various musical organizations and gone around to publishers offering his compositions. "Songs of Innocence" were melodious and appealing, but it seemed the music was trite and thin; they were not suited to the concert stage, and music in sheet form was not salable unless first made popular by a concert artist. Even had Augustus's talents been salable, they could never realize enough money to support him, let alone a wife and family. Augustus at twenty-six was unattached, but he was of an age to hope he might soon form an attachment and either marry money or make it. There was no future for him in the musical life of London. His connection with music must henceforth be confined to the enjoyment of it, a hobby whose pursuit could be followed only in a large city, one where he could find other, gainful employment. He resolved to seek his fortune in America, where it was said fortunes were to be made overnight. Hence he journeyed down to Wrox to talk to Arthur and found his arrival coincided with that of the New Zealand cousins.

It was one too many arrivals for Arthur, who had only recently welcomed back Edward from Mr. Plumptre's school. Mr. Plumptre had agreed with the new young doctor at Wrox, Mr. Jenkyn, that Edward should be not only permitted but actively encouraged in the use of his left hand, and he had proven to be very apt at writing, producing essays and letters that might have been composed by a grown man. Constant daily association with his contemporaries at school, where he was teased about his stammer but not excoriated, had caused the impediment in his speech almost to disappear; it did recur on occasion, when he was under stress.

Such an occasion arose a few days before Augustus's arrival from London. Arthur had received a communication from Uncle Cuthbert that called for a confrontation. He sent for Edward.

"Come in, Edward, and shut the door."

Edward obeyed, eyeing an open letter held in his brother's hand. He sat down.

Arthur passed the letter across the table. "Did you write this?"

Edward took the sheet of Motherdear's writing paper that had been much folded and refolded—obviously much read and reread. He recognized it and recognized the handwriting as having been done with his own right hand, secretly.

"Read it," said Arthur.

Edward began to read his own words to himself.

"Out loud, if you please!"

Edward coughed and swallowed. " 'Aunt Augusta,' " he began, aloud, " 'I was told I must write to you to thank you for having me to stay at Chipping, the reason being that you are very rich and I am poor, so I must do as I—as I . . . am—am told. If things were the other way around and I was th-the r-rich one, I—I would—' " He stopped reading. The sheet of paper was shaking in his hand like a leaf in the wind.

"Go on," Arthur said, feeling sorrier for his young brother than he ever had, even on the train journey from Stoke to Wrox.

Edward pulled himself together and smoothed out the paper. He had courage. He got on with it and somehow came to the end of the page. It read:

"I would not invite you to stay with me, because I would know you hated it and only came because your mother wanted me to leave you my coal money. Since things are not that way around and you are rich and I am poor, I must tell you that I do not want your coal money, and I am not ever coming back to Chipping for the purpose of making you feel sorry for me and leave it to me. In fact, the person I am sorry for is you, and that is the truth. What is the use of being rich if all you do is sit around and eat and never see the world? Do you ever wonder what happens to all that coal? Do you ever think of all the hearths it warms? Do you ever imagine the voyages made by the ships it powers? Or the lives of the men in the ships' holds, who sweat black, feeding your coal into the hot furnaces? Men are under the earth digging out your coal, and others are on top of the earth riding across it in coal-fed trains. In a way you, Aunt Augusta, are going all over the world as you sit there in your dining room spilling soup on your front.

"Please give my love to Aunt Tass.

> Your nephew,
> Edward Hampden"

"Where did you get this?" Edward asked at the end of his ordeal, as he handed the letter back.

"Uncle Cuthbert. Evidently it was returned to Stoke by Aunt Tass, acting for Aunt Augusta. Well, Edward, it appears you have done yourself out of a possible fortune. You will have to make your own way in the world. Don't count on any coal money."

"I never did!" cried Edward, indignant. "I would sooner have run away!"

Arthur walked around the table to lay an arm across his brother's shoulders; they were thin; he felt the bones under the worsted of the jacket. "It is a wonderful letter, Edward," he said. "I wish I could have written it. I not only love you but admire you. You have the stuff of greatness."

Augustus asked Arthur to go for a walk on the downs so they might talk without interruption. The brothers set off in the direction of Knip barrow, crossing the railway tracks and closing the gates carefully behind them. The day was mild and sunny, the countryside all green underfoot, with a blue sky above, and everywhere drifts of white: white blossoms of the cherries lifted on the breeze, newly shorn sheep cropping the downland, clouds crossing overhead. When they turned to look back the way they had come, they saw a Gypsy caravan headed on the road to town, stopped at a level crossing to let a train go by. The approach of the train could be seen and heard to the east. "Gypsies!" Arthur exclaimed. "They have not been seen hereabouts for years, not since—"

"Since the summer when Letty disappeared," said Augustus. "I wonder if they know where she went—or, rather, where she was taken." Tears started to his eyes as he thought of the little sister, snatched away on her third birthday.

The brothers continued their walk up the slopes. "They know a lot, the Gypsies," said Arthur. "Strange people, carrying their shells about on their backs like tortoises. They have no home yet are not homeless."

"Constable Frakes will keep an eye on them," Augustus said, "and let us hope the vicar will lock up his communion vessels; he has grown slack since the Romanies stopped coming." He wiped his tear-stained cheeks with the back of a hand. He felt a pang when he realized it was his intention to leave this place where he belonged but where there was no place for him. He told Arthur he now knew he could never make a living in music but did not want to live without it.

The brothers walked on for a time in silence, moving at the unhurried pace of country life, of the cattle grazing and the horse pulling the heavy plow, of plowman and shepherd; they alone were walking with no purpose other than the walk itself. Arthur tried to tell his brother how he was endeavoring to keep land and family together; he regarded it as a trust and a duty. He begged Augustus to take his part in achieving this purpose. "I have worked hard," said Arthur. "Do not let it be in vain."

But Augustus wanted to look upon more distant horizons. So Arthur decided to assume further debt and to give his young brother his inheritance outright; the farms had been showing a profit, and Samuel Hole had said this year's wool harvest (as he called it) had been of top grade. Augustus was to go to the New World with the sum of five thousand pounds and his brother's blessing.

Augustus went back to London for the last time, in order to collect his belongings and make his farewells; Glückstein still owed him two lessons, and all his music sheets were with the teacher of harmony. He traveled to the city in company with his half brother, Robert Fox, and Benjamin Share, who was to stay, like himself, at the Piccadilly house.

Mr. Share's purpose in going to London was twofold. First, he was to confer with his publishers on the proposed book about places on the Continent. His sketches of ruins, churches and castles were more valuable than ever because they could be reproduced on the same paper—even on the same page—as the text, whereas photographs required an expensive process done on specially treated paper, which made their use prohibitively expensive. Second, Mr. Share intended to consult a London specialist about his health; he was troubled by an annoying cough.

On learning this, Augustus looked more closely at the old friend of his family. Mr. Share was noticeably thinner than he used to be; the mustache that circled both sides of his mouth like parentheses was definitely gray, while the hair at his temples, although thinning, was certainly, suspiciously, black. Although Mr. Share was forced to stop occasionally and get out a handkerchief, his cough did not prevent his recounting to Augustus and Robert, as the train carried the three men toward the metropolis, all the latest pieces of interesting gossip.

Mr. Share dealt frankly and unashamedly in gossip. It was his stock-in-trade. He deplored its being called trivial; the adjective "malicious" was even worse. "It is the vital news of daily life," he maintained. "It is talk over a cup of tea; it is concerned with births, deaths and marriages, visits and travels, friendships and enmities, ballrooms and playing fields, sickness and health, christenings and funerals."

Speaking of funerals, Mr. Share told his listeners, he had recently attended that of the great Duke, who had died from having eaten a poisonous mushroom. Mr. Share had been on the scene because he happened to be staying at Edge Park.

"It was His Grace's own fault," said Benjamin; "he ate it at his own insistence. The species was called the *Amanita*, and it is known that most varieties are deadly, especially the 'death trap' and the 'destroying angel.' However, it is said to be delicious beyond imagining. The Duke had come upon a beautiful specimen and wished to determine its qualities for himself. His physician advised against so much as tasting it, the chef refused to cook it, but His Grace could not resist taking just a tiny bite, it could not hurt him, it was his own mushroom, growing in his own field, where any passing animal might have eaten one like it, and there had been no deaths reported from eating mushrooms. The *Amanita*'s appearance was inviting, and it proved to be indeed food for the gods, delicious beyond human imagining. So exquisite was the flavor that the Duke could not resist an overwhelming desire to consume the entire fungus. After a very short period of utter bliss, he had suffered agonies beyond description, and Death, when at last it came, was welcome."

The daughters had gathered at the castle (all but Lady Eleanor, who was in Canada), and Lady Anne had told the newspapers that her father's death was accidental. To have eaten the *Amanita* on purpose would have been to commit suicide, so the truth had to be covered up. There was talk of charging the chef or the physician with murder and of requiring by law that everyone of ducal rank employ a taster, like a tyrant who feared poisoning or a king whose life had been threatened. Of course, this talk had come to nothing, no blame could be placed anywhere and the Duke's standard was flown at half-staff for the period of a month's mourning.

All this was fascinating to Robert and Augustus, who wished the journey from Wrox to Paddington were twice its length.

Mr. Share told them about the mummy case in the castle chapel, made of syenite, that contained the remains of an Egyptian queen. "It was the Duke's wish that this sarcophagus should serve for his own," Mr. Share continued. "He was by way of being an antiquarian, you know. The daughters had promised to carry out his wishes. However, it appeared to be an impossibility that the Duke could ever be made to fit into the sarcophagus. I myself have measured it personally, with my own eyes, and I am of the opinion that the fit could never be managed."

Mr. Share paused, got out his handkerchief and asked Augustus to close the window, which was open a few inches at the top. Flecks of soot like big black raindrops were being blown into the carriage and settling on everything in sight. To boot, the noise of the engine made it necessary that the raconteur raise his voice, causing him to cough.

"What did they do?" asked Robert eagerly, as soon as the three were settled, he and Augustus facing Mr. Share.

"The Duke was not a tall man—although, it is to be assumed, taller than a woman of ancient Egypt, albeit a queen. His daughters thought that if he were to be placed in the mummy case with his knees raised and his head on one side, as one sometimes sees that of Our Lord, hanging from the cross—without the arms extended, of course—I mean no disrespect, I simply want you to picture how it would be . . . thus—" Benjamin held his arms straight at his sides and bent his head down toward his right shoulder. "The ladies thought it might be possible to carry out their father's last request. It was a task for Procrustes. No one gave any thought to the disposal of the Egyptian mummy, which would obviously have to be removed to some other resting place." Here Mr. Share stopped again, coughed into his handkerchief and asked if anyone had thought to bring water. No one had.

"We are due at Reading station in a few minutes," said Robert. "They have tea on the platform there. *Do* get on, Benjamin. Was His Grace fitted in?"

"Just," said Mr. Share. "It was a tight squeeze, and not a very dignified position, especially for a duke."

"And what became of the mummy?" asked Augustus.

"It wasn't there. She was gone. The daughters were terribly upset because when their father bought the sarcophagus at Thebes, it was guaranteed to contain the mummy of a queen. The ladies are afraid he was 'had,' as they say, and possibly the whole sarcophagus is a fake and might even have been of recent manufacture, expressly for the export trade."

Robert Fox, in going to London at this time of the year, was following in his own tracks established as he went about his pleasure. He was now looking forward to a taste of high life after the quiet of the country and to the semiannual visits to haberdasher and vintner. He proposed that Augustus should join him for dinner at his club and a theater or music hall afterward. "Meet me at White's at eight o'clock," he said.

The half brothers dined well, with two wines plus champagne accompanying dinner, brandy and cigars afterward. Robert Fox was not surprised to learn that Augustus knew nothing whatever of London life, which he undertook to show him. At about ten o'clock they walked to Chelsea, where there were all sorts of activities available at the Cremorne Gardens. "They put on a capital show," said Robert. "It is a respectable place. The girls do not approach you—you need not fear that —but they give you plenty of opportunity to observe *them* and pick out one who suits."

Cremorne Gardens glittered with thousands of flickering gaslights illuminating the platforms, gardens and circles where as many souls of both sexes, many obviously alone, were strolling, dancing and enjoying all sorts of amusements. A fresh breeze blew from the river, where boats were being loaded and unloaded of pleasure seekers, the women in pretty summer frocks. It was a well-dressed crowd, but Robert and Augustus stood out in it as being obviously a pair of swells. Robert was dressed with the best of taste in fawn-colored trousers and jacket, a glossy top hat over carefully curled hair, carrying gloves and a gold-headed stick. He was looking about with an air of amused disdain when a stout gentleman of middle years came forward and addressed him. It was Mr. Sleepe, who knew very well it was Mr. Fox of Mount Street to whom he spoke but who knew better than to call him by that name in this place.

"Oh, hello, Sleepe," Robert said carelessly. "Are you not some distance from home?"

"Looking for you expressly, sir." Mr. Sleepe touched his forehead where a forelock had existed once upon a time long ago. "Two young gentlemen of quality," he said, including Augustus in a fawning glance. "I had me eye on you." He looked about. There were no police in sight and no one to overhear. Mr. Sleepe had been hoping to meet up with a gentleman or two of title, but so long as they were gentlemen (as was obvious) and rich (as he knew) he was satisfied he had found what he sought, and the money was more important than the title. "I have a young girl lately come from the country," he said in a confidential tone. "Absolutely fresh, untouched goods, I guarantee it. There is no possibility of infection or unpleasant consequences. I would not give her, neither, to one who might infect her, I would not do that. You know me, sir, you know Mrs. Sleepe's and my accommodation is of the highest order."

Robert was interested. It might be amusing to bring his inexperienced younger brother together with a girl equally virginal. "What would you say is her asking value?" he inquired of Mr. Sleepe.

"For two gentlemen, a special price." Mr. Sleepe spoke and looked like a businessman discussing the sale of valuable merchandise. "She is one of a kind. Wellborn, you can tell it to look at her. Lovely, she is. I could not let just anyone have her—for the first time, mind you—for anything less than"—he paused, and named a sum far greater than the gentlemen could possibly be carrying on their persons at the moment, but he knew Mr. Fox to be a man of integrity who would honor his debts —"a hundred guineas."

If Robert was surprised, he did not show it, and he would never have condescended to haggle on the street with the likes of Mr. Sleepe. "Very good," he said. He turned to his young half brother. "You will not forget this night in London," he said. "You will remember it all your life, however far you may go across the sea."

Mr. Sleepe moved away and started along the path with the two gentlemen following. He led them up onto the pavement along the embankment, through Pimlico, past the Abbey to Westminster and the house near Waterloo Bridge. It was a long walk but calculated by Mr. Sleepe to arouse the appetites of the gentlemen for the delicacies of food and drink prepared by Mrs. Sleepe and the rare sweets to follow.

The Sleepes' parlor was softly lighted behind closed curtains. The furnishings were comfortable, even luxurious. On a white damask cloth were laid out dishes of jellied eggs, tropical fruits, biscuits and rare cheeses, bottles of still and sparkling wines. At the far side of the room a door stood open to a back chamber, lined with mirrors, containing a large bed and everything necessary for making a toilet. From this room Mrs. Sleepe brought forward a young girl, introduced her as Betty and withdrew to the hallway, closing the door behind her, having first shown the gentlemen how to lock it from the inside.

Betty was above average height for her age, which looked to be about sixteen or seventeen. She had an abundance of copper-colored hair with eyes that matched. Her skin was a smooth, warm tan, with rosy cheeks. She was simply dressed in a clean cotton frock of a shade of fresh spring green, and she was barefoot. The feet were well shaped and strong, the same tan color as her face, as if they had never been confined in shoes. She wore no artificial paint, and no ornament but a gold chain that hung from her neck and disappeared into the front of her frock.

"You are lovely, child," said Robert. He had removed hat and gloves, and now his jacket. Betty was obviously as fresh as Mr. Sleepe had promised, else she was a remarkable actress, and Robert knew from experience that for a hardened prostitute to look and act like an innocent girl was virtually impossible. "Come and have a glass, my dear," he said, pouring brown sherry into three goblets. "I am glad for your sake as well as for ours that it is we who came to you tonight, as we shall treat you gently and be kind to you. Do not be afraid."

Betty was not afraid. She was more curious than anything else. She was used to seeing men in all stages of dress and undress, but never dress like the clothing of these gentlemen. She accepted food and drink, sitting in a large armchair with her bare legs drawn up under her. She stared at the two men with big eyes, following their every movement, while pushing food greedily into her mouth with her left hand.

"So your name is Betty?" asked Robert.

"Yes."

"Have you another name? A surname?"

She looked puzzled. "*Another* name? I am Betty." Her voice was accented in a way with which neither of the men was familiar.

"She reminds me of someone," said Augustus.

"No one I know," Robert said. "Sleepe told me she was wellborn, and I can see she did not come out of Whitechapel. She is of the country. She looks as if she might have Romany blood." They were discussing her as if she were unable to understand.

"If she is . . . fresh," Augustus began, "I do not feel it is right to—to —to—you know what I mean."

"That is precisely why we must do it," Robert told him. "Another might be cruel, whereas we shall make sure her first experience is pleasant." He rose and went over to the girl, who looked up at him trustingly with the great amber-colored eyes.

She licked her fingers and wiped them on the green frock. Mrs. Sleepe had trained her in preparation for her future career, and she began to carry out that lady's instructions. "Let me offer you refreshment," she said, getting up and moving to the table. "We need not hurry; we have all night."

Robert was now convinced that she was in truth fresh—fresh from the country, not used to serving the baser needs of men but not afraid of them either. She smiled at him with great simplicity and held out a rosy peach in her strong, well-shaped hand. "She does indeed look to be wellborn," he said to Augustus.

Augustus was trembling, in a fever of nervous anticipation, waiting for Robert to make the first move. Robert removed his elegant bespoke shirt and folded it carefully, looking steadily the while at Betty, who looked back politely, then put out a finger and touched him on the bare chest. Augustus took off his jacket and unbuttoned his shirt.

"Let us go in there," said Robert, indicating the bedroom. Betty followed him obediently, and Augustus followed her.

"Take off your frock," Robert told her hoarsely. He reached toward her to lift the hem of the green cotton frock. Betty's hands reached down to cover his, and together they lifted the frock up the length of her body and over the copper-colored hair. She wore nothing underneath.

"Oh, my God!" exclaimed Augustus suddenly. "Stop! Stop it!"

Robert looked over at him in disgust and exasperation. Betty was surprised.

"That is my sister Marietta's locket!" Augustus cried. He reached out for the chain and removed it from the girl's neck. "That is the picture of Aunt Augusta Pounceby, before she was married, Augusta Hampden! It is Marietta's locket that was lost . . . years ago . . . at Wrox . . . I was a little boy . . . we looked for it everywhere, all of us, Marietta had lost it!" He was babbling.

Robert stared at his half brother's face, from which all color had drained. Augustus breathed in and out, panting, as if he had been running. He closed his mouth, swallowed and spoke. "It is Letty," he whispered. "Robert, we have found Letty."

There was a moment of silence in the room while Robert Fox took in what his half brother was telling him. Then he felt a prickling of his scalp, and he shivered, as goose pimples rose along the skin of his arms. He experienced that which he had never known in his life before: a genuine, deep emotion. He looked from Augustus to Betty, and saw that it was so: they were both Hampdens; the "someone" of whom she had reminded Augustus was Edward, the boy at Wrox who was her twin. Robert thanked God—again, for the first time in his life—that it was he who had been the chosen *deus ex machina*, that he had arrived in time to save his sister, that he had been stopped in time from committing the awful crime of incest: the ultimate taboo.

Augustus was aghast; he looked terrible. Betty knew there was a crisis of some kind, connected to herself, and feared she had done something wrong. She picked up her frock and held it in front of her nakedness.

Robert pulled himself together. "We must take her away from here," he said to Augustus. "Immediately. Get your clothes on." He began dressing himself in haste, not forgetting hat, gloves and gold-headed stick. "Put on your frock, Betty. You are going home with us."

"No, *no!*" she cried, backing away. "I am not to go. It is forbidden. I must stay here."

"You cannot stay here. Get ready to leave at once. I shall find the Sleepes." Robert unlocked the door and went into the hall. Mrs. Sleepe was there, sitting behind what in France would be called a *caisse*. She was knitting a woolen cap and listening for the sounds of the house.

"I must see Sleepe," Robert said urgently. "Fetch him immediately!"

Mrs. Sleepe saw that something out of the ordinary had occurred. Mr. Fox looked so much upset and sounded so angry that she dropped her needles and went in search of her spouse. They returned to the hall together.

"This child, Betty," Robert began, without preamble, "I know who she is. Where did you find her?"

"What has she been telling you?" asked Mr. Sleepe. He remembered uneasily that the girl had been in the room when money had changed hands between himself and the Gypsy.

"She has told me nothing. That is why I am asking you. I know who she is, and who is her family. How did she come here?"

Mr. Sleepe shifted his weight from one foot to the other. He avoided looking directly at Mr. Fox. "She just showed up one day," he said. "Maybe six weeks back. We took pity on her, she was alone in the world, we took her in, gave her a home; it was done from goodness of heart—"

"She is leaving as of this moment," said Robert, "with me and my brother. We are taking her to her family." He turned his back on the Sleepes and walked away from them.

" 'Ere, sir!" cried Mr. Sleepe, following. "You can't do that! She's not for sale, she belongs 'ere, you can't take 'er away."

"We are leaving with her now."

Betty did not want to go. She had been abandoned by the Romanies— the only family she had known—and for the first time in her life had been six weeks in the same place, a comfortable place, where she had had plenty to eat without begging for it and a warm bed to herself. She put up a fight, kicking and scratching, until Robert and Augustus between them overcame her and reduced her to submission. Mrs. Sleepe was begging them to be quiet, not to disturb the clients upstairs, not to draw attention from the passersby in the street.

"Do you go to fetch a cab," Robert said to Augustus. "We shall wait for you outside." To Mr. Sleepe, who was still protesting, he said, "The police will be interested to find out how you happened to have this girl in your house."

At mention of the police Mr. Sleepe fell back and watched the three leave without further remonstrance. "A hundred guineas was agreed upon, I believe?" he murmured hopefully at the door. Robert did not answer. He had no intention of notifying the police about any aspect of this sorry business; he was praying it might never come out that Letty had been found in a house of accommodation.

Out on the pavement Robert and the girl waited until Augustus appeared with a cab. As they got in, the cabman turned it around and started at a brisk trot toward Westminster.

"Where are we going?" Robert asked Augustus.

"To Piccadilly."

"No, no, Mount Street!" Robert commanded. "Do not be a fool! Benjamin Share is at the Piccadilly house. If ever he were to find out about this—" The sentence was left unfinished.

Betty had begun to wail. "I wants me locket, I left me locket, I wants it, it's me own locket—"

"Oh, my dear child," said Robert, overcome with compassionate pity. "Do not cry. We are taking you home, where you will see your own mother." He put his arm around her in a gesture of protective love. He had never done such a thing in all his life, any more than Betty had felt warm arms around her, holding her close. She leaned back against her half brother and rested her head on his shoulder as she was carried through the dark streets toward a new life that was at the same time a return to the old. She was taking nothing with her but a single garment, the green cotton frock.

Augustus was sobbing, hunched over on the small folding seat facing the others. He was just beginning to realize how narrowly they all had escaped falling into the dark, bottomless abyss of eternal damnation. In a roundabout way, and quite by accident, Aunt Augusta Pounceby—of all people—had been responsible for their salvation, Aunt Augusta, who had never in her life done a good deed intentionally. Nor had she ever given anyone a present welcomed by its recipient. At Marietta's christening she had presented the baby with a gold locket containing *her own picture* —of all unwanted things! And now, more than thirty years later, Aunt Augusta was unknowingly responsible for a miracle. God's ways are mysterious indeed.

Robert Fox, too, was beginning to realize what had happened: He had been spared, at the very last moment, from the commission of a most terrible, unforgivable sin. A mortal sin. Would the fact that he had not intended incest have made it any less a sin? The sin would have been the same, whether committed intentionally or not. It was not from good intentions on his part that he now had his arms around the girl in love rather than in lust. He decided that it was not himself God had spared but the innocent girl. He had been the instrument chosen by God to save her from a terrible fate.

Both men knew it was a brother's duty to protect a sister, to keep her safe at all costs from that great wrong they themselves had been about to do her. Each of them was overcome by shame, but mixed with that base emotion there was a kind of joy; theirs was the burden of shame that might have been hers. Violet was still "fresh," and so she would be when returned to her family.

The cab arrived at Mount Street. Robert paid off the cabby and let himself, Augustus and the girl into the dark house. "We must decide how to proceed now," he said to his half brother.

❧ 40 ❧

THE TWINS ARE REUNITED

When Benjamin Share took his departure from Edge Park, he left behind for Marietta a letter that read, in part:

> I am shortly to leave England for more southerly climes, not to return. Now that I am a figure of note in the literary world, it appears I have contracted the disease that is the bane of literary men, such as Keats, a disaffection of the lungs that makes it advisable to take up residence abroad. It is amazing how many writers suffer from this ailment—almost as if it were a hazard of the occupation. Fortunately I am commissioned to produce books about Switzerland, the south of France and northern Italy that will provide me with the means to live and travel in those salubrious parts of the Continent. My friend Thomas Hood, whose "Literary Reminiscences" you so much enjoyed in "Hood's Own," was a victim of the same malady, and I only hope I may bear my affliction as cheerfully as did he. I shall, of course, keep in touch with you and with all my many friends and let you know where I may be found when you visit the Continent. . . .

Oh, poor Signor Partay! Marietta thought, no longer to be the ever-welcome guest—it would be unsafe to have him near the children—but there was something of gallantry in his mid-life change of career, and she rejoiced for him that he would not have either to call on friends for money or to live upon charity. He was even proud to have contracted an illness that put him in the company of Keats and Hood.

Marietta was preparing to move the family back to London after its holiday in the country when the telegraph operator at Wrox station brought the message. This new method of instant communication had been lately installed and was used mainly to convey bad news. She tore open the paper fearfully: "COME LONDON MY HOUSE MOUNT ST SOONEST POSSIBLE TELL NO ONE STOP FOX."

"I shall go with you, of course," said James.

They had missed the passenger train for London, so James decided they would go by carriage and pair, and it was after nightfall when they arrived at Mount Street. The servant showed them into the drawing room, where they were soon joined by Robert and—surprisingly—Augustus. The men shook hands.

"Well, Fox, what is all this about?" James demanded. "You have upset my wife. And why is Augustus here? We thought him to be with Mr. Share at Piccadilly."

Robert closed the door, making certain no one was near to it on the other side. "Pray be seated," he said. "We have something to tell you that is of utmost importance to all of us." He and Augustus had agreed how it was to be told to Marietta—in strictest confidence—and that they would then rely on her for advice as to what to do next.

When they were settled, he said, "I must tell you, first, that we have found Violet."

Marietta swayed, and the color left her cheeks, as if she were about to faint.

James rushed to her side to support her. "How can that be?" he demanded. "Are you certain it is she? Where is she?"

"She is upstairs. There can be no doubt as to her identity. I shall have to tell you how we happened upon her, and the story must never be heard outside this room. No person except we four here now is ever to know what I am about to say. I am not proud of my part in it, but I am bound to confess that in view of our having found the girl, it is impossible that I should regret the manner of the finding. Bear with me."

The Edges listened in silence to the story of the meeting with Mr. Sleepe, the walk to the house of accommodation near Waterloo Bridge, the introduction of the "fresh" girl and the discovery of the locket that Augustus had recognized as being Marietta's, lost so long ago.

"It was not lost," said Marietta. "Lucy gave it to the Gypsies. She bribed the Gypsies and made me say I had lost it."

"Violet has been with the Gypsies all these years," said Augustus.

"We must warn you what to expect," Robert said. "She can neither read nor write. She knows nothing beyond a life with the Romanies. You will barely understand her speech."

"My God!" exclaimed James Edge as he took it all in. There was a moment of silence.

Marietta sat up very straight. "Who knows she is here?"

"No one."

"Then she must stay here until I can take her home."

"She has not even a pair of shoes," said Augustus.

"Oh, the poor child!" James exclaimed. Marietta had begun to cry. "Don't, my darling, it will be all right. We must decide how we shall say she was found."

"Let us say Augustus saw her on the street and recognized the locket," Robert suggested. "She was begging on the street. Not soliciting," he emphasized. "Begging for money. That is what she was taught by the Gypsies. That is how they used her, and that is true. She has told us so."

"Who will believe this?" James asked.

"There is the evidence of the locket," said Marietta.

Robert told them the locket was gone, left behind at Mr. Sleepe's.

"But without the locket what proof is there?" Marietta asked. "She was only three when they took her; she will remember nothing of Wrox or of any of us—"

"She resembles the Hampdens, *au fond,*" Robert said, "underneath the Gypsy."

They talked until nearly morning. Then the Edges went to Piccadilly, Marietta promising to return next day with clothing and toiletries for Violet, in preparation for taking her home to Wrox. "She will have to be taught everything," said Marietta. "Do you suppose the Reddles would come back?"

"No, they would not," Augustus said. "Mr. Reddle has been appointed president of a college near Philadelphia. Why should they come back where they are nobodies just to teach one Gypsy girl? But there is Miss Theodora Smallwood. Perhaps she can be persuaded to remain in England. She would be glad of a home at Wrox, I should think. She does not really wish to emigrate and face a whole new world of strangers."

"How shall we tell Mama? Who will tell her?"

"Arthur and Lottie must be told first," Marietta said. "Then we can prepare Mama."

It was one morning a week later that Marietta took the girl over to Wrox from Edge Park. They were to meet Lottie by prearrangement outside the house before proceeding indoors to tell their mother about the return of Letty. Lottie had told Norah, the nursemaid, who now took care of the youngest Hole girl. Both she and Norah were skeptical. "I think my sister has been taken in," said Lottie to Norah, "and I really fear for my mother's mind if it should prove to be a hoax." Lottie missed the little sister more than had anyone else; she had been like a mother to Violet and had made up for the loss of that child by doting on her own three little ones. She was now dreading the meeting with the Gypsy girl, for if she proved not to be Violet, it was her own heart that would break before her mother's.

Betty, as she persisted in referring to herself, was still sullen and resentful, demanding her locket, refusing to wear shoes in the house, but so much impressed by the unimaginable grandeur of her strange new surroundings that she was no longer actively rebellious and showed no desire to run away. She had been told Marietta was her sister, Augustus her brother, that she had two other brothers and another sister and a mother. She had been lost, they told her, they had all been looking for her, and now they had found her they wanted her happiness above everything. She could not seem to understand why this should be so. Why should these people wish her happiness? The very word was not in her vocabulary.

Marietta and Letty were driven around to the stableyard at Wrox and descended from the carriage near the paddock. Marietta looked closely at the girl to see if she showed any sign of recognizing the house or its surroundings. She did not. She stood awkwardly in her new clothes, waiting to see what was expected of her. Her eyes were blank. Her arms hung limply at her sides.

Lottie and Norah appeared, walking from the lane at the end of the shrubbery. They came closer. The Gypsy girl saw them and lifted her head, while on her face appeared an expression of delighted wonder. "Wotty!" she cried, running toward the two women. "Nowah!" She smiled at them, a brilliant smile, her teeth shining white against the dark skin; then she went right past them to the head of the lane. "Squiwwels!" she shouted, and began running along the lane between the hedgerows as fast as she could go, calling "Squiwwels! Squiwwels!" She ran head-long until she came to a gate that was closed. She stopped, panting, trying to get her breath, looking into the field beyond. There, with an empty gunnysack in his hand, stood the Gypsy Tony.

They stared at each other across the gate. They had last been together on the Stepney embankment, two months before.

Tony said, "*Betty?*"

She turned and ran back the way she had come, along the lane that led to the Hall, leaving a shoe behind, running so hard she could taste blood in her throat, running away from the Gypsy, home to Wrox.

Half an hour later the Gypsies had taken to the road, moving more quickly than was their habit. By nightfall they were somewhere beyond Glanbury, headed north. They were never seen again in the neighbor-hood.

In the drawing room Arthur was preparing his mother for the return of Violet. "The Queen has been on the throne seventeen years today," he began.

"The twins' birthday," said Maria. "It is fourteen years today that Letty was taken." She was standing by a window, looking out past the stables and paddock in the direction of Sheerwater.

"Come and sit down, Mother," her son said gently. "I have wonderful news."

Afterword

June 1993

The author is indebted to Maria Hampden Riddle (Mrs. J. W. Clothier Riddle) of Bryn Mawr, Pennsylvania, for the following information about her ancestors. She is the great-great-great-granddaughter of Augustus Hampden, who emigrated to the United States in the year 1884. He settled in Philadelphia, where he became a successful merchant, owner of the department store A. W. Hampden & Co. He married Susannah West, of the West family of Quakers. He was a philanthropist and amateur musician, founder of the Philadelphia Philharmonic Society.

Professor Osbert Reddle, president of Chester College from 1848 to 1861, published many textbooks on various subjects, especially that of the education of the young of both sexes. He died in 1865 and is buried in the Friends Cemetery in Chester, next to his wife, Elizabeth.

The seventh Viscount Edge served as Governor-General of New Zealand from 1867 to 1870 and as the Queen's Ambassador to the protectorate of Rome under Napoleon III. The twelfth viscount and present peer, James Mountjoy Wrox Wellington Churchill, of Edge Park, is the lord lieutenant of the county.

Wrox is a manufacturing town (population 169,544) on both banks of the river Sheer, with large woolen factories, paper mills and fish hatcheries. It is served by the Great Western Railway and an airport with direct connecting service to Gatwick, Prestwick, Shannon and Dinard, on the Channel coast of France.

Wrox Hall is now a hotel, called Wroxhall, in a small garden and park entirely surrounded by the city. Wrox church and churchyard are on Plum Road. Among the graves there are those of Maria Wrox-Hampden (d. 1861); her son, Arthur; the Reverend Jonathan Smallwood (d. 1856); his wife, Ada, their daughter, Theodora, and two children who died young; and several generations of the Hole family, rich merchants of Wrox, who lie in a mausoleum that is a replica of the Erechtheum. It is built against the south wall of the church. The churchyard has been full since the year 1900, when a former mayor of Wrox, Kenneth Frakes, was the last person to be buried there. The present rector of the church is Peter Algernon Thomas Scrimbold, a direct descendant of Violet Scrimbold (née Violet Wrox-Hampden), who was famous in her day as "Gypsy Betty."

Mrs. Thomas Pounceby (née Augusta Hampden) died in 1855 and left her large fortune to a nephew, Edward Charles Hampden.*

Robert Fox, Esq., of Foxbridge Abbey, married an Italian woman, reputedly his longtime mistress, and spent the last part of his life in Rome. The Abbey is now the property of the National Trust.

"Young Arthur" Wrox, the son of Maria, married at the age of forty the youngest daughter of the great Duke of the family Stuart, to whom he had been introduced by his brother-in-law, Viscount Edge. They had one child, whose descendants live today in a small manor amid large grounds on the outskirts of the city, a place once occupied by the Wrox overseers. These Wroxes are well off and could afford to live anywhere but have no wish to leave the little piece of England where their forebears were settled for so many generations.

---

* Mrs. Riddle told the author that research among old family letters and documents disclosed that Mrs. Pounceby's will (the last among many) was written on September 2, 1853 and that on September 15, she sent for her lawyer for the purpose of changing it again. Miss Catherine Hampden wrote to her brother Cuthbert, the archdeacon, to say that Augusta wished to name the two of them as beneficiaries rather than the nephew named in the will of September 2. The lawyer was actually in the room with Augusta and had the new will awaiting her signature when Augusta suffered the stroke that rendered her totally incapacitated and unable to change it as she had intended to do. Augusta Pounceby lived on for two years longer in a state of hibernation.

Mrs. Riddle, on a visit to England, called upon these distant cousins at Wrox. They had in their possession many old family letters, among them correspondence between Marietta Edge (Viscountess Edge) in Rome and her brother Arthur at Wrox Hall, dated 1865, which revealed that Lucy W-H had borne a son out of wedlock in Rome in the year 1838. Lucy had died in childbirth, but the boy had lived, having been adopted in infancy by a prominent Roman family. Nothing more was known of him beyond the fact that he had been baptized Benito. Lady Edge's husband was, in 1865, British Ambassador at Rome. At the embassy was a young Italian attaché (Marietta wrote) called Benito San Matteo, who bore a resemblance to the Hampden family, being sandy-haired and well over six feet tall—an uncommon height in an Italian. Lady Edge's letter contained the following enigmatic paragraph:

> James believes this young man to be our nephew, Lucy's child. It is confirmed that he is 27 years of age, whether adopted or not we cannot discover. James attempted in every way possible to find out about the young man's feet, asking him to recommend a bootmaker, requesting that he remove his shoes when entering a sickroom, even suggesting that they visit the Baths together, which shocked the young man, as it seems that that is an improper suggestion. In fact, all these attempts on James's part to see his feet were taken on Benito's part as unwelcome advances, and he has requested transfer to another post.

From the *Oxford Companion to English Literature*, third edition: "HAMPDEN, EDWARD (1837–1893), the son of a ——shire squire, published in 1878 'Poems Descriptive of a Traveller's Life.' He traveled widely in the Pacific, living in New Zealand from 1861 to 1877, where he was a commissioner for crown lands. He edited the 'Collected Letters of Benjamin Share' (q.v.) 1882. He left to the nation the Hampden collection at Chipping that contains examples of Grinling Gibbons, William Kent, Thomas Chippendale and Hester Bateman."